Storms Gath

CLARE FLYNN

Storms Gather Between Us

CANELO

First published in the United Kingdom in 2019 by Canelo

This edition published in the United Kingdom in 2019 by

Canelo Digital Publishing Limited
57 Shepherds Lane
Beaconsfield, Bucks HP9 2DU
United Kingdom

A CIP catalogue record for this book is available from the British Library.

Print ISBN 978 1 78863 564 6
Ebook ISBN 978 1 78863 263 8

Look for more great books at www.canelo.co

Printed and bound in Great Britain by Clays Ltd, Elcograf S.p.A.

For my siblings Tom, Sebastian, Eileen and Anne-Marie

Ah, love, let us be true
To one another! for the world, which seems
To lie before us like a land of dreams,
So various, so beautiful, so new,
Hath really neither joy, nor love, nor light,
Nor certitude, nor peace, nor help for pain;
And we are here as on a darkling plain
Swept with confused alarms of struggle and flight,
Where ignorant armies clash by night.

Dover Beach,
Matthew Arnold (1822–1888)

Former coal mine owner executed for the murder of his son

John William Kidd, aged 57 years, was hanged at Willagong Prison this morning. Kidd was convicted of the murder of his eldest son Nathaniel Kidd, aged 29 years, an Anzac who served his country at Gallipoli.

Kidd refused the chance to say any last words before the execution was carried out at six thirty. A witness said Kidd appeared resigned to his fate.

Sentenced in May after a three-day trial, Kidd's crime shocked the town of MacDonald Falls where the Kidd family lived and where John (known as Jack) Kidd was the owner of the Black Rock Colliery.

Sydney Mail, July 12, 1926

Body recovered from Glebe Harbour was murderer's daughter

The body of a young woman pulled from Glebe Harbour three days ago was that of Mrs Henrietta Winterbourne, aged 22 years. Mrs Winterbourne was estranged from her husband, Michael Winterbourne, who is believed to have left Australia a year ago. The coroner recorded a verdict of suicide, possibly while of unsound mind. The victim was the daughter of John William Kidd of MacDonald Falls, NSW, who was executed at Willagong Prison last year for the murder of his eldest son, Nathaniel, 29. Police reported that efforts had been made to notify Mrs Winterbourne's surviving brother, William Kidd, next of kin, but without success.

Sydney Mail, March 6, 1927

Chapter One

Zanzibar, Africa, October 1937

When the SS *Christina* slid into the dock, the sun was burning down and the cool ocean breezes were now behind them. Will Kidd loved to feel the sun on his skin – the heat was like food to him, nourishing, burning the life back into his body from where it had been drained away by the cold gloom of the transatlantic runs he'd been doing the previous year. The sun reminded him of home, Australia, where he knew he'd never return, no matter how much he wanted to.

He breathed deeply, drawing the warm air into his lungs, savouring the smell of the land after weeks at sea. Standing on the foredeck, Will watched the gulls circling the boat hungrily, ready to swoop and dive to the surface of the water to scoop up any scraps of food thrown from the ship or the dockside. Ahead, the land throbbed with heat and, under the distorting haze of the sun, the port was a vibrant splash of primary colours, as brown-skinned bearers carried sacks of grain and cotton, bales of bright-hued fabrics and baskets overflowing with tropical fruits and spices. Will could smell the rich aroma of those spices in the air, mingling with the tang of salt from the ocean and the sharpness of sweat from the procession of labouring men as they carried produce between ships and warehouses.

It took several hours to partially unload the *Christina* of the cargo designated for Zanzibar and replenish her hold, then Will and most of his shipmates were at liberty. This would be only a brief stopover – the ship would sail on the first tide next morning, not long after dawn, but until midnight they were free to enjoy the sights and sounds of Zanzibar, to explore its bazaars, drink their fill in its quayside bars, and sample the delights of its spicy cuisine.

The ground on the dockside underfoot was hot as a gridiron. Prostitutes were evident everywhere, calling out to the men as they swaggered by, knowing the sailors could have been weeks at sea without the comfort and pleasure of a woman's body. Some men succumbed, peeling away from the group, happily led by the hand by smiling white-toothed women with skin like burnished ebony. Will never gave them a second glance. A seasoned sailor after ten years at sea, he knew the best-looking women didn't need to go near the quay, didn't need to hunt their own game, because it came to them.

With his crew-mate and friend, Paolo Tornabene, Will headed straight to a tall, narrow building in the heart of Stone Town. It was a bar, not a drinking dive, a meeting place not a brothel. Tonight it was doing a brisk trade when the two men arrived. Efficiently run by a Lebanese woman, it was always packed, known to serve the best food this side of the Indian Ocean. Men were being turned away at the door, but there was always a place for Will here at Rafqa's.

The owner, Rafqa Papas, was a widow. She had moved to Zanzibar, as a newly-wed, nearly twenty years ago from

Beirut with a husband who died soon after they arrived, leaving her childless and penniless, with only a run-down, ramshackle building. Rafqa had transformed it into this thriving bar, restaurant and guest house. These were the only facts known about her. Yet if Will were to be honest with himself, he also knew she was more than a little in love with him – but he chose not to let himself think about that.

Rafqa's place was always buzzing, the food and drink accompanied by live jazz music – the singers handpicked by Rafqa as much for the beauty of their faces as the melody of their voices.

Tonight there was a mixed crowd at the tables, mostly men: crews from other ships, merchants and traders, British and German settlers in Zanzibar to do business, assorted consular officials of varying nationalities, the odd policeman and, this evening, a table of four Germans, two of them in naval uniform and sporting the sinister-looking swastika. Someone had once hinted to Will that Rafqa was a spy – possibly for more than one country. Will didn't know if there was any truth in the rumour, and to be honest he didn't care. A place like Zanzibar was probably full of spies and no one would be better placed to fill that function than Rafqa Papas, whose establishment was patronised by men of all nations and stations. Everyone who was anyone went to Rafqa's.

Will walked into the bar with Paolo, navigating their way through the crush to the only vacant table. All he wanted was to drink. He'd probably eat some food, not out of hunger, but because Paolo would insist upon it – the young Italian had evidently appointed himself Will's protector and conscience. All Will wanted – all he ever wanted – was to find oblivion, to drink as much as he could, then pass out, preferably in the arms of a woman, and tonight that woman would probably be Rafqa.

She saw him as soon as he came in, and threw him a wide grin, but carried on with whatever she was doing behind the bar. Will liked that about her – she never demanded anything, never allowed herself to appear needy, didn't pepper him with questions. Instead, she just accepted what he offered when it was offered. He had no illusions that she lived like a nun between his visits – but whenever he was on the island she was there for him. As Zanzibar was a regular call for the *Christina* he had seen a lot of her.

Right now, though, he wanted to get drunk, to feel the bitter tang of the spirit in the back of his throat, the burning warmth as it spread through his veins, the feeling of numbness that soaked through his whole body as the liquor hit his bloodstream and deadened the pain. Oblivion. That was what he craved. To wipe out the thoughts that crowded his head when on dry land, clouded his judgement and screamed at him constantly that he was a failure and, at barely thirty, had squandered his life away.

Once they had eaten, Paolo left to return to the ship, after reminding Will to be back on board by midnight. 'I tell you again, my friend, don't be late. *Il Capitano* has said one hundred times that next time anyone late, they off his ship.'

Will just waved a hand, impatient for his friend to be gone and off his back. He lifted the bottle and refilled his glass. The table of Germans had been joined by Rafqa. He could hear her low laughter across the room. She was flirting with the four men. Suppressing a momentary spasm of jealousy, he moved his chair to face away from them and towards the band. After a few minutes, he glanced around and saw that Rafqa was now in conversation with one of the non-uniformed Germans. There was no laughter now – and whatever they were discussing appeared to exclude the other three. A few minutes later, out of the corner of his eye, Will saw the man go outside. Rafqa was leaning over the table laughing with the others, then she followed the first man, slipping through a side door, unnoticed by anyone but Will. What was she doing? He told himself it was none of his business. Ten minutes or so later, she was back at her usual station perched on a high stool at the bar.

It was after eleven when Rafqa finally wove her way between the tables to join him. By now, Will was enveloped in a warm shawl of fuzziness. Drink always helped to numb the pain and assuage some of the guilt that had plagued him since his father's death.

She slipped into the seat opposite. Her perfume was light but heady and Will would have liked to bury his face between her breasts and breathe it in.

'You drink too much, William,' she said, sighing lightly and smiling. She stroked his hand briefly, but tenderly. 'It makes you imagine things are better but it doesn't change anything.'

Her voice always excited him. Warm treacle, slightly breathy, rich, resonant, wrapping him up. He looked up from his whisky to study her. She was a beautiful woman. Older than him – maybe even by as much as ten or fifteen years. Her dark brown eyes were silent promises and he felt a sudden wave of lust crash over him.

Rafqa leant forward and brushed away a lock of hair from his brow. 'You look tired, William. Maybe too tired?' Her voice was husky.

'I'm not tired,' he said. 'Not any more. And never for you.'

She smiled, and for a moment he glimpsed the sadness behind the smile – the finest of frowns, the hint of forlorn hope in the two dark pools that were her eyes. Then the expression had vanished, replaced by the brisk efficiency that characterised her.

'Everyone seems happy enough.' She swept her arm expansively around the room. The bar was packed: more women here now, the band playing softer, more romantic tunes and a few couples moving slowly around the small dance floor. 'I think they can get on with it now and I can leave them in Bebe's capable hands.'

She looked towards the portly, silver-haired Arab behind the bar, then inclined her head in the direction of the table of Germans.

Will saw the uniformed men were getting to their feet and were leaving with four young women.

'I thought I might have some trouble from them,' she said. 'But they're full of schnapps and have just settled the bill. Now they've other things on their mind.'

Will too had other things on his mind and reached over the table for her hand. He pulled her to her feet and drew her towards him.

Rafqa pushed him away. 'Not here. It doesn't look right. I don't want people getting the wrong idea about me. Give me five minutes, then come upstairs.'

She moved off, pausing on her way between the tables to say the odd word to a customer, then she was gone, through the curtained doorway at the back of the room.

Will drained his glass, studied his watch impatiently, then when the five minutes had passed, crossed the room and went through the beaded curtain.

To his surprise the whisky had dulled neither his desire nor the ability to satisfy it. Had it done so, he was certain that the sight of Rafqa standing naked in a pool of moonlight, her hair tumbling around her shoulders, her perfume filling the room, would have been sufficient to revive him.

Afterwards, exhausted from their efforts, Will lay on his back while Rafqa got up from the bed, draped a silk robe around herself and went to sit cross-legged on a rug by the window, where there was a large hookah. Will watched her, desire coursing through his body again, as she mixed some of the contents of a tobacco tin with that of a small wax-wrapped parcel, and placed everything in the bowl of the hookah. 'Nothing but the best for you, William.' She stirred a few drops of honey into the mixture, then covered it with mesh, placed charcoal on top and lit it. Putting the pipe in her mouth, she took a long, slow inhalation, then signalled Will to join her.

He breathed in the hashish, drawing it deep into his lungs, immediately feeling his nerves numbing, his heart pounding, pulse racing, thoughts fading away into a sublime nothingness, a mellow intensity of perception. Time slowed down. He looked at Rafqa. She was bathed in the moonlight again and her silk gown had slipped from one shoulder. Suddenly he felt an overwhelming tenderness for her. It was more than desire. In that moment he loved her. Would have laid down his life for her. His usual

7

reticence gave way to a wish to tell this woman everything, to lay himself bare, pour out his heart, reveal the innermost workings of his soul.

-

Next morning, Will woke in a tangle of limbs. Unravelling himself from Rafqa he went to stand at the open window, which looked out over the roofs of the city. On some of the nearby buildings he could see women already up and doing their washing on the flat rooftops, in the half-light before the sun came up fully and made working more arduous.

His head was pounding, his mouth raw and his stomach queasy – the delayed penalty for the deadly combination of hashish and whisky. Glancing back at the bed, where Rafqa lay, naked, her long hair spreading across the pillow, he heard the soft snoring stop, and she opened her eyes and smiled at him. The smile conveyed much and, although he could remember little of what had passed between them the previous night, he felt a twinge of guilt. He knew he had shown her more tenderness and affection than their casual relationship warranted. The drugs did that sometimes – suppressed lust and replaced it with strong feelings of affection and tenderness that were closer to romantic love than Will intended. While the details were blurred he knew they had made love rather than having sex. He turned away and stared out of the window. He didn't want her getting the wrong idea about his feelings for her.

Behind him she rolled off the low bed and moved across the room. He could hear rattling and realised she was making coffee. Rafqa made great coffee, so thick you

8

could stand the spoon up in it, the sweetness of sugar softening the bitter strength of the arabica. Worth waiting for. Pulling on his trousers he looked at his watch. It was after five and getting light already. He needed to get a move on. But he didn't want to forgo the coffee and knew there was no likelihood Captain Palmer would fulfil his threat to sail without him. He was already hours past the midnight deadline.

Rafqa handed him the cup. The liquid was boiling hot and he blew on the surface to cool it. She was wearing the silk wrap again and in the cold light of the dawn he could see the fine lines around her eyes. Still beautiful though. She moved towards him, reaching out with her hand but Will pretended he hadn't noticed and stepped backwards, trying not to acknowledge that she had flinched, trying to ignore the hurt in her big soulful eyes.

Desperate to lighten the tension between them and restore some normality, he said, 'Who were those Germans last night?'

She shrugged. 'Two from a ship that docked yesterday. Naval officers. I don't know who the other two were.'

He looked up at her as he sipped his coffee. He knew she was lying. Rafqa knew everything that happened in Zanzibar. 'I saw you talking to one of them. Didn't look like you didn't know him.'

She gave a throaty laugh. 'Jealous, William?'

'I didn't like the look of him. I don't like to think of you hanging around with Nazis. I'm fond of you, Rafqa.'

Another dry laugh. 'Business.'

'You should keep away from the Germans. I don't trust them.'

9

She brushed the hair away from his brow. 'There will be a war, William. Maybe not this year or the next, but soon. You need to wake up and make some choices. Stop letting life just pass you by. Decide where your loyalties lie.'

'Are you telling me yours lie with the Germans?' He was incredulous.

'How can you even ask me that? How could I ever support such a regime with its plan to people the world with the so-called master race.' Her voice was angry, contemptuous. 'My country was under the rule of the Ottomans and now has to suffer decisions being made for us by the French. I've seen so much hatred and fighting because of religious differences. I am a patriot and a believer in freedom. Do you have any idea what Hitler has been doing in Germany, in Austria and Czechoslovakia? Do you have any idea what he's capable of?'

'I'm not interested in politics.'

She snorted in derision. 'Politics! You don't know the meaning of the word. My freedom and yes, your freedom too, William, are at risk if Hitler isn't stopped.'

'And how exactly does hanging around with those Germans help you do that?' He knew he was being cruel and dismissive but he couldn't help himself. His head was pounding as though his brain was pressing against his skull, confined by it.

'The Germans are all over East Africa, from the Cape to here and beyond. Their friends, the Italian fascists, too. Mozambique is a hotbed of intrigue. South Africa, too. Nazi sympathisers everywhere. You are naive, William. But fortunately there are a few enlightened people who are awake to the threat.'

'You're telling me you're spying on them?'

She gave a little shake of her head. 'Of course I'm not. Who would be interested in using a woman like me as a spy?' She laughed, but he thought there was a hollowness to it. 'Now you must go. You told me your ship sails at dawn. It's past that now.'

He turned and looked at the orange glow on the horizon as the sun lit the surface of the sea.

Putting down the cup, he pulled her towards him, brushing her forehead with a light kiss. She leaned away, unconvinced, then placed her hands on his cheeks. 'Ah, William. I am too fond of you for my own good.' She hesitated a moment then added, 'But thank you for last night. It was special.'

A hammering on the bedroom door broke the silence between them. When Rafqa opened the door, Paolo Tornabene was standing on the landing, red-faced and breathless. He pushed past her into the room.

'I told you, Kidd, *il Capitano* will sail the ship without you. You must come now or I will be left behind too.'

'Shit!'

No time for any lingering farewells with Rafqa. Will tried not to show his relief, threw her a quick smile, pushed away his guilt about his treatment of her, and ran down the stairs behind his Italian crew-mate.

The pair raced through the narrow streets of Stone Town, back to the waterfront and the waiting ship. The dockside was deserted but the deck of the *Christina* was a hive of activity as the crew made ready for departure. The hatches were closed, cargo checked, derricks secured, the steam already up, and the crew were everywhere checking everything moveable was safely stowed.

Moments after Will and Paolo scrambled on board, the gangway was lifted and the moorings were slipped. The horn sounded and the ship eased away from the quay. They had made it by the narrowest of margins.

Any hope that Will might sneak on board the *Christina* undetected was dispelled when he heard the booming Australian accent of the bosun calling him across the deck.

'Thought I wouldn't notice you slipping back on board six hours late, did you, Kidd? You're nothing but a bludger.'

'Not yet six hours.'

'Don't split hairs, you dirty bastard.' His voice was strident, and his anger evident in the way he sprayed spittle as he spoke.

Before Will could answer, the ship's master appeared behind Cassidy. 'Shore leave was until midnight. It's now nearly six. Get on with your duties, Kidd. I'll see you at ten o'clock in the day room. But I'll tell you this now, there'll be no shore leave for you and Tornabene between here and the Med.'

'Please, sir, don't punish Tornabene. He was only trying to—'

'Don't interrupt.' The master narrowed his eyes. 'Now you've cost him Naples too.'

Will wanted to kick himself. Paolo's home town was Napoli and the Italian had been looking forward to the stopover there and the rare chance to see his mother. But Will knew protest was futile and likely to cost them both further. He bit his lip and struggled to swallow his fury.

The hurried coffee with Rafqa had scalded his mouth but done nothing to banish his headache. If anything, it was getting worse. The sun was already hot and Will felt slightly dizzy. The hash had been strong stuff.

Fortunately, his long experience as a mariner meant he could carry out most of his tasks without thinking. The sea was calm, the skies clear and most of the crew were used to the passage in and out of the harbour here. They had called at Zanzibar many times in the six months they had been travelling up and down through East African waters. Now, their time here over, they were heading to the Arabian Gulf, the Suez Canal and then through the Mediterranean and back to England. To Will this trip had been a pleasing change from the misery of trans-Atlantic voyages, where it was a dull shuttle back and forth across cold, grey and often hostile seas.

The *Christina* was a tramp steamer on a long circular voyage, picking up and depositing cargo as she went, in a series of short runs along the way. They followed no regular route, but went where the loads were, discharging one cargo and seeking a replacement. Their cargo changed constantly, depending on the port, everything from sugar, salt and spices to scrap metal and machine parts. If it needed moving and the price was right, then they would transport it. Men like Will and Paolo didn't want to join a national navy – tramping offered freedom, variety and most believed the merchant mariners were more skilled sailors than their naval counterparts. The crew were of many nationalities, including many lascars, from the Indian sub-continent, renowned as great sailors and cooks, so the rations were better than Will had been used to on the Atlantic crossings.

He had been delighted when he'd got the opportunity to sign on for this voyage and didn't want to lose his place on the *Christina*. With the exception of the bosun, he liked all the crew and respected the officers. Until now, he'd got along well with Captain Palmer too, despite the odd disciplinary lapse. Will had sailed under the Englishman six years ago on the 'the Millionaires' ships' of the Furness Bermuda Line, ferrying wealthy industrialists and their guests to and from their Caribbean retreats. But Captain Palmer had moved on and been replaced by a skipper who Will had managed to rub up the wrong way. Will lasted just one trip under the new regime before being laid off. That plum job had been followed by three years of service on crowded passenger ships plying their way between Liverpool and New York or Halifax – until a chance meeting in a Liverpool pub had brought him back under Palmer's patronage and to his job as an able seaman on the *Christina*. And now he'd jeopardised it all because he'd allowed himself to get stoned. He cursed his stupidity.

Tornabene was leaving the day room when Will arrived for his meeting with the ship's master. The young Italian's expression was glum. Palmer had made good on his threat to cancel his Neapolitan shore leave.

'Did he dock your pay too?' asked Will.

Paolo shook his head. 'But I'd rather have lost the pay than the shore leave.'

'I'm sorry. He had no right to take it out on you.'

'*Cazzo!* When will you take responsibility for your own actions, Kidd? I don't blame *il Capitano*. I blame you.' He shoved Will aside and made his way back along the companionway.

When Will pushed open the door, Captain Palmer was at a table in the otherwise empty day room. Will went to stand in front of him and tried to look appropriately penitent.

'You're wearing out my patience, Kidd. I warned you before I won't tolerate disobedience on my vessel. You act as if you're a law unto yourself. Bosun Cassidy is constantly bringing complaints to the mates about your conduct.'

Will lowered his head, fixing his eyes on his shoes. 'I seem to have got on the wrong side of the bosun, sir.'

Palmer said nothing for a moment, studying a leather-bound book in front of him. 'According to the other officers your behaviour gives no cause for complaint. But it's essential my crew gets on with the bosun. I want a happy ship.'

'Aye aye, sir.'

'And I also want a punctual one. Next time you're late you'll be left behind. And let what you've done to Tornabene be a lesson to you. You will go ashore in Naples and I'll make sure you have to walk past your crew-mate, knowing that he has missed a chance to visit his family. Maybe then you will reflect on the selfishness of your conduct. And don't even think about offering to swap with him or any other crew member.'

'Sir.' Will felt shame mix with anger that the captain was doing this to Paolo.

'Dammit, man, isn't it time you grew up?'

Will kept his eyes fixed on the floor, his hands behind his back clenched into two tight fists.

'What disappoints me more than anything is that you have so much potential if you'd only apply yourself and show some discipline. You could be an officer one day, even captain your own ship. By now a man of your skills and experience should be ready to become a bosun.

Instead, you risk getting yourself thrown off my ship altogether.'

It was stuffy in the room and Will's head still felt as though it was being squeezed in a vice. He wanted to go below and sleep off his hangover. Sweat was beading his forehead.

'I'm docking you three days' pay. No shore leave between here and the Mediterranean. I want you to reflect on what I've said to you today. You need to make a choice, William Kidd, whether to throw your life away or try to make a career for yourself. It's as simple as that. I'm a patient man and I've put up with more than most would. But there's only so far I'm prepared to go if you won't help yourself. Do I make myself clear?'

'Yes, sir.'

'I've told the second mate and the bosun to keep a close eye on you. Now get out of my sight.'

Will left, fuming with resentment. The last thing he wanted was Jake Cassidy, the only other Australian on board, breathing down his neck. There was no love lost between the two men. As far as Will knew, there wasn't anything particular he'd done to cause this. Cassidy had taken an instant and irrational dislike of Will and lost no chance to find fault in everything he did. As a seasoned, able seaman, Will took exception to this. But protest was futile, so he tried to keep out of the bosun's way.

It was the middle of the afternoon before Will began to feel human again. As they made their way along the coast under a clear blue sky with barely a breeze, he forced himself to think about what the ship's master had said. He would be a fool to risk losing this posting. Being in the tropics had lifted his spirits – as far as he believed them capable of lifting – and the prospect of returning to the northern hemisphere didn't appeal.

Yet he felt hemmed in, unsatisfied. All his life he'd longed to go to sea. As a teenager in the outback, he'd supplemented the few bob his father had paid him to work the land, by selling rabbit skins for a shilling a-piece. The money accumulated, ready for the day when he'd plucked up the courage to leave home and the bullying of his father, and set out to seek his fortune at sea.

Never having visited the coast, the sea was something he'd imagined and dreamed of, based on the stories his mother had told him as a child and the books he read: *Treasure Island*, the adventures of Sinbad the Sailor, and *Robinson Crusoe*. Enough to fuel his imagination during the years spent on an isolated smallholding in the bush. But Will soon learned that a dream can sour when it is pursued out of necessity rather than desire. His longed-for maritime adventure had become a furtive running away from the shame of a father who had been hanged. While the anonymity of being among an international crew had liberated him from the gossip of parochial Australia, he found that the guilt about his father being put to death for saving Will's life stayed with him. Guilt too, that he'd never visited him in prison, unable to face the enormity of what Jack Kidd was about to go through.

–

It was several hours before Will was able to talk to Paolo. The young Italian was avoiding him, but Will eventually found him on deck as the sun was sinking. He was sitting on top of the hatches, leaning against the bulkhead. It looked as though he'd been writing a letter – presumably to break the news to his family that he would not be visiting them as planned.

The sun disappeared rapidly as it always did in the tropics, moving from day to night in a moment. Will sat down beside his friend. He swallowed, forcing himself to say the words he knew to be true but struggled to admit. 'I'm sorry, Paolo. I've been stupid and selfish. You tried to help me and you've paid the price for it. I wouldn't blame you if you told me to go to hell and never spoke to me again.'

Paolo spoke without looking at him, his voice spitting out the words. '*Vai al diavolo. Mannaggia a chi t'é muort! Mannaggia a chi t'é vivo!*'

Will tried to ease the tension. 'You're going to have to translate that for me, cobber.'

Paolo grunted. 'I did as you asked. Told you to go to the devil. Then I added in a special Neapolitan curse – that your dead relatives go to hell too – and that your living ones are also damned.' He gave a little snort. 'Yes, I am *incazzato*. Very, very angry with you.'

'Well, I hate to disappoint you, matey. But my mother died when I was a lad and since her life was a living hell, I expect the real thing would be a blessed relief. My brother's dead too and whatever it was you said, I'll willingly say that too. He's certainly rotting in hell already. As for my old man, since His Majesty's pleasure was that he should hang by the neck until he was dead, there's a pretty good chance he's down there too.' He sighed a long breath. 'Even though the old bastard didn't deserve to be hanged.'

'I'm sorry, Will. I didn't know.' Paolo's face in the dim light looked stricken.

Deciding that he would unburden himself of everything to his trusted friend, Will said, 'And as for my living relatives, all I have is an older sister. And I haven't spoken to her since the old man was sentenced to swing. As far as I'm concerned it was her bloody fault he was convicted, when all he'd done was save my brother from killing me. So if you call your curses down on her, I'm not going to argue with you, mate.'

As he spoke, a hand grabbed his shoulder from behind with a powerful grip. 'I've got news for you, then, Kidd, you piece of filth. Your sister's dead too. And certainly burning in hell.'

Will spun round to face Jake Cassidy. 'Keep out of other men's conversations, Cassidy.'

'You had no idea, did you?' The man curled his lip. 'You didn't even know your own sister died ten years ago. Some brother you are.' He moved round in front of Will, arms folded. 'Well, she's well and truly a dead relative now and quite certain to be burning like a crisp because she topped herself, didn't she? A mortal sin for those of us like me and *Turnybainy* here, who are members of the one true Holy Catholic Church.'

'Rack off, Cassidy. Peddle your lies to someone else.' Will tried to inject confidence into his voice but it sounded unconvincing, even to him. What was Cassidy talking about?

'Drowned herself in Glebe Harbour. Word was she was legless – drunk as a skunk. I was in port at the time and watched them pull her body out. You could smell the gin fumes a mile away. And the fishes had nibbled her eyes out.' He was grinning widely. 'I only made the connection this morning when I was wondering how a fellow Aussie could turn out to be such a feckless bludger as you are, Kidd. Then I remembered the papers saying that girl was the daughter of one of Australia's finest murderers, Jack Kidd – the man so rotten he killed his own son. Word at the time was your sister was on the game as well as being a drunk and rather too fond of snorting white powder up her pretty little nose.'

Will lunged at Cassidy, trying to grab his arms but the bosun was a powerful man and held him off by the shoulders.

Cassidy looked down at the stupefied Tornabene. 'Find yourself some better company than this loser, Eyetie. He's going to be thrown off this ship before we're back in Liverpool, you mark my words.'

Chapter Two

Lying in his bunk that night, Will thought again about Rafqa. He let his mind recreate the image of her lustrous black hair, her long, lithe limbs and the way they had wound themselves around him. His desire for her was undeniable, but as much as he would have liked to, he knew he couldn't love her.

Will didn't know what love was any more. Had he ever? All he did know was that it had taunted and eluded him. Years ago, he had believed himself to be in love with his father's wife. His stepmother – although he hated to use that word in relation to her. But Elizabeth had made it clear his feelings were not, and never could be, reciprocated. Will had always known that she had not loved his father but had made a marriage of convenience. But discovering that she had been in love all along with the man Will counted as his best friend, his brother-in-law, Michael Winterbourne, was more than any man should be expected to bear. Betrayed by both of them – was it any wonder that the capacity to love was no longer in him?

Poor Rafqa. He felt more for her than for anyone else. But love? Impossible. He was an empty husk. Squeezed dry, desiccated. And while he no longer loved the sea, he hated the idea of being stuck in one place. It would be like a slow suffocation. As to marrying, settling down with one woman, even one as desirable as Rafqa, was never going to happen. He didn't want it to happen. He would never allow it to happen.

He lay back on his bunk in the darkness, listening to the chorus of breathing and snoring around him. If only sleep came as easily to him as it did to his crew-mates. Lying in the dark, his memory of the previous night solidified. In a half-sleep, he felt himself transported back to that upstairs room and realised he had indeed said more than he should have said and had shown Rafqa more tenderness than he had intended. He felt the blood rush to his face so he could feel the heat of it. If only he could wind back the clock, take back what he had said, and what he had done.

The first thing Will felt after smoking the hash, was a sharp hunger as if he hadn't eaten in days. This was a familiar experience – cannabis always brought on a desire to eat, even when there was no reason to be hungry. He watched Rafqa as she walked across the room to the curtained corner where she brewed her coffee. She emerged a moment later, carrying a plate of sweetmeats dripping in honey and studded with pistachios and almonds. Sitting beside him on the rug, naked, she began slowly feeding him with her fingers, while he did the same for her, each relishing the sticky sweetness of the pastries, licking the honey from each other's mouths and fingers in a slow, sensual interlude that seemed to last for hours but could only have been a matter of minutes.

'You're so beautiful,' he said. 'More lovely than anything I have ever seen. More beautiful than the night sky. You shimmer like the stars.'

Instead of laughing at his unprecedented and uncharacteristic poetic outpouring, Rafqa silenced him with her lips, drawing him into a honeyed kiss that was tender and moving.

Looking back now, he knew it was the terrible magic woven by the drugs, but then, caught in the sensual music of the moment, he had believed it almost divine, spiritual, holy.

He spent he knew not how long, running his fingertips over every inch of her, then lay back as she did the same to him, until it seemed that he no longer inhabited his own body but had moved outside it into another dimension where everything happened more slowly and intensely. He wanted to stay there forever, inside that room on that Persian rug with Rafqa.

Then they made love. Slowly. Tenderly. All the pleasure he had experienced hitherto, the many women he had enjoyed, paled in comparison with what he and Rafqa were doing. Every sexual experience he had had before now – even with Rafqa – had been just that: having sex, mostly pleasurable, rarely emotional, and never before like this.

After the long, slow lovemaking, they had talked. He had told the Lebanese woman more than he wished he had.

'Tell me, Will. Where have you left your heart?'

'What do you mean?' His voice harsh, nervy.

'You have taken your heart out and locked it away where no one can find it.' Her eyes were full of sadness. 'Not even me. Not even now, when everything says that you are opening it to me. But you and I know you are not.'

'I love you, Rafqa,' he said at last, cupping her chin in his hands and locking his eyes onto hers.

'Do you really, Will?' Her voice was doubtful.

He pulled her into his arms again and fastened his mouth upon hers. Then they didn't talk any more until morning.

It had been like no other night. At the time, to Will it had been deeply meaningful.

But it wasn't meaningful.

Now, in the cold light of day, on the high seas, Will knew his mind and body had deceived him. His feelings for Rafqa were affectionate, sometimes passionate, but never meaningful in that way. He decided then and there, lying in his bunk, listening to the symphony of snoring around him, that he would never again take narcotics. Never again would he risk forgoing control, allowing another part of himself – for he could not deny that it was indeed a deeply buried part of himself – to come to the fore.

Will shivered in spite of the heat of the night, still ashamed. The *Christina* was shadowing the coast and it was a close atmosphere, heavy, thick, hard to breathe. In those few hashish-heavy hours he had indeed believed he loved Rafqa, God forgive him. But their tragedy was that once the drugs washed away, he felt nothing, only the kind of attraction any man would feel for a woman such as she.

Now he knew he should have admitted to Rafqa that loving her was impossible. Loving anyone was impossible. He had realised that, the moment he knew that Elizabeth, his beloved Lizzie, would never love him back. Rafqa was right: he no longer had a heart. Elizabeth had torn it out of him and thrown it away.

Acknowledging that sleep was not going to come, he made his way up to the deck, where he stood in the dark, leaning on the port-side rail, watching the dark mass that was the coast of Africa slipping past in the far distance. While less muggy up here on deck, there was little breeze. They were travelling at around eight knots and as he looked towards the bows, he could just make out the pale pinpricks of lights that were Mombasa. The *Christina* wasn't stopping there, but steaming straight for Aden and beyond to the Suez Canal and into the Mediterranean. Will had liked what he'd seen of Africa so far, and was sorry that the short back-and-forth hops up and down this coast had now come to an end. Palmer was right. He had to make some choices. If he was to stay in the merchant navy, he had to think about making a proper go of it. Despite the unfairness of today's punishment of Tornabene, Will respected Palmer. He was the best skipper he'd served under – and there had been a lot of them. If he wanted another stint on the *Christina* he had better work his way back into the master's good books.

What choice did he have? He couldn't go back to Australia. There was nothing there for him. His family were dead. The scruffy excuse for a homestead that was Wilton's Creek had doubtless been sold after his father's execution. Sold to pay off the accumulated debts of Jack Kidd's failed coal-mining business. And Elizabeth. He couldn't bear the thought of seeing her again. Of knowing that she was probably married to Michael Winterbourne now. If Jake Cassidy was telling the truth, Harriet's suicide would have removed the last obstacle for them.

Poor Hattie. They'd been so close when they were small, but they had been separated after the death of their mother when Harriet was sent into town to live with the local schoolmistress. The separation pushed them apart, until in the end they had nothing in common and had become like strangers. But for her to be dead – and at her own hand – shocked him deeply. And not knowing for ten years. Hattie had always made bad choices. She'd messed things up more than he had. Maybe all the Kidds were cursed. Every one of them had died prematurely and violently.

If Will were to avoid that curse himself he'd better start to change things. If, some day, he was going to return to a life on the land it would have to be somewhere other than Australia – America maybe. Since the Depression and Prohibition ended, things were looking up there. But to make a success of a new beginning he'd need some solid cash behind him. That would mean cutting back on his spending, saving his wages and studying for his mate's ticket.

When both Rafqa and the skipper had told him that he needed to make choices, to grow up, he hadn't liked to hear it, but he knew they were right. Until now, he'd let life wash over him and carry him along passively, like a piece of flotsam swept along by the currents. From now on he would set his own course.

–

One day drifted into another as the ship made its slow, stately progress through the Indian Ocean.

Will cursed his own stupidity, which meant he would be confined to ship during their planned stops at Aden, Jeddah and Port Said. Being stuck on board during a protracted stay in port was never pleasant. The land-based delights were visible and tangible, and being cooped up on a hot, airless ship was a trial. All the crew had to do it from time to time, but on a rota, and mostly with at least a couple of hours to go ashore to dispatch mail, buy essentials and drink a few beers. Denial of shore leave was a very effective punishment.

Confinement, and guilt about Paolo made Will determined to keep his nose clean for the rest of this voyage. He wanted to avoid giving Cassidy any ammunition that would allow him to make good on the promise that Will would be thrown off the ship before they reached Liverpool.

One morning, as they were moving through the Red Sea towards the Suez Canal, Cassidy appeared beside Will, who had just finished scraping rust off the guard rails at the stern, ready for re-painting. He enjoyed the meticulous nature of such tasks, allowing himself to concentrate on the work in hand and blot out everything else.

'Call that done, Kidd?' The bosun ran his fingers underneath the rail. 'Feels bumpy. There's more rust there.'

'But I'm down to the next layer of paint. I've scraped all the rust off.'

'There's rust underneath the paint, so get that off too. I want it smooth as a baby's bottom.' He grinned. 'But you wouldn't know about babies' bottoms would you? So let's say a Lebanese tart's arse.'

Will was about to jump up and thump him, but a voice in his head told him to swallow his anger and let it go. He'd get his revenge on the bully one day but there was no point in risking incurring the captain's wrath again. Cassidy, realising he was not going to get the satisfaction of a response, moved away, thrusting his hips in a parody of the sexual act as he went.

The man was sick in the head. Yet Cassidy seemed to get along with the rest of the crew well enough. For a reason known only to Cassidy himself, it was just Will who was the target of his bullying and snide remarks.

Will was counting the days until they arrived in Liverpool. Not because he wanted to be there – he didn't – but because he'd heard that Cassidy planned to switch to the White Star Line with its regular runs to Australia.

As long as Palmer would take him on again, Will only had to hang on a little while longer and he would be free of Cassidy for good. One thing was sure. He'd never sign on to another vessel that the bosun was sailing on.

–

When they docked in Naples, the sun was shining. It was late morning and there were two full holds to unload. The harbour was busy and all hands were needed to man the operation which took until after dusk. Captain Palmer had meetings with cargo aggregators and deals to be done to finalise the replenishment of the cargo for the onward leg. He advised a happy crew that shore leave would be until eight o'clock the following evening, with sailing soon after dawn the day after.

Paolo's face was a picture of misery. He hadn't seen his family in more than a year and was heartbroken that he would be missing a rare opportunity to enjoy his mamma's cooking and tell his extended family all about the places he'd visited, during what had only been his third year as a seaman. The fact that they were to be in port for so much time only made it worse – a prolonged torture.

Will was deeply ashamed. 'I'd give anything for you to be going ashore in my place today. What I did was unforgivable. You're a better friend than I deserve. You should have let them leave me behind in Zanzibar.'

Paolo looked up. '*Non fa niente.* There will be other times in the future when I can see *la famiglia*. It would be worse being on the ship without you, my friend.'

'What can I do for you while I'm ashore? Would you like me to call on your family?'

Paolo's eyes lit up. 'Would you? You don't mind?'

'Hell, mate, it's the least I can do. I'm ready for your mother to give me a sock in the jaw.'

'*Madonna!* You're a brave man. I have some gifts that maybe you take to them? It will stop *la mamma* getting too angry with you.'

Will shouldered the bag of gifts for Paolo's family. It was packed to the brim. In his pockets he had letters for Paolo's parents and each of his siblings and a hand-drawn map to show him the way. Evidently the Italian had passed all that time confined on board to better effect than Will had. But Will had no one to write letters to anyway.

Stopping off in a marketplace to buy flowers for Signora Tornabene, Will made his way through the narrow crowded streets, dodging the numerous bicycles and carts and ducking to avoid the washing that hung from every window. Although it was after dark, it was still hot. Barefoot children were playing, faces dirty and clothes threadbare. Naples clearly had more than its share of poverty. Despite the evident deprivation, people were smiling and the children looked as carefree as any Will had seen on his travels. It struck him then that the same was true of much of Africa. People accepted what life flung at them and didn't spend their time complaining or wishing for more.

He had gone a short distance from the market, occa-sionally consulting the pencil-drawn directions Paolo had sketched for him, when he heard the noise of shouting – no, more like chanting. He turned a corner into a small piazza and came upon a crowd of black-shirted men, holding banners, some bearing the symbol of the Italian Fascist party – a bundle of wood with an axe – some carrying slogans which Will could not understand. They had raised arms and were shouting in chorus; the only words he could recognise were '*Viva Il Duce*'. The sight was a chilling one. While Will had no interest in politics, and largely ignored world affairs, the rise of Mussolini had not passed him by. Running across this group of Fascists was the first time he had ever encountered adherents of the dictator and he didn't like what he saw. Shivering involuntarily, he doubled back the way he'd come and took a transverse street, giving the square a wide berth.

The Tornabenes lived in a third-floor apartment in a building that was as rundown and shabby as its neighbours. Nervous, he knocked on the door. It opened and a small boy of about seven stared up at him. It was only then that it occurred to Will that he spoke no Italian and it was unlikely that the Tornabenes spoke English.

The boy called something over his shoulder into the dark interior and after a couple of moments a stout lady wearing an apron appeared. She looked Will up and down and then evidently reassured by the canvas kitbag, seaboots and black bell bottoms, she swung the door wide open.

'*Entra! Devi essere un amico di Paolo.*' Signora Tornabene wiped her hands on her apron then extended one to Will, untying the apron with the other one. She called out something in a rapid quick-fire speech that Will assumed was Neapolitan dialect – although if it had been pure Italian he would still have been none the wiser.

He was ushered inside – the door leading straight into a kitchen with a makeshift wooden table and an ancient stove. Signora Tornabene gabbled some instructions to the small boy, who left the apartment, the sound of his rapid descent echoing from the stairwell.

A man came forward and shook Will's hand. '*Sono il papà di Paolo,*' he said. Will knew enough to work that one out, but was surprised that this was Paolo's father since the man looked about sixty. But then so did the mother. Life in Naples must take its toll.

'*Buonasera,*' said Will, wishing he had sought some lessons in Italian from Paolo, as he had now reached the limit of his knowledge. He looked around him, unsure what to do next. The door burst open and the small boy, followed by a long line of Tornabenes, entered the room, all lining up to greet Will.

He was astonished and relieved at the reception he was receiving, having expected anger. The family crowded around Paolo's brother as he read the letter aloud and it occurred to Will that perhaps the older members of the family couldn't read. There were sighs and shaking heads and many hand movements but no anger directed at Will. Paolo must have shouldered the blame for his absence rather than blaming it on him. His shame deepened. His friend was generous to a fault, and now as each family member greeted him, the young men with embraces, the two daughters with shy smiles, Will, for the first time in years, experienced a sudden sense of loss at his lack of any living family. What would it have been like if his mother hadn't died, if his brother hadn't been the rotten core that had ruined his family, if his father hadn't sacrificed his own life to save Will's? What would it have been like if

Hattie had remained at home, under the positive influence of her mother, instead of being overindulged by the timid schoolmistress who had brought her up after their mother's death? How would his life have been different if, instead of falling in love with Elizabeth, he had been content to continue having her in his life as his stepmother? What if he'd visited his father in prison – might he have persuaded him to appeal his conviction?

All this rushed through Will's head in a moment, before he was led to the table, around which, somehow, the entire family managed to squeeze. He picked up the bag Paolo had given him and emptied the contents onto the table top. Paolo had tied each item with a label and string and the family members scrambled to grab at the booty, until Paolo's mother shouted something, then began passing the gifts to their designated owners, who took them with shrieks of delight. The gifts were mere trinkets – ten a penny in the local African markets – yet the Tornabenes accepted them as if they were the most precious treasures.

Looking around the room, Will saw how basic it was, how it lacked anything without function. His home at Wilton's Creek had been a squalid hovel until Elizabeth had arrived and transformed it with little touches, so Will was no stranger to shabby surroundings. Yet *Casa Tornabene* was spotless, even if completely lacking adornment. It was only then that Will spotted the grey-haired lady sitting, like a tiny gargoyle in a wooden chair in the corner – *la nonna* – the grandmother Paolo had so often spoken of. When *la mamma* handed her a small carved giraffe, the old woman began to weep, a profusion of tears coursing down her cheeks.

Bewildered by the cacophony of voices around him, Will was about to make his exit, when he was pressed back into his seat, offered a glass of wine and a bowl of what looked like some kind of vegetable soup, along with a basket of fresh bread. He tried to protest, using hand movements but *la signora* was having none of it.

'*Mangia, mangia!*' she said, as she passed out bowls to each family member. '*Minestrone!*'

Will had never tasted a soup so delicious. To his surprise it was also filling, especially accompanied by the crusty bread. Unaccustomed to drinking wine, preferring beer, he appreciated the robust flavour of the local wine, after *il signor* Tornabene had poured it into a pottery jug from a huge flagon in the corner, then handed him a tumbler. It may not have been the finest of vintages, but this everyday, rough-and-ready *vino rosso* went down well.

The simple meal over, the Tornabenes lined up to embrace him again, one by one, each giving him a wide grin.

Will clattered down the stone stairs and into the street. By now it was after eleven, but there were people everywhere, even children. Old men sat on steps and low walls smoking and putting the world to rights, while young men stood around, also smoking, but posturing like peacocks as they eyed up any attractive passing woman. It was strange how Italian women were so fresh and vital when young and single, yet appeared to advance rapidly into premature old age once they were married with children – there seemed to be no middle ground. But, as most of them had big families and small incomes, it was not surprising that life took its toll on their looks and figures.

The Tornabenes home was on the side of the city closest to Mount Vesuvius and he could see its dark slopes in the distance, looming threateningly over the city. There was a breeze from the south and he could discern a slight sulphurous stink in the air, mingling with the strong smell of fish and the sweetness of ripe tomatoes. There was also an undercurrent – a faint aroma of damp and decay where the ancient buildings crowded together and the heat and light of the sun didn't reach. A city of contrasts – of brilliant sunlight and dark shadows – also reflected in its architecture. An ancient city, with relics from Rome through Napoleon and the Bourbon kings, all leaving their marks in a melange of buildings and monuments, elegance jostling with symbols of power and strength – all intermingled with the ad hoc, haphazard sprawl of homes crammed with people, where poverty and disease were no strangers.

Will debated whether to grab a few beers before returning on board. Once, he would have headed straight to the fleshpots of the city and sought out a woman, returning to the ship the following day at the last possible moment. Instead he decided to find Paolo and let him know how warm and welcoming his family had been – even if there had been a complete inability on both sides to understand a word of each other's languages.

Hearing the sound of running footsteps behind him, he hesitated, suddenly cautious. Naples was renowned for its pickpockets and robbers and Will had no wish to be found with his throat cut in a deserted alleyway. He moved to stand with his back against the wall, close to a pool of light from an upstairs window, turning to face the person following him.

It was a young woman, her face illuminated by the light. '*Signore*. Wait. Please.' She reached out to touch his sleeve. 'I am Loretta. Friend of Paolo.'

She was about twenty, with long, almost black, hair sweeping over her shoulders, and cautious eyes in a face that reminded him of one of the many statues of the Virgin Mary that crowded shop windows all over Naples. Wearing a simple cotton dress, low-cut and fitted close to her body, her breasts were rising and falling visibly as she regained her breath.

He held out a hand in greeting. 'I'm William. You speak good English, Loretta.'

She shrugged, brushing off the compliment. 'Please to give this to Paolo and say him Loretta wait for him.' She pressed something into his hand, then ran back the way she had come, disappearing into the network of narrow streets.

It was a small silver chain with a locket. A cheap trinket. Possibly made of tin, but nonetheless precious to its owner. Slipping it into his pocket, he headed to the ship, stopping to buy a couple of bottles of beer on the waterfront. He stuffed them in the haversack, on top of the jar of homemade tomato sauce and the carefully wrapped pastries Signora Tornabene had given him for Paolo.

How would it feel to have a mother to cook treats for you? To worry about you? A girl prepared to wait, no matter how long, for you to come back and marry her; he presumed that was what Loretta had meant when she said she would wait for Paolo. If Will was drowned at sea, who would mourn him? Possibly Rafqa – but she was realistic enough to know there was no possibility of a future for them.

–

He found Paolo sitting on the fo'c's'le, his back against one of the big black drums of the windlass. The Italian was staring miserably at the bay of Naples, his gaze towards Vesuvius and the area where his family lived. Will climbed up and sat down beside him, handing him a bottle of beer.

They chinked their bottles together.

'You are back soon. You see *la famiglia*?' Paolo's expression was worried.

'Of course I've seen them. That's why I came straight back. I didn't feel like going drinking tonight.' He let out a long sigh. 'You have a wonderful family, Paolo. So warm and welcoming. Meeting them made me sad that I have no family of my own. I was feeling lonely so I thought I'd come and find you so we can both feel lonely together.' He pulled a tragi-comic face.

Paolo laughed. 'Did you give them *i regali* – the gifts?'

'Yes, they loved all of them. Your grandmother was very taken with her giraffe. It made her cry with joy.'

'*Madonna! Mi manca la nonna.*'

'Give the lingo a rest, mate. I spent the whole evening trying to work out what they were all saying, but was none the wiser.'

'I said that I miss my grandmother. We are very close.' He rubbed his eyes, turning his head as he did so, in an effort to prevent Will noticing that he was on the verge of tears.

'She's a good egg, your *nonna*. Well, the whole bloody lot of them are, actually. And the tucker was great. I haven't eaten that well in years. Talking of which—' He pulled the packages out of his rucksack and handed them to his friend, who took them with whoops of joy.

'You will eat with me tomorrow, my friend.' He held up the jar of tomato sauce. 'I will cook the pasta – *la mamma* has a special recipe for her sauce.' He kissed his fingers. 'The best *pomodori* in the world grow on the slopes of *Vesuvio*.'

'There's more.' Will handed him the paper-wrapped pastries.

Paolo squeezed his hands into fists and waved them in the air. '*Sfogliatelle*. Now I die happy!'

When Paolo had calmed, Will reached inside his pocket and handed him the locket. 'After I left your folks, I ran into your friend Loretta and she asked me to give this to you.'

It was as if the bubble had been pricked: Paolo's ebullient mood deflated.

Will, conscious of the change in mood, said, 'She must have followed me from your parents' place. She told me to give you a message.'

Paolo looked away.

'Look, mate, I didn't know you didn't want to have anything to do with her. I had no choice. She just came up to me from nowhere.'

Paolo said nothing.

'She asked me to say that she's going to wait for you. That was all.'

'She said that?'

Will nodded.

Paolo's head was still turned away, facing seaward now. Will realised that he was weeping, silently.

Uncertain what to say, he tried to make light of the situation. 'She's a real looker, that Loretta. You've done well there, mate.'

Paolo turned to him, his eyes glistening with the held-back tears. 'We can never be together. Her *famiglia* will not permit it.'

'Well, you need to tell her fam*eelia* to go take a long walk off a short pier.'

Paolo's forehead creased in puzzlement.

Will quickly said, 'Never mind, I was only trying to say you don't want to pay attention to her family. If you and she think a lot of each other, all power to your elbows.'

Paolo shook his head. 'Her family has much power. My elbows have no chance against the *Camorra*.'

'You've lost me there, cobber.'

'They are powerful people, but bad people. Loretta's father is important in the Camorra. He wants Loretta to marry with another *Camorrista*.'

'You saying they're criminals?'

Paolo gave a dry laugh. 'The worst. And now that Mussolini tries to stop the Camorra and the Mafia and all the other criminal gangs, some of them have joined the Blackshirts so they can carry on their crimes from the inside.'

'I ran into some Blackshirts on the way to see your family.'

'*Stronzi!* They are the shit of the dogs. I hope you stay away from them?'

Will nodded. 'They looked a bunch of thugs. I kept well clear.'

'*Cazzo!* I hate these people. They want to destroy my country.' He slammed his fist against the metal drum. 'And the brothers of my Loretta are the worst.'

–

The *Christina* sailed on through the Mediterranean, steaming on its course towards Liverpool and stopping, briefly, only at Lisbon. Will worked hard to avoid the bosun but it was a near-impossible task. Cassidy was like a hawk circling over its prey, ready to pounce.

When they docked at Lisbon, Will and Paolo took advantage of the meagre three-hour shore leave, like thirsty men happening on an oasis. It was early afternoon, the sun warm, so they headed for one of the many cafés near the quayside and shared plates of grilled sardines and salted roasted peppers.

As they ate, Cassidy walked past, and Will heaved a sigh of relief that he hadn't noticed them. They chinked their beers together in celebration.

'Tell me, *amico mio*, you think it is true what the bosun say about your sister, that she kill herself?'

Will looked away. He hated talking about intimate matters, about his past, about anything personal. Yet Paolo's family had welcomed him into their home and he felt a stronger kinship with the Italian than he'd felt for anyone, since his friend Michael Winterbourne. But that friendship had turned sour. Michael had betrayed him. Will's caution was deep-rooted.

'Yes,' he said at last. 'I think it's probably true. Hattie was pretty mixed up.'

Paolo crossed himself. '*Santa Maria, Madre di Dio*, how terrible to take her own life.' He shook his head. 'Your

39

sister must have been very sad, *molto disperata*, to do such a terrible thing.'

'Maybe she *was* desperate.' Thinking of the Tornabene family, Will could understand his friend's incredulity. 'Hattie was never happy. Always wanting what she couldn't have.'

'What did she want?'

Will stared out at the water and shrugged. 'Who knows? To be rich? To be accepted by the country club people? For our mother not to have died when we were still kids? To have had a different life? To be loved?' As he said the words, he wondered himself. Hattie had been an enigma to him. 'But if she had wanted to be loved, she'd done everything she possibly could to prevent it from happening. She married a friend of mine and made him lead a dog's life. Only got hitched to get away from home and wangle a settlement from my old man. As soon as the ink had dried on the marriage certificate she told her husband, Michael, she was going to spend most of her time living apart from him, in Sydney.' He drained his beer bottle. 'I reckon she blamed herself for our father being condemned to death.'

Paolo's face was astonished. 'Why? How could it be her fault?'

'She opened her big mouth in the witness box and put her foot in it.'

'But did he kill him? His own son?' Paolo was horrified.

Will pinched the bridge of his nose. 'He had no choice. My brother was bad. Rotten. Used to beat my mother up. Bashed the daylights out of her. And that day he was going after my stepmother.' Will realised he was actually finding the telling therapeutic. He'd kept all this bottled up inside for so long. Paolo didn't judge, just listened quietly and intently. 'When I got there he was trying to have his way with her. Had her blouse half torn off.' Will stared out towards the sea, frowning at the painful memory. 'I stepped in and got a knife in my belly for my trouble. Nat would have finished me off and raped her, but Pa came along and shot him dead.'

Paolo's expression was grave. 'Then your papa had no choice. So why was he executed?'

'Because the silly old fool said he was glad Nat was dead and wished he'd killed him long ago. Then my sister told the court that Nat had found out Elizabeth was having an affair. Made the jury think Pa killed Nat because he was mad at him for wrongly accusing his wife.'

'So, they found him guilty? That is very sad.' Paolo's eyes reflected his concern.

'The lawyers reckoned they could have got a retrial and the charge reduced to manslaughter and a long jail sentence, but the old man wouldn't hear of it. Said dying was no more than he deserved.'

Paolo frowned. '*Madonna. Che storia triste!* Very sad story.' He looked at Will intently. 'And you, *amico mio*, what do you want?'

Will gave a dry laugh. 'Me? I want nothing, mate. A bed to sleep in, wages paid at the end of the week, and a girl in every port.'

'You make fun, Will, but inside I see you too are *triste*. Maybe not like your sister, but you are sad.'

Will laughed. 'No, mate. Not sad.' He gave a dry laugh. 'I'm not the one whose girlfriend comes from a criminal family.'

Paolo looked at him with amazement, then scraped back his chair and got to his feet. Without another word he turned away and headed back to the ship.

Will sat at the table, appetite for sardines gone. He called the waiter to bring him another beer and put his head in his hands. Why did he strike out and hurt the only people who cared for him? He'd done it to Rafqa and now he'd shown careless cruelty towards Paolo. As soon as anyone got close to him, he pulled down the shutters and locked them out. Why?

–

Crossing the Bay of Biscay is often a challenge. The seas there are predictable only in their volatility. The weather in the bay is frequently angry, its shallow waters attracting abnormally high waves that cause many a merchant ship to founder when caught in a storm. The winds blow in all the way from America, so that the waves grow in power as they cross the Atlantic and reach the shallow waters of Biscay with a ferocity that can challenge even the most seasoned sailors.

Will had only crossed the bay a few times. On the voyage south eight months ago, it had been calm and placid. The crossings he had made while working passenger ships between Sydney and Liverpool after he first went to sea had been rough but manageable and no test for his strong sea stomach. He was used to the rough waters of the Mozambique Channel and so now approached Biscay with respect but no fear.

The day started tranquil. Had they been a boat under sail, instead of a steam-powered ship, they would have been becalmed, but Will knew enough about the weather to understand that you could never count on it. About an hour into the crossing, the rain began, light at first, then growing in strength as the morning progressed. By midday the winds began to squall, and the sea swelled, rising and falling, causing the *Christina* to pitch about as it struggled to move through the increasingly choppy waters. Where this morning a dark flat sea met a pale grey sky, now these elements were reversed. The sky was dark as pitch and the sea now rising in towering waves and crashing down again, tossing the *Christina* in a terrifying cauldron of water.

Will was fortunate – one of the rare few who are immune to seasickness, no matter what the conditions. Paolo had claimed he was too but had never experienced seas like those they encountered that day. As the ship rose and fell, it rolled sideways as the force of the giant waves gathered. Paolo ran to the guard rail, ready to empty his stomach. Will dragged him by the arm. 'Move leeward, now!'

Paolo jerked his arm away. Sick he might be, but not yet ready to be reconciled with his crew-mate.

Ignoring the slight, somehow Will dragged his friend to the lee of the wind, holding his head over the railings as Paolo vomited.

'You don't want to throw your guts up into the wind and have it come back all over you.'

Paolo was pale and sweating.

'Look to the horizon. Keep your eyes fixed on it.'

Paolo groaned.

Will supported him and screamed again for his friend to focus on the horizon as everything else in this upside-down, crashing and pitching world moved in an uncontrolled and violent ballet. 'Keep your eyes on it – it will help you get your balance back. Remember to roll with the ship. Don't fight it.' He took a small lump of raw ginger out of a tin in his pocket and told Paolo to chew on it. 'It'll help settle your stomach, pal.'

The sight of the shrivelled piece of ginger seemed to make Paolo feel even more nauseous.

'Trust me. Chew it slowly and it'll sort you out. Now, best way to fight it is to take your mind off it. Come on, we need to go below. It's getting worse.' Will shouted to be heard over the crash of the breaking waves.

As they lurched like a pair of drunks towards the companionway, one foot on the deck and one on the bulkhead, trying to stay upright against the pitch of the ship, they saw Jake Cassidy in front of them, lashed with a rope to the bulkhead and shouting at two of the lascars. The Indians were clinging onto the guide rail, their eyes wild with fear. It was clear that Cassidy was exhorting them to move to the bows to fasten down an untethered crate which was sliding across the deck.

The lascars were terrified – the bow was lifting upwards as the ship crested the giant waves which crashed over the deck in a torrential cascade that threatened to sweep them overboard. In just a few brief minutes the sea had grown angrier and the boat was being tossed about as if it were a piece of flotsam, not an iron-clad steam ship.

'Get below! All of you,' Will yelled, pushing Paolo through the hatchway that led to the lower deck. His voice was being swallowed by the wind and waves so he grabbed at Cassidy's arm and jerked his own head towards the hatch. 'Come on, get below! Staying up here is suicide.'

Cassidy shoved him away, eyes blazing, then turned back to the two Indian men. His voice was hoarse as he strained to screech orders at them above the sound of the storm and the elemental force of the breaking waves. 'Tie it down – now!'

One of the two lascars must have heard the order as he stepped forward to grab the dangling end of the rope attached to the crate. The moment he caught it, he was swamped by a wave and tossed upwards. Will watched, powerless, as the man was lifted up above their heads and swept overboard. It happened in a fraction of a second, the screams of the man drowned out by the roar of the ocean. The second lascar, now hysterical, lurched towards Will, who grabbed onto the sleeve of his jacket and dragged him back against the bulkhead.

Yelling, 'Man overboard!' Will, soaked to the skin, pushed the surviving lascar through the hatchway and turned back to face Cassidy. 'You have to get below. No point staying up here now. He's gone.'

Before Will could do anything, Captain Palmer appeared in the open hatchway. 'Below decks both of you. Now! Cassidy, go and relieve the second officer in the wheelhouse. Kidd, get below and close the hatch behind you.'

Cassidy's eyes fixed on Will, burning with hatred.

The three men waited at the top of the ladder. All knew it was critical to match their movements to those of the ship. As the boat rose on the next wave, Will grabbed the rails and slid straight down the ladder to the deck below, letting the ship's opposing momentum carry him. Cassidy followed on the next upward movement, with Captain Palmer bringing up the rear. Trying to get down a ladder as the *Christina* moved downwards would be like trying to wade through setting concrete – better to let the forces of gravity take the effort away.

'We've lost a man overboard?' The master's face was grave.

Cassidy responded, 'One of the lascars – disobeying my order to go below.'

Will was too stunned to speak. He stood there dumb, mouth open.

The master glanced at Will, but gave no sign that he had registered his shock. 'Nothing we can do for him. Poor wretch has no chance in these seas.' Palmer shook his head, his face grim. Losing a crewman to the anger of the seas was never easy for a captain. 'Who was he?'

Cassidy shrugged. 'They all look the same to me.'

'His name was Ashok.' Will addressed Palmer, avoiding looking at Cassidy and barely able to control his anger. He wanted to tell Palmer the truth about what had happened but knew it would do no good. Cassidy would deny it. He ranked higher than Will, and the attitude towards lascars in the merchant navy was that they were expendable.

Yet Will didn't want to let it go. The surviving man, Sachin, could corroborate his story. But would they be believed? If only Tornabene had witnessed it too, but by then he was already through the hatch door. Will knew he had to tell Palmer. Even if the master chose not to believe him.

The storm lasted for several hours but the *Christina* withstood the buffeting through the bay. Will sat beside Paolo's berth as his friend continued to throw up the contents of his stomach – even the water that Will kept urging him to drink. Half the crew were vomiting – even some of the old hands.

By now Paolo's anger at his friend seemed to have dissipated. Will rubbed the Italian's back as he bent over a bucket. 'No shame, my friend. They say even Lord Nelson got seasick in a storm.'

It was early next morning before Will had a chance to talk to the Master. He went to his stateroom and knocked on the door. Palmer listened as Will told him how Cassidy had ordered the two lascars to batten down the loose crate, even though they were not lashed to the ship.

'And Cassidy himself?'

'Lashed to the bulkhead.'

'Witnesses?'

Will shook his head. 'Tornabene went below just before it happened. Only me and Sachin.'

Palmer let out a long sigh and rested his forehead on one palm. 'I spoke to Bosun Cassidy last night. He was categoric that the lascars defied his orders to go below.'

Will stared straight ahead and swallowed. This could cost him his career.

'Then he was lying, sir. The two men were terrified. The deck was awash. Yes, we'd have lost the crate, but we wouldn't have lost a man.'

'Perhaps I should summon Bosun Cassidy back and have you repeat your allegations in front of him.'

Will groaned. 'He'll deny it, sir.' He dug his nails into his palms as he clutched his fists behind his back.

Palmer studied Will's face for a few moments, then gave a little shake of his head. 'I don't want trouble on my ship – especially now we're on the last leg home. In the absence of corroboratory witnesses, Cassidy, as the senior man, will carry the day among the crew. He's a popular crew member. You know that as well as I do.'

'Sachin was there too, sir. It's not just me.'

Palmer looked embarrassed, then shook his head again. 'I believe you, Kidd, but you know the drill. I don't like it any more than you do.' He steepled his fingers under his nose. 'But hear this – and it's to remain within these walls – I will never work with Cassidy again, and I'll make sure that every master I know understands why.' He picked up his pipe and lit a match, then put the pipe down again without lighting it. 'Today we'll have a small ceremony of remembrance for the poor unfortunate – what did you say his name was?'

'Ashok, sir.'

'We'll give Seaman Ashok a good send-off. Now, get back to your duties, Kidd.'

Chapter Three

The wind pulled at the grasses on the dunes, bending them over, throwing up a fine spray of sand that forced Hannah Dawson to turn her head, cover her eyes, and face the other direction. She pulled her coat tight about her and tried to push the unexposed parts of her ears under her felt hat, wishing she'd remembered to put on her scarf.

Slithering down the slope into the valley between two dunes, she huddled out of the wind, knees bent in front of her, and taking the library book out of her handbag started to read, fumbling at the pages with gloved hands. It was this or no reading at all. Hannah hated having to be so furtive, but books were forbidden in the Dawson household, apart from the Bible. Her father was resolute on that point. All books, with the exception of the 'Good Book', were the work of the devil. Hannah had learnt that the hard way when she was a child. Her father had caught her reading a battered copy of *Oliver Twist*, borrowed from a schoolfriend, and had thrown it on the fire. Ever since, her love for reading undiminished, she had found ways to indulge her passion clandestinely. She shuddered to think what her father would do if he found out about her secret trips to the library. And were he to find the book she was reading now, his rage would be boundless. Rosamund Lehman's *The Weather in the Streets*. The 'oh, damn, oh hell' of the first paragraph would be enough to condemn it, never mind the adultery, divorce and worse. Charles Dawson's volatile temper was a cause for fear for Hannah, her younger sister, Judith, and her mother, Sarah.

Just that morning, during breakfast, Judith had mentioned that she would be home a little later than usual from the dressmakers where she worked, as there was a rush order for a wedding gown. She'd directed the remark at Hannah but the explosion from Charles Dawson was titanic.

'You are employed to work between the hours of eight and four-thirty and I expect you to be inside this house by a quarter to five every day. No exceptions.'

'But, Father, there's a good reason. Mrs Compton asked me specially. Miss Finch was ill earlier in the week and so we've fallen behind and the wedding is on Saturday. If I don't work a little late tonight the bride's fitting will be delayed.'

The hand thumped the table so hard that the crockery rattled, tea slopped into saucers and a fork fell onto the floor. Before Hannah could bend down to pick it up, her father had kicked it across the room, where it clattered against the skirting board.

'I should never have allowed you to go to work. You should be at home until you are married.' He swiped his napkin across his mouth and flung it down on the table. 'Wedding dresses are a disgraceful vanity. I had no idea you were involved in the making of such things.' He scowled at his wife. 'You told me she'd be making coats and hemming blankets.'

Sarah Dawson looked away and said nothing.

'But Father—' Judith's face showed a mixture of fear and anguish.

'Shut your mouth. You'll be back inside this house at four forty-five. And I want no discussion.'

With that, Dawson rose from the table, picked up his hat from the sideboard and left the house, banging the front door behind him.

When he was gone, Judith burst into tears. 'It's not fair. Why is he like that? Why can't he be like a normal father? Why can't we be like other people? Now I'll probably lose my job. If the dress isn't finished what's the bride going to do?' She dissolved into more sobbing.

Hannah placed a comforting hand on her sister's arm. 'You could always work through the dinner hour, Jude. That might help. If you explain to Miss Finch she'll understand.'

'How can anyone understand? How can anyone else know what it's like to have a father like ours?'

As all this was going on, Sarah Dawson finished her cup of tea, got up from the table then said, 'I don't feel well. I'm going to lie down for a while. Clear up, Hannah.' She said it as though it were unusual, but Hannah had done most of the housework since their father had dismissed the maid, complaining that she was lazy and he couldn't afford to pay her. Sarah Dawson had limits, and housework was one of them. Born into a wealthy merchant family, she wasn't going to work as a skivvy, not even in her own home. Recently, it seemed to Hannah and Judith that their mother spent more time in her bed than out of it.

When Sarah had gone upstairs, the sisters exchanged a look, and Hannah rolled her eyes. Sarah Dawson had become passive, withdrawn, submissive. The sisters remembered it hadn't always been that way; but over the years their father had knocked the stuffing out of their mother until she had become silent and reclusive. The loss of her only son, two years younger than Judith, to whooping cough, when he was a small child, the death of two other daughters in infancy and a series of miscarriages, had killed her capacity for joy – indeed for life itself.

There was no predicting Charles Dawson's behaviour. Sometimes he acted as though the three women didn't exist, eating his meals in silence before withdrawing to the small front parlour that he referred to as his study. Hannah wondered how a room that contained neither books nor writing materials could be worthy of the designation 'study'. She suspected he fell asleep in front of the fire but couldn't be sure, as they were all forbidden entry when he was in there. On other occasions, like this morning, the slightest thing was a provocation to him, causing him to explode in a fury that left his daughters bewildered and his wife mute and cowed.

After the incident with *Oliver Twist*, Dawson had insisted the two girls be withdrawn from school and educated at home, a task that fell to their mother, who had neither the inclination nor the energy for it. Reading and composition, foreign languages, history, as well as natural sciences and geography were deemed unsuitable subjects by Dawson, leaving only simple mathematics, Bible studies and domestic economy, none of which interested Sarah Dawson in the slightest. Hannah and Judith were mostly left to their own devices, with their father regularly testing them on their knowledge of the scriptures but doing little else. Any education they had acquired was down to their own natural curiosity, fed by illicit trips to the library in Hannah's case, and being taught to sew and embroider by the lady next-door, in Judith's.

Their educational needs were of no interest to anyone, once the occasional enquiries of the school board inspectors ceased when Judith turned fourteen. Judith's talent for sewing had recently led to her apprenticeship with a ladies' tailor. Today's outburst from her father indicated this was unlikely to be a lasting arrangement.

Hannah had shown some aptitude for figures and so, from the age of fifteen, she was required to attend her father's business premises three afternoons each week to assist with the book-keeping, with a view to her taking over when the clerk responsible retired. Four years on, his retirement did not appear to have come any closer. Hannah's part-time employment did not arise from any belief on her father's part that women should be allowed to make their way in the world, but entirely from his desire to reduce the firm's outgoings. She was expected to perform her duties for no more than her bed and board in the family home, a considerable saving for her father. Given his extreme parsimony, Hannah was surprised he hadn't pressured Mr Busby, the clerk, into relinquishing his role, but she was grateful he hadn't, as what little liberty she did enjoy would be curtailed once she was under the scrutiny of her father full-time.

The business, *Morton's Coffee Importers*, was a struggling enterprise. Charles Dawson had an unshakeable belief in his own prowess as a businessman, against all evidence to the contrary. He himself had started out as a clerk to the company, which had belonged to his wife's family. After Hannah's maternal grandfather had emigrated to Australia when she was a small child, the firm had been sold, but her father had continued to be employed there. Hannah didn't know the circumstances behind his eventual take-over of the business but his management had brought about no reversal in the downward fortunes of the business. Ten years ago, the family had been forced to move from Trevelyan House, their once-elegant town house north of Liverpool, to live in a small redbrick terrace in one of the crowded streets close to the docks. Her mother had never got over the humiliation.

Hannah's reading was disturbed by the screams of a group of seagulls that were wheeling and diving close to the water's edge. She looked up. The wind had whipped up the waves so the dark grey mass of the water, where the Irish Sea met the River Mersey estuary, was broken by the foam of 'white horses'. It was hard to concentrate on her book when she was so cold. Before long she'd need to head back along the waterfront to the area where the sands gave way to the concrete and brick of the docks and their hinterland. Stuffing the book inside her bag, she clambered onto her feet, deciding a brisk walk was a better idea. Her attempts to concentrate had been clouded by errant thoughts, so better to give free rein to them while she tried to warm herself.

Lately, Hannah had been doing a lot of thinking. She had started to feel anxious. Very anxious. About what her father might be planning for her and her sister.

Chapter Four

The *Christina* sailed onwards towards Liverpool, the final destination of their eighteen-month voyage. As was the normal practice at the end of a long trip, all the ratings would be dismissed, left to find another position, take some unpaid shore leave, or wait to sign articles again with the same ship. The merchant navy was a hard task master. If a ship was unlucky enough to sink, the wages of its crew were stopped as soon as the ship went down, regardless of whether they survived or not, or the time taken to be rescued. Had rating Ashok arranged for some or all of his pay to be transferred to his family back home, the payments would have ceased the moment his body was washed overboard.

Will felt ashamed that, apart from knowing the man's name, he knew nothing of the lascar. Was he married? A father? Would a whole family be both grief-stricken and immediately impoverished as a result of his death?

At the ceremony to mark Ashok's demise, Jake Cassidy acted as though the dead man had been an intimate friend. He lowered his head respectfully and shaped his features into a mask of tragic concern. But the sly smirk on his face when he thought no one was looking was proof enough to Will that the bosun felt no remorse. As the captain concluded his brief eulogy for the lost seaman,

Will glanced again at Cassidy and tightened his fists as he saw the falsely pious expression back on the bosun's face. He burned with indignation that Cassidy was not to be called to task for the negligence and cruelty that had cost the lascar his life. He tried to take comfort from the fact that, if Palmer were right, word of the bosun's behaviour would spread faster than Cassidy could sign his next articles. He may not be charged for the negligence, which in Will's eyes was tantamount to an act of murder, but at least he might have to join the ranks of the unemployed.

—

The Pier Head took shape through the early morning mist, and Will and Paolo leaned on the railings, watching as the ship moved closer. The Liverpool skyline was familiar to most merchant sailors, with its three elegant dock-front edifices – the Cunard Building, the Royal Liver Building and Port of Liverpool Building.

Will turned to Paolo, 'What will you do now? Will you wait for the *Christina*?'

'The second officer say me it will be many weeks – and I must save money. You know… I have to get Loretta away from Napoli and her family. I want to take her one day to America. So, I cannot wait for work. Maybe I find a job on a ship for the Mediterranean.' His lips formed a smile, but his eyes were sad.

'Good luck with that. There's not much work going. You know as well as I do how many shipping lines have gone to the wall recently.'

Paolo frowned, puzzled. 'Gone to the wall? What wall?'

'Gone out of business. You could try one of the Norwegian lines. They've bought up a lot of the British ships. And most of them are converted to oil – better than these dirty old coal-burners. Or you could try and join the Royal Navy.' He winked at Paolo. 'Nah! They wouldn't take an Italian.' He grinned.

Paolo shook his head, indignant. 'I would never wear the uniform of the British Navy.'

'You could always join the Italian one.'

Paolo grunted. 'To serve *il Duce*? Never. Mussolini is a very bad man.'

Will looked at his friend. 'Well, you're a good-looking fellow, Paolo. And all that Italian charm. Maybe you should try for a job on a passenger ship. Cunard? Or the White Star? Work as a steward. On the transatlantic crossings they say the tips from rich Americans are worth a fortune.'

'*Certo* – but that means the wages will be very bad.' Paolo laughed. 'I will see what I can get. I must eat the soup or jump out of the window.'

'What?' Will pulled a face.

'It's an Italian expression – *o mangi questa minestra o salti questa finestra*. It's not the same in English?'

Will snorted. 'If it is, I've never heard of it, but don't ask me: I'm an Aussie. I think you'll find most people prefer to say beggars can't be choosers.'

Paolo laughed and repeated the idiom. 'I will remember that. It will be very useful.'

Their laughter stopped when the voice of Cassidy interrupted them. 'Get forward you miserable malingerers. There's five holds to be emptied and scrubbed out and we need the covers off the hatches before the wharfies come on board. If I find a single bleeding cockroach when you're done, you'll be scrubbing the holds out again. Just the two of you. Now move!'

Will swallowed his indignation. Not much longer to put up with Cassidy now. While on the surface the merchant navy might appear more relaxed than the Royal Navy, with no uniform and often a reputation for bolshie behaviour, its vessels were regimented and operated to the timing of the ships' bells, and the rostering of the bosun was under the orders of the officers and ultimately the master. A voyage could be hell if the officers or the bosun chose to make it so.

It took all day for the dockers to empty the *Christina*'s holds of their cargo of salt, palm oil, cotton, and coffee beans, at the Queen's Dock, and most of the next for the ship's crew to clean the holds from top to bottom to Cassidy's satisfaction. The deck of the ship looked chaotic: a mess of tarpaulins, rope, hatch boards, hoses and cables. When the discharging and cleaning was complete, the *Christina* manoeuvred into the graving dock where the necessary repairs to her hull and superstructure would be taking place. There they were expected to scrub down the decks, stow all the unloading gear and generally ready the ship for its period in dry dock.

It was after six the following evening before the crew members were all discharged, wages and discharge books in their pockets. While this was the last pay they would receive until they found new employment, most of them were eager to get inside an English pub and drink some English ale, before beginning their search tomorrow for ships needing crew.

Will, having no family to concern him, enough cash in his pocket to see him through several weeks – months maybe, if he was careful – thought he might wait around in Liverpool for the *Christina* to sail again. But before disembarking, the master had told him that the ship was likely to be in dry dock for a few months. Repairs that had been planned anyway were now more extensive after the battering the ship had taken in the Biscay storm.

'Use the time wisely, Kidd. Get some more experience under your belt. You ought to be studying for your Mate's certificate.' He took a pen from his pocket and wrote something on a piece of paper which he folded and handed to Will. 'If you go along to the Coastal Line and ask for this man and tell him I sent you, you might get some work. It's short runs between here and Dublin, but it will help towards getting your ticket and keep you out of trouble. Then, when the *Christina*'s done, come and find me. You never know, I might just be looking for a new bosun.'

'Thanks, sir.' Will stuffed the paper into the pocket of his donkey jacket, but thought it unlikely he'd do as Palmer suggested. Chugging back and forth across the Irish Sea didn't sound like the kind of job he'd come to sea for. If the *Christina* was out of the picture for a while, then maybe he'd try for another tramp ship heading south.

The extensive dock area of Liverpool offered up a plentiful supply of public houses. Paolo and Will chose one at random and headed inside. The Old Brown Jug was packed with dockers and sailors, most of the latter with only a few hours in port, all keen to make the most of the beer and the chance for some relaxation.

The two seamen pushed their way to the bar, bought a couple of pints and headed for a table in the corner, away from the noise of the crowd. Most of the men in the pub seemed to be discussing the previous day's football results. The two local teams had enjoyed different fortunes with Liverpool winning 4:0 at home, while Everton lost away to Preston North End. Will had been to a couple of games in the past when in port and, impressed by the prowess of Dixie Dean, had decided he'd cheer for the Toffees. He gathered Dean had now moved on and the team was missing his magical goalscoring.

Paolo pulled a face. 'How I wish I were in Napoli. My father used to take me to watch the *calcio* when I was a *bambino*. Now I am stuck here with your dirty English weather, dirty football game and I will never get used to your horrible English beer.'

'It's not mine, mate. I keep telling you, we Aussies hate warm, flat beer as much as the next man.'

Someone had left a newspaper on the table and Will drew it towards him and glanced casually at the headlines, then picked it up and started to read. 'Strewth! Hitler's gone and invaded Austria. Rafqa said she reckons there'll be a war in Europe before long. Maybe she's right.'

'I don't like it. Very bad.' Paolo started to read over his shoulder. 'Mussolini is *troppo* friendly with the Germans and I don't want to think what will happen if there is a war.'

'We could end up on opposite sides.' Will tried to make it sound like a joke but Paolo was frowning.

'I have to find a way to get Loretta out of *Italia*. Or I must go back and join her. But her family will kill me if they find out we are still together. And if I go back I might be forced to join the *Regia Marina*, and you know what I think about the regular navy.'

'If we do end up at war, and Italy backs the Germans, you could be in trouble here too. They might treat you as a foreign spy and lock you up.' Will grinned at his friend, believing it was the most unlikely of prospects.

But Paolo's face was serious. 'Then we must pray to the Madonna it will not come to that. Maybe this Hitler is playing a game. Showing his strength. But he won't go further. Will he?'

Shrugging, Will said, 'You know more about it than I do. I pay no attention to what's going on in the world. Well up to now, that is. Maybe I need to start reading the papers.'

He stood up, took the two empty glasses from the table and started to move towards the bar.

It happened so quickly that Will didn't even register Cassidy's presence until the bosun's fist made contact with his chin. Thrown backwards by the blow, he stumbled, dropping the glasses which clattered and smashed. The crowd of men around the bar drew back, leaving a space around him and Cassidy.

Will's jaw was ablaze with pain and he could feel the taste of blood from a cut lip.

'You piece of shit, Kidd. You miserable son of a bitch. You've cost me a job with the White Star.' He drew back his fist ready to strike another blow, when Tornabene stepped between them, arms outstretched.

Cassidy pushed Paolo aside as though he were inconsequential, knocking him into a table and sending more beer glasses flying. The bosun grabbed Will by the front of his jacket, pushing his face close to his. 'You told the skipper

I caused that towel-head's death. You lying bastard.' His teeth were bared so he looked like a wild dog. 'I only got a "Satisfactory" rating in my discharge papers. How the hell am I going to get work with that?'

As the older man thrust back his arms to strike the next blow, Will got in first, landing a punch in the solar plexus and winding the bosun. 'That man would still be alive if you hadn't ordered him to go forward. You murdered him. And his name was Ashok.'

'You know all about murder, you fucking bushie. You, with a father who was hanged for it. And a brother who tried to kill you. A family of bludgers and killers.'

Will lunged at him, rage and adrenaline coursing through his body. Before he could plant another blow, he felt his shoulders being jerked backwards as several men rushed forward and pushed the two of them apart. Two of them held Cassidy back, but such was the rage in him that he bit down on the arm of one his restrainers, broke free and before anyone realised what was happening, he'd drawn a knife and was lunging towards Will.

In that moment, Will was transported back to Wilton's Creek, to his brother pulling a knife and thrusting it into him. Plunging it into his stomach and almost killing him. It wasn't going to happen to him again. He wasn't going to let a man like Cassidy get the better of him, cut him down, snuff him out, like poor Ashok. A new energy surged through Will. He wasn't ready to die. He stepped sideways, quickly dodging the thrust and, sticking out his foot, caused Cassidy to trip over and fall. The knife skittered across the floor of the pub, its progress slowed by the sawdust.

As soon as the commotion had started, the barman must have reacted quickly, because two policemen came into the bar and made a beeline for the brawlers. Without waiting to ask questions, they clipped handcuffs on both Cassidy and Will, and grabbing them each by the collar, led them, protesting, out of the pub.

Paolo ran after them. 'Why are you taking my friend? He do nothing wrong. It was that man.' He pointed at Cassidy. 'He had a knife. He started the fight.'

'Unless you want to be arrested too, I'd run along, Eyetie.'

The policemen shoved Cassidy and Will into the back of a waiting 'paddy wagon' where Cassidy continued his tirade.

'You fucking bushie bastard. You filthy piece of scum. You'll pay for this. Ever since you came on board you've pissed me off with your arse-licking to the old man. The master never normally speaks to ratings. Who the bleeding hell do you think you are to get special treatment? I'd like to kill you, you piece of shit.' Then his threats were drowned out by the wail of the siren as the van headed away on the short trip to the police station.

After being relieved of the contents of his pockets, Will was led away to a cell, grateful that he was at last separated from Jake Cassidy. The room was cold and empty, with only a stone bench built across one end and a bucket to use as a toilet. There wasn't even a window. He sat hunched forward on the cold slab, then got up to pace around the confined space, movement being preferable to sitting shivering. He lost track of time but had no desire to sleep and, even if he had, it was unlikely he'd succeed on the hard bench without so much as a blanket.

As he prowled the narrow measure of the cell with small steps, he thought of his father. How had he coped during the weeks and months he was locked away? Will knew he'd go mad if he were held here for long. Perhaps his father *had* gone mad – maybe facing the executioner had been preferable to more time in prison waiting for an appeal. Even if his sentence had been commuted to manslaughter it would have meant years locked away.

Ever since, Will had convinced himself he hated his father – yet deep down he knew that wasn't true. When Will's mother was alive he'd been a different man, kinder, capable of humour. Her death and Nat's part in that had changed him. He'd become bitter, closed off, cold. But his marriage to Elizabeth had begun to soften that hardness, and while Jack Kidd would never have outwardly shown his son affection, Will knew that his father had cared for him in his own way.

There on that hard bench in that small cell, Will was forced to admit to himself that his hostility towards his father stemmed from his own insecurities and from his conviction that he had been a disappointment to him. He felt as though he had failed every test his pa had ever set for him. Forced to work in the coal mine Jack Kidd owned, Will had been terrified, miserable and claustrophobic. The cold dark netherworld of the pit had been a living nightmare to him.

His reveries were interrupted by the sound of the bolts being drawn back. The desk sergeant who'd processed him stood on the threshold.

'You're free to go,' he said in a strong Scouse accent. 'Keep out of trouble now. Go'ed, lad, I don't want to see you back again.'

'The other man? Have you let him go too?'

The sergeant shook his head. 'He'll be up before the beak tomorrow for assault. The publican and one or two others all 'ad the same story, like.' He gave a chuckle. 'Still screaming his head off, giving it down the banks, he is. Don't mind telling you I've learnt a few new words from him. You're lucky you came away with just a cut lip for your trouble. And the lads who brought you in heard the threats he was making on the way here.'

Relieved he was free and that Cassidy was not, Will tried not to resent his miserable night in the cells. He pocketed the possessions that had been taken from him when they brought him in and made his way upstairs, behind the sergeant.

Paolo was waiting on a wooden bench when Will emerged into the police station lobby. The clock on the wall showed it was after six in the morning.

'G'day, cobber' said Will. 'You're a real pal to wait for me. How do you like the sound of a big fry-up? The tucker's on me.'

Chapter Five

Hannah walked into the Morton Coffee Company premises, a pair of cramped rooms, close to the docks, and dwarfed by an adjoining line of warehouses. The space was unworthy of the term offices, with its piles of unpaid bills, its unwashed windows, unswept floors, cobwebs and mouse droppings. When she'd first started work here, Hannah had taken a broom, intending to clean up, only for her father to remind her that she was the proprietor's daughter, not a common worker-woman. She'd started to answer back, only to see his eyes narrow and his mouth set hard, so she mumbled an apology and put the broom in the corner where it had remained since, gathering dust.

She was relieved to discover that her father wasn't at his desk this afternoon. Charles Dawson's rages and ill humour usually lasted a few days and it was always wise to give him a wide berth until he eventually returned to a state of silent moroseness.

Greeting the clerk, Mr Busby, Hannah hung up her coat, stuffed her gloves inside the pockets and placed her hat over the hook. The hat was a battered felt, long past its best. With no money of her own, apart from a paltry allowance for the most basic essentials, she had no means of replacing it. Her father believed clothes served only to protect the wearer from the elements, preserve their modesty and reflect their sobriety. Changing fashions were, in his eyes, an indulgence encouraged by the devil. Wearing long-out-of-date hand-me-downs from her mother's younger, affluent days made Hannah feel a frump. Her sister's skill with a needle helped – Judith was able to re-fashion items in acknowledgement that it was 1938 and not 1918 – but the cuffs and nap of Hannah's coat were threadbare and her shoes were worn down at the heels. She had to console herself with the miserable thought that in any case she had nowhere to go, even had she had something better to wear.

Mr Busby, who had not responded to her greeting, looked up at last and nodded to her, pushing a pile of invoices across their shared desk for her to enter in the ledger. He was a man of around sixty, parsimonious in words and expression. Hannah was used to sharing the office in silence punctuated only by the loud ticking of the clock on the wall above her head, Mr Busby's nervous cough, and her occasional request to use his pencil sharpener – an item which he guarded with a ferocity more appropriate to the conservation of a valuable historic artefact.

The time always dragged. The work was undemanding, repetitive and unfulfilling. If her colleague was going to retire, she prayed it wouldn't be soon, as working here day after day as her father's full-time, unpaid minion was a horrible thought. When, one day, she had dared to challenge her unsalaried status, Dawson had flown into such a terrible rage that it still made her shudder to think about it. That had also been the first occasion he had struck her, leaving a large welt across her cheek. Her mother's expression when she saw the bruising was a wordless acknowledgement that she herself had long been the victim of her husband's violence. Hannah wasn't sure whether her mother's eyes were signalling solidarity or resignation. Either way, her father's attack was not something she wanted to repeat.

Sometimes, walking on the shore, or pausing in the tedious addition of columns of figures, she would imagine running away. Would it be so hard? To walk out of the house and never come back. But where would she go? How could she survive without a penny to her name? What about Judith and her mother? Judith would never agree to come with her. And without Hannah to do the cooking and cleaning, how would her mother get by? It was too much to expect her mother to ever take on the running of the house herself. Besides, if her father were to find her – as he surely would – the beating he would give her was more than she wanted to contemplate. Instead, she allowed herself to dream, to travel on a flight of fantasy, far away from Liverpool, away from the miserable shabby little house they inhabited, away from this scruffy office.

She felt in her skirt pocket and pulled out an old photograph, looking at it under the edge of the desk. Its precious nature was demonstrated by the way she kept it safe between a piece of folded cardboard, but even so, it was already well-thumbed and faded. Hannah had found it in the attic of Trevelyan House, one afternoon when her mother was sleeping. It was not long after the last of Sarah's many stillbirths, and her grief and despair meant that Hannah and Judith were left unsupervised. The attic was forbidden to the thirteen-year-old Hannah – but who was to stop her? When she came upon a trunk full of books, a violin, and a silver-framed photograph with its glass shattered, the distant memory of a much-loved aunt had returned in a vivid flash, along with the recollection of music filling the house. Music – something long forbidden by her father. Hannah had removed the picture from the frame, hidden it inside her blouse and kept it safe on her person ever since. That night, before the light faded, she had lain in bed, studying the portrait. Aunty Lizzie, her mother's older sister, had been a daily presence in her life, until one morning, when Hannah was five, she'd woken to find her aunt gone. From then on, any mention of Aunty Lizzie's name led to a smack from either parent, or to being sent to her room – until eventually the memory of her aunt had faded. Finding that photograph was like finding buried treasure, a secret she shared with no one, not even Judith, who'd been too young to remember.

The office was cold. There was an ancient coal stove in the corner which, when lit at all, benefited Mr Busby, but only took the worst of the chill off by the time its feeble output reached Hannah's side of the desk. She shivered, wondering whether to put her coat back on.

Looking through the grimy window at the activity on the dockside, Hannah watched the stevedores calling out to each other, trundling two-wheeled carts piled high with boxes or sacks, moving them from ship to warehouse, or the other way round. Overhead, derricks swung, winches turned, and ropes and pulleys carried sacks and bales from deck to dock. Sometimes she'd try to guess what the cargo was before it was landed – although this dock dealt mainly with grain and cotton from America.

The coffee business was going through something of a slump. Britain was a nation of tea drinkers and the rising price of coffee, set against the falling value of wages and the high levels of unemployment during the Depression had been a blow to Morton's. The company's cash reserves had disappeared and the balance sheet made dismal reading.

'Mr Busby?'

The clerk looked up, his irritation evident.

'Has my father ever tried to deal in other commodities than coffee?'

Busby looked horrified. 'This is Morton's Coffee. Always has been since your great-grandfather founded it.'

'But if no one wants to pay the necessary prices for coffee, couldn't my father experiment with something else? Something that people *do* want to buy.'

Mr Busby snorted. 'I wouldn't know about such things. It's not my job to speculate. I just add and subtract the figures and prepare the accounts.'

'Exactly. So you can see as clearly as I can that we can't go on like this.'

Another frown creased Busby's forehead. 'Don't let your father hear you say such things. God in his infinite wisdom will provide. We are here on earth only to do His will, and that means we don't question matters that are not our concern.'

Her colleague bent his head back to his work and Hannah chewed the end of her pencil as she studied him. Small and thin, with a face that was gaunt as a rat's, he had thinning hair, plastered to his head with plentiful quantities of brilliantine. The collar of his jacket was dusted with dandruff. She wondered whether there was a Mrs Busby, and if so was she as dour as her husband was? There was no point in asking any personal questions of either the man himself or her father, so she picked up the next invoice. Like everything in their view, it was none of her business.

As she worked away, she continued to wonder about the company. As Morton's outgoings were so low – nothing had been spent on the premises since her father took over and Mr Busby had not had a pay rise in years – it was hard to understand why Morton's was in such dire straits. Even though sales were down, they were still selling the coffee – yet there was apparently nothing to show for this. It had never occurred to her before to question the oddness of the situation, as she had always accepted the incontrovertible fact that times were hard and the market depressed, but as she stared at the columns of figures something struck her as not being quite right.

She squeezed her lips together and decided to ask Mr Busby. 'Do you know why the previous owners decided to sell Morton's to my father?'

Mr Busby looked astonished. 'What's got into you today, Miss Dawson?' He looked around him nervously as though expecting Charles Dawson to pounce on him any minute. 'It's really not your concern. Mine neither. I do what I'm paid to do and then I go home.'

'Yes, but you've been at Morton's a long time, haven't you?'

'I worked for your grandfather since leaving school.' He looked up at the ceiling as though trying to picture those days. 'Things were different back then before the war. We had much grander offices, off Lord Street and our own warehouse at the Queen's Dock. Your father and I were two of about four clerks. Morton's had the lion's share of the coffee import business through Liverpool.'

'So things went downhill after my grandfather sold it?'

'It started before then. Your grandmother died and it was as if Mr Morton lost his spirit and his interest in the business. When he emigrated to Australia he instructed his solicitors to sell. The buyers lost interest very quickly once they realised it was no longer the goldmine it used to be. That's how your father was eventually able to take over for next to nothing.'

This was all news to Hannah. There was never any discussion of the business at home. She half suspected that to her father commerce was an ugly concept, something grubby and ungodly. He appeared to show little interest in the fortunes of the company, treating it only as a source of personal status.

'Why do you think he bought Morton's? My father doesn't seem to have much appetite for the business.'

Busby coughed. He took out a handkerchief and wiped his brow. 'I am in no position to comment on such matters.'

'But Mr Busby, you've been here so long, you must know more than anyone. You must have your theories.'

For a moment she thought the clerk was blushing. He opened his mouth to reply, but the door burst open and Charles Dawson walked into the room. Busby dropped his eyes and got on with his work. Dawson gave the two of them a quick look before going into the inner office – a partitioned-off section of the room – and slammed the door behind him.

Hannah returned to the pile of invoices and carried on working, frustrated, as for a moment she had actually believed she was beginning to get somewhere in her questioning of Mr Busby.

Chapter Six

Will and Paolo enjoyed a hearty fried breakfast, washed down with mugs of tea. After two years at sea on a British merchant ship, Paolo had come to appreciate bacon and eggs but still regarded tea as an eccentricity, and constantly moaned that he longed for a decent cup of real Italian coffee.

After he finished his last mouthful, Paolo spoke. 'I have news, *caro amico*. Last night, before I went to find you at the police station, I talk to a man who is first mate on an Italian ship, *Il Montefeltro*, bound for the Mediterranean. He say me they leave from the Queen's Dock tomorrow and need more crew. It is perfect for me. A ship of my own country. Why don't you come too?' He moved his hands in a supplicatory gesture.

Will grinned. 'That's bonzer, mate. Just what you need. But not for me. I don't speeka da lingo.'

'I did not speak *inglese* before I went to sea but I learn fast. You learn *italiano* too. I teach you.' Paolo's stretched out his hands.

'No, mate. It'd mean going back to the beginning. If I'm sticking at sea, I have to go forwards not back. And I'm not as clever as you are. Too old to start learning a new lingo now. I'm already going to have my work cut out trying to learn enough to go for my mate's ticket.'

He rolled his eyes. 'I've never been one for studying. School of life, that's me.' He paused then added hurriedly, 'Assuming I do try for the ticket, which I'm not even sure about.'

'You are a good sailor, you teached me much. You must do what the old man say and study. He's right you could be *il Capitano* one day.'

Will gave him a weak smile. Why was he still so uncertain? What was the alternative? Even were he to leave the sea and go to America, he'd need money, and the best way to get more of that was to progress in his job. The pay was abysmal now, but getting a position as bosun and eventually mate would be an improvement, even if a minor one. Better than nothing. 'The skipper gave me the name of a man who might be looking for crew. Said I could get some experience with a different line then maybe I might be up for the bosun's job when the *Christina* sails again. What do you Eyeties say – better to eat the soup than jump out the window? So maybe I'll try me some soup.'

'*Bravo!* That is a good plan. Beggars can't be choicers.' He grinned at Will. '*Ma mi mancherai moltissimo.* Yes, I will miss you very much, my friend.'

After saying goodbye to Paolo, and swearing to each other that they would meet again one day, Will made his way to the offices of the Coastal Line near the Nelson Dock. He owed it to Captain Palmer to start with his recommendation – and at least short haul trips to Ireland would mean he'd be on hand to rejoin the *Christina* as soon as she was ready to sail again.

He tried to push the thought of Paolo Tornabene from his head. The Italian had been the only man – only person – he'd allowed to get anywhere close to him. There had been something about Paolo's sunny nature, cheeky grin, desire to learn, that had got under Will's skin. Unlike most of the crew he'd known over his eleven years at sea, Paolo was quiet, happy to sit in a companionable silence, knowing when to keep his counsel and not to pry – so that Will had begun to confide in him in a way he'd never done with anyone else. Perhaps it was the fact that they were so different – language and culture, family background, everything about their circumstances. Yet in many ways, Paolo was similar to how Will had been as a younger man: naive, eager, hungry for life. But most of all, Will had been moved by the way the young Italian had risked everything to get him safely back on board in Zanzibar, thus ensuring Will avoided the ignominy of a return to home port via the consulate and the next passing ship. Paolo had paid a heavy price for his kindness and Will would always feel indebted to his friend. He hoped that one day he might find a way to repay that debt.

–

When Will called at the offices of the Coastal Line, any thought that getting a post on a small Irish cargo ship might mean a promotion to bosun was quickly dispelled. Although unemployment had declined since the height of the depression, the shipping lines could still take their pick of the available work force, and Will found that his choice was between settling for a post as an ordinary seaman or carrying on looking. And at least they agreed he could work as casual labour and sign off as soon as the *Christina* was ready. He decided to 'eat the soup' as Paolo had put it.

He had two days at liberty before he needed to join his new ship, the *Arklow*, now *en route* from Dublin and due to dock that night, so he shouldered his kitbag and headed off to the Sailors' Home on Canning Street. From past experience he knew that here you could get a bed for the night with breakfast for a few bob.

The building was of a grand design with twin turrets and a pair of impressive wrought iron gates which were locked at ten o'clock every night in a strictly enforced curfew. Those heavy gates had collapsed and crushed to death an old lady, then a policeman some years later. Both were rumoured to haunt the place. Will didn't believe in ghosts but he always stepped quickly through the portal with a nervous look upwards to check that the structure wasn't about to collapse on him.

The ground floor of the institution was the home of the 'Pool' where sailors came to seek their next ship. A series of counters were staffed by clerks who exerted their power to make or break men's lives by finding them suitable jobs, consigning them to months of misery on a bad ship, or turning them away with no job at all. Will stood in line, just in case he found something better than the Ireland job, but the only other options on offer were a tramp ship heading for the Arctic Circle or a place on the Mersey ferries. He decided to be grateful that he had secured a job that would keep him employed until the *Christina* was ready to sail. The Arctic tramp would have meant signing articles for the next year or more – and not knowing the clerk responsible for deck jobs, he would have been at the back of the pecking order for any other available options.

Will's quarters here at the Sailors' Home were basic but no worse than what he'd been used to on board ship.

The cell-like rooms, although on dry land, were known as cabins. Wood-panelled and painted an ugly green, they contained only a simple iron bed and a chest of drawers, known, like the onboard equivalent, as a locker, even though it had no key. The men shared a communal toilet and washing facilities. The place was reminiscent of a Victorian prison – with galleries surrounding an open central space, but finer than those of a prison, made with intricate wrought iron balustrades, featuring mermaids and sea creatures. Blind to the lavish carvings, all Will needed was a bed to lie on and some food to keep him going. And the place was cheap. Beggars can't be choosers, he told himself, then remembered Paolo saying the same thing that morning but getting his words wrong. He'd miss him.

Will was rootless – little more than an itinerant. No one waited for him to return home from each long voyage. There was no home for him at all for that matter, no family, no wife to greet him with a decent meal and a warm and welcoming bed.

He stowed his few possessions in the locker, lay down on the bed and stared at the cracks in the tobacco-stained ceiling. Residents were not permitted to lie around in their rooms all day. Just as there was a curfew for night time, so too the cabins had to be unoccupied during the day, so he swung himself off the bed and headed back downstairs and out of the building.

His board settled, Will went for a walk around the city, savouring the solid feel of the ground beneath his feet. It would take a long time to lose the involuntary sailor swagger that came from constant adjustment to the swell of the sea.

Liverpool, as always, was thronged with people, the jangle and ding-dong of the trams, the blare of horns on motorcars and buses, and the background buzz of the population going about their business. It was a grey grizzled day and he missed the brilliance of the African sun. That made him wonder what Rafqa was doing now but he pushed the thought away. Walking through these crowded streets past the grandiose soot-blackened Victorian buildings, the memory of Zanzibar was a distant dream, a different planet, an impossibly vibrant palette of explosive colour in contrast to the monochrome of these charcoal-coloured streets and sky.

For the first time since he had left his home in Australia more than ten years ago, Will admitted he was lonely. It wasn't that he had a need for company, conversation, conviviality. No, it was a deeper, darker gnawing inside him, a kind of despair. Is this all there is? All there will ever be? The future stretched in front of him and he didn't like what it looked like – a long empty road to nowhere, marked out by a series of ships and ports, miles of empty oceans and endless skies. What was the point of it all?

On impulse, he headed into a public house and ordered a beer. But the drinking did nothing to lighten his mood. He drained his pint quickly and ordered another, staring down into the dark liquid, while all the time the words 'is this all there is?' eddied around his brain.

Over at the bar, two men, the only other occupants of the hostelry, one of them the barman, were evidently discussing Hitler's annexation of Austria – or the *Anschluss* as the newspapers were now calling it.

'There's no question about it, Ron,' the barman said. 'One way or another we'll be at war with those bastards again before long. I'm glad I was too young last time and with a bit of luck I'll be too old this time around – and there's me bad leg too.'

'I'm too old myself of course. I did my bit last time around. But they wouldn't touch *you* with a bargepole. They'd never be that desperate.'

'Less of the lip, old man. One thing's sure – we won't be lining up in trenches and blasting the crap out of each other this time. I was reading in the *Echo* that future wars will be mostly fought from the air. That little Kraut with the silly moustache will get what's coming to him as soon as we drop a big fat bomb on him. Blow him and his bleeding Reichstag and goose-stepping idiots to blazes. Won't know what's hit them!'

The old man chuckled in response, and the laughter turned into a fit of coughing. He stretched out his empty glass to the barman. 'Another one in there, pal, when you're ready. Believe me, it'll take more than a bomb to stop that devil. The rate he's been building up his armies he's probably already got a damn sight more bombs than we have.'

The barman shook his head as he pulled the pint. 'Didn't they tell us there'd never be another war and here we are, not yet twenty years later, and we're already talking about the possibility.'

'I've four sons under twenty-five and I don't want to see them in uniform.'

'In uniform or out of it, if they do drop bombs we'll all cop it. Women and kiddies too.'

'Nah! They'd not do that. Not wage war on civilians.'

'Says you. They dropped bombs from those Zeppelins last time. I'll bet they wouldn't hesitate. You can't trust the Hun.'

Will couldn't avoid listening. They were talking loudly, the pub was otherwise empty and there was nothing else to distract him. It seemed the whole world was more up to date with the threat of Adolf Hitler than he was and everyone seemed to think there would be a war. Part of him wished there would be. At least then he might be expected to do something that might make a difference. And war also brought the possibility of an end to everything. Then at least he'd be past this terrible empty pointlessness.

Twenty minutes later the old man was still droning on about the possibility of war. Will decided he'd had enough. He downed the last of his pint and left the bar.

It was too early to return to the Sailors' Home, so he went towards the waterfront and carried on walking until he reached the shore at Seaforth. Hands thrust into pockets, collar drawn up and woollen hat pulled low over his ears, he walked along the sand between the sea and the dunes. He must have walked for an hour before turning round and heading back the way he had come. It was already dusk. He lay down on the slope of one of the dunes and, overcome by a sudden tiredness, dozed off. Waking with a jolt, he saw it was now fully dark. He stared up at the black of the sky. It was a clear night and he gazed at the stars, trying to make out the various constellations.

A vivid memory of the first time he had met his new stepmother, Elizabeth, suffused him. He had come upon her at Wilton's Creek trying to light a fire outside, with no thought to the risk. Will had shouted at her, kicked out the fire and then discovered to his astonishment that this young English woman was his father's new wife. She had been equally astonished to discover that her husband had a teenage son. Never had been much of a conversationalist, Jack Kidd. Will found himself smiling as he remembered that evening: how he'd shown her how to build a safe fire and they'd baked potatoes and the fish he'd caught and then talked and watched the stars together and he had called her Lizbeth. She had been surprised that the southern skies were different from the northern ones she was used to in England. He had been instantly and hopelessly smitten, and had loved her with a wretched, hopeless passion to which she had been oblivious. Lying here in the sand now, Will still felt the sting of shame and embarrassment he had experienced when he had finally confessed his feelings and Lizbeth had shown him a kindness that had cut him to the bone. He'd never forget her words or the expression on her face when she'd admitted that she loved his friend Michael Winterbourne.

'Right now, Will, you believe you love me, but I promise you, it's just a crush.'

Just a crush! Here he was, more than ten years later, and his feelings were as strong. His love for her had shaped his life and ruined the possibility of him ever loving anyone else.

She'd told him, 'Your time will come.' Her face had been full of sadness and pity and he hadn't been able to bear it any longer. That was the moment when he'd decided to go to sea.

He'd told Lizbeth that day that he wanted to look at those stars she'd told him about, in the northern skies. Now his eyes moistened as he looked up and studied them.

Brushing the threatened tears away, he jerked himself upright and got to his feet. Stuffing his hands deep in his pockets and fixing his eyes on the lights of the city, he walked briskly back towards the Liverpool docks.

When he was nearing the Sailors' Home, he ran into a large group of fellow sailors, including many of the lads from the *Christina*.

'Come with us, Kiddo!' one of them called out to him. 'There's a dance on tonight at Atlantic House.'

'I'm not feeling very sociable.'

'Get away, pal. You'll feel a lot better once you've twirled a lass round the dance floor. They're all nice girls. No tarts.' The speaker was the second mate. 'A good-looking fellow like you should be looking for a wife to settle down with, someone to come home to after a long voyage.'

'What? Just like you, Fred?' The second mate was unmarried.

'Why do you think I'm going along? I live in hope!'

'They'd have to be blind to pick you,' said one of the crew to much laughter, which didn't seem to bother Fred at all.

Maybe that was what Will needed – a bit of mindless banter among men he knew, a few dances with a pretty girl or two, then back to the Sailors' Home for a good night's sleep. Enough of the introspection, enough of the despair. The idea of music, laughter, and a soft-skinned, bright-eyed, smiling girl in his arms began to have appeal. 'All right, lads. Let's go!'

The sailors' social club, Atlantic House, was a haven to crews in port. Run by a Catholic priest, the place welcomed sailors of all creeds, races and nationalities.

The beer was cheaper than in the pubs and the regular dances were well attended by young women willing to spend some of their free time with lonely sailors. It was all above board, with strict rules of conduct – the girls were vetted by Father O'Driscoll and forbidden to date the men. Despite these restrictions, many courtships arose from encounters at Atlantic House, and many sailors went along in the hope that they might meet a future wife or girlfriend. Whether that happened or not, there were worse ways to spend an evening in port.

For the first hour, Will leaned against the bar, watching the dancing. The band was pretty good and the dance floor was packed. One of the attractions for the crew was the fact that the young women were all there because they believed it was their Christian duty and so rarely refused a dance invitation. Fred was red-faced and happy after dancing with one after another and was now enjoying his third dance with the same girl – a homely looking lass with generous proportions and twinkling eyes.

'Looks like the Second's got lucky tonight. That girl's stuck to him like a limpet,' said one of the seamen.

'At least they won't spoil two fireplaces,' said one of the boiler men.

'She's not that bad. Give them a break.' Will gave the man a gentle shove.

'Go on then, Kiddo. Interrupt them and ask her to dance. Rescue the poor girl.'

Will shook his head.

Despite the crowds, the cheap beer, the pretty girls and the lively dance music, his mood remained dark. It wasn't self-pity. Instead, he felt as though he were caught in a void, numb to the world. The past was a place he didn't want to think about – his murderous brother, his father's execution, his sister's suicide. He didn't want to confront these things. Most of all he didn't want to think about Lizbeth.

The future stretched in front of him, vast and empty. He felt nothing, couldn't imagine feeling anything again. Even fear would be welcome. Maybe if there was a war, he'd experience that, and right now he thought he'd embrace it – anything rather than this sense of passivity, of nothingness. What would it be like? To have fear clutch at his innards? Years ago, when he'd had to go underground in his father's coal mine, terror had gripped at his guts, bringing sweat to his face, causing his stomach to lurch. He'd hated it but at least it was a sensation. Better than this hollow vacuum. He looked across the room and saw a girl sitting alone. In an instant he decided to ask her to dance. Maybe the music would wash away his melancholy – and the warmth of her body against his might breathe some life back into him.

He took another swig of beer, put his empty pint pot down on the bar and nodded to one of the crew members he was drinking with, a Nigerian. 'Your round, Abuchi.' Then he moved across the floor and approached the young woman. She was a freckled redhead with blue eyes. Nothing special, but pretty enough.

'Would you like to dance?' he asked.

The girl flashed him a smile, looked around her, uncertain for a moment, then said, 'I promised the next dance to someone else. He's gone to buy cigarettes and he hasn't come back yet.' She looked up at him and grinned. 'Yes. Why not? Thank you.'

Will steered her towards the dance floor as the leader announced the next number – a tune called Harbour Lights – and the band struck up. She was a good dancer, moving naturally and letting him lead her. He relaxed into the dance and realised that right now, in this moment, he was actually enjoying himself. He looked down at the top of her head and asked her what her name was.

'Peggy. Yours?'

He told her, and they danced on, one tune merging into another as they swirled around the floor. Lost in the beat, he allowed his head to empty of everything but the music, the feel of the girl against him and the sharp scent of the eau de toilette she was wearing. Then he felt a hand grab his shoulder and before he realised what was happening, he was spun around and separated from Peggy. A blow landed in the centre of his chest, knocking the wind out of him and sending him careening across the dance floor, cannoning into other couples, until he landed on his bottom, his back against a table, a sticky trickle of spilled beer running down his neck.

A familiar voice boomed out. 'You fucking bastard, Kidd. You got me arrested. You stole my job. Now you're trying to steal my girl.'

Cassidy's eyes were narrowed, full of hatred, his words coming out like gun shots, his rage radiating off him like heat. There was a strong smell of drink. Several of the sailors, including the second mate, rushed forward and held him back as he tried to lunge at Will again.

Will scrambled to his feet as Cassidy struggled against the men restraining him.

'Take your hands off me, you pommie bastards. Let me kill that ocker.' Cassidy's face was red and he spat in Will's direction.

'What in the name of heaven's going on?' Father O'Driscoll moved into the fray. 'Stop that filthy talk.'

The red-headed girl was now in tears, her eyes darting between Cassidy and Will and back again. 'All I did was dance with him. I did nothing wrong, Father.'

'No, Peggy, you did nothing wrong at all. Go and sit down in my office and I'll have someone bring you a glass of warm milk and see you home.' The girl was led away by one of the other women.

'Now who's going to tell me what's going on with you two fellas?'

Will started to answer but Cassidy cut in. 'This man's cost me my job. I spent last night in the police cells because of the lying bastard.'

'Is this true?' The priest turned towards Will.

'We were on the same ship, Father. Last night he attacked me in a pub and we both ended up at the police station. They let me go this morning and told me they were detaining him in order to press charges.'

Cassidy was swearing like a trooper.

The priest rounded on him. 'Shut that filthy mouth of yours, young man, before I shut it for you and summon the constabulary. You'll be back in that cell in a flash.' He looked around. 'Anyone here who can corroborate what either of these two fellas is saying?'

By now, all the men present who were from the *Christina* had gathered around.

Abuchi stepped forward. 'Bosun's had it in for Kidd all the time since I came on board.'

'He's picked on him since Kidd joined the ship. Eighteen months ago. You'd think both being "diggers" they'd stick together,' said another sailor.

The boiler man added, 'I was in the Brown Jug last night and Kidd was having a quiet drink with one of the other crew when the bosun came in and landed a punch on him. Just like now.'

Several men were speaking at once and the priest held up his hands. 'One at a time. Who's the senior man here? Any officers?'

Fred stepped forward. 'Me, Father. I'm the second mate on the ship these lads came in on. It's true what they're saying.' He turned to address the bosun. 'I don't know what's come over you, Cassidy, man. Kidd's done nothing to you.'

'He only went and told the master I'd caused that darky's death. It's cost me my ticket.' Cassidy's face was flushed red and the sinews in his neck were standing out. As he spoke, he sent a spray of spittle into the air. 'Now I'm out on bail and up before the courts next week. The fucking bastard has ruined me. I'm going to kill him.' He jerked forward, his eyes bulging, but the crewmen held him back.

'Sounds to me as if you need to wash out that dirty mouth of yours, fella,' said the priest. 'Unless you want to spend another night in the cells you'd better calm down. Where're you staying tonight?'

'What's it to you?'

The priest took a step towards him, immune to intimidation. 'I want to be sure you've a roof over your head, as if you've not, I'm sure His Majesty's finest can offer you a cell tonight. What's it to be, laddie?'

Cassidy took a gulp of air and seemed to calm a little. 'I'm staying at my brother-in-law's in Everton. Just off Scotland Road.'

The priest looked at the gang of men. 'Anyone willing to walk this man home to the care of his family?'

Two of the crew members stepped forward.

'Now, straight there, mind,' said Father O'Driscoll 'No stopping off at pubs along the way. Looks to me like he's already had more than a skinful.'

After they had gone, the priest clapped his hands and called over to the band. 'Let's get on with the evening, boys and girls. And no more nonsense.' He laid a hand on Will's arm. 'Take it easy now, fella. You all right?'

Will nodded.

'Good. No harm done then. Get on and enjoy yourself. Plenty of nice girls here to dance with.'

But Will had had enough. His appetite for dancing had disappeared and after downing the beer Abuchi had got for him, he made his way outside and walked slowly through the streets back to the Sailors' Home.

Chapter Seven

It was with a heavy heart that Will woke up in the Sailors' Home the following morning. It was his last day of freedom before joining the crew of the *Arklow*. The run-in with Jake Cassidy, the force of the man's malevolence, had weighed on him, keeping him awake for most of the night. Had he been unfair to the bosun? Had he really cost him his job?

For a few minutes Will doubted himself, then remembered that Seaman Ashok had lost his life in a pointless and cruel manner. And there was no doubting the violence in Cassidy. Two assaults in as many days indicated the man had an anger inside him that was irrational. Will was still at a loss as to why his fellow Australian hated him with such passionate intensity.

Rather than relishing his last day off, Will was restless and anxious to be at sea. He didn't want to run into Cassidy again, and had a feeling that the bosun would not be content to let matters go. This last day of liberty was a frustration – there was nothing he particularly wanted to do, no one he knew in Liverpool. Again, that empty feeling he'd experienced the previous day washed over him.

After buying a few essentials from the shop inside the Home in readiness for his new ship, he went to the sitting room, where he settled down with a news-paper and caught up on the news. There was more about the growing threat of Hitler, matched by other columns declaring that the possibility of a future war with Germany must be avoided at all costs. He turned to the back pages and scanned the sports reports. Still restless, he decided to go to the pictures. Sitting in the dark of a cinema, he could doze off if he wished, and at least it would be warmer than walking the streets.

The first picture house he came upon was showing a film about a Royal Navy ship getting caught up in a coup in South America. That would feel like a busman's holiday. He walked on and came upon another, grander, cinema. Here they were showing *Young and Innocent*, a thriller directed by Alfred Hitchcock. Will had enjoyed *The 39 Steps* by the same director a couple of years earlier, so he paid his shilling and went inside. The film proved a good choice, and he lost himself in the story of incompetent policemen hunting the wrong man for the murder of a movie star. Inevitably, the fugitive was helped by an attractive young woman with whom he, of course, fell in love. Everything was so simple in films – even a man wrongly accused of murder ended up with the pretty girl. Things like that never happened in real life. At least not in Will's experience.

When it was over, he set off to walk back to the Sailors' Home. He headed towards the Pier Head and stood smoking a cigarette as the crowds poured on and off the Mersey ferries. What would it be like to go to work in the same place every day, crowding onto ferries, trams and buses and slaving away in factories, on the docks or in an office? Better perhaps to be at sea. The life might be lonely but at least each day was different.

He decided to take the overhead railway to the Gladstone Dock, where the *Arklow* was moored. Although he wasn't due to report for duty until the following morning, he wanted to take a look at the ship.

It was a short ride and as he walked away from the railway towards the ship, a young woman emerged from a rundown building. His first thought was that it was unusual to see women on the docks. There was something about her that made him study her as she approached. She didn't look like a prostitute – her clothes were too modest, rather old-fashioned, her hairstyle simple, and her face unadorned with makeup. When she was within a few feet of him, Will's heart missed a beat.

Elizabeth.

He stopped dead in his tracks, blocking her pathway and called her name.

The woman halted, looked him straight in the eyes, her face recording surprise. She hesitated momentarily, then skirted around him and started to speed up. He must have frightened her.

'Please wait! I need to speak to you.'

She began to run. He could hear her taking in big gulps of air. He started to go after her, then sense prevailed. No wonder she was frightened. He was a stranger on a deserted dock front at dusk, and she was alone. He was a fool.

Of course, it couldn't be her. He looked after her receding figure. By now Elizabeth must be in her forties and this woman looked as though she were barely out of her teens. Yet in every other respect she was the living image of the woman who had made such an impact on his life and been the cause of his lingering unhappiness.

Will remembered the last time he had seen his stepmother. Telling her about his feelings had been hard. Yet he'd nursed the tiniest hope of a sign that she felt something for him. But she'd broken his heart with the gentlest of words and made it clear that her feelings for him were only maternal. His face flushed at the memory of that humiliation.

But the girl he'd just seen had to be related to Lizbeth in some way. Her daughter? A younger sister? The resemblance was too strong for it to be coincidental. He had to find out.

The building she'd emerged from was a brick-built single-storey construction – a storage facility or office. Too small for a warehouse. There was a wooden sign above the door, its lettering faded by the years. Morton's Coffee Importers Ltd.

Yes! There was a connection. Morton had been Elizabeth's maiden name. And hadn't she once told him she came from a town just north of Liverpool? It had meant nothing to him at the time – Will had never expected to visit England then. And now that he thought about it, she had mentioned that her father had been a coffee importer.

But he'd let the young woman get away, missing his chance to talk to her, to find out her relationship to Lizbeth. She'd been terrified, her eyes – Elizabeth's eyes – telegraphing her fear. Will cursed himself. Why had he spoken to her like that?

He went towards the building and tried to peer through the filthy grime of the windows to see if there was anyone inside. An elderly man was sitting at a desk. Will pushed open the door and went inside.

'Excuse me. Are you Mr Morton?'

The man looked up. 'There's no Mr Morton. Not for many a year. It'll be Mr Dawson you're looking for and he's not here. Can I help?' His expression was dubious as he looked Will up and down.

'The young lady I saw leaving here just now. I was wondering—'

'Best not to wonder.' The man scowled at him. 'If he catches you asking about his daughter there'll be trouble. If you're a sensible man you'll stay away. Miss Dawson wants nothing to do with the likes of you.' The man got up from his desk and moved towards the door, holding it open. 'Good day.'

Will had no choice but to leave.

That night Will cursed the fact that he had to sail for Dublin the next day. All he wanted was to go back and wait to see if Miss Dawson returned. At least he now knew her name and that she was unmarried. Her father must be Elizabeth's brother-in-law. Lizbeth had never really talked about her family. It was as if the memories were too painful. He'd got the idea that she had been very unhappy before leaving for Australia.

These thoughts ran through his head until he drifted off to sleep, the image of the frightened young woman on his mind.

–

Hannah had always hated having to come to the office near the docks. She felt uncomfortable at being surrounded by so many strange men and didn't like the way, when she walked past, some of them looked her up and down as though mentally removing her clothing. When her father wasn't with her, they often wolf-whistled. Telling herself that most of them meant no harm didn't make her feel any less vulnerable.

She'd tried to tell her father that she was nervous about being here on the docks, only for him to demand that she learn the 91st Psalm by heart and recite it to him until the words were burnt onto her brain. *I will say of the Lord, He is my refuge and my fortress, my God, in whom I trust.* But no matter how many times she repeated the verses of the psalm, it didn't reduce her discomfort at those men looking at her. And Hannah knew from the books she secretly read, that words and prayers were not enough to stop the evil that was present in some men. She resented her father's complacency, his insistence on wrapping her in the cloak of his religion yet leaving her unprotected against real potential dangers. Walking out of the docks in the hours of darkness unaccompanied would always be a source of fear, so, whenever alone, she kept her head down and walked home rapidly.

But this man today. He hadn't looked at her like that. He had not catcalled, or whistled, or made rude gestures. He'd spoken what he must have thought was her name. *Elizabeth.*

It had chilled her, frightened her. It was not the first time someone had commented that she resembled her missing aunt. One day she'd been walking back from her secret refuge among the sand dunes, when a smartly dressed lady had called out the name Elizabeth. She'd turned round, and the woman had apologised.

'How remarkable. I took you for someone else. Someone I haven't seen in years. I wonder… perhaps you are related. Her name is Miss Morton. Perhaps—'

Mindful of her father's edict not to speak to strangers, she'd said nothing and hurried away, leaving the woman standing looking after her. Hannah had regretted it ever since. It had been her one opportunity to find out something about her aunt. She'd often returned to the same street but had never seen the woman again.

Now this man had called her by her aunt's name. She'd not been able to see his face very clearly. He was wearing a cap pulled low over his brow; it was already dusk, and this stretch of road, poorly lit. His voice was unusual – some kind of accent. She didn't know from where – it had an almost musical lilt and was not the scouse or Irish accent of most of the dockers.

Hannah ran until she was within sight of her own street. Yet again she'd missed her opportunity to find out about Aunt Lizzie and the mystery of her sudden departure. All her mother had told her was that she was never coming back. Hannah had always imagined she had gone to join her father, Hannah's grandfather, in Australia. But if she had, then why had she never written?

Safely inside the house, she went upstairs to the bedroom she shared with her sister, stuffed her library book into its customary hiding place underneath the mattress and sat down on the bed. She took the photograph of her aunt out of her pocket and studied it. Did she really look like her? She would like to think so. But who was the mysterious man? How did he know Aunt Lizzie? She now regretted failing to stop and talk to him and not just because of her aunt. There had been something about him – she couldn't say what – that made her wish she had waited to hear what he had to say. As she tried to sleep that night her thoughts kept returning to the man on the docks and the sound of his voice.

–

The *Arklow* was similar to the *Christina* in build and capacity but the waters it sailed over were very different from those Will had known around Africa. Here the sea was dark, as grey as the sky it reflected. He had been told most of the crew were Irishmen, the rest drawn from the wide variety of nationalities that sailed out of Liverpool. Friendly enough, but none of them inspired the close affinity he had experienced with Paolo Tornabene.

The day passed uneventfully, as the crew loaded up the now empty holds with cargo, ready to return to Ireland. While the heavy lifting was done by the dock workers, the crew had to drag the tarpaulins over the hatches, keep the decks safe and operate the derricks and winches. It was hard work and the tarpaulins were huge – the size of a tennis court sometimes – and heavy.

One of the dockers was an Irishman. He was friendlier than the others – dockers tended to keep themselves apart from the crew. There was an unofficial rivalry between the seamen and the stevedores. The seamen generally saw themselves as superior to these landlubbers and the dockers thought the sailors were wimps. Will had no truck with this animosity. He took all men at face value. The old naval expression 'You scratch my back and I'll scratch yours' deriving from the days when the cat o' nine tails was the common currency of punishment, had always made sense to him. When the man offered him one of his cheese and pickle sandwiches, Will accepted gratefully and offered the man a friendly grin and a handshake.

The man told him his name was Eddie O'Connor and he had only recently relocated to Liverpool. 'There's more work and better money here than back home, you know. I thought I'd be giving it a go. But I miss the *craic*.'

When Will looked puzzled, Eddie said, 'You've not been knowing many Irishmen then? *Craic* mean the company, the chat. These Scousers are a close lot. Takes a bit to be accepted.' He laughed. 'Even though most of the buggers come from over the water themselves – or their mammies and daddies did.' He drew on his cigarette. 'You know anyone in Dublin?'

Will shook his head.

'Then take this.' He scribbled with a pencil stub on a cigarette paper. 'I've four brothers, three working the docks and one a seaman like you. The mammie's a widow. The old fella was killed when a crane toppled on him ten years ago. If you need lodging or a bit of craic, go and see them. Mammie's always glad of an extra bob or two since me da died. She'll put you up. Cheaper than the seamen's hostel.' He searched in his pocket and pulled out a ten-bob note. 'You'd better give her this. Tell her I'll try and send more when I'm able.'

Amazed that a stranger should show him such trust, Will grinned and shook the man's hand. 'Thanks, mate. I'll see your ma gets it.'

'And when you're back in the Pool we'll have a few jars together. You'll find me in the Baltic most nights.'

They would be away for four days: there was the crossing to Dublin, unloading and reloading, one night in port, then the return to Liverpool via Birkenhead where they were dropping off a quantity of live cattle. Will wasn't too impressed when he discovered that fact. He disliked live cargo. It made for a messy ship, strong smells, and the cattle made him think of the slave trade – helpless creatures being shipped towards an unknown fate. In the case of the cattle, it was the abattoirs of the Wirral peninsula.

For the first time since he had run away to sea eleven years ago, Will found himself looking back towards the land, thinking of someone in particular and wishing he was still in port. The image of that scared young woman haunted him. She'd been so like his Lizbeth – but he had frightened her away. He wouldn't make that mistake again. As soon as he was back in Liverpool he would make it his mission to track her down and this time find a way to talk to her.

Chapter Eight

Judith burst into the bedroom like a small tornado.

Hannah quickly tucked the photograph of their aunt under the welt of her cardigan, hoping Judith wouldn't notice.

'Where's Father?' Judith looked annoyed. 'We still haven't finished that bridal gown so I missed my dinner hour again and ran all the way home because I waited until the last possible minute, and he isn't even here. I could have stayed late and finished that dress. Now I'll have to go in early tomorrow and work through the dinner hour again.' She pulled a face.

'I have no idea where he is. He was only in the office for about half an hour this afternoon and you know he'd never consider telling me where he was going.'

The two sisters chorused together, '*Aspire to live quietly, and to mind your own affairs.* Thessalonians, Chapter Four.'

They started laughing. 'Bet you can't remember the verse number,' said Hannah.

'You're right about that – but don't let Father hear you using the word bet.'

They started laughing again, this time helplessly. Then Judith stopped and looked at her sister, head tilted on one side. 'Has he talked to you yet about getting married?'

'No!' Hannah's heart began thumping. Her worst fear might be coming to pass. 'What do you mean? What do you know?'

'Nothing. Just something Mother said.'

'What? What did she say?'

'That Father said it was time for you to be married. I reckon he's hatching a plan to marry you off.'

Hannah flung herself on her back on the bed. 'He can't do that. I'm not his property.'

Judith gave a wry laugh in response. 'Oh, no? Try telling him that.' She sat beside her and pushed a stray lock away from her sister's forehead. 'Don't get all sulky about it, Han. You've always known it would happen eventually. Father would never consent to either of us choosing our own husbands.' She shook her head and sighed. 'Even if we ever had a chance to meet any men, which we don't. And at least it means you'd get away from him. You'd have your own home and be able to do what you like.'

'If you believe that, then you're dafter than you look, Jude. He'll have made sure to choose some pompous Bible-basher just like him.'

'Hannah! Don't say that! He is our father after all. And it's wrong to show disrespect for the Bible.'

'I don't care.' She grabbed at Judith's arm. 'Did Mother say anything else? Did she say who it is?'

'No. I don't think she knows. Father only tells her what he chooses and that's not much.'

'I'll run away. Like our aunt did.' She bit her lip and wished she'd not let that slip out.

'Aunt? What aunt? We don't have any relatives since Grandmother Dawson died.'

Hannah had no choice but to go on. 'We used to have an aunt. Mother's sister. I can remember her. You were just a baby.'

'I don't believe you. You've such an imagination, Han.'

'It's true.'

'Then why does Mother never mention her?'

Hannah squeezed her lips together. 'I don't know. I think they must have quarrelled.'

Judith snorted, her expression sceptical.

'A lady once stopped me in the street and called me by her name.'

'Silly! She probably meant somebody else.'

'No, she said Elizabeth Morton.'

Judith frowned. 'There are probably lots of Elizabeth Mortons. Just because the surname is the same as Mother's maiden name doesn't prove anything. And anyway I'd have known about her if she existed.'

'They never spoke of her. She just disappeared. I got into trouble whenever I asked about her so in the end I stopped asking. And you were too small. I forgot all about her, until...'

'Until what?'

'Nothing.'

'You can't get away with that. You have to tell me now.'

Hannah let out a long breath, then reached under her cardigan. 'Until I found this.' She handed the photograph to her sister.

Judith gasped. 'Where did you get this? It could be you.'

'I found it in the attic in our old house, years ago. Before we moved here. It was in a frame with the glass shattered. Her music and her violin were there too. The violin had been smashed to bits. It was thrown in an old trunk. Sheet music too. It's probably all still up there, unless the new owners threw it out.'

'I'd no idea.' Judith studied the photograph, running her hand over the image. 'She's so like you, Han. Beautiful. Is she really our aunt? Where do you think she is now?'

'I've no idea.' Hannah grinned. 'Maybe she fell in love and eloped. Ran off to Gretna Green with some handsome chap.'

'There you go again. Always making up stories.' She handed the image back to Hannah.

Once Judith was out of the way, she would put it under the mattress with the book she was hiding. Better that her sister know nothing of her secret library book cache. It would only mean she'd be in trouble too if their father ever found out.

'I think we should ask Mother about her,' said Judith.

Hannah immediately wished she'd never mentioned Elizabeth. She grabbed her sister's hand, relieved that she hadn't gone on to mention the man on the docks that afternoon. 'No, Jude. Please, no. Mother used to fly into a rage if Aunty Lizzie was mentioned. And as for Father. Please, please, I beg you. Don't tell either of them. Let it be our secret.'

Judith looked doubtful, but said, 'Very well. But don't you go thinking any more about running away. Even if Father does want you to get married. It has to be better than living here under his thumb. He doesn't pay you any wages and I have to hand mine over and we're still poor. You never know, your future husband might be rich and handsome.'

Hannah gave a dry laugh. 'More likely old, fat, ugly and broke.'

'Look on the bright side. No one can be as bad as Father. And you'll have a home of your own and, before long, babies to care for. So much nicer than our lives now.'

'Perhaps I should suggest to Father that *you* marry whoever it is then.' She saw the look of horror on her sister's face. 'Exactly. You'd hate the idea as much I do. Easy to dole out your advice to someone else, isn't it?'

Judith smiled and shrugged. 'I'm only trying to help. It will happen to me too, I suppose, in time. Right now, though, I think Father's glad of my wages coming in.'

'I know.' Hannah smoothed out the surface of the bedcover with the flat of her hand. 'Judith, do you ever wonder why we're so poor? Morton's used to be a prosperous business when Mother's father ran it. Mother told me she used to have fine clothes and go to balls and things. And they had a big motorcar when hardly anyone had cars. And Trevelyan House was huge compared to this place.' She swept her arm around the room. 'Just look at it.'

Their shared bedroom was little more than a box room. The wallpaper was stained and peeling away, and there was a cracked pane in the window that they covered with a piece of cardboard, reducing the daylight but keeping out the worst of the elements. The curtains were threadbare and stopped just short of the ledge. The floorcloth was worn and had shrunk so that it didn't reach as far as the skirting. A moth-eaten carpet brought from Trevelyan House lay on the top of it – it was serviceable but had seen better days. Charles Dawson believed that spending money on rooms used only for sleeping was an unjustified expense. The sisters were grateful there were only four of them in the house – the adjoining properties in Bluebell Street were home to much larger families.

'Maybe Father's not very good at business.'

'That's certainly true. But there should still be enough for us to live comfortably, even if not in the grand style.'

'Didn't he say once that the market was bad?'

'People still buy the coffee. Just not for very high prices.'

'Maybe people don't drink much coffee. We never do. Always tea. Even though it's Father's business.'

'Exactly. Don't you find that strange?'

'Not really. I don't ever think about such things. I'm not like you, Han.' She smiled at her sister, fondly.

'Now where's that hat of yours? I smuggled out an off-cut of grosgrain ribbon and there's just enough for me to trim it for you.'

'Oh, Judith. What if you'd been caught?'

'It was on the floor and Miss Finch told me to sweep everything up and put it in the bin. Waste not, want not.'

Hannah leaned over and flung her arms around her sister. 'Thank you, I don't know what I'd do without you.' She jumped off the bed. 'Time I got the supper ready. It won't cook itself.'

Chapter Nine

Will was on the fo'c'sle as they sailed up the Liffey into Dublin. He was ready to operate the steam windlass and release the heavy ropes they would fasten to the bollards on the quayside. It was a sunny day, the cold biting into his face, but the azure blue sky lifted his spirits.

This was his first time in Dublin and he was looking forward to exploring the place. The bad news was they would only be in port for one night, before they were due back in the morning to load up the return cargo and any passengers. At least the cattle would be managed by drovers – he wasn't keen on the idea of chasing angry bullocks round the deck. The Dublin cattle market began at three o'clock in the morning and it would be early afternoon when the drovers brought the beasts onto the ship. The rest of the cargo needed to have been loaded before then – it wouldn't do to have heavy sacks and crates winched on board over the heads of the cattle, which were kept in open pens on the deck.

The dockers having finished the unloading, Will was free. Other crew would be on hand for the task of supervising the loading up for the home run. He now needed to make a decision on what to do with his free time. He didn't relish the idea of lodging with Eddie O'Connor's family. The thought of staying with unfamiliar people didn't appeal so he decided to return on board to sleep instead – but after he'd enjoyed a few jars first. There was no harm in calling on the O'Connors and finding out if one or two of Eddie's brothers might be up for a bit of *craic*, as Eddie had called it, and a couple of pints of the black stuff. They'd know the best pubs to go to – and hadn't Eddie told him that the Guinness tasted better in Dublin than the exported stuff they served in England?

The *Arklow* was moored on the north side of the Liffey. Remembering Eddie had told him his family lived close to the North Wall, Will set off, stopping occasionally to ask the way.

The O'Connors home was in a tenement building about fifteen minutes' walk from the docks. Will was reminded of his visit to the Tornabenes in Naples. Here though, there were no fascists marching through the streets and at least they ought to be able to understand each other, although the thick Irish brogue of many of the crew was sometimes a struggle to comprehend.

As he climbed up through the stairwell of the building he could hear shouting. With a sinking heart he realised it was coming from the second floor where Eddie's family lived. He hesitated outside, then knocked loudly. A woman's voice boomed out from behind the door. 'If it's the rent you're after you'll have to come back tomorrow.' Then the door was flung open.

'Who are you?' The woman was about sixty, with dark grey hair loosely pulled back into a bun. She was wearing black – a skirt that was long and looked like it was from decades ago. Her face was heavily lined and her eyes had a cloudy look. 'You can tell your boss he'll get his money at the end of the week. There's none now.'

'I'm not a rent collector.' He extended a hand towards her. 'Eddie told me to call on you, Mrs O'Connor. My ship docked this morning from Liverpool.'

She raised her eyebrows. 'Eddie?' She made a snorting sound. 'That no-good eejit. If it hadn't been for him wasting all his wages I'd be able to pay the rent on time. A terrible fella, he is. And now run off over the water instead of staying here with his own kin and supporting his poor old mammy.' She wiped her hands on her apron and her expression softened slightly. 'You say you've seen him?'

'Yesterday. He was helping load the ship.' He grinned at the woman. 'He shared his tucker with me.'

'Tucker?' She looked aghast. 'What in heaven's name is that?'

'His food. He gave me a cheese sandwich.'

Mrs O'Connor tutted. 'Cheese sandwiches! And here's his poor mother too broke to pay the rent man.' She gave a long deep sigh. 'Well, I suppose I should be thankful that he's putting food in his belly and not gambling it all away to some card sharp. And that he's still full of the Christian values he was brought up to have. A real Good Samaritan he is, giving his sandwiches to a stranger. Right then, mister, you'd better come inside.' She called over her shoulder as she swung the door open. 'This fella says he's a pal of our Eddie.'

The room was cramped, gloomy and cold – but clean and tidy.

Will remembered he still had Eddie's money. He took out the ten-shilling note from his breast pocket and handed it to the woman. 'Eddie asked me to give you this.'

'Oh, he did now, did he? So, he hasn't forgotten his poor old mother after all.' She stuffed the money into her apron pocket.

'He said sorry it isn't much. He'll try and send some more soon.'

She snorted her doubt. 'He's a good boy is my Eddie but I'll believe it when I see it.' Then she smiled at Will. 'Look at me forgetting me manners. Sure, you'll be having a cup of tea, won't you, mister. Now I didn't even ask you your name, did I?'

'Kidd. William Kidd.'

'William Kidd – well then, Willy the Kid.' She gave a loud guffaw. 'That's a good one! Sit yourself down. Bridget, put the kettle on. Lads, get in here!'

As she spoke, a young woman wearing a woollen shawl and a dress of a similar vintage to her mother's got up from a chair by the unlit fire. Her hair was dark and glossy and hung in curtains either side of a thin, but not unattractive, face. She gave Will a big, beaming smile that revealed a small gap between her front teeth. 'Pleased to meet you, Mr Kidd, I'm sure.' She moved to a corner of the room and put the kettle on the hob.

The men of the family, all evidently younger than Eddie, trooped in and stood, awkwardly, their arms folded in front of them.

'This is Eddie's friend. A sailor over from Liverpool. Says he saw him yesterday.'

They each stretched a hand out in turn and shook Will's, telling him their names: Dermot, Seamus and Liam.

An awkward silence followed. Will doubted any of them would be accompanying him to the pub. Mrs

O'Connor was unlikely to stand for that if money was as tight as she was saying. He felt only relief. The men looked a miserable bunch. Even though the language had been a barrier, he'd communicated more easily with the Tornabenes than he was likely to do with this lot.

The matriarch pointed to a chair and he sat, accepting a tin mug of tea from a still smiling Bridget. The menfolk shuffled their feet. Will wished he'd never agreed to make the visit. He couldn't wait to get outside and away from the oppressive atmosphere in the room.

The older woman leaned forward and studied him intently. 'Are you a married man, Willy?'

'I'm not.' He squirmed in his chair under her scrutiny.

'Aye, well. The sea's a hard mistress. There's not many women willing to share a man with her.' She looked at her daughter, then turned to face him again. 'But you're a good-looking fella, I'll say. And every man needs a wife, Willy. Someone to mend his clothes, cook his meals, keep his bed warm and give him children to support him in his old age.' Again she looked towards her daughter, who looked away, clearly embarrassed.

Will slugged his tea down, uncaring of the fact that it was burning his mouth. He couldn't wait to be out of the room. The three brothers were watching him but remained silent.

He finished the tea and looked around unsuccessfully for somewhere to deposit the empty mug. 'Well, I'm due back on board soon. We've a lot to do and we're heading back to Liverpool tomorrow.' He got up. The O'Connor women, like Eddie, were friendly and approachable – but the men seemed dull and inscrutable.

The three brothers stared at him, but remained silent.

'Goodbye to you all, then. I'll tell Eddie I saw you.' He handed the mug to Mrs O'Connor and left.

Hurrying down the stairway, he was halfway to the bottom when a door slammed above him then he heard the sound of several feet on the steps above. He looked up. The O'Connor brothers were clattering down at speed.

He waited for them in the hallway at the bottom.

Seamus waved the ten-shilling note at him. 'The Mammy must like you. She said we can all have a couple of pints on her.'

'But the rent?' Will knew it was none of his business yet he couldn't help himself. He wasn't sure Eddie would be happy at his hard-earned money being drunk away by his brothers.

'We get paid tomorrow so this is a wee bonus,' said Liam, winking. 'Come on, let's not be wasting valuable drinking time.' He slung an arm round Will's shoulders and the four of them set off.

Will was astonished at the transformation in the three once they were away from their mother. No wonder Eddie had fled to Liverpool. The brothers chattered away to him, explaining that Fintan, their oldest sibling, was sailing somewhere in South America. Another escapee then.

When they reached the public house, Liam shouldered open the door and ushered Will inside. The place was packed. From the look of the clientele they were mostly other dockers. Big muscly men. Will was swept towards the bar by the O'Connors, who did a round of introductions – they appeared to know everyone. He discovered that there was a Dublin dockland tradition to give each docker a nickname. He was given no choice in his own, as

Dermot introduced him as 'Willy the Kid'. Will groaned inwardly – he had often been called Billy The Kid when on the Transatlantic ships, and had thought he'd escaped it by returning to Europe. At least they hadn't called him 'Matilda' as one of the other dockers suggested, picking up on his Aussie accent. Cormac was known by his co-workers as 'Cocky Corm'. Seamus as 'Pockets' and Liam as 'Knees O'C'. No one troubled to inform Will as to the basis for these names but it was clear that they were now as familiar to each man as his Christian name – probably more so.

After a round of Guinness, Seamus clapped a hand on Will's shoulder. 'So you're a single man, Willy? Not even a girlfriend then?' Will saw the men look at each other.

'No time, lads. As your mother said, the sea doesn't appeal to many women.' He didn't like the direction the conversation had taken. 'And it looks like you're all single men yourselves.'

None of the brothers replied. Will speculated to himself that marriage plans no doubt required the approval of Mrs O'Connor – who was probably unwilling to forgo their weekly wage packets.

'It's my round,' he said, breaking the silence, deciding that once he'd discharged this obligation he'd head back to the ship. The O'Connor boys were pleasant enough fellows but he wasn't comfortable at the exchange of glances between them as though he were the only one not in on a joke.

'Mammy told us to tell youse, you can sleep at our place tonight. No charge. Her guest. She'd like you and our Bridget to get better acquainted.'

So that was it. His fears were grounded. 'Thanks, lads,' he said. 'But I'll be going back to my ship after this one. I have to be up at the crack.'

'What's the name of your ship?' The speaker was a man who'd identified himself earlier as Chins Gilligan.

When Will told him, the man laughed. 'Me and Topper here are loading that ship. Do it every week. You're not needed back till morning.' He laughed. 'Plenty of time for some more craic – and maybe a spot of courting.'

Will was now decidedly uneasy. The prospect of spending a night in the O'Connors home was as appealing as walking the plank. By now he was certain there was a plot afoot to marry him off to Bridget. They were clearly crazy. While he was sure Miss O'Connor was a charming and not unattractive lass, he was hardly about to start courting her on the basis of a ten-minute acquaintance. Will had no intention of courting anyone. Hadn't he resisted the call of matrimony for all eleven years he'd been at sea?

Leaving his almost full pint on the bar he went off to the Gents and was about to slip out of the side door of the pub and head back to the *Arklow* when he felt a hand grab his shoulders. It was Liam.

Will's face must have reflected the panic he felt, but Liam burst into peals of laughter. 'Trying to do a runner were you? Did you think we were about to kidnap you and marry you off to our Bridget?'

Seamus and Dermot were falling about, holding their stomachs.

Liam said, 'Sure, and you thought we were. You did!' He hauled him back to the centre of the bar where everyone was in tears of laughter.

'The face on you, Willy, lad! Blind panic. Did you think you were about to have a shotgun wedding?'

Will could feel the blood rushing to his face as the realisation that he had been the object of a prank dawned on him. Relief overwhelmed him and he too began to laugh.

One of the men handed him a fresh pint. 'Don't youse worry, Willy. It's a standing joke. Every man who crosses the threshold is a potential son-in-law as far as Mary O'Connor's concerned.'

'And there's many of us would be more than happy to marry Bridget. But the lass will have none of us.'

Dermot winked at Will. 'She's her heart set on marrying Jesus. Wants to be a nun, a bride of Christ, but the Mammy's dead against it. She's been praying up a storm that some man will come along and change her mind. But we know our Bridget. Her mind's made up. Soon as she's had her twenty-first birthday she'll be hammering on the convent door.'

While relieved that he wasn't about to be kidnapped and forced into marriage by a crazy Irish family, Will couldn't help agreeing that it was an awful shame that a young woman like Bridget should embrace the religious life.

–

When he got back to the ship that night, the bullocks were already on board, having been driven through the streets of Dublin from the main cattle market at Stoneybatter, weaving between traffic and trams, all the way to the docks. The drovers and their dogs were evidently a common sight on the streets and a habitual disruption to the business of north Dublin on market days. Will thought it strange that this should be taking place in a capital city as though it were a rural market town.

Will's dislike of live cattle as cargo was not diminished by the return crossing to Liverpool. The sea was lively throughout the eight-hour sail back over the Irish Sea and the cattle bellowed in protest as the ship rose and fell with the surge. His worst fears about the smell were vindicated and he was glad to see the back of the beasts when the *Arklow* docked on the other side of the Mersey in Birkenhead.

As soon as they reached Liverpool and discharged the rest of the cargo, Will went in search of Eddie O'Connor. The man owed him a few beers for the prank his brothers had played on him in Dublin.

But once Eddie heard what had happened, he was having none of it. 'Come on now, Will, it's a long-standing tradition to pull the leg of a fella who's new to Dublin. And aren't you as green as the grass in Connemara to think me poor old mammy and me little brothers would be off and kidnapping youse and forcing yer to marry me sister!' He grinned at Will. 'And what makes you so sure she'd even've had you? I tell you there's far better men than youse that have tried to court our Bridget.'

Will raised his eyes and nodded his head. 'Yeah, yeah, I know. But she's going to marry Jesus. Your brothers told me. The evil bastards.'

Eddie roared with laughter and clapped Will on the shoulders. 'You're right about that. They are evil bastards.

But I love the bones of them all. Oh God, Willy boy, I miss the family.'

'Then why not go back to Dublin?'

Eddie gave a sly laugh. 'Maybe one day. Now, I'll be dying of a terrible thirst if you don't get yourself over to that bar and get me a drink.'

When they were settled with their beers, Eddie took a long slug then winked at Will. 'But it's not surprising the boys were getting a rise out of youse, with you being a bachelor and all. It seems a strange thing that a fella like you doesn't have himself a wife. You're not one of those fairies are you? A shirt-lifter?' He pulled a face.

Will rolled his eyes and chose to ignore the question. 'I could as easily ask you the same thing. You and your four bachelor brothers.'

'That's down to the mammy. Rules us with a rod of iron, she does. It's why I came over here. There's a girl I'd like to marry but as long as I'm under the family roof I've not a chance to save up enough that I can ask her to marry me. Her name's Maureen.' He fished in his jacket pocket and pulled out a photo. 'Now, isn't she the prettiest thing you've ever clapped eyes on?'

Will made some appropriate noises, then settled into his pint.

'You still haven't told me, is there a girl waiting back in Kangaroo-land for youse then?'

'No. Nobody.' He spoke with a note of finality that must have registered with Eddie, as the docker didn't argue. In a couple of minutes, the conversation moved on.

'When do you sail again?'

'Tomorrow on the first tide. I'm due back on board tonight.' He glanced up at the clock. 'I need to go now in fact. I'm on cargo watch.'

Eddie put a hand on his sleeve. 'I don't suppose you could lend us a few bob? Just to tide me over. And after all you helped the lads drink through that ten shilling note I gave you for the mammy.'

Will took a note out of his pocket and handed it to Eddie. 'Don't drink it all at once, mate.'

Chapter Ten

Hannah approached the closed door of her father's so-called study, terrified. The only reason he would have summoned her was that she must have done something wrong.

But Hannah was always careful. Most of the time Charles Dawson was likelier to find fault with her younger and more careless sister. Judith seemed to irritate him, so she kept out of his way. Hannah was the favourite, if a man like Dawson could be said to have a favourite. Not that he spoke to her often. Most of the time he shut himself away either in his study or in his office at work. But there was something about the way she sometimes caught him looking at her that made Hannah feel uncomfortable. She couldn't put her finger on the reason it did – she just knew that he never looked at Judith or their mother in that way.

She knocked on the door and was told to enter.

Charles Dawson was sitting in a winged chair in front of the fireplace. A roaring fire was burning in the grate and Hannah immediately felt the difference in temperature compared with the back kitchen where her mother, Judith, and she spent their time. He was, as always, sitting ramrod straight in his chair, his knees splayed apart and his arms folded. As she looked at him, Hannah reflected that she couldn't remember ever seeing her father laugh.

'Father?' She heard the tremor in her own voice.

He stared at her, his face rigid and inscrutable, but said nothing. She could feel the anger radiating off him.

Hannah's heart almost jumped out of her chest when he brandished the library's copy of *Weather in the Streets* at her.

'You have defied me. I am ashamed of my own child. The fruit of my own loins. This book is filth. Utter filth.'

Hannah began to shake and felt the tears rising in a mixture of fear and anger. Anger at the injustice of it all.

He looked at her with loathing. 'I have been reading a few pages and I feel I have swallowed poison. It has contaminated me. Even on the very first page.' He was shouting now. He held the book in front of him, his spectacles low on his nose as he read from the opening page. '"*Oh damn, oh hell*" – words that speak of the devil, thrown out so casually by this… this adulterous woman. How could you bring such foul depraved matter into this house? You, my own daughter? This book is about a woman having a relationship with a married man. It's filth.'

Before she could answer, he began to tear the pages out of the volume and flung them onto the fire.

'But, Father! It's not mine. It belongs to the library. Please, stop!'

He continued to tear at the book in a frenzy. 'I will tell those godless people exactly what I think of the degenerate, immoral, perverted works they are peddling to young women. It's a disgrace. Is this what I pay the rates for? You will never enter that place again. I am ashamed of you.' His body shook as though possessed.

Hannah looked at the fire, watching the crackling flames as they consumed the pages he continued to feed it.

Until she made an apology and suffered the inevitable punishment, she would be kept standing there in front of him. Hands clutched behind her back, she pressed her fingernails into the flesh of her palms. The words pained her. 'I'm sorry, Father; I was only curious. I had no idea. I haven't read any of it yet. I just liked the title. That was all. I didn't know it was a bad book.' The lies flowed like a river.

'There is only one good book. All others are the work of the devil.' He continued ripping the book apart and turned to look at her, his eyes cold and angry. 'And this book is written by a *woman*. A sinful daughter of Eve. Jewish too – one who has turned her back on the teachings of the Lord. And you dare to bring this abomination into my home.'

The subsequent silence was protracted, and Hannah was about to ask if she might be allowed to leave the room, when he spoke again.

'You are a viper in the midst of this home. You are a liar. You had hidden this wicked and sinful book beneath your mattress, where you thought it would be undetected. You are a deceitful Jezebel.'

Who had found the book and given her away? Hannah couldn't believe her mother would have had either the energy or the volition to lift the mattress. And surely it wasn't Judith? Her sister would never betray her trust, and she didn't even know the book was there. Did she?

It was not long before that question was answered. Her father reached in his breast pocket and brandished the photograph of her aunt. The blood drained from Hannah's face.

'You told your sister about this... this... woman. I overheard Judith asking your mother whether she had a sister. She said you had a picture. I found it concealed with that dirty book underneath your mattress.' He was speaking so fast the spittle flew as he waved the offending image above his head. 'Deceitful creature! You're just like *her*. Just as bad as that filthy, dirty harlot. A temptress. An adulteress.' He looked at her in that way that always made her feel uncomfortable. Now she knew why. It was a look partly of hatred and contempt, and partly a kind of longing. If she hadn't known it was impossible for a father to have such feelings for his own child she would have thought it was desire. Hannah was suddenly afraid. This was her own father. It wasn't right that he looked at her as if he wanted to tear her clothes off, hurt her and then kill her.

Before she could do anything, he had torn the picture of Elizabeth in half and thrown it onto the flames where Hannah watched it catch, blacken and burn away. She gave a little sob.

The blow landed on her face before she saw it coming. She reeled backwards, her hip knocking painfully into the side table, the only other furniture in the room. The Bible, which was on top, fell onto the floor. This enraged Dawson further. He grabbed Hannah by the arm, hauled her towards him and struck her a second time across the face.

The pain lashed her, cutting, burning, stinging. Taste of blood in her mouth. Metallic, warm. She fought back her tears. Don't show him any weakness. Don't give him the satisfaction. Don't let him win.

He bent down and picked up the heavy leather-bound Bible. Pushing her onto her knees, his hand twisting in her hair, he began to read aloud.

> 'The lips of an immoral woman are as sweet as honey,
> and her mouth is smoother than oil.
> But in the end she is as bitter as poison,
> as dangerous as a double-edged sword.
> Her feet go down to death;
> her steps lead straight to the grave.'

Tears and blood mingled on Hannah's face, but she couldn't reach her skirt pocket to extract her handkerchief. She gave in to the sobbing. This enraged her father further and he pulled her hair, jerking her head back so she couldn't avoid his face.

'The Book of Revelations says, "But I have this against you, that you tolerate that woman Jezebel, who calls herself a prophetess and is teaching and seducing my servants to practice sexual immorality and to eat food sacrificed to idols."'

He struck her again and Hannah lost consciousness.

–

When she came to, she was lying on the rug in front of the fire, her cheek hot from the heat of the blaze. Judith was speaking and Hannah made out her sister's features through her hazy vision. 'It's all right, Hannah. He's gone. He's left the house. You're safe now. We'll take care of you.'

Hannah felt a hand on her forehead and realised it was her mother's.

'He should never have done that.' Sarah looked at her, tenderness replacing her usual glassy stare. 'Did he do anything else to you? I mean – apart from hitting you?'

Hannah pushed herself up into a sitting position. 'What do you mean? Apart from hitting me? Isn't that enough for you? He struck me twice. He knocked me out.'

'I mean... Never mind. Judith, go and make some tea for your sister. Plenty of sugar.'

Judith left the room, throwing Hannah a rueful smile as she left.

'I mean did he touch you? Interfere with you.' Sarah's face was pale, her eyes narrowed.

Hannah was aghast. 'What are you saying? That's too horrible. He's my father! How can you even ask that?'

Her mother's voice was calm and controlled but her resignation was underlaid with sadness. 'Because I've seen how he looks at you. Because I know what he's capable of.' She brushed away a strand of hair from her daughter's face. 'He forced himself on one of the maids when we lived in the other house. Denied it of course. I had to pay her not go to the police.' She turned her head away. 'I am afraid I married a monster and it took me years of closing my eyes to his misdeeds before I could admit it to myself, much less to you.'

'But, but... he's a God-fearing, church-going man. He is full of religious beliefs. He's always condemning the sins of the flesh. How can what you're saying be true? I can't believe it.'

'You need to believe me. Your father is the worst kind of hypocrite. He has ruined this family. He has ruined my father's company. He has ruined my life.'

'What are you talking about, Mother? I don't understand.'

'I warned you years ago not to provoke him by ever mentioning Elizabeth's name. And now it turns out you've been keeping a photograph of her.' Sarah Dawson dipped a cloth into a bowl and wiped it over Hannah's brow. 'Foolish girl. You should know by now what he's like.' She paused. 'Where is the photograph?'

'He threw it on the fire.'

Sarah turned her head to look at the dying embers, her face contorted.

Hannah, suddenly defiant, said, 'Why? Why can't we speak of my aunt? She's your sister. Why should she be unmentionable?'

'He drove her away. I chose to believe him rather than her. As long as I live I'll never forgive myself.' She put her fingers to her lips. 'I'll tell you everything some time, but not now. Judith will be back in a moment.'

'Hasn't she a right to know too?'

'Judith's headstrong and lacks caution. She's also fragile. It's bad enough he's beating you. If he were to start on her too—'

Judith backed into the room, carrying a small tea tray. 'Here you are, Han. This will make you feel better.'

Sarah got up from where she was kneeling beside Hannah on the rug. 'Stay out of his way. Both of you. Now, I'm going to bed. I don't want any supper. If you've any sense you'll go to bed as soon as you've had yours.' She moved to the door then looked back at them. 'And lock your bedroom door.'

—

Charles Dawson didn't come home for several days. Hannah had no idea whether he was absent from the office too, as she didn't go into work. Her face was bloated and bruised from the blows he had dealt her but there was no serious damage. Worst of all was the realisation that she was afraid. Terrified of seeing her own father. For two days she remained indoors, ashamed to show her face in public.

If Hannah expected that the display of concern from her mother marked a new beginning, she was soon disappointed. Sarah returned to her usual state of torpor, spending hours in bed. There was no sign she was ready to share any further revelations about her past or her sister Elizabeth.

On the third day, desperate for fresh air, Hannah decided to go for a walk on the sands. She pulled an old tam'o'shanter low on her brow and covered as much of her face as possible with a knitted scarf and set off, avoiding the main thoroughfares. It was a cold and blustery afternoon and she knew it was unlikely there would be many people around on the seashore.

She went by way of the library, needing to confess that *The Weather in the Streets* could not be returned. Waiting until the young librarian she knew best was alone at the counter, Hannah approached and told her what had happened. She'd originally intended to make up a story about a pet dog destroying the book, but she was a poor liar. No, the truth was always better. She explained that her father belonged to a religious sect that believed any books, apart from the Bible, should be destroyed.

The woman looked at her open-mouthed. 'He threw it on the fire?'

Hannah nodded. Conscious of the librarian staring at her, she hoped her scarf and hat still covered the bruising.

The woman looked up at the clock behind the desk. 'It's time for my break. Come with me.' She moved from behind the counter and ushered Hannah by the elbow to the back of the room and through a doorway into a small anteroom. As well as half a dozen upright chairs there was a wooden trolley holding an electric kettle and a collection of cups and saucers.

They sat down side-by-side.

'Your father hit you, didn't he?'

Hannah's hand went involuntarily to her face.

'Let me see.' The librarian eased the scarf down and winced as she saw the extent of the bruising. 'He shouldn't be allowed to get away with that. No one should, and certainly not your own father. Maybe you could try telling a priest – or even the police?'

'No. Please. It would make matters worse.' She stood up. 'I just wanted to tell you I was sorry about the book and to warn you that he might come here and make a fuss.' She pulled her scarf up again and, waving her hand towards the kind-hearted librarian, pushed open the door. 'I have no money. But I will try and find a way to repay the library.'

'Don't worry. Lots of books go missing. And if he does turn up here, he'll get a piece of my mind. Burning books! Is his name Adolf Hitler?'

Hannah was starting to walk away.

The librarian softened her tone. 'Please wait.'

Hannah shook her head and left the library, wishing she hadn't come.

Walking towards the shore, she was filled with regret about telling the woman the truth. Her kindness had almost made things worse. Hannah hated feeling sorry for herself, much less to invite the pity of others, and now she had the added worry that the woman might tell someone else. It would have been better to have said she'd left the book on a tram. Her nerves tingled in anxiety and her stomach churned. What had she done? Why had she been so stupid?

As she'd hoped, the beach was devoid of people. The tide was on the turn. Hannah walked briskly along the hard, wet sand, still thinking about what the woman had said. What if she did go to the police? Might they be able to help her? Something told her that her father would brush any enquiries away – even supposing the police would be interested in a matter between family members – he would find a way to convince them it had been an accident. Then she would be left unprotected to face his even greater rage.

She had been unable to forget the night a few years ago when she and Judith had lain in bed weeping as they listened to their father beating their mother in the adjoining room, and repeatedly shouting, '*WIVES, SUBMIT YOURSELVES UNTO YOUR OWN HUSBANDS, AS UNTO THE LORD*.' It had gone on for nearly ten minutes and their mother's screams had chilled them to the bone. The next morning, when they tried to comfort her after he had left the house, Sarah had pushed them away.

Hannah kept on walking, further than usual, beyond Waterloo and Crosby, almost to Hightown. Looking up at the sky she saw there were banks of dark clouds. Deciding to turn around and head back as she had no umbrella, she saw, in the far distance, the outline of a man walking towards her. Inside her pocket, Hannah crossed her fingers hoping that he would turn off the beach before their paths crossed. She looked around her, now anxious, but the shore was otherwise deserted. Fixing her eyes on the distant city she increased her pace and tried to walk purposefully and confidently, pulling her scarf higher to cover her face.

He was about fifty yards away from her now, and the dunes were encroaching closer to the sea at what would be their point of crossing. There was no room for her to move further away from him, other than by scrambling up the dunes or stepping into the sea. Something about him seemed familiar. She lowered her eyes and kept walking.

She was almost level with him and he raised his cap in greeting. Recognising the man from the docks the other evening, she heard him gasp in recognition too. 'It's you again. I've been looking everywhere for you. Please, wait! I mean you no harm. It's just that you look exactly like someone I once knew.'

Hannah carried on walking, mindful of her father's strictures, but the man swung round and was now walking beside her. 'I think you might be related to her. Her name is Elizabeth Morton. Please, Miss Dawson.' That funny accent again.

Hannah turned to face him. 'How do you know my name? What do you want with me?' She was uncertain what to do; fear mingled with curiosity. The man was older than she was, probably around thirty. His expression was sincere, his face open and friendly. And she did have so many questions. But the last thing she wanted right now was for this man, who had known her aunt, to see her with a face that looked as though she'd done a few rounds in a boxing ring against the champ.

'I made enquiries in the building you came out from. They said you were Miss Dawson. The man in the office told me. The building had a sign saying Morton's Coffee. I realised you must be related to her, to Elizabeth.' He held out his hand. 'Sorry, I have the advantage over you – my name is William Kidd. Elizabeth Morton was my father's second wife. In Australia. That's where I come from.' He brushed his hair away from his brow and put his cap on again.

Australia. That was the accent then. She accepted his hand with her gloved one. 'You knew her? My aunt?'

'Yes.' His face broke into a wide grin and he clenched his fists in front of him in a gesture of triumph. 'I *knew* you had to be related. You're the living image of her.'

Hannah felt a little surge of pleasure at that. He had a nice face and laughing eyes. She decided she liked him. Liked him a lot.

'Your mother? Is she Elizabeth's sister?'

Hannah looked around her, fearful of someone seeing her speaking to this man. But the beach was empty. 'Yes. My aunt left when I was a small child. I had no idea where she went, until now. I did have a photograph but not anymore.' She felt a rush of emotion and struggled to conceal it. 'Is she still alive? Is she all right?' She searched his face, her excitement growing.

Will closed his eyes for a moment. 'As far as I know, but I haven't seen her in more than ten years.'

'Oh.' Disappointment sapped her. She had to know more. 'You said she was married to your father?' Hannah frowned, puzzled.

'My father's been dead for many years. I'm afraid that's why I lost touch with Elizabeth.' A frown darkened his features and he looked towards the sea, avoiding her eyes.

After a moment he turned to face her again and this time looked at her intently. Hannah felt the blood rushing to her face. What was it about him that should have that effect on her? It must be the way he looked at her. Hannah couldn't remember anyone ever looking at her that way before. As if she were the only other person in the world. As if the world didn't exist beyond this empty beach and the two of them. Her stomach gave a little jump. Then she remembered her bruising and pulled at her scarf, tugging it tighter around the lower half of her face. She could feel his eyes still on her. She wanted to get away before he could see what her father had done to her – and yet she didn't want to stop talking to him, didn't want to move away from him.

'Would you like to get a cup of tea somewhere, Miss Dawson? We have a lot to talk about.'

She wanted nothing more. But that would mean he would see her whole face. See the ugly blue bruising around her jaw and the cut to her lower lip. 'I can't' she said quickly. 'I have to get back. I'm expected at work. I'm sorry. I can't talk to you, Mr Kidd. I'm really glad you knew my aunt. Goodbye.' Heedless now of getting sand in her shoes, she stumbled up the dunes towards the nearby road and didn't look back. Her last words must have sounded incoherent. As she scrambled up through the slippery sand, she could feel his eyes on her.

—

Later, she cursed her stupidity. Why had she run away? Why hadn't she arranged to meet him again another day. The damage to her face would soon be healed. Why did it matter so much what her face looked like when all she wanted to do was talk to him about her aunt? But she knew that wasn't the truth. Talking about Aunt Lizzie was a means to an end. She was afraid if he saw the cuts and bruises on her face, he wouldn't feel the kind of attraction for her that she was already beginning to feel for him.

Why was she even thinking this? *Pull yourself together*, she urged herself. Mr Kidd was a stranger with whom she merely shared a common acquaintance. No more than that.

—

Will stood on the shore, watching the young woman hurrying away. Something wasn't right. Why was she hiding her face behind that scarf? It was cold but not that cold. What was she concealing? All he'd been able to see were her eyes. Big beautiful eyes. Lizbeth's eyes. She'd seemed frightened and he didn't think it was because of him.

He remembered what the clerk at Morton's had said: that her father would be angry if he knew Will was asking about her. Even though they had only spoken for a few minutes, he felt drawn to her. He decided to go after her but by the time he reached the other side of the dunes she had disappeared into the network of residential streets.

The impact of seeing this young woman was greater than, by all rights, it should have been. Will was convinced he was meant to know her. Why else would he have run into her again in the few hours of free time he had in port, before the *Arklow* returned to Dublin? For someone who had believed himself to be immune to women, this one was already exercising a strong pull on him. Instinct told him that she was in some kind of trouble.

Trudging back towards the ship, he mulled over Miss Dawson's behaviour, asking himself why he cared so much. Elizabeth was gone from his life. But the feelings this young woman had evoked in him weren't only because he'd loved Elizabeth, it was something about the girl herself. In such a short time she'd got right under his skin.

Chapter Eleven

He'd come home. Hannah, her mother, and sister were eating supper when Dawson arrived, slamming the front door as he came into the house. The three women glanced at each other, put down their cutlery and waited for him to enter the room, anxiety showing in their faces. But he didn't come in. Instead, he went straight into his 'study'.

His voice boomed through the walls. 'Why is there no fire lit in here?'

Hannah started to get up. Her mother – unusually – stayed her with a hand to her arm. 'I'll go.'

After Sarah had left the room, Judith rolled her eyes at Hannah. 'If there'd been a fire lit he'd have screamed at us for wasting fuel in an empty room.'

'I know. We can't win.'

They both sighed and picked up their knives and forks but neither had much appetite left. A few minutes later the shouting began.

The rooms were small but the walls were thick and the two women strained to hear what was being said. Silently, as though reading each other's mind, they rose from the table and went into the hall and stood outside the door to their father's study. Wood was thinner than brick.

Their father's voice was an inaudible rumble, but their mother's was clear. 'I must have been out of my mind when I chose to marry you.'

'You married me because no one else would look at you.' Dawson's raised his voice and now clearly enunciated his words. '*I* married *you* because of Morton's Coffee. *I* married *you* because I thought your no-good father would have done the right thing and handed the company over to me. But he must have despised you as much as I do. That's why he cut me out and sold the business.'

'He sold the business because he knew you were incompetent. He knew you'd do what you did as soon as you managed to get your hands on it: run it into the ground. Morton's used to be a healthy business. You ruined it.'

Judith and Hannah looked at each other. They couldn't remember the last time their mother had spoken out against their father.

The reply from Charles Dawson was inaudible – at least the words were. But the sound of their mother being struck was evident, even through the door.

Defiant in pain, she spoke. 'That's your only response. Always the fist.'

'Be silent, woman! Show respect! I am your husband and master. *I own you.*'

'You're not a man. You're weak. You're useless. A coward. My father was right.'

Another blow, followed by Sarah's muffled whimpers.

Hannah reached for the door handle but her sister stayed her hand. 'Don't. It'll make it worse for her. For us all.'

'You revolt me.' Dawson's voice was rising, consumed by rage. 'You're like a fat slug. You were always plain. The ugly one. But your sister was a whore. And your daughter is one too.'

Hannah gasped.

'Don't you speak of my sister or my daughter. Who, in case you've forgotten, is your daughter too.' Her words were followed by the sound of her crashing against the door.

Hannah was shaking, terrified at what her father might be capable of. 'Let's go in. There are three of us. We can stop him.'

'No. Please, Han. You'll only make it worse.' Judith whispered, tears running down her cheeks.

'I should have believed Lizzie.' Sarah's voice rose almost to a scream. 'I was jealous of her. I was stupid. She gave me no cause. It was my fault. All my own stupid fault. And God knows why.' Her words were engulfed by sobbing.

The scream was bloodcurdling as he struck her again. '*Thou shalt not take the name of the Lord thy God in vain.*'

'You're a hypocrite. All your Bible reading and piety and you're just a dirty pervert who can't control his own lust. I've seen how you look at Hannah. And it's exactly what I saw before. The looks you gave Lizzie. My *sister*. I know what you did to her. I always knew. I just pretended to myself that I didn't.'

Judith clutched Hannah's arm, her eyes wide and filled with tears.

Hannah tried to pull her back into the kitchen, but Judith shook her off and stood rooted to the spot.

'You raped Elizabeth. You forced yourself on her. Then you made me fling her out of the house. You sent her away. All these years and I've no idea where she is. My own sister. You destroyed her, and you've destroyed me.'

'Your sister was an adulteress. She plied me with drink and came to my bed.'

Sarah's voice was rising. '*Your* bed? You mean her bed. You went into her room and raped her. I saw you in there, passed out drunk on top of her bed.'

'She lured me there. She is Jezebel.'

'For God's sake, stop lying.'

Another sound of a blow, then, 'I've told you – *Thou shalt not take the name of the Lord thy God in vain.*'

After a brief silence, Sarah's voice. 'Go away. Now. I will tell the pastor exactly what kind of man you are.'

'And why would the pastor listen to a *woman*?' He said the last word as though it were something dirty.

Hannah and Judith realised their father was laughing. 'The pastor knows what a poor wife you have been to me. He knows what a poor Christian you are. A lazy, idle, useless wife. Only able to give me one son and now barren and shrivelled. You couldn't even manage to keep my son alive.'

They could barely hear their mother's weeping any longer. Those last words seemed to have killed the fight in her.

Hannah found Judith's hand. They looked at each other and went up the stairs to their bedroom and locked the door. A few minutes later they heard the slam of the front door as their father left the house.

Hannah said, 'Come on. We have to go to Mother now. She needs us.'

They opened the door to their father's study and gasped. Their mother was on the floor in front of the empty fireplace, her face bloodied. She moaned and cradling her left hand in her right, said, 'I think it's broken.' Wincing with pain, she added, 'My wrist took the weight of the fall.'

Hannah helped her into a sitting position. 'We need to get you to hospital.'

'No!' Sarah looked anguished. 'They'll ask questions.'

'Well, they need answers. He's gone too far this time.' She looked to her sister for support.

Judith was in tears. 'Oh, Mother. I can't believe he could be so cruel. We have to get you to hospital. Maybe I should run to the phone box and call for an ambulance.'

'No!' Sarah grabbed her younger daughter's wrist with her own undamaged one. 'They might tell the police. Then he'll take it out on you too.'

Hannah knew her mother was right. 'We'll make up a story.' She thought for a moment. 'We'll tell them you caught your heel in a tramline. You tripped and fell and hit your head on the kerb.'

Judith glanced at her, sceptically.

Hannah frowned. 'We must stick to the same story. Now, come on. We need to get you there before he comes back.'

But he didn't come back that night. By the time the three women returned from the hospital it was almost midnight. Sarah's wrist had been painfully re-set and plastered and she had been given some painkillers. Judith made them all a cup of tea and they retired to bed, grateful and relieved that the hospital had treated Sarah, without requiring payment.

The following morning, when Judith left for work, Hannah went in to see her mother. Sarah's face was taut and strained. She signalled Hannah to sit on the bed beside her. Hannah took her mother's hand and asked whether she'd managed to get some sleep.

'Why are you being kind to me when I don't deserve it? I've been a bad mother to both you and your sister.'

Hannah was about to deny it but Sarah jerked her hand away.

'Don't tell me it's not true when we both know that it is.' She stared past Hannah through the grimy bedroom window. Outside the sky was clear above the lines of roofs and chimney pots. There were no trees. Just long streets of ugly red-brick terraced houses, each identical to the other.

'I never thought I'd end up in a place like this.' Sarah's voice was wistful, distracted, as though her words were involuntary rather than considered. 'It was all so different when I was your age. No shortage of money. New clothes every season. Our house was a happy home. Full of music. Joyful.' Her eyes remained fixed on the window as though she were picturing the scene. 'My mother was a good, kind woman. Caring. Loving. My father was devastated when she died. We all were. Everything changed for all of us. You were a baby so you won't remember her.'

Her mother's eyes were brimming with tears. Hannah had never seen her like this. Sarah never betrayed her emotions. Suddenly courageous, Hannah asked, 'Why did you marry Father?' As soon as the words were out she regretted them, remembering the cruelty of her father's words the night before.

But Sarah gave the ghost of a smile. 'I was a little crazy then. Headstrong. Thoughtless. Defiant. My parents didn't like your father. Sometimes I think that's why I did it. To get attention. To be different.' She turned her head and looked at her daughter. 'I've never admitted this to anyone, even myself, but the main reason was because I was jealous of my sister.' She looked down at her hands, twisting her fingers together. 'Of Elizabeth. She couldn't bear Charles.'

Hannah squeezed her lips together. It was hard to believe that her mother was at last opening up to her.

'Elizabeth's fiancé, Stephen, was killed in the war. I suppose she must have really loved him, as she had many other suitors after the war but refused them all.' She closed her eyes and took a breath. 'Including your father.'

Hannah suppressed a gasp.

'I suppose I resented her because she seemed to have everything. She was popular. A talented musician. She understood the coffee business better than I ever did and so she was Papa's favourite. She and Mama loved to read, and they were both musical. I felt left out. All I wanted was to be married and have children. Lizzie didn't seem to care about that herself. Maybe that's why I did it.' She wiped her eyes with the back of her hand. 'I went after your father. Threw myself at him. I was very young, and it was my way of getting attention. Mama and Papa had to take notice. Charles is fifteen years older than me and that made me feel special too. More sophisticated.' She gave a dry brittle laugh. 'What a stupid fool I was. What a pathetic, silly girl.'

Hannah was dumbstruck.

Sarah reached out and squeezed Hannah's hand briefly, then let it go. 'But I can't ever regret having you and Judith.' She shook her head. 'It's a miracle how you both turned out so well with such a useless mother and that…

that… man as a father. I should have taken you both and walked out long ago, but there was nowhere to go. No money. And I had your brother to think of until he died, and then each time I was expecting I thought it would be all right but it wasn't. His anger never went away. It got worse. When Timothy died, your father took it out on me. I was grief stricken and he hit me for the first time. As if it were my fault that Timothy was dead.'

'Oh, Mother! Why did you never tell me this before?'

'I was ashamed. I was hoping you'd never find out. I blamed myself. He kept telling me it was my fault. That I hadn't taken enough care of Timothy.' She fixed her eyes on Hannah's for the first time. 'He drove Lizzie away. Or rather he made *me* do it. I threw my own sister out of her home. Our family home. In the middle of the night. Eighteen years ago, and since then I have heard nothing more of her. She could be dead.' She started to cry again.

'I don't think she's dead, Mother.'

'What do you mean?'

'A man. On the beach. He asked me if I knew her. He told me I look like her.'

'You do. Oh, Hannah, every time I look at you it breaks my heart as I remember what I did to my own sister.'

'The man was from Australia.'

Sarah pulled herself upright. 'Australia?'

'He said his name was Will Kidd and Elizabeth had been married to his father.'

Her mother's hands flew to her mouth. 'She married him? Mr Kidd?' The colour had drained from Sarah's face. 'I always thought she must have used the ticket my father sent her and gone to Sydney. But I never thought she'd marry that man. What else did he say?'

Hannah was confused. 'What do you mean about her marrying that man? Did she know him already? Will Kidd's father?'

Sarah ignored the question. 'What else did he say?' She repeated.

'Nothing. I didn't know whether he was telling the truth.'

'He was telling the truth.' Sarah clutched at her hand, squeezing it tightly. 'Where is Elizabeth now?'

'The man doesn't know. He said his father is dead and he lost touch with his stepmother ten years ago. He's a sailor.'

'You must find him. I must see him. I have to find out. I have to have her forgiveness. I have to tell her I was wrong.' She gripped Hannah's wrist tightly. 'On no account tell your father about this. Never, never, never. Promise me. You have to find this Mr Kidd and tell him I want to meet with him.'

'Please, Mother. Tell me what's going on.'

Chapter Twelve

Hannah decided to go into the office as usual. She had missed several days after her father had struck her, but now the bruising had faded, and she didn't want to give her father any further excuse to focus his anger on her.

'I thought you had the flu,' said Mr Busby when she walked into the office.

'I'm well now,' she replied, avoiding the need to lie. She glanced towards the closed door to her father's office.

'Mr Dawson is out,' said the clerk. 'He's hardly shown his face here these last several days.' The elderly man tutted loudly and pointlessly shuffled the pile of papers in front of him.'

Hannah said nothing. She took her place on the other side of the desk and stifled a sigh.

'You been in the wars, Miss Dawson?' Busby was uncharacteristically conversational today.

Hannah touched her cheek. 'No. Why?'

'Your face… I mean… Oh, nothing.' He looked embarrassed.

Hannah kept her head down as she worked through the columns of figures and piles of bills. Where was her father? He was increasingly absent from home and his violent temper had become more volatile and unpredictable than ever. Once again, she wondered whether she ought to go to a police station. He had attacked both her and her mother, so her younger sister could well be next. Judith was not as resilient as Hannah. She was frailer, flightier, and, at only just seventeen, less mature and worldly than Hannah. The recent outburst from their father about Judith working longer hours could well lead to something worse. And Judith wasn't careful enough – sometimes sailing too close to recklessness in her dealings with her father, governed by her own naivety and gaucheness.

She must focus. Stop daydreaming. The pile of paperwork had grown during her absence. She picked up another invoice and was about to enter it into the ledger when she paused.

'Mr Busby, do you know what this relates to?' She read out the name of the supplier, Merseyside Maritime Services. 'I don't think we've had anything from them before. What do they do? It's for a lot of money. Forty-seven pounds.'

'Just get on with it, Miss Dawson. Isn't it obvious? They must do what the name suggests.'

'Yes, but what kind of services?'

Busby gave a protracted sigh. 'Maritime ones. Don't you know what the word means?' He looked at her irritably then lowered his head again.

'But that could mean anything. What services can we possibly require? The coffee goes straight to the wholesalers. We don't ship it on anywhere else. There's just warehousing and transport costs.' She waved some other pieces of paper in her hand. 'I have the bills for that. This is for something else. And we've never had an invoice from them before.'

Another sigh. 'I have absolutely no idea, nor am I expected to know. If you are determined to find the answer then I suggest you ask your father.'

Hannah wasn't going to do that. Frustrated, she carried on working her way through the bills. It was mind-numbingly boring, but also requiring her full attention so there wasn't even a lot of scope for daydreaming. One thing that was testing her though was the question of how she was going to find and then conceal books to read. The brutality of her father's reaction to the discovery of *The Weather in the Streets* ruled out the library – and she didn't want the librarian pushing her to go to the police. It was too risky. And where in their small sparsely furnished house could she hide a book? How would she afford to buy any now that the library was ruled out? She would have to find another library and go there to read, without withdrawing the books. That was a reasonable plan. Easier as well than trying to read on the seafront or in the park, especially when the weather was cold. Life without the stimulus and escape that books provided was unthinkable.

Mr Busby scraped back his chair at four o'clock. 'I have to go early this evening. If Mr Dawson hasn't returned by the time you leave, please lock the door and leave the key under the fire bucket. And make sure no one sees you doing it.' He pulled on his overcoat, grunted in farewell and left the building.

Relieved he had gone, Hannah picked up the bill from Maritime Services again and studied it. The address was unfamiliar. Like most of the other invoices, it was on printed letterhead, but the balance due was written by hand, not typed. Not very professional. She grabbed a scrap of paper and scribbled down the address.

Just before a quarter to five, she tidied her desk and was putting on her coat when there was a knock on the door and before she could react, it opened. Hannah gasped as the man who had called her Elizabeth stepped inside.

'Are you alone, Miss Dawson? Can we talk now? Please.'

He looked desperate for her to agree.

Her heart pounding, she said, 'Not here. We can't talk here. And not now. My father—'

'Wouldn't like it, I know. Your colleague told me. Can we go somewhere else?'

'Where?'

'We could get a cup of tea. There's a café round the corner.'

'No.' Hannah knew if her father should pass by and see her inside a café there'd be ructions. 'I have to go home.' She was about to suggest he walk her home, but decided it wasn't a good idea for him to find out where she lived. She couldn't risk him turning up on the doorstep as he had done just now. 'Perhaps tomorrow morning. We could go for a walk on the beach. It's too dark now.'

'My ship sails tomorrow morning. I have to be back on board tonight. Please.'

Curiosity about what he wanted to tell her, and a strong desire to spend time with him, fought against her sense of self-preservation. His expression was so sincere. But if her father were to catch them… He seemed to take her hesitation as a signal, as he said, 'Please let me walk you home. Where do you live?'

Hannah battled with herself again then said, 'Close by. Just north of here. In Bootle. You can walk with me part of the way.'

He held the door open for her and followed her outside. Hannah remembered Mr Busby's instructions about locking up and hiding the key. She locked the door, made a rapid character judgement, and put the key under the fire bucket without trying to conceal what she was doing from him. Will Kidd showed no reaction. Anyway, what was there worth stealing in there? Mr Busby's pencil sharpener?

They walked in silence for a few minutes. Hannah hoped he couldn't hear her thumping heart. Conscious of the mounting tension between them, she started to speak, only for him to speak in the same moment. Hannah conceded, then immediately wished she hadn't.

'Why did you have your face covered up when I saw you the other day?' he asked, his eyes full of concern.

'It was cold.' She knew she sounded unconvincing.

'You've not been at work. I came several times. When I was in port. That man said you were ill with the flu. But it wasn't the flu, was it?'

'Why would I lie? I told you, my face was covered because I was cold.'

Will said nothing.

'Look, Mr Kidd, I thought you wanted to talk about my aunt.'

'I'd rather talk about you.'

She pulled up.

'I'm sorry. I shouldn't have said that. What would you like to know about Lizbeth?'

'Why do you call her that?'

He gave a little laugh. 'I always called her Lizbeth. My special name for her. It was something between just the two of us.'

'My mother called her Lizzie.'

'Lizzie? Really?'

Hannah couldn't see his face clearly in the twilight, but she sensed he was smiling.

'Tell me about her.' she said. 'What was she like? I was only small when she left, but I remember crying for days when she disappeared.'

'I loved her.' He quickly added, 'I mean she was a wonderful woman. I was so happy that she was part of our family. She and I would talk for hours. About everything – the names of the stars, how she loved music – and I taught her the names of our Aussie birds.' He became animated as he spoke about Elizabeth, and Hannah suppressed an unexpected twinge of what she realised must be jealousy. She longed for someone to speak about her in that way – no, more than that – she wished Will Kidd were speaking about her.

Telling herself not to be foolish she asked, 'Did she love your father?'

Will Kidd stopped walking. 'No. She didn't. How could she?' His tone was surprisingly aggressive.

'I don't know. I don't know anything. How could I? I was only a small child when she went away. It was very sudden. My parents would never speak of her. I was hoping you were going to tell me about her.' She spun round. 'I think you should go now.' She felt the prick of tears behind her eyes.

Will took her arm and looked stricken. 'Please. I'm sorry. I shouldn't have said that. It's just...' He drew her under the light of a lamppost and looked at her, his eyes were full of sincerity and – if she were to describe them – sorrow. 'Please. We need to have a proper time to meet and talk. Not like this, walking along, in a hurry. I want to get to know you.'

Hannah looked up at him, at his face that was such a nice face, a face that she wanted to keep looking at. She felt the blood rushing through her veins and hoped in the half-light that he wouldn't notice she was blushing. Before she could help herself, she said, 'I want to get to know you too.'

He clenched his fists in a gesture of triumph.

'I get back from Ireland in three days' time. Can you meet me on Friday? Somewhere we can talk without being interrupted?'

Excited and exhilarated, she tried to make herself sound disinterested. 'It will have to be in the morning. I have to work on Friday afternoons.'

'That's fine. On the shore at Crosby – where I saw you the other day. Ten o'clock all right?'

Hannah nodded. 'You'd better go now. And promise you won't try to follow me.'

He put his hand over his heart and said, 'Sailor's honour.'

As she hurried towards home, she felt a thrill of anticipation. She was going to find out about her aunt at last. But it was more than that. She had to acknowledge that it was mostly at the prospect of seeing Mr Kidd again.

Neither Hannah nor Judith knew any men apart from those their father vetted – and there were few of them and they were all much older men like Mr Busby or Mr Henderson, the pastor from their father's chapel, who occasionally called on him at home. None of the Dawson women were permitted to attend the chapel with their father. Their religious observation was entirely supervised by Dawson and consisted of them reading the scriptures and learning chunks of it to recite back to him. It was as if Charles Dawson believed women were unworthy to bear witness to God directly – everything had to be channelled through him. So Hannah's knowledge of men was limited to men she passed in the street or saw working on the docks – always at a distance and never in direct conversation. When they'd moved to Bootle from Northport, the boy next door had tried to engage her in conversation over the back wall, but her father put a stop to that. As the neighbour was a pimple-faced youth whose conversational skills didn't appear to extend beyond the weather, Hannah did not feel this was any great loss. None of these brief encounters had made her eager to explore male company further. But Mr Will Kidd was different and the way she felt drawn towards him was a strangely disturbing experience for her. The prospect of seeing him again and having time to talk properly with him was one that filled her with a mixture of excitement and dread. What could she possibly have to say that would interest him?

–

Will headed to the Baltic pub, where he thought it likely he'd find his new friend, Eddie. The public house was crowded with men swilling pints and the buzz of voices and laughter carried outside. He pushed open the door to the Public Bar and immediately saw Eddie, standing apart from the throng, a pint glass in his hand.

'I was wondering when I was going to see you again, Willie lad. Did ye see my folks when you were over in Dublin?'

'Not this time. It was a fast turnaround.'

'Pity. Now, I'd be after buying you a beer, but I'm a bit skint at the moment.'

Will concluded he was unlikely to see the return of the cash he'd lent him.

'Only I had a horse that was a sure-fire bet and the little bugger tripped at the last fence just as I was sure I'd be retiring on the profits!' Eddie chuckled and took a swig of beer, draining the glass. 'I don't suppose…'

Will caught the eye of the barmaid. 'Two pints of mild.'

'Ah, you're a good lad, Willie boy.'

'Do us a favour, mate, the name's Will. Less of the Willie if you don't mind.'

'No offence. Will it is.'

They took their drinks and retreated to a table in the corner away from the crush around the bar.

'So, you're fond of the horses are you Eddie?'

'Sure, I keep telling myself to give up the gee-gees as it's a fool's game. The only winner's the bookie himself.'

'No doubt about it. I thought you said you were saving to get married?'

'I was so certain this nag was going to bring home the bacon I thought I'd be hurrying along the wedding fund.'

'How much did you lose?'

'I told you. I'm skint. Cleaned me out it did, the useless nag. Fit only for dog food and Belgians.'

'When do you get paid again?'

'Day after tomorrow.'

Will pulled a couple of half-crowns out of his pocket and passed them to Eddie. 'Now, I don't want to hear you've handed that to the bookie. It's all I can spare and I'm gone tomorrow.'

'Ah, you're a good man, Will, you are. I'll be paying you back every penny when I see you next.'

They supped their beers in silence for a few minutes. Eventually Will spoke. 'I met this girl—'

'That's grand!' Eddie clapped him on the back.

'No. It's not like that. We're distantly related – through marriage. Her aunt married my father.'

'Is she a looker?'

'I told you, it's not like that.'

'Then what's it about?'

'Nothing really… I just think her father might be bashing her.'

'Bashing her?'

'Hitting her. Beating her. The other day she had her face almost completely covered when I bumped into her on the shore. She'd a scarf right up to her eyes.'

'Well, there's often a cold wind by the sea. Maybe you're used to it, being a sailor and all, but for a lady. They feel the cold more.'

'Perhaps.' Will stared into his pint. 'But I have a feeling there was something she was trying to hide. She didn't want to stop and talk.'

Eddie gave a guffaw. 'Can you blame her? Poor lass was probably scared stiff of a big lump like you. Maybe she thought you were going to carry her off and sell her into white slavery. Nice girls don't talk to sailors.'

'They're even less likely to talk to dockers, mate.' Will nudged his friend with his elbow. 'Anyway, I told you. There's a family connection.'

'If she is getting beaten by her old man, there's not much you can do about it.' Eddie shrugged. 'What goes on behind closed doors in a family is their concern.'

'You think it's all right for a man to bash a woman?'

'No. Of course not. But there's some wouldn't agree with me. There's many as think a husband has a right to discipline his wife if she steps out of line. And as for a father? Didn't your da give you a clout every now and then?'

'That's different – we're both men. And he only did it when I was a kid. Gave me a lick with his belt or his slipper. But he never touched my ma or my sister. It was my brother who was the violent one in our house.' He drained his pint and got up to go to the bar. Why was he telling Eddie all this when he barely knew the man? He decided to change the subject.

Later that evening as he headed back to the *Arklow*, he was still thinking about Miss Dawson, increasingly sure that she had been hiding some kind of facial injury when they met on the beach. He barely knew her, and yet he felt an overwhelming desire to protect her from whoever had hurt her. Clenching his fists, he thought of her beautiful calm face and wanted to kill the man who had struck it.

Chapter Thirteen

The weather was fine when they sailed into Dublin again and Will decided to take advantage of the few hours he had free before they loaded up, by exploring the city. He wandered along the waterfront until he came to the O'Connell Bridge. To his right up the wide street was the General Post Office where the Easter Rising had taken place just over twenty years ago. Having no interest in politics and a limited education in history, he had not been aware of the Irish troubles – but Eddie O'Connor, horrified at his ignorance, had given him chapter and verse when they were in the pub. Eddie himself had missed the uprising as he'd been conscripted as a young lad into the British army and sent off to the Belgian front.

Will stood looking back up O'Connell Street, trying to imagine it wreathed in smoke and with the sound and smell of gunfire as the rebels fought it out with the British army. A rather maudlin Eddie had told him the stories of the men who were arrested for leading the uprising and almost immediately executed without trial. Not for the first time it occurred to Will that politics was a dangerous game. Maybe his ostrich-head-in-the-sand approach was the best way. He couldn't imagine wanting to lay his own life on the line for a cause. But then, who better to do such a thing than a man like him – without family ties and encumbrances? Would he be prepared to step up and do his bit if asked to? Were all the murmurings of war just that – murmurings that would come to naught?

'Penny for them.' The voice was soft. Will spun round to find Bridget O'Connor looking up at him.

'Miss O'Connor. A pleasure to see you.'

'Where are you off to, Mr Kidd? Are you lost?'

'I'm just having a walk. Thought I'd explore the place while I've an hour or so to spare.'

'Would you like a guide?' Her voice was hesitant but her smile was broad.

'Wouldn't I be taking you out of your way?'

'Not at all. I'd be happy to show you around. I'm on my way back from Confession. I was heading over to the other side anyway.' She jerked her head in the direction of the Liffey. 'I usually take a walk myself and seeing you gives me an excuse not to hurry home, where Mammy will have a hundred chores for me and a hundred lectures to go with them.' She gave him a little wink. 'I'll have to tell that in my next Confession.'

They fell into step together and crossed the bridge to the south side. She led him over to College Green, through the grounds of Trinity College and then past the National Library and eventually into St Stephen's Green. They sat side by side on a bench beside one of the lakes, watching the ducks swimming, dappled by sunlight filtering through the trees.

'Hard to imagine this place being a battleground,' said Bridget at last. She told him how it had played a part in the Easter Rising. 'One of the rebels fighting here was a woman, you know. Constance Markievicz. They said she shot a policeman. She was sentenced to death by the Brits

– but they ended up letting her off as she was a woman.' She gave a dry laugh. 'I wonder if they'd do that today? Somehow I doubt it.' She kicked her feet out in front of her.

Will didn't know whether to agree with her or not – but she didn't seem to expect an answer.

'I'm sorry about the mammy trying to marry us off.' Her face was in shadow but he sensed she was smiling. 'I can promise you it's a source of mortification to me. As I imagine it was to you too. But the mammy is a law unto herself.'

Will squirmed on the seat beside her. It felt ungallant to acknowledge that it was a relief not to be viewed as a serious matrimonial prospect, but to show disappointment would be as bad.

Bridget carried on. 'I'm sure the boys have told you I have a vocation and I'm determined to follow it, no matter what my mother thinks.'

'They did.'

'Funny isn't it. She'd be proud as punch if one of those boys decided to enter the priesthood – but it's another thing altogether when it comes to me.'

'I suppose you being the only daughter?'

'Maybe.' She looked thoughtful. 'Now, let's just relax and enjoy this beautiful spring day and treat each other as old friends. No barriers.' She held a hand out for him to shake.

He took the proffered hand and felt at once a weight lift off his shoulders. There was something reassuring and comforting in Bridget O'Connor's presence. He leaned back against the wooden bench and felt the warmth of the spring sunshine on his face. They remained a while in companionable silence, until eventually Will broke it.

'Why is your mother so dead set against you becoming a nun?'

'I don't think she is, to be honest. I think it's more that she wants to cling on to me. She knows I'll never agree to getting married and she'll have to let me go to God in the end, but she's trying to put it off as long as possible.'

'Why do you go along with it? Why not just tell her you're going to enter a convent and be done with it?'

'Grief's a terrible thing, Mr Kidd. It gnaws at a person and eats them away. My poor old mammy hasn't got over Daddy getting killed. It's five years now, but I still sometimes wake in the night and find her lying in the bed beside me, eyes wide open staring at the ceiling. And that's the trouble, you see. She puts on a happy face to the world and has never let herself give in to the tears – even during sleepless nights. It's all bottled up inside her. A person can't let all that pressure build up without finding an outlet for it and I'm terrified that one day she'll stop functioning and have some kind of breakdown. So I've decided God wants me to stay with her right now.' She pushed her hands deep into her coat pockets. 'I pray that perhaps she might come to the convent with me. Give herself over to God too, but there's no sign yet of that happening. Still I put my trust in Our Lady.' She smiled at him. 'You're not a religious man yourself, then, Mr Kidd?'

Will shook his head. 'The only times I've set foot in a church were for my sister's wedding and the funeral of my half-brother and sister – they died when they were small. Of the diphtheria.'

'So, you've known grief too.' She placed a hand on his arm.

Will shrugged. 'It was a long time ago.'

'Do you see your family often? It must be hard them being in Australia and you away at sea.'

'I have no family now. They're all dead. Ma, Pa, my sister, Harriet, and Pa's two kids with his second wife.'

She turned in her seat and gave him a long look. Will squirmed, knowing she was thinking he was bottling up his own grief too. And perhaps he was.

'I'm so sorry,' she said at last. 'I'll remember you in my prayers. It must be sad to be so alone in the world. I've been blessed in having five healthy brothers.'

'I told you, it's all a long time ago.' He looked at his watch. 'I must be getting back to the ship.'

Bridget's face flushed. 'I'm sorry, Mr Kidd, I've upset you. I didn't intend to.'

Will forced a smile. 'Not at all. I do need to get back though.'

They rose from the bench and walked out of the park.

'I'll take you back a different way.'

They walked more briskly this time and Bridget pointed out a few places as they went, but there was a strained atmosphere between them. Once they'd crossed Butt Bridge and they could see the *Arklow* further downstream, she bade him goodbye.

'I enjoyed our walk, Mr Kidd. I hope we'll get a chance to talk again. And I'm sorry if I offended you with my tactless comments. I will definitely remember you in my prayers.'

'It's me that should apologise, Miss O'Connor. Sometimes I'm like a bear with a sore head. And I'm not accustomed to the company of a lady, being at sea all the time.'

She reached for his hand and held it in both her gloved ones for a moment. 'God bless you, Mr Kidd. And I'll also say a prayer that that won't always be the case. You don't deserve to be lonely.' She turned and hurried away.

Will stood on the quayside, watching until Bridget disappeared from view. Was it that obvious? When he'd never even admitted to himself that he felt that way?

Chapter Fourteen

They were late docking, and as a result Will was more than an hour late for his rendezvous with Hannah. Was there any point in him turning up now? he asked himself, feeling frustration and disappointment. There had been no way for him to get word to her. What must she think of him? Surely, she wouldn't still be hanging around waiting for him on a deserted beach on a cold spring morning. But on the off chance that she might be, he raced towards Seaforth, running along underneath the overhead railway – the Dockers' Umbrella as it was commonly known.

When he reached Seaforth Sands, the shore stretched in front of him, an empty expanse, with no one in sight, apart from a couple in the far distance throwing sticks for their dog. Disappointed, but with nothing else to do, he kept on walking, hands thrust deep in his pockets, collar turned up against the chill wind. The weather was fine but cold, with a pale sun emerging from heavy clouds. He shivered, suddenly wishing he were back in Australia. Granted, they had their fair share of cold winters up in the Blue Mountains, but the summers were often hot and the air always clear and easy to breathe. Here the atmosphere was choked with the smoke from coal fires, the buildings blackened with it, and the weather often a depressing drizzle.

His mind wandered back to his conversation with Bridget O'Connor in the park the previous day. All that talk of grief, the look in her eyes as she touched his arm. It wasn't exactly pity, but more a sense of deep compassion. Maybe she was right, and he was like Mrs O'Connor – in all the years since he'd fled Australia never allowing himself to grieve the losses and sadness he had lived through.

A flock of seagulls swooped low in front of him, screaming their shrill cries. And in that moment, he brushed off the maudlin feelings and increased the pace of his walking. It was habitual with him – never let the demons get to him, never dwell on the past, never think of what might have been, live only in the moment. And above all, never allow himself the indulgence of self-pity.

He didn't see her until he was almost upon her. She was sitting in the lee of one of the dunes, her coat wrapped tightly around her and a beret pulled low on her head. Her gloved hands were clasped around her knees. His heart soared and he wanted to punch the air, but was wary of frightening her again.

Will walked towards her. 'Miss Dawson, I am so sorry for my lateness. We had a rough crossing and were delayed docking and then I was held back as there was a spillage in one of the holds and we had to clear it up. I didn't know what to do to let you know.'

She smiled at him and her smile lit up her face. 'I was just about to give up on you, Mr Kidd.' She began to gather herself together to get up, but Will put a hand out. 'Don't get up. I'll join you. It looks out of the wind here.' He saw her blush and liked that about her.

Hannah looked uncertain for a moment, then she smoothed the sand beside her. 'I don't think my father would be too happy about me sitting amidst the dunes with a young man but what the eye doesn't see…'

Will grinned at her and settled himself down beside her. Suddenly nervous, he fumbled in his pocket for his tobacco and began to roll a cigarette. 'Do you mind?'

She shook her head.

'Tell me about your life, Miss Dawson. Your family? Your work?'

Hannah gave a little laugh. 'There's not much to tell and what there is isn't very interesting. I lead a very dull life. I live with my mother, who is the younger sister of Aunt Elizabeth, my father and my sister, Judith. We used to live in a town to the north of Liverpool in a rather grand house, but things became hard – the family business hasn't flourished – so we moved to a little house close to the docks several years ago.' She looked up at him, her eyes darting over his face and then dropping down.

She was so like Elizabeth, that same shade of brown hair, the flawless bright skin you wanted to touch, the same big beautiful eyes. And yet there was a difference. Will tried to put his finger on what it was and then concluded that Hannah was her own person – the expression in those eyes was unique to her, the tone of her voice, the rise and fall of it, the way she kept pushing her hair out of her eyes where the wind blew it, the soft swell of her lips, the shape of her nose, slightly longer than Elizabeth's. He couldn't take his eyes off her. Every time he tried to look away, he was drawn back to her as if an invisible thread was tugging at him, tying him to her. He wished they could stay here forever, sitting side by side in the sand, with him listening while she told him the bare facts of her life and her work in her father's company.

'What's your first name?' he asked. 'Please call me Will.'

She hesitated just a moment then said quietly, 'Hannah. My name is Hannah.'

He repeated the name twice. 'It suits you. Unusual.'

'It's from the Bible. My father lives his life by the Bible. It's the only book he allows in the house.'

Will jerked his head in surprise. 'Really? Are you religious too?'

Hannah hesitated. 'No, but I'd never let him know that. I know enough of the Bible myself that it's easy enough to convince him that I believe it as strongly as he does.'

'And don't you?'

She waited a few moments before answering as though weighing up how to respond. 'No. I believe in God. In Jesus, and the good things he did and said. But my father appears to be governed more by the God of the Old Testament, the God of anger and vengeance.' She stared out towards the grey waters of the Mersey. 'He belongs to a group of men who interpret the words of the scriptures literally in every possible sense.'

'I know very little about the Bible, but isn't that the whole point of it? If you believe it, don't you have to go along with it all?'

Hannah smiled at him. 'Stoning people to death, condoning slavery, committing human sacrifices? As soon as I read the passage about Abraham being ordered by God to sacrifice his only son, and then *going along with it*, I started to have doubts about a lot of things. I mean, how can it possibly be a good thing for God to demand that someone do such a terrible thing? So pointless. So cruel.'

'And did he? Did Abraham kill his son?'

'No.' She sighed and smiled at him. 'God sent an angel to step in just in time and let him off the hook – but that doesn't make it all right, does it? After he'd already got him trussed up and stuck him on top of a pile of wood ready to burn, and had his knife at his neck. Only then did the angel appear and tell him he didn't have to do it. What a cruel, nasty joke to play on someone! What kind of relationship could Abraham and poor old Isaac possibly have had after that? How could Isaac ever begin to trust his father again? How could he look him in the eye? He'd have to spend the rest of his life looking over his shoulder, terrified his dad was going to creep up behind him, stick a knife in him and turn him into a burnt offering. And even if he didn't – just knowing his father would be prepared to kill him on a whim of God's. And what kind of God would demand such a pointless killing – never mind a father killing his only son? It would have been murder! Of his own son. His *only* son.'

She was breathless and indignant in telling him all this and Will looked at her with new eyes. He liked her passion, her spiritedness.

'And your father believes this to be right? How come?'

She heaved a big sigh. 'He justifies it by saying that it was a test of Abraham's love of God. Because God sent the angel in time to save Isaac that made it all right.' She thumped a fist into the sand. 'But it wasn't all right. Was it? Not if Abraham was actually ready to murder him.'

'So, what about the Hannah in the Bible? Did her father try to sacrifice her too? Why did your father choose that name?'

She turned her head and stared right at him. Will felt his insides turn to jelly and an unexpected desire caught him by surprise.

'Hannah was the childless first wife of a man who wanted children so he took another wife and had lots of children with her. Poor Hannah remained barren – what a horrible word that is. She prayed to God and promised that if he gave her a son she would give her son back to God.'

'Like Abraham?'

'Not that bad. After years of being taunted by the second wife, she had a son at last and handed him over to serve God – I imagine that means he became a priest – and then she had lots of other children as a reward and was barren no longer.' She scooped up a handful of sand and let it sift through her fingers.

Will imagined those fingers laced through his. What was happening to him? He forced himself to return to Biblical Hannah. 'It seems odd for a man to name his child after a childless woman, but I do know that Hannah is a beautiful name.'

She looked at him with that same direct look that felt as though she was looking straight into his soul. Another clutch of desire was tempered by an overwhelming feeling of tenderness towards her. Instinctively, he reached for her hand. Then, before he knew what was happening, he had pulled her into his arms and was kissing her. It was not premeditated or planned. It just happened. At first her mouth responded and he drew her closer. Then, as if she had been stung by a bee, she pulled herself away from him and he watched, dumbstruck, as she scrambled to her feet and started to stumble up the sand towards the promenade at the top. Will grabbed at her hand and held her back. Her eyes were frightened, desperate even. 'Please, let me go.'

Will dropped his hold. 'I'm sorry! I shouldn't have done that. Don't go away! I don't know what came over me. Please forgive me. I promise I won't try to do it again.'

Her slight hesitation was all he needed. He clambered after her, feeling the sand sliding away under his feet as he tried to get purchase and move up the slope.

She waited at the top until he reached her. 'I shouldn't have let you do that,' she said. 'It's my fault. I shouldn't have put myself in that position.'

Suddenly bold, he said, 'Why not? You're not courting anyone are you?'

Her face flushed. 'No.'

'Then what's wrong?' He took a big gulp of air, deciding that honesty was the best policy. 'Look, Hannah, I couldn't help it. I really like you. I know we barely know each other but I feel as though I've always known you. You remind me so much of your aunt and it feels...' His voice trailed away.

'What?'

'Look, let's go for a walk. I promise I won't touch you, but I need to explain.'

Hannah had a dubious expression on her face, but she nodded. 'Just as far as Blundellsands then I have to head back. Father expects me at work in a couple of hours.'

They walked without speaking for a few minutes, while Will searched for the right words to say. At last he said, 'I had a teenage crush on your aunt.'

'A crush?' Hannah's eyes widened, and the hint of a smile played around her lips.

'Yes. Even though she was nearly fifteen years older than me.' He coughed and then decided there was no point beating about the bush. 'She was much younger than my father and she and I got on really well. I thought she was the most beautiful creature I'd ever seen. I was only a kid and she seemed like an angel to me, appearing from nowhere. She was far too good for my father and I was angry that an old misery like him should be married to her. I used to lie awake thinking about her all the time. I suppose it was puppy love, but I thought it was deadly serious.' He paused, embarrassed. 'In fact, until recently, I still believed I was in love with her.'

Hannah was staring at him wide-eyed. 'Did she know?'

'She probably guessed. In the end I told her how I felt. I was nineteen by then and convinced it was love.'

'What did she say?'

'She didn't laugh at me. Thinking back now I'm amazed that she didn't – but I'm grateful too. That's what Lizbeth is like – always kind and caring. She let me down gently and told me that one day I would meet someone else and realise that what I'd felt for her was just a crush.'

Hannah was watching his face intently as they walked, her own eyes wide.

'I was angry with her. Angry with everything. Angry with life, with the whole injustice of everything.' He looked at her, trying to decide how much to tell her, then realised it would have to be everything. 'My father was in prison, condemned to death for shooting my brother dead.'

He heard her draw in breath, shocked.

'The poor old devil was only defending Lizbeth. My brother had attacked her – he'd torn her blouse open –

then when I tried to stop him, he stabbed me. I passed out, but before Nat could do anything to Lizbeth, Pa came along and shot him dead. In the back.'

'But surely that wasn't enough for the death sentence? Since he was defending my aunt, and your brother had already stabbed you, wouldn't that have counted in his favour?'

Will winced. The memory was painful. 'Trouble was, Pa admitted he was glad Nat was dead. He told the doc who came to patch me up that he should have shot him long before. Then when Hattie–'

'Hattie?'

'Harriet, my sister. She was married to my pal, Michael...' His voice trailed away. He realised he'd said too much, but there was no going back now. 'What I didn't find out 'til later was that Elizabeth and Michael Winterbourne were in love. They'd met on the ship coming out to Australia and then got separated. Your grandfather had died just a few days before Lizbeth landed in Sydney and she was desperate. No money. No family. I still don't fully understand why, but she married my old man.'

'Why did she marry him if she was in love with this Michael person?'

'Beats me. I suppose she was desperate and thought she'd never see Michael again. But then, after she'd married Pa, Michael turned up in her life again – working for my old man. I've no idea what went on between them, but he ended up getting hitched to our Hattie. God knows why, as it was obvious they felt nothing for each other – maybe he did it to get back at Lizbeth for marrying Pa.' He paused a moment, checking to see if she was following his convoluted tale. He saw she was frowning but appeared to be listening closely. 'I know Hattie only married Michael to get away from the Falls – that was the town we lived in – and she knew the old man would settle some cash on her once she married.' He kicked at a heap of seaweed. 'It was an unhappy marriage. Hat went off the rails. Drugs and drink. She was always a wild child. After Pa was arrested, she turned up in court and might as well have tied the noose round his neck.'

'How? What on earth did she do?'

'I think she thought she'd be helping him by implicating Lizbeth. She always hated her. Jealous, I suppose. Resented her for taking Ma's place. She and Ma were always close. Hattie hated the idea of Pa marrying again – specially someone young and beautiful like Elizabeth.'

He rolled a cigarette as they walked along, then cupped his hand round a match and lit the roll-up, drawing the smoke into his lungs slowly. 'She told the whole court that Nat had found out that Lizbeth and Michael were lovers, and the Prosecution twisted it to make out that Pa killed Nat to stop him going round telling lies about Lizbeth having an affair with her husband's right-hand man. The old man couldn't bear to think that she and Michael were actually in love. Michael was the manager of Pa's coalmine, you see, and Pa thought the world of him. Anyway, it was enough, along with what the doc said, to give the jury a motive – so he went down for it.'

'He was executed?' Her voice was barely more than a whisper.

'Hanged by the neck until dead.' Will's voice betrayed his sudden rush of emotion. 'I didn't stick around for it. Didn't even visit the poor devil in jail. I was too cowardly to face him.' He turned to look at her. 'So that's the kind of man I am, Hannah.'

He expected her to walk away, sure that after this she'd want no more to do with him, but instead she reached her arms up and clasped them around his neck, laying her head against his chest. He could tell his heart was thumping and knew that she must be able to hear it too. His arms went up around her back, holding her tightly against him. For what seemed to Will an eternity, but could only have been a few moments, they stood like that, motionless, holding each other, as above them the seagulls screamed and the waves lapped at the shore.

When they eventually broke apart, Will knew things were different now. He had experienced an intensity of feeling, a strange mixture of desire and a wish to protect her, maybe even from himself. Hannah was vulnerable, inexperienced, innocent, yet he longed to kiss her again, to hold her, to make love to her. He took her hand in his. The feel of her skin against his own made even this small act one of intense intimacy. They continued their walk along the sands.

'Is Harriet older or younger than you?' she asked.

'She was older.'

'Was?' Hannah's face telegraphed her surprise. 'You mean—'

'Yes, she's dead. Apparently...'

Her expression was astonished. 'You don't know?'

'After what happened to Pa and her role in his conviction, I didn't want any more to do with her – I was angry – and like I said, she'd gone off the rails. I didn't even say goodbye when I went to sea.'

'How do you know she's dead?'

'There was a fellow on my ship from Australia too. For some reason he had it in for me. I never figured out why as I never did him any harm, but he told me a couple of months ago that she'd drowned herself in Sydney Harbour. She was drunk or drugged up to her eyeballs.'

'He might have made it up. How would he know she was your sister?'

'My old man's trial was headline news. And Hattie's intervention in it. She was dressed to kill and the flashbulbs were popping. Once Cassidy knew who I was and realised I didn't know she'd died, he took great pleasure in telling me.'

Hannah's eyes welled up. 'Oh, Will, I'm so sorry. I can't imagine how I'd feel if my sister died. I wouldn't want to go on living.' He felt the pressure of her hand squeezing his.

'Hat and I were close like that when we were kids, but we'd grown apart. She left home to board at the school in town after Ma died. She got all full of airs and graces, then when she married Michael she made his life a misery.' He turned away to look towards the sea, afraid that his emotions would break through under the intensity of Hannah's sympathy. 'I miss how she used to be my friend as well as my big sis. But I don't miss the woman she turned into.'

They walked on in silence for a few minutes, until Hannah spoke again. 'If my father were to die, I wouldn't mourn him at all. I don't love him at all. I can't. I've tried. Really hard. But I just can't. Do you think that makes me a bad person?'

Will smiled, longing to kiss her again, but fearful of frightening her away. 'I could never think of you as a bad person, Hannah. If you don't love your father, then that must mean he doesn't deserve to be loved.' He wanted to ask her again about the reason she had covered her face that other day on the beach, but something made him hold back.

'He has been very cruel to my mother. I think he may have been cruel to Aunt Elisabeth too and that's why she went away.'

Will smiled. 'Well, he can't be all bad: if he hadn't caused her to come to Australia I'd never have met you.'

'I must go,' she said, her demeanour changing.

'Let me walk back with you.'

'Only as far as Seaforth. I don't want to risk anyone seeing us.'

'Why not? We've done nothing wrong.'

'My father wouldn't agree.' Her eyes welled up.

Will felt a rush of emotion. 'Then let me talk to your father. If you feel you like me at all, maybe you would go out with me? I know we barely know each other, Hannah, yet I feel I already know you so well. And I want to get to know you better.'

She looked up at him and, in that moment, he knew with unshakeable certainty he loved her. Her eyes told him she felt the same way. It was as if they were already bound to each other.

But then she turned her head away. 'You mustn't talk to Father. Please promise me you won't even try. He'll never agree, and you'll make things worse for me.' She turned back to look at him. 'He has a terrible temper. When he discovered I was hiding a photograph of Aunt Elizabeth he threw it on the fire. If he found out I've been talking with you… if he knew you wanted to see me… I can't tell you what he'd do. He's capable of anything.

'Now, I have to go, Will.' She started to walk away, then stopped and hurried back. He felt his heart lift.

'I forgot to tell you. My mother wants to talk with you.'

Will felt a surge of hope and must have shown it in his face, as she frowned, holding up her palms in front of her in a blocking motion. 'She wants to speak with you about Elizabeth.' She reached into her coat pocket and pulled out a scrap of paper and wrote on it with a pencil. 'This is the address. 15 Bluebell Street. Please go one afternoon so you won't run into my father.'

'Wait!' He called. 'When will I see you again?'

'I don't know.' Her face looked anguished. 'I often come here. Maybe we might meet again here on the seashore. But please, don't go near the office, and apart from when you call on my mother, please, don't go near our house.' Her eyes were filled with fear.

Will stood motionless as a statue, watching her walk away up the beach towards the docks. Lighting a cigarette, he remained fixed to the spot on the empty beach, watching, until Hannah had disappeared from view. Her absence was like an ache inside him. For a moment he had been sure she felt the same way about him, but the fear of her father was evidently greater. The idea of someone hurting her, threatening her, was like a knife being twisted inside Will. He had to find out what was happening to terrify her so much and put a stop to it.

–

Hannah was in turmoil as she hurried towards Morton's Coffee. She had taken a terrible risk in meeting Will Kidd and knew that if her father found out he would be enraged. Her fear of the consequences of that rage were not only for herself but for Will too, and – as always – for her mother and sister. Yet the morning she and Will had spent together had been like no other morning. Hannah felt as though she were riding on a giant wave of emotions.

She replayed the morning in her head. The growing disappointment she'd felt when she'd thought he wasn't going to turn up. The surge of joy when he appeared around the corner of the sand dune. How it felt as though the story Will told her about his own personal tragedy, and her aunt's role in that, had created an intense bond between them. Yet it was the moment when he had drawn her into his arms and kissed her that she wanted to relive again and again. Her heart had wanted that kiss to go on forever, to drown in it, to be held in Will's arms and for him never to let her go, but she knew desire was dangerous, and so she'd pulled away from him. The hurt in his eyes had caused her to wait for him at the top of the dune. All she'd wanted to do was to kiss him again, but she couldn't take that risk.

How was it possible that, already, Will's absence had opened a chasm in her life that had not existed before she met him? How was it possible that one could live one's entire life until now unaware of such feelings, and in such a short time be completely governed by them? With a bewildering mixture of unconstrained joy and crippling fear of the consequences of that joy, she walked into the office and forced herself to behave as if nothing had happened.

Four days later, Hannah was walking on the shore. She had gone there every day in the vain hope of seeing Will again. Maybe he was at sea. Why hadn't she made a firm plan to meet? Had her standoffish behaviour convinced him she didn't want to see him again?

Hannah was confused by her own feelings. One moment she was exhilarated at the memory of him, and the next despondent that she might have driven him away. She told herself he was older than her, more worldly-wise. He probably thought she was a foolish girl, and had already forgotten her. What was it they said about sailors? A girl in every port. There was no point anyway, as her father would never permit her to go out with Will. She'd taken too many risks already. Better to forget Will Kidd and get on with her life.

But she couldn't forget him.

Trudging along the shore, her collar turned up against the wind, Hannah started to wish she'd never met Will. It was more than she could bear to have known him and then so swiftly lost him. All her own stupid fault.

She was about to turn around and head for home, when she heard her name. Will was half running, half sliding down one of the dunes. Her heart somersaulted under her ribs and she began to run towards him. He slid to a halt in front of her, took her wrist and drew her against him. Before Hannah could stop him, he was kissing her, and she was kissing him back.

'I docked at five this morning. I've been walking up and down this beach ever since. I was afraid you wouldn't come.'

She flung her arms around his neck, no longer caring who might see them. 'I've been here every day. I was terrified you wouldn't come back.'

He held her close, kissing the top of her head. 'How could I not come back, my darling? I've been counting the days, hours and minutes until I'd see you again.'

Chapter Fifteen

Will stood on the doorstep of 15 Bluebell Street, nervous about what might be in store. He knocked tentatively, half hoping Hannah's mother would be out.

Mrs Dawson opened the door immediately. She was wearing a sling on one arm, which was in plaster.

Behind her, the interior of the house was gloomy and cramped. There was a small hall – little more than a porch, with two doors leading off it.

He told her who he was, and she showed him into the rear of the house, a poky parlour with an open grate, where there was a fire laid but unlit, and a small deal table and chairs. Beyond was a scullery tacked onto the back of the building. She apologised for the lack of ceremony. 'Mr Dawson uses the front room as his study. We make do in here.'

Will sat down and Mrs Dawson pulled out a chair opposite him, her good elbow on the table, leaning forward. Her gaze was an intense and penetrating appraisal. 'I never thought I'd tell anyone what I am about to tell you, let alone a man, and a stranger at that.'

He was going to reassure her that whatever she said would go no further, but decided against it, and kept his eyes fixed on her face. Sarah Dawson didn't look much like her sister or her daughter – at least not at first glance.

Her face was slightly puffy, her complexion pale like uncooked pastry, so that the definition of her features seemed blurred. But now, as he looked at her, he saw her eyes were like theirs, and as he looked into them he began to recognise the connection. He was conscious that she seemed nervous, jumpy. She was picking at the plaster cast on her arm with her fingernails.

'You knew my elder sister, Elizabeth?'

He nodded. 'She was my stepmother.'

'Was?'

'Is. But my father is dead.'

'I'm sorry.'

Will ignored the expression of condolence, wishing she would get to the point. 'I was very fond of Elizabeth. She was good to me. A true friend.'

'Yes. Everyone was fond of Elizabeth.' She gave a long deep sigh. 'She was a loveable person.'

'So what caused you to lose touch with her? Why did she go to Australia?'

'You come straight to the point, don't you, Mr Kidd?'

'Please call me Will.'

'Well, I suppose we are practically related.'

He waited, expecting her to answer his question, but it hung in the air between them.

Eventually, Sarah broke the silence. 'Was she happy?' She leaned forward, her eyes still fixed on his. To his surprise, she reached out and touched his hand lightly, then withdrew hers so quickly he started to wonder if it had happened at all.

'Elizabeth had a hard life when she first married my father,' said Will. 'He was not the easiest of men to get along with. He didn't treat her well—'

'He beat her?'

'No. He wouldn't have done that. At least I don't think he did. But he was cold. Distant. Didn't tell her things. Didn't appreciate her. At least not at first. He was a wealthy man but he kept it well hidden – from me as well. He dumped Elizabeth at our place in the outback and left her to get on with it.' He looked down. 'A man and a teenage boy living in a shack. You can probably imagine what kind of state the place was in. But she cleaned it up. Turned it into a home again.'

Sarah leaned back in her chair, her eyebrows raised. 'Lizzie did housework?'

Will nodded. 'Until we moved into town. The old man had a fancy place there. A great big mansion. That was one of his secrets. Servants as well. He moved her there in time for Mikey being born.'

'Mikey?'

'Her first child. He was as cute as a button. A really good kid.'

'I'm glad she has children.' Sarah smiled for the first time. 'How many?'

'Two. A little baby girl later. Susannah.' He squeezed his lips together. 'But they both died. Diphtheria. It was a terrible thing. Mikey was only three. Susannah was a baby.'

He looked at her and saw she was crying.

'I know how that feels. I miscarried several babies, and I lost my only son to whooping cough.' She fidgeted, still plucking at her plaster cast, crumbling tiny pieces of plaster onto the table. 'Poor Elizabeth.'

'She had a lot of sorrow in her life,' he said. 'But she always made the best of what was thrown at her. That's one of the things I loved about her.'

Sarah nodded.

'But we shouldn't talk of her in the past tense. I'm sure she's alive and well.'

'But you don't know where?'

'I expect she's still living in MacDonald Falls. Unless…'

'Unless what?'

'Unless she wanted to get away from a place where everyone knew who she was and who she was married to.'

Sarah was frowning. 'You need to tell me why that might be the case.'

So Will told her about what had happened to his father. About the terrible night when his brother Nat had turned up after years when they'd believed him dead, tried to molest Elizabeth and stabbed Will when he'd defended her. About how their father had shot Nat dead. In the back. How Jack Kidd had refused to show any remorse. Will told her about the trial, the verdict and the sentence and how his father wouldn't pursue an appeal.

Sarah listened in silence. 'All this is my fault. If I hadn't sent Lizzie away. Disowned her. Thrown her onto the streets.' Tears were rolling freely down her cheeks. Will dug in his pocket and pulled out a clean handkerchief and gave it to her.

'Now it's my turn to tell you why Elizabeth went to Australia,' she said. 'My husband is a violent man. A cruel and cold-hearted man. He has never loved me. Never shown me any kindness or affection. Nor has he offered any to our daughters. The only person on this earth I have ever witnessed him show any respect or fondness for was his mother. And she was as bad as him. Maybe worse. She died not long after he moved her in with us. Maybe it makes me a bad person but I never mourned her for a moment. I rejoiced that she was dead. She was a bitter, nasty, petty-minded woman, who did all she could to make my life a misery and to goad Charles into doing the same.'

Will was uncomfortable. He barely knew Sarah Dawson, had met her today for the first time, and it seemed wrong to hear her speaking ill of a woman long dead.

'When the old witch died, what was already a strained relationship between my husband and me, became poisonous. Mr Kidd, you seem to be a man of the world? I presume I may speak frankly?'

He nodded, but wished he had some means of escape. He dreaded to think what she would tell him next.

'While he shared a bed with me, he rarely wanted marital relations. And when he did, it was usually accompanied by violence. He likes to inflict pain. It makes him feel powerful.'

She stared Will straight in the face and he felt himself blushing.

'Two days after our son died, I miscarried my next baby and then lost another when he was two months old. It was undoubtedly due to the beatings he had started giving me. They happened without warning. Without reason. Even when he had relations with me, he made it a kind of punishment. He tried to hurt me. To cause me pain, physically and emotionally.' Again her gaze was steady, as though challenging Will to look away.

Will swallowed and moved his weight in the chair.

'Charles Dawson is a sadist. I imagine he is a lot of other things too that I don't know the words for. But I do know he's a coward.' She closed her eyes for a moment. 'And a rapist.'

Will felt the blood drain from his face. He felt his stomach churn. This was Hannah's father.

'He raped my sister. Elizabeth. I chose to believe him rather than her. I accused her of committing adultery with him. Of seducing him. Getting him drunk.' She clenched her fist and brought it up to her mouth. 'This is very hard for me, Mr Kidd, but I have to tell you everything. It's important that you should know. Our father had written from Sydney with a ticket for Lizzie's passage to Australia as he had found a husband for her. It was your father. Mr Jack Kidd. She would never have gone. It was unthinkable of Father to expect her to travel across the world to marry a stranger, an older man. She laughed when she read the letter and said Father must have lost his mind.' Sarah dug a fingernail into the wooden table surface. 'We argued. I told her that our father had put the family home in my husband's name and Charles wanted her to leave to make room for his mother.'

She cupped her forehead with her hand and was silent for a moment, breathing audibly. She lifted her head again. 'Then I took away her choice. My husband had started sleeping in the box room. I was expecting Timothy, my son, and he wouldn't come near me. I used to see the way he looked at her. I knew he wanted her. Then that night – the day Father's letter came – I'd gone to bed early but something woke me up. The bathroom door was locked so I went into Lizzie's room. He was lying on top of her bed. Passed out and stinking of whisky. His dressing gown was open and he was naked. Lizzie came out of the bathroom with her blouse torn and bloodied, and her lip cut.'

Sarah closed her eyes but carried on speaking. 'I knew what he'd done to her. I knew he'd forced her. Lizzie would never have had anything to do with him. She didn't like him. She had warned me against marrying him. She never understood what I saw in him. Yet I accused her because I didn't want to let myself believe my husband had raped my sister.'

She made a choked sound and the tears ran down her cheeks. 'I pushed her through the front door in the middle of the night and threw her things out onto the street after her.'

Sarah got up and went to stand at the window, her back to Will. She stared at the outhouses in the rear alleyway, on the far side of which were the backs of other terraced houses. Whoever had planned these dwellings had evidently been motivated to cram as many as possible into the smallest amount of space. Rain ran down the windows, making an ugly outlook even grimmer.

Neither spoke for a few minutes and Will wondered if she'd finished and what he should say in response. He was numb with shock, and angry on Elizabeth's behalf. He wanted to find Charles Dawson and wring his cowardly neck.

Sarah turned round suddenly. 'When did she have her son? How long after she married your father?'

'I don't know.' He felt foolish. 'I was only a lad and didn't think too much about these things. She turned up at the Creek already married to him and soon after I realised she was expecting a baby. I thought she must have married him a while before he brought her up from Sydney.'

'Our father? Was she with Father? Did he come too?'

Will shook his head. 'She told me he was dead by the time she got to Australia. Drowned in the Harbour.'

Sarah gave a cry and buried her head in her hands.

'I'm sorry,' he said. 'I thought you would have known that.'

'I didn't know he was dead. I thought he must still be with Lizzie. That was the only thing that stopped me going mad – believing that Father and Lizzie were together. That she was taking care of him – that they were caring for each other.' She dissolved into tears.

Will squirmed in his chair. He'd had no idea he would be causing so much pain when he'd agreed to meet Sarah Dawson.

After a few moments, she seemed to calm herself and she asked him, 'What date was it when your father brought her home?'

'I don't know, Mrs Dawson. I told you, I was still a kid. It was a long time ago and I can't remember.' He closed his eyes and tried to recall. 'I got mad at her for lighting a fire outdoors when the ground was still as dry as a dead cow in a drought.'

'What month?'

He shook his head. 'It's so long ago, Mrs Dawson.'

Sarah appeared to be mentally calculating, using her fingers to work out the months. 'But it was still 1920?'

'Yes. I think so. Yes, it must have been.'

'How long after she arrived did she have her baby?'

He told her, and she returned to sit at the table and leaned her head on her good hand. 'Her child must have been my husband's. Unless she became pregnant on the voyage out, but whatever I might have felt about my sister fifteen years ago, I know better now. She was not the kind of woman to behave that way.' She picked at her plaster cast nervously. 'No. Her son was my husband's child. I'm certain of it.'

Will took a few moments to take in what she was saying. 'Mikey was Hannah's half-brother?'

Sarah burst into tears. 'It's a good thing that he died.'

'Don't say that. He was a good kid. A bonzer little fella. We all loved him. Lizbeth loved him.'

He looked down at his hands then raised his eyes to meet Sarah's. 'Hannah's also your husband's child. And I love her too.' He swallowed. 'More than I can say. I've only known her a short time but it feels like a lifetime. Everything you've told me about her father fills me with horror, but nothing can change how I feel about her. I love every bone in her body. She is the best thing that ever happened to me. She has given me a reason to want to live, when all I used to want was to get through life. To serve my term.' He knew his eyes were welling up. 'Hannah has made me want to live forever. I want to marry her. I *have* to marry her. She mustn't marry someone else. She has to marry me.' As he spoke the words, he had never felt surer of anything.

Sarah Dawson looked at him, then she stretched out her hand and squeezed his. 'And she feels the same way?'

Before he could confess that he hadn't yet told her of the true depth of his feelings, she continued. 'If she does, then you must marry. But I warn you, Mr Kidd, my husband will move heaven and earth to prevent it happening. He wants to marry Hannah off to some man in his church. I don't know who. I don't know any of those people.'

'But why? Doesn't he want Hannah to be happy? I'll take care of her. I promise you I'll do anything to make her happy.'

Sarah laughed. It was an ugly laugh, hollow, bitter. 'Hannah's happiness doesn't even enter my husband's calculations. All Charles Dawson cares about is himself. Hannah is an asset, something to barter or sell to the highest bidder. Marrying her off is something he will only do if it furthers his own ends.' She laughed again. 'Her happiness? If he cared about her happiness, he wouldn't have beaten her the way he did when he found she was keeping a photograph of Elizabeth.'

'He beat her?' He slipped both palms against his forehead.

'She didn't tell you? No, I expect she didn't. Out of a sense of shame I expect. That's what my husband has done to us all. When he exhibits violence and anger, we have been made to believe it's because we have done something terribly wrong. Years and years of him telling the three of us that he is God's agent on earth has to have an impact. It kills the fight in a person, the self-belief, the confidence. It caused me to give up so that I neglected my daughters and left them unprotected.' She laughed again, mirthlessly. 'There you are! I'm proving my own point. Shouldering the blame for what he's done. Even now.' She pointed to her plastered arm in its cotton sling. 'Who do you think did this?'

'I'm going to kill him. I'm going to make him pay. He's going to face up to what he's done to you and your daughters and to Elizabeth and then I'm going to kill him.'

'Don't be a fool, Mr Kidd. All that would do is get you hanged like your father.' She lowered her eyes. 'I'm sorry. I shouldn't have said that. But it's true, and you of all people should know that. If you really love my daughter, then you need to focus on getting her away from here. Away from him.' She glanced out of the window. 'It's getting late. We've talked long enough. You need to go. If he catches you here it will make things bad for all of us. You'd better leave by the back door.'

She led him through the scullery and opened the door into the back yard.

Will turned to face her, 'We have to talk to the police.'

She shook her head. 'Oh Will, you're so kind but you know nothing. The police won't care. As far as they're concerned it's a domestic incident. They can do nothing when it's inside a family. If they investigated every case of men beating women in our street alone, they'd never be done. Men get angry. Sometimes it's the drink. Sometimes it's hunger. Often just because a wife or a daughter is close to hand and not strong enough to fight back. A man three doors down battered his wife to death with a saucepan. Broke her skull. He told the police she fell downstairs. He got away with it. My husband—'

'—can do what he pleases? Even if he ends up killing you or Hannah?'

She looked away again. 'Pray God it won't come to that. But that's why we can't afford to provoke him.

He looked down at her. 'Do you know, for years I thought I was in love with your sister. When I finally confessed my feelings to her, she was incredibly kind and told me one day I'd find real love and see that what I felt for her was a shadow of that. I was angry at her.

But she was right. Seeing Hannah for the first time was like stepping into the light. When I saw her there was an instant recognition – I don't mean the physical resemblance – it was much more than that. It was like coming home. Until then I hadn't realised how lonely I was, how unhappy.' He looked away, avoiding her gaze for a moment, then turning back to face her. 'When I started to know Hannah, it was the first time I began to know myself too. Maybe even to like myself a bit. I've been living a half-life, Sarah, seeing the world through a fog, only partly experiencing it. But now the veil has lifted, and I can see.'

Sarah Dawson looked up at him, her eyes welling. 'You are a dear man. I can see that. My daughter is a lucky woman. I promise you, Will, I will do everything I can to help you and Hannah find the happiness you both deserve.'

Chapter Sixteen

As soon as Judith left for work, Hannah, as usual, got up from the table to clear away the dishes. Her mother stretched out her good arm and stayed her. 'I'll do those later. I want to talk to you first.'

Surprised, Hannah sat down again. 'What is it? Has something happened?' She felt a shiver of fear run through her body.

'I met him yesterday. Your friend, Will, Elizabeth's stepson.'

Hannah felt the blood rush to her face and her cheeks burned. Her heart hammered inside her rib cage.

Her mother gave a little chuckle. 'You're the colour of a ripe strawberry. So, you feel the same way about him then.' It was not a question.

'What do you mean? What did he say?'

'Only that he's fallen for you. In a big way. Worships the ground you walk on.' She smiled at her daughter. 'He's a nice-looking fellow. You're a lucky woman.'

Hannah couldn't control the smile that broke over her face. 'He said he likes me?'

'He said he *loves* you. Wants to marry you.'

Hand clamped over mouth, a rush of joy ran through her body.

'So, he hasn't told you that, yet?'

Hannah shook her head, mute with happiness. 'We've had so little time.'

'Sorry, if I'd realised you didn't know, I'd have held back some of what he told me so he could have told you first himself.'

'It doesn't matter. Oh, Mother!' She jumped to her feet and rushed around the table and scooped her mother into a hug.

'Mind my arm, you daft girl!'

Hannah returned to her seat. She couldn't remember the last time she and her mother had hugged each other. It must have been when she was a small child.

'So, you love him too?'

Hannah nodded her head, too happy to speak.

'It's all very fast, but I can tell you both feel the same way.'

'You think it's too fast?' Hannah was sure her face telegraphed her alarm.

'Who am I to say? You both seem sure.'

'I've never been surer about anything. But I'm afraid. About Father.'

'The only way you are going to be able to marry Will Kidd – and marry him you must – is if you do it soon and do it secretly. Your father will go off like an erupting volcano when he finds out, but once it's done, it's done and there's nothing he can do about it.'

'But what about you? If he discovers you knew.' She closed her eyes and covered her mouth with her hands. 'Oh, Mother, he might take it out on you and Jude.'

'Don't worry about me. And we'll leave Judith out of it. You mustn't tell her about Will or what you're doing. You mustn't even tell me. The less we know the better.

You and Will must come up with a plan to get yourselves wed and you can leave your father to me.' She paused. 'But if you want my advice, you'll get him to take you away from here, somewhere your father can't find you. He told me he sails regularly between here and Dublin – perhaps he can take you over there.'

Hannah was excited but also terrified. Fear of her father wasn't the only element. It was also fear of the unknown. After years of intimidation by Charles Dawson, confinement within a limited sphere, governed by strictures – and scriptures – she was about to be plunged into a whole new world. A new city, a new country, marriage, love, and who knows what else. And with a man she'd met only three times and barely knew. Yet she did know him. She knew without a shadow of a doubt that she loved him, that they were meant for each other.

Sarah said, 'Enough chat now. Get yourself over to the Gladstone Dock before his ship sails this morning. Whatever you and he cook up together, don't tell me or Judith. And I'm going to say this now as we may not get another opportunity – please write and let me know where you are. Don't send the letter here. Write to me care of Mrs Compton next door. But only once you're safely out of the way. Put it inside an envelope addressed to her and tell her only to give it to me when your father's not around. And whatever you do, Hannah, however much you're tempted, don't breathe a word to Judith. Once you're settled, we can see about getting away from here ourselves too, but if Judith gets wind of what's happening she won't be able to keep her mouth shut. Look at all the trouble she caused by asking me about Lizzie.' Sarah got up and began to gather the dirty crockery together. 'Now get a move on. Before you're too late.'

When Hannah reached the docks, she couldn't find him. She ran up and down the quayside, dodging between carts, sacks, and crates, ignoring the stares and wolf whistles of the dock workers. Where was Will?

Just as she was about to give up in despair of locating him, she was grabbed from behind, spun round and found herself wrapped in Will's arms. The chorus of catcalls was now deafening. Throwing one hand upwards in a gesture of dismissal to the men, Will took her other hand in his and pulled her, half running, off the quayside and towards the exit to the dock.

Once outside, they walked along beside the tall brick wall, hand-in-hand, needing no words, until they reached the entrance to another dock. 'We can go in here. It's quieter. There's no ships in there this morning.' He led her towards the waterfront, beneath the tall Victorian warehouses that surrounded the dock. They sat down on the edge of the quayside, legs dangling over the side, above the oily water below.

They turned to look at each other and Hannah felt her insides melt. She looked into Will's eyes and gave a little cry before moving to meet his kiss. This time she didn't resist it at all. She let him kiss her, and was unable to stop herself kissing him back, feeling a hunger for him that she had to feed.

When at last they broke apart, breathless, he held her head against his chest and stroked her hair.

Hannah was bursting with happiness. 'Mother told me what you said about me. That you really like me. I had to see you straight away… to make it right – after pushing you away when you kissed me the other day.'

He cupped his hand around her face and looked into her eyes. 'I love you. That's the truth of it, Hannah. I've never felt this way about a woman before. I didn't believe it was even possible. I don't want to be apart from you. I want to marry you. Will you marry me? Please.' He took her hand. 'I've not much to offer. I'm only an Able Seaman but I've already started studying to become an officer. I never took it seriously before, but I'll work so hard. I promise you. One day I can get my master mariner's ticket then I'll be—'

She lifted a hand to his face and placed it against his cheek. 'I love you too, Will. And the answer's yes! I want to marry you. Yes, yes, yes!'

Their mouths met again. Hannah held onto Will as though if she let go, he'd disappear. The kiss went on, neither wanting it to end.

This time when they finally drew apart, Will's face was serious.

'Why didn't you tell me what your father did to you?'

She looked away. 'I was afraid. I didn't want you to be angry and go after him. I didn't want you to cause problems for Mother and Judith by making Father angry.'

'You realise he wants to marry you off to someone from his church? Another bloody religious maniac, no doubt.'

Hannah looked down, then suddenly confident, she looked him in the eyes. 'He won't do that. At least not for a while. I keep house and do the books for him. Unpaid slave labour. He won't give that up in a hurry.'

'Your mother's not so sure. She told me to make a plan to get you away from Liverpool.'

'I know. She said the same to me. Told me I can't even let Jude know what's happening. But I still can't believe it's so urgent. Father's hopeless at business and I'm sure he won't be any better at making arrangements to marry me off.' She gave a little laugh, but it sounded false.

'I'm not taking that risk.' He looked at her and unable to stop himself, kissed her again. 'Besides, I don't think I can control myself when I'm with you. I want you so much. And I respect and love you too much not to put a ring on your finger first.'

She raised her eyes to look at him, at his beautiful kind, world-weary face. Then she lifted her hand and stroked his cheek, feeling the texture of his skin, the early traces of stubble – he'd evidently not had time to shave that morning. As she gazed into his eyes, they clouded over, suddenly expressing worry.

'I'm older than you, Hannah. I've been around the block many times.' He stopped, evidently struggling to find the right words.

Hannah leaned forward and put a finger against his mouth. 'It's all right. Nothing matters apart from how much we love each other, Will. And nothing you can say could change how I feel about you.'

'But… there's been lots of women. Some that I've treated inconsiderately. I've led them on and then walked away. I'm not the good chap you think I am. I've lived my life as if I didn't care about anyone or anything. I've drunk until I've fallen over; I've taken drugs and passed out with no memory of what has happened. I've—'

'I don't care. None of that matters. It's all in the past. I love you, Will. No matter what you've done.'

'All my life I've been searching for something, but I didn't know what. I thought I was running away from my past. From Elizabeth. From what happened to my father. From my whole rotten life. But now I know that I was floundering about in the dark, waiting.'

'Waiting?'

'Waiting for you. For you to come along and give me a reason for living.' He jumped up and pulled her onto her feet beside him. 'With you I believe I can do anything. Go anywhere. Be anyone. Because whatever I do, I'll be doing it for you. With you. You'll make me a better man than I could ever be without you.'

'Shut up!' She put her hands over his mouth. 'Stop talking, William Kidd. I want you to kiss me again and keep on kissing me until I beg you to stop.'

He bent towards her as she said, 'But – word of warning – that will never happen!'

They were interrupted by the sound of three sharp blasts from a ship's horn.

'Damn! I have to go,' said Will.

'When will you be back?'

'In four days.' He took her hand and they walked back towards the Gladstone Dock. 'While I'm in Dublin I'll arrange for somewhere for you to stay over there. I'll buy you a ticket for the next crossing. I'll sort out a room. We can get married there. I've friends in Dublin who'll help us. Good people.'

She clung to him, unwilling to let him go.

Will kissed the top of her head. 'I'll be back soon, my darling girl. I'm going to make it my life's mission to care for you and protect you. Soon we'll be together.'

–

It was pouring with rain. Too wet to walk by the sand dunes. And what was the point since Will would still be in Dublin. While Hannah longed to be with him, she knew that she had to try to put him from her thoughts until he returned. By then he would have worked out a plan. In the meantime, a sleepless night had led her to the conclusion that something bad was going on at Morton's. It had been nagging away at her for some time and now she was certain. There was surely something nefarious happening. Were she to uncover some serious wrongdoing it might give her a reason to go to the police – something that they would have to act upon. That could help her mother and Judith.

Charles Dawson was a crook. As the word crook formed in her head she realised that that was indeed the way she now thought of her father. A criminal. A man capable of causing grievous bodily harm to his wife and daughter and who made their lives a soulless misery, would surely be also capable of some other crime. The more she thought about it the more she was convinced that he was involved in some kind of financial fraud.

She decided to go to the Picton Reading Room at the main library in the centre of Liverpool to try to find out something about the sender of the strange invoice. On the walk there she knew there was little risk of running into her father, as he avoided the heart of the city, claiming it was a cesspit of commerce and corruption. Hurrying along, she dodged the puddles on the pavement and jumped away from the splatter of passing cars and trams. It took longer than she'd expected to get there and she felt intimidated, standing in front of the grandiose William Brown Library with its six-columned portico. If it hadn't been for the increasing intensity of the rain, she'd have probably chickened out of going inside. She scaled the steps and went in, trying not to be intimidated by the vastness of the place.

When she entered the Picton Reading Room, she was unable to prevent herself gasping out loud. The dimensions of the rotunda took her by surprise. Capped by a large dome, it rose through three levels with spiral staircases giving access to the higher galleries. She had never seen so many books before. Her father would be horrified and she took satisfaction from that knowledge. In the centre of the room was a tall wooden column bearing an enormous lamp in the form of an upturned bowl. So taken with the place, she lost track of time as she wandered among the shelves, awed by the volume and variety of books. Coming upon a collection of local street directories, she remembered the task she had come to do, and took down the latest volume of Kelly's Directory. She thumbed through the pages looking for the address. She found Sutherland Street but there was nothing listed for number 101, the address on the invoice. The only businesses listed in Sutherland Street appeared to be retailers and none of them with street numbers higher than eighty-seven. Puzzled, she went off to find a librarian and asked him if it were possible to search for a company by name – perhaps since the invoice was handwritten it had been a transcription error. He pointed her to another directory and she carried the volume over to a table and settled down to search for Merseyside Maritime Services. Again, she drew a blank. The nearest she could find was a firm called Mersey Marine, which appeared to supply cranes and lifting gear for shipping. It was also in a different part of town. There was only one thing for it, she decided, now unable to suppress her conviction that something was amiss. She must go and look for what, if anything, was at 101 Sutherland Street.

It didn't take her long to find a street plan and locate Sutherland Street. It was a long road leading down towards the docks near Kirkdale. She glanced at the clock. If she left now, she could pass that way without too great a diversion on her way to the Morton's office at the Bootle docks. She was going to have to get a move on, as it was a fair distance and she had no money to pay for the bus or the tram to take her even part of the way.

Sutherland Street started out as a typical street of redbrick Victorian terraced houses. There were dirty-faced children playing hopscotch, skipping games and tag, while their mothers leaned in doorways chatting to each other. Hannah hurried past, checking the numbers as she went. There was little evidence of any commercial activity, other than a couple of corner stores, a green-grocer and a dairy. There was no sign of any building that could possibly be Merseyside Maritime Services. She reached number eighty-seven, which was a cobbler. Beyond it, were half a dozen more domestic dwellings but then the road ended, with another larger one intersecting it. On the other side, the street bore a different name. She retraced her steps and walked down the opposite side of Sutherland Street but found no sign of anything connected to Merseyside Maritime Services.

A woman leaning in a doorway looked at her curiously. 'You lost, love?' she called out.

Hannah asked if she knew where Merseyside Maritime Services might be.

The woman snorted. 'Never heard of it. It's just houses round here. Try nearer the docks, love.'

Hannah thanked her and went on her way. A dead end. If she wanted to find out who or what was Merseyside Maritime Services, she would have no choice but to ask her father. But that was no choice at all.

As soon as she walked into Morton's, she knew something was not right. She could hear voices coming from her father's small private office. As she hung up her coat, Mr Busby looked up. 'Your mother's here,' he said.

Hannah looked at him with wide eyes. Her mother never left the house any more and she couldn't remember the last time she had visited the Morton's premises.

Busby hissed at her. 'Don't go in. There's been raised voices. In fact now you're here I think I'll slip out for a while. I have some errands to do.'

He pulled on his coat and left the building. Hannah suspected that he wanted to avoid witnessing any confrontation.

She slipped into her seat behind the desk, all thoughts of Merseyside Maritime Services now gone, replaced with anxiety for her mother. Something extraordinary must have compelled her to venture into the business realm of her husband, especially with her arm still plastered and in a sling. Hannah was amazed. Then she realised that perhaps that was the reason. Charles Dawson was less likely to strike his wife if they were in a place where others could bear witness. Straining her ears, she tried to make out what was being said but it was now a low rumble. The raised voices Mr Busby had mentioned had given way to a more controlled exchange. Hannah thought she heard her own name mentioned, but she couldn't be sure.

She was about to get up to go and listen with her ear against the door, when it opened. Her father appeared, his body filling the space. Behind him she could just see her mother.

'Hannah, walk your mother home. Then come straight back here. After her accident she shouldn't be out of the house.'

Her accident? Now he was trying to pretend to them all that it was an accident – knowing full well that she and Judith had been present in the house when he had struck Sarah. Hannah looked at her mother but Sarah avoided meeting her eyes.

Hannah grabbed her coat and shrugged it on.

It was only once they were out of sight of Morton's that Sarah at last looked at Hannah. 'I married a madman,' she said. 'Not only have I lived to regret it for my own sake but now for yours and Judith's. I am paying the price for my own folly and it is my fault that you are soon to pay it too.'

'What do you mean, Mother? Has he threatened you?' She linked her arm through her mother's undamaged one. 'Should we go to the police?'

'The police won't care. They won't bother with the likes of us. Their attitude will be that your father is within his rights. Coppers don't care about women. They think they have more important things to do. And you know how plausible he can be. He'd have them eating out of his hands in no time while he plays the upstanding, God-fearing man worthy of respect.'

'Then we have to leave. We could go away somewhere he won't find us. Judith too of course. Will can arrange it all. We can all go to Ireland.'

Her mother looked at her with an expression halfway between cynicism and sadness. 'And where will we find the money to get away? You know as well as I do your father keeps us all without a brass farthing.'

'Will could help us. Or we could just go. Walk out. We could find shelter somewhere. I could get a job. Judith too. We can look after you, Mother. We could earn the money to get us *all* to Dublin.'

'Silly girl. You always were a dreamer. I've made my bed and I have to lie in it. Maybe you and Judith can get away, but I can't.'

'I'll never leave you, Mother.'

Her mother didn't argue. 'I'm sorry, Hannah,' she said. 'He's going to try and force you to get married. And not to Will?'

Hannah nodded. 'I hoped it wasn't true. I didn't think he'd get round to that for ages. Can he even do that?'

'He who holds the purse strings has the power. Unless you run away, you have no choice but to obey him. I am going to pray that if he does this, he will choose wisely for you, since I'm powerless to stop him. Have you heard from Will?'

'He's in Dublin. Trying to arrange things. He'll sort it all, Mother. Don't worry. I'll talk to him as soon as he's back.'

Sarah stroked her daughter's hair. 'I hope so, but I'm afraid it may be too late. I pray one day you will find it in you to forgive me for letting things get this bad. Now go. If you're late getting back, you'll provoke him.'

As she hurried back to the office near the docks, Hannah asked herself how one man had the power to ruin so many lives. She conjured up the image of Will Kidd with his eyes looking into hers and begged God that Will would be able to make things all right.

Chapter Seventeen

Hannah stood in front of her father, hands clasped behind her back, palms sweating. She tried to stop herself shaking, but the truth was, she was terrified of him. His violent outbursts towards her mother and herself were increasingly getting out of control and more and more often he had shown an unaccountable anger. Was he about to hit her again? Had she done something else he thought wrong? She'd been so careful. Perhaps he had found out about Will? Had one of the neighbours seen him when he'd called on her mother? Her heart hammered and she prayed her father couldn't sense her fear.

Dawson smiled at her. It was a smile made by stretching his narrow lips apart to reveal small pointy teeth. A smile that failed to reach his eyes. It made Hannah think of a china doll she had been given as a child by her grandfather – a doll with a painted smile unmatched by its cold glass eyes that stared blankly into nothingness.

Fear of being struck gave way to a different kind of fear. Why was he smiling at her? What could he possibly want with her? Her mother's words about the imminence of his plans for her to marry, chilled the blood in her veins and she felt her stomach clench.

Dawson gestured at an upright chair in the corner, signalling her to draw it near and sit down.

Perching on the edge of the seat, she tugged at the hem of her skirt, making sure it was well below her knees. Her father was still smiling that sinister smile. It was worse than his anger. A smile was so rare that she couldn't help but feel suspicious – in fact she couldn't remember ever seeing him smile at all.

'Remind me how old you are, Hannah.'

'I'm twenty-one, Father. Almost twenty-two.'

He nodded. 'Good.'

She waited, too frightened to speak.

His eyes swept over her, lingering a moment too long on her bosom. She pulled her cardigan closed and folded her arms over her breasts. Why did he look at her that way? It made her squirm and want to run out of the room. At last his eyes settled on her face and his fake smile disappeared.

'A good age to be married. Your mother had already had you at that age.'

She closed her eyes, dreading what was coming. All she could think about was Will and how he would be in Dublin by now. Would he have arranged her passage to Ireland, her lodgings, their wedding?

'Hannah?'

'Yes, Father.'

'Well?'

She swallowed. He was baiting her, tormenting her. 'I don't think I'm ready for that yet.' She looked at the floor, noticing, absently, how scuffed her shoes were. 'Besides I know no one who might want to marry me.' As she told the lie she suddenly thought that maybe he actually meant Will. Perhaps her mother had told Dawson about him and won him round to the idea.

But that faint fleeting hope was dashed when her father said, 'Of course you don't. And that's how it should be.'

She swallowed again. Suddenly defiant she said, 'Or who I might choose to marry.'

He snorted. 'Choose? You? You have no choice. A woman is not capable of judging who would make her a suitable husband. A woman is made by God to serve her husband, her lord and master. The scriptures are clear: "*Neither was the man created for the woman; but the woman for the man.*" The only person fit to make such an important choice is your father. Just as Abraham chose Rebecca to be wife to his son Isaac. It is the gift of a father. A gift to God. And woman is a gift to man. The Bible has laid it out and we must follow.'

Hannah felt sick. 'But, Father, marriage is a lifelong commitment. Surely I should not be forced to commit myself to a husband for whom I have no feelings?'

Her father stretched his mouth into another of his false smiles. 'Your feelings are immaterial, Hannah. God will guide me to make the right choice for you. Your role is to show humility and do my bidding, then once married, you will do your husband's bidding, just as every woman is intended to do. The Holy Scriptures have determined it this way.' He raised his eyes to the ceiling as though calling upon God himself. 'Now let us pray together that this wilfulness will be driven from you and you will bow to the will of the Lord, as channelled through me.'

He reached forward and grabbed her by the collar, jerking her from the chair and pushing her down onto her knees. The sudden impact with the cold hard floor made her gasp, but she didn't protest, knowing it would only make things worse.

Dawson took up his Bible and read a series of verses designed to demonstrate his contention that woman was made solely for man. He asked her to repeat the words after him and, shivering with fear, she did so. After about half an hour, her kneecaps aching, he permitted her at last to return to her chair. He flashed his sharp-toothed non-smile at her again.

'I suppose you would like to know who the man is God has guided me to choose for you?'

Her mouth was dry and she began to shiver. 'Have you chosen already, Father?'

He nodded. 'It's all arranged. I have spoken with the pastor and he is willing.'

Hannah's chest tightened in fear and horror and she tasted bile. Not the pastor. Mr Henderson was older than her father. A stern-faced widower with beetling eyebrows and a bulbous red nose. She'd never spoken to him, as she and Judith always kept out of the way whenever he visited their father. The thought of being such a man's wife filled her with disgust and fright. 'But… Father… he's so old.'

Dawson laughed. 'Stupid child! Do you honestly believe such a great man as the pastor would be prepared to marry you – a silly young woman? While I can imagine no greater honour than for a man of such wisdom and so filled with God's spirit to take a daughter of mine in marriage, I know that I could never be worthy enough.' His obsequious tone made Hannah think of Dickens's Uriah Heep

Hannah breathed again. No one could possibly be as bad as the pastor. But a future without Will in it was in any way unthinkable.

'Pastor Henderson has however bestowed a great honour upon me and this family as he has agreed that you will be given in marriage to his son, Samuel.'

'His son? I don't even know this Samuel.'

'There will be time enough for that. Samuel is his only son.'

'Does Samuel himself have any say in this?'

'Samuel lives his life by the examples set down in the Good Book. He will emulate Isaac, to whom Rebecca was given in marriage. I want you to read that chapter now. Tomorrow I will expect you to have read and understood their example. Now tell me in which book of the Bible you will find their story.'

Hannah wracked her brain, fearing his rage if she misremembered. 'Is it Genesis, chapter twenty-four?'

Dawson bared his teeth in another *faux* smile. She'd never seen so much smiling from him before. 'You have done well. Now go to your room and study it, until you know it backwards.'

'When will I meet him?'

'So many questions. You will meet Samuel Henderson when I consider fit. Remember Rebecca went to marry Isaac without having met him. She followed the will of God and you will do the same.'

'But I will meet him first?'

'Yes. Your future husband wishes to meet you first.'

Feeling suddenly defiant she said, 'So he's not like Isaac then. Trusting his father's servant to make the choice for him.'

'His father has chosen for him and he will obey. It is God's will.'

'And the marriage will be when?'

'Likewise. When I decide. Now go. I'm done with your prattle.'

Hannah got up and left the room, rushing upstairs to where her sister was waiting anxiously.

'Well?' Asked Judith.

'You were right. He's selling me into slavery.'

'What?'

'As good as. He says I am to be married to Samuel Henderson, the pastor's son.'

Judith frowned. 'So, it's really happening?'

'Did you doubt it?' Hannah flung herself on her back on the bed, her hands covering her eyes. 'For a few moments I thought he meant I was to marry the pastor himself. I was ready to throw myself under a tram.'

Judith gave an exaggerated shudder. 'I wouldn't blame you. Did he say anything about me?'

'No.'

Judith's sigh of relief was audible.

Hannah rolled on her side, her back to her sister. 'So that's all right then, is it? As long as you're not involved.'

'Don't be like that, Hannah. You know it's only a matter of time before it happens to me too.' She stroked her hand over Hannah's hair. 'Don't let's quarrel, Han. That would be letting him win.'

Hannah rolled over to face her and smiled up at Judith. 'You're right.'

'Did he say when it would happen?'

Hannah shook her head. 'I'm not even sure this Samuel knows himself. We're just pawns in the hands of our fathers. I'm hoping it could be weeks – even months. He said there'd be plenty of time to get to know him.'

Judith grinned. 'Perhaps this Samuel won't like you.' She giggled. 'No. I can't see that happening. Any young man would be thrilled to have you as his wife.'

Hannah gave her a sad smile. 'Oh, Jude, what shall I do?'

'Pray to God to give you the strength to bear it. Pray to God that this Samuel will be a kind, handsome and loving husband.'

Hannah punched the pillow. She asked herself why she was unable to stand up to her father's bullying – but she still had the faded bruises to remind her, as well as the sight of her mother's broken arm. And a lifetime of constraint and being worn down by this patriarch had all but crushed her spirit.

But there was still time to get to Will, to get him to speed up his plans to help her, to take her away with him. He would back in Liverpool in a few days at the most.

-

'He's not at all ugly! He looks quite presentable. He's not a bit like his father.' Judith was standing, her nose pressed up against the grimy bedroom window, looking down into the street. It was Sunday afternoon and they had been instructed to stay in their room until summoned. 'Come and have a look, Han!'

'Get away from the window. They might see you.'

'They won't. Aren't you even curious?'

'Why should I be? I'll soon have the rest of my life to look at him. I want to postpone that for as long as possible.'

'You're daft. I'd be bursting to know what he's like.'

'Pity you're not the one having to marry Mr Samuel Henderson then.'

A loud rap at the front door. Judith stepped onto the landing and looked down the stairs. 'They've gone into Father's study.'

A low buzz of voices rose through the ceiling.

'Is Mother with them?' Hannah looked up from her horizontal position on the bed.

'No. I think she's in the back kitchen. She told me she wanted no part in this and intends to keep out of the way.'

'Can you hear what they're saying?'

Judith shook her head. 'I'm not risking going downstairs. Father would go berserk if he caught me listening in the hall.'

As she spoke, the two women heard a door creak open and their father's voice called up the stairs. 'Hannah, come down.'

Hannah got off the bed, smoothed her dress and patted her hair into place. 'Wish me luck.' She gave her sister a sad smile then went downstairs, feeling like a martyr heading for the scaffold.

Samuel Henderson was standing in front of the fireplace, his father sitting in the chair that was habitually her own father's. Dawson sat down opposite and Hannah stood between the two older men, there being nowhere else to sit. She kept her eyes lowered, to avoid looking at the stranger whom her father intended to be her husband.

'You've met my elder daughter, Hannah, sir?' Dawson's tone was obsequious and sycophantic as he addressed the pastor.

Mr Henderson grunted and gave Hannah only a passing glance.

Dawson turned to the younger Henderson. 'Samuel, this is Hannah.'

Should she offer to shake his hand? She decided that would be inappropriate and instead stood rooted to the spot, waiting for Samuel Henderson to speak.

He looked as if he wished he were in another place. Any place but here. Half-turning, he let his eyes run over her quickly then turned to focus them on her father. 'Miss Dawson,' he said, addressing her father rather than her.

The pastor got up from his seat and to Hannah's surprise he knelt down in front of the hearth. For a moment she had the mad thought that he was about to lay a fire, then he said, 'Now we will pray together and seek God's guidance and blessings.'

Dawson immediately knelt too, jerking his head towards Hannah to indicate she should do the same. Samuel continued leaning against the wall until a cough from his father caused him to kneel beside the other three.

Hannah closed her eyes. It was excruciating. She wished the ground would open and swallow her up. Henderson senior led the prayers, his voice stentorian and declamatory. With her eyes squeezed tightly shut, she tried to pretend it wasn't happening but, unable to shut out the pastor's voice, she listened to the sound of the words rather than their meaning. Eventually he quoted from the Biblical passage Dawson had made her study. 'Behold, Rebekah is before thee, take her, and go, and let her be thy master's son's wife, as the Lord hath spoken.'

Looking out of the corner of her eye she saw that Samuel Henderson appeared to be as embarrassed by the whole performance as she was. He was biting the nail of his thumb. His face was in profile and she didn't want her father to notice that she wasn't concentrating, so she looked away again. There was a protracted silence before the older Henderson got to his feet, followed by the rest of them. He nodded to Dawson who said, 'Hannah, you may take Mr Henderson into the parlour. His father and I have matters to discuss.'

The parlour was an overly grand term for what was usually referred to as the back room. The prospect of entertaining her betrothed there for an indeterminate amount of time was not an appealing one. As she went to open the door, her mother emerged from the room, nodded and muttered a greeting to Samuel Henderson then went straight upstairs. Hannah felt abandoned.

They sat down on opposite sides of the table – the only available seating in the poky room. She offered him a glass of water but he shrugged away the offer. 'Tea?'

He shook his head. 'Look, Miss Dawson, I don't imagine you're any happier about this farce than I am. St Paul said it was better to marry than to burn but quite frankly the idea of being tied to the stake is not unappealing right now.'

She was taken aback, unsure whether to laugh or be affronted. She stared at him, but saw he was quite serious.

'Then why are you going along with this?'

'Why are you?'

'I have no choice.'

'Neither do I.'

'Surely not. In my case I'm entirely financially dependent on my father. But you?'

'That's my business. But rest assured if it were up to me, I wouldn't be doing this.'

'Well, that's clear then. You'd better say so before it's too late.' She jerked her head at the wall dividing the two rooms.

'I can't.'

Hannah screwed her eyes up and studied him. He was about mid-twenties, blond-haired, and blue-eyed. When he leaned forward, signs of premature balding were revealed that were otherwise invisible. His face managed to be both thin and slightly puffy, as though his features had been smudged, and he had an arrogant rather patrician air about him – but Judith was right – he was certainly not ugly. A sulky look played about his eyes, like a child who'd been denied access to a jar of sweeties, but otherwise he could be described as a good-looking man.

'Please, call me Hannah,' she said at last, deciding she must try her best to get along with this man. 'May I call you Samuel?'

'Sam.' He leaned back in his chair, exhaling a long breath. Until this point he had avoided her eyes, but now he studied her closely. 'Do you have a boyfriend, Hannah?'

Taken aback, she lied and told him she hadn't. 'To be honest, my father keeps my sister and me from mixing with people in general. His views are somewhat old-fashioned, since he is a devout man with strong religious beliefs.'

Sam snorted.

'Are you implying he isn't?'

'I'm *implying* nothing. "Woe unto you, scribes and Pharisees, hypocrites! for ye are like unto whited sepulchres, which indeed appear beautiful outward, but are within full of dead men's bones, and of all uncleanness."'

Hannah gaped at him.

'One of the few Bible verses I've never forgotten as the same description is true of my father as well. He too is a whited sepulchre, a hypocrite of the highest order. That's why I have no truck with religion.'

She felt her eyes widening. Sam Henderson was not at all what she had expected. Glancing nervously at the closed door, she said, 'You're not a believer yourself, then?'

He shrugged. 'I suppose I believe in some kind of higher power, but certainly not the angry vengeful god that my father bangs on about, and certainly not the literal interpretation of every word of the Bible. It was written thousands of years ago. Actually it wasn't even written. Old stories. Folklore. Most of that Old Testament stuff is no different from the myths of the Norse gods or the ancient Celtic deities. Old stories passed down by word of mouth.'

Hannah felt a smile appearing at the edge of her mouth, but then suppressed it. What he was saying was shocking. If their fathers should overhear him she could imagine how they would react.

'If you don't believe in it then why are you going along with all that stuff about us following on the same path as Rebecca and Isaac?'

'Because that's all it is. Playing a part.' He got up and began to pace back and forth as far as was possible in the restricted space. 'Ours, Hannah will be a marriage of convenience. It gets me off a hook I don't want to be dangling from. In your case, I can't imagine why you're prepared to go along with it, but I suppose I have to accept that perhaps you are indeed under the thumb of your father.' He pushed the empty chair back under the table, then seemed to change his mind, pulled it out again, sat down and crossed one ankle over the other knee. 'So, let's agree then. We will play along with this charade and come to some kind of arrangement once we are free of the parental yoke.'

'Some kind of arrangement?'

'As I said, a marriage of convenience.'

'Is it because… is there… is there another woman you would rather be marrying?' She felt her face reddening and was incredulous at the turn the conversation had taken.

He looked at her steadily, eyes narrowed. 'No. There is no other woman I would rather be marrying. You will do well enough.' He got up. 'I think those two have had long enough to hammer out the deal, don't you think?'

She didn't know what to say. Her mouth was open as she stared at him.

He turned to address her again with his hand on the door knob. 'Anyone would think we were in the last century, not in 1938.' He shook his head rapidly in a sudden jerky action like a wet dog shaking water out of its coat. 'Still, needs must, eh?'

She followed him into the tiny space between the two rooms which the family over-generously referred to as the hall and waited at the foot of the stairs while he went inside, then she climbed slowly upstairs to find her sister.

A few minutes later they heard the Hendersons leaving. Judith leaned out of the window to watch them go while Hannah, lay on her back on the bed, staring aimlessly at the ceiling, where she spotted several cobwebs. She'd take a broom to them later.

After a couple of minutes, Judith pulled the sash back down and turned to her sister. 'I got a good look this time. He's very handsome, Han! Lucky you. I can't believe Father has picked him. I hope I'm as lucky when my turn comes. He's started thinning a bit on top – but you can't expect perfection!' She started giggling.

Hannah said nothing.

'Look, you can't just keep sitting there like a deaf mute' said Judith. 'Tell me all about it. What did he say? What did Father say? I want to know everything.' She was actually grinning.

Hannah let out a deep sigh. 'There's not a lot to tell. The pastor treated us all to a lengthy Biblical discourse and we had to kneel together and pray. It was awful.'

'I'm not interested in that. What about what the son said? You and he were in the parlour for ages. And Mother wasn't even there! Did he kiss you?'

'Of course he didn't kiss me.'

'Well, he *is* going to marry you, isn't he? Wasn't it all settled?'

'Yes, I believe so.'

'Gosh, you are *so* infuriating, Han. Don't be such a beast! I want to know every detail. When's the wedding? I'll make your dress, of course. What's he like? Oh my goodness, there's so much I want to know.' She plumped down on the bed beside Hannah and took her hands, pulling her round to face her. 'I'd have thought you'd be excited, bursting to tell me. Why are you being so cagey? You must be so relieved he isn't some fat, old bloke.'

'To be honest, Jude, it makes no difference, as I have no choice in the matter anyway. But if you really want to know, I think he is as unimpressed by what's happening as I am. I think if it were up to him he'd run a mile.'

'What? I can't believe that. You're gorgeous. Any man would be over the moon to marry you. Stop running yourself down, Han.'

Before Hannah could reply, their father's voice boomed up the stairs, summoning her back to his study. She threw a look of resignation at Judith and hurried down the stairs.

When she entered the room, Dawson signalled to her to sit. 'You acquitted yourself well, Hannah. Pastor Henderson was satisfied you will make his son a suitable wife.'

He didn't seem to expect a reply so she sat and waited.

'We have agreed that the nuptials will take place as soon as the licence is obtained. The pastor will conduct the ceremony himself.'

Hannah was stunned. 'So soon?'

'No reason to delay. Once the matter is settled that's an end to it.'

'But the preparations?'

'What preparations?'

'I will need something to wear. Judith wants to make my wedding dress. And the wedding breakfast to organise.' These things mattered not a jot to her – other than as a means of delay.

Her father scowled. 'There will be none of the fripperies that ungodly people use to disguise their denial that a marriage can only be made by God. Your mother and sister won't even be there. You know the chapel doesn't permit women to attend.'

'Not even for a wedding?'

'Certainly not.'

'Then how can *I* be there?'

'Your presence is unavoidable.'

'But Judith—'

'Judith will do as she is told. She and your mother will mark the occasion by studying the Bible. I will select some suitable passages. They will pray for you here.'

Hannah gaped at him. He had always been fanatical in his religious devotion but lately he was taking matters to a different level. Not for the first time she questioned his sanity.

'So, no new clothes. No wedding breakfast. No guests.'

'Correct.'

'And when the marriage is done?'

'You will live with your husband.'

'And where might that be, Father?'

'Samuel Henderson lives in the family home. Near Aintree.'

'The family home?'

He looked at her as though she were an irritating fly he would like to swat away. 'So many questions. You and your husband will live with Pastor Henderson and will abide by any strictures he lays down. I understand the boy has been somewhat wayward. The pastor hopes that the care and consolation of a wife will steady him and set him on the right course, as determined by God.'

'What has he done?'

'What has who done?'

'Sam, er Mr Henderson.'

'That is not your business. Your role is to care for the needs of your husband and father-in-law, keep house, and in good time and when the Lord wills, bear your husband children. Now I will have no more questions. Instead you can go to your room and read First Corinthians Chapter 7. There you will find the basic rules for married life. You will also see that Paul says a man who gives his daughter in marriage does right, but a man who doesn't give his daughter in marriage does right too. I am a righteous man and I have two daughters. I have decided that while you will be given in marriage, your sister won't. She will remain here to act as a help to your mother and to devote herself to the Lord and contribute to the upkeep of the household.'

Hannah felt her throat constrict. 'You mean Judith may not marry?'

'You have understood me.'

'But… in that case, Father, perhaps Judith could marry Mr Henderson and I will remain single? Judith would be more than happy—'

'Judith's happiness is no concern of mine. Judith would do well to concentrate on serving the Lord and looking after this home.'

'But—'

'Shut your mouth. I'll hear no more from you, Hannah. Now go to your room. I want you to commit the verses I have set you, to memory. I will hear you recite them tonight after supper.'

Hannah, numb with shock moved towards the door.

As she turned the knob, he said, 'Send Judith to me now.'

–

After the visit of the Hendersons, Dawson told Hannah she was no longer to come to work at Morton's Coffee. He contended that it was inappropriate for a married woman – or one soon to be married – to be employed in an office. For two days after the meeting with Hannah's future husband, Charles Dawson remained at home, instead of going to work himself. Hannah and her mother were unable to talk in private and it felt as though they had both been confined to a jail. Dawson was closeted in his study, doing they knew not what, but calling out for refreshments to be brought to him from time to time.

Each morning, Mr Busby arrived punctually at nine to confer with Dawson and remained with him for up to an hour before returning to the office. As Hannah was showing him out on the second day, he said, 'You ill again, Miss Dawson? Leaving all your work to me?' He scowled at her. 'Notice he doesn't pay me any more for taking up your slack.' He was holding a handkerchief over his nose and mouth.

So her father hadn't told the clerk the real reason for her absence. She decided she wasn't going to tell him herself. 'Don't worry, Mr Busby, it's not contagious.' Then, with a sense of devilment she added, 'Just women's troubles,' and enjoyed a brief moment of amusement as he scuttled away red-faced.

Most of the time, Hannah sat at the table in the back parlour pretending to read the Bible verses her father had assigned her to study in preparation for her marriage. Sarah had resorted to spending her days up in her bedroom – although no longer lying in bed.

Confined to the house, Hannah thought constantly about what she could do to prevent her imminent marriage, to escape the house and go to find Will. Imminent – but what did that actually mean? This week? Next? Next month?

'You have to go and find Will,' said her mother in a whisper, when she brought her up a cup of tea on the second afternoon. 'Get him to take you away.'

'I don't even know when he's back in port.'

Sarah, her listless attitude now a thing of the past, counted the days on her fingers. 'It must be about now. I think he probably docked yesterday and will be leaving again today.'

Hannah covered her face with her hands. 'But Father's downstairs. Guarding the door.'

'Leave him to me. I'll distract him while you slip out the back door. But you'd better be quick. I'll tell him you're feeling unwell. Get back here as soon as you can. Tell Will he needs to act fast.' She paused, pulling her daughter towards her and hugging her against her chest. 'In fact if you get hold of him I think you're better to stay with him. There may not be time otherwise.'

'But that means... you and Judith...'

'I'll explain everything to Judith when you're safely away.'

'But it means I can't say goodbye. I don't know when I'll see you and Jude again.'

'I told you: once you're safely married you can write, care of next door. Then once he knows you're married and has some time to get used to the idea we'll see about you coming back to visit us.'

'Only when he's not here. Oh, Mother, I honestly don't want to see him again. Is that terrible of me?'

'No. Of course it isn't. I wish I'd taken you girls and run away with you years ago. But...'

'I know. You couldn't leave.'

'When I was expecting babies, I couldn't leave. I still hoped and prayed we'd be a proper family. If the babies hadn't died. And then losing Timothy...' She closed her eyes tightly, sucked in a breath and squeezed her daughter's hand. 'Go! Now. I'm going to take him in some tea and I'll tell him you've gone to lie down with a headache. 'Go!' She pushed Hannah towards the door.

Hannah ran as fast as her legs would carry her towards the docks. She burst through the gate of the Gladstone Dock just in time to see a ship moving out into the estuary, ready to sail into the waters of the Irish Sea. There were no other vessels in the dock, just another ship waiting to enter.

Lungs bursting, she ran towards one of the stevedores who were wheeling empty barrows to the dockside ready to unload the incoming ship. 'Excuse me. That ship that's just left, what was it?'

'*Arklow*, heading for Dublin.'

'But I thought it wasn't due to leave until later today.'

'Well, you thought wrong, love.'

'When will it be back?'

He shrugged. 'Dunno, doll. Two or three days? Maybe more.'

Disappointment flooded through her and she walked to the edge of the dockside and watched as Will's ship sailed into the distance, leaving a churning wake behind it.

With a sinking heart and an overwhelming sense of abandonment, she headed back to the house. All she could do now was pray that Will would be back before it was too late.

Chapter Eighteen

Once in Dublin, Will went straight to the see the O'Connors.

He was disappointed that Hannah hadn't managed to get away to see him this time. He'd even passed by the office, looked through the window and had seen she wasn't at work. The temptation to go to her house had been enormous but he kept the promise he'd made to Hannah not to go near. It was probably best not to rouse the suspicions of her father until the time came for her to leave, and anyway Will had yet to finalise the plans for her escape. Better to focus on getting all that ironed out. He couldn't afford to overlook any details. They would probably only have one chance.

His previous crossing to Dublin had not allowed him time to visit the O'Connors as he'd been assigned to port watch duty and hence confined to the ship. This time though, he would have plenty of time to talk to Mrs O'Connor and make the necessary arrangements. He had enough money put aside to rent a place of their own for Hannah, but there wasn't sufficient time on this trip to go looking. Anyway, he wanted the decision on where they would make their first home to be Hannah's too – and being alone in a strange city she would probably prefer to stay with some friendly faces at first. Eddie had assured him that his mother would be only too happy to take Hannah in, and Will was confident that Bridget would prove a good friend to her.

Will tried to imagine being married. Coming off the ship after each trip and into her arms. He thought of the two of them sharing a meal and sitting in front of their own fireplace, listening to the wireless. Maybe they'd go dancing. To the pictures. She loved books – he'd buy her a shelf-ful to occupy her while he was at sea. Beautiful clothes too, to replace the threadbare, old-fashioned garments she usually wore. He imagined lying with her in their own bed, making love for hours, then going out to walk together, lost in the pleasure of each other's company.

It was hard to believe that in such a short time he had come to feel this way. Before the *Christina* had docked in Liverpool, all he'd cared about was his next drink, the next woman, the next port, whether he'd get shore leave, which roster he'd be on. A pointless, aimless, empty existence. Now he let himself imagine having children with Hannah, holding their first child in his arms, watching her feeding their baby. He hoped it would look like her. A beautiful bright happy child. A child like little Mikey, his poor dead half-brother. Only he knew now he probably wasn't *his* half-brother – but Hannah's. That thought made him think of Charles Dawson – not something he wanted to do. He felt his hands form fists and his anger rising inside him. The man was pure evil. He had to get Hannah away from him.

As he had hoped, Mrs O'Connor and Bridget were only too willing to take Hannah in. 'If she doesn't mind roughing it and mucking in with us,' said the mother.

'Bridget and I share a bed but we can squeeze a mattress in for her in our room. Two of the lads can share for a while. They won't care. And we can't have her bunking down in here with the boys.' She gestured around the small room. 'It's not much, but it's home and your intended will be very welcome.'

Bridget was grinning at him. 'I can't tell you, Will, how happy I am for you and I can't wait to meet Hannah.'

Her mother gave her a wistful look.

'My prayers for you were answered. Thanks be to the Blessed Virgin Mary.' Bridget's face was glowing with happiness. 'I told you, you deserved to be happy, that day when we had our walk to St Stephen's Green and I've been praying up a storm ever since.'

Mrs O'Connor looked sideways at her daughter. 'You didn't tell me you'd been walking with Willy. And over the other side and all.' She looked indignant.

Bridget laughed. 'I didn't tell you, Mammy, as you'd have read all kinds of things into it that weren't there at all.' She threw another grin at Will, who thought, not for the first time that it was a terrible pity the woman was set on becoming a nun.

Stretching her lips and giving her head a little shake, Mrs O'Connor said, 'Oh well. Aren't we all helpless in the will of the good Lord?' She turned again to Will. 'We'll take great care of the lass. Just get her over here and you can rest assured she'll be safe with us. Now you will be marrying in the Church – I can have a word with Father O'Leary.'

'Neither Hannah nor I are Roman Catholics. It will have to be a civil wedding.'

The two women looked at each other. 'We know nothing about that,' said Mrs O'Connor, rather primly. 'But we'll make enquiries.'

'It might be more straightforward if we marry in Liverpool before we leave.'

'Aye, it might.' Mrs O'Connor was tight-lipped.

'But risky. I told you about her father. I was thinking to wait until just before the ship sails for Hannah to slip away. If we have to get married first there's always a chance of her father finding out and having time to get her back. I know nothing of the procedures for getting married over there either.'

'I thought captains could marry people at sea,' said Bridget. 'Can't you get yours to marry you during the crossing?'

'That's just a myth. There's nothing to say a ship's master can legally marry a couple – and absolutely not on a short eight- to ten-hour hop across the Irish Sea.'

'Oh, that's a pity.' Mrs O'Connor gave a rueful smile. 'I'd always thought it was possible. Well, for the non-Catholics anyway. And so romantic.' She corrected herself quickly. 'But of course, it wouldn't be a marriage in God's eyes. We Catholics need the priest for that. But you being a Calathumpian, that's different.'

Before Will could ask what a Calathumpian was, Bridget jumped up and went to fill the kettle. 'Don't you worry, Will. We'll make all the necessary enquiries for you to have a civil marriage here. By the time you come back with your bride-to-be, we'll have it all straightened out.'

'And we'll be throwing a party for you,' her mother added. 'The boys will insist on it!'

Bridget returned with the teapot and three mugs. As she poured the tea, she said, 'And don't you forget to ask your captain for a few days' leave. You have to have a honeymoon. It'll be a chance to see a bit of Ireland and discover what a beautiful country it is.'

'And how would you know, Bridget? You've never set foot outside Dublin.' Her mother folded her arms across her ample bosom.

'That's not true, Mammy. Have you forgotten when I went with the parish on the pilgrimage to Knock?'

'You did. And, yes, I had forgotten.'

'You're right,' said Will. 'I'd forgotten about asking for some shore leave. I'll ask the master. He's a decent fellow. I'm sure if he knows I'm getting wed he'll let me take a few days off.' He grinned at Bridget.

–

Her father gave her no warning. The family were eating breakfast when he put down his teacup and announced that Hannah was to be married that morning.

'No!' Her reaction was instant. Spilling her tea, she jumped to her feet.

Charles Dawson narrowed his eyes. 'What have I said about your defiance, Hannah? I will not tolerate it. Remember what the Bible says. "It is better to dwell in the wilderness, than with a contentious and an angry woman."'

Hannah turned to her mother, who looked stricken. 'This is too soon, Charles. Hannah needs time to prepare herself. She's only just met Mr Henderson. She needs more time to get used to the idea.'

'I am the judge of what is best for my daughter. It's all arranged.' Turning to his younger daughter, he said, 'Judith, it's time you left for work.'

'But you just said the wedding is today.' Judith's eyes darted to her sister's.

'The wedding is Hannah's, not yours. Now be gone.'

'Can't I be there?' Judith's voice was anguished. 'Please! Mother?'

'Neither you nor your mother will be there. Say your goodbyes now. Hannah, you will be living with your husband's family from today.' He turned to his wife. 'As for you, you'll actually need to start doing some work around here from now on.'

Dawson rose from the table, and indicated that Hannah follow him. He looked at his watch. 'Get a move on, girl. I don't want to be late.'

'No. I won't. I can't.' She felt tears of anger rising. 'I won't do it.'

Dawson grabbed her upper arm in a vice-like grip that made her shriek with pain. 'Dare to defy me, you shameless creature, and you'll suffer not just my anger but the anger of the Lord God. As will your mother for feeding your head with this defiant nonsense. I am God's instrument and I am doing his will.' He jerked her violently across the room so she hit her shoulder against the door.

Tears now streaming down her face, shock pumping through her body, she looked to her mother. Would she help her? Should Hannah just run? But her mother shook her head then buried her face in her hands. Judith was open-mouthed and also tearful.

Numb with shock, Hannah threw a last look back at her mother and sister as her father pushed her in front of him out of the house.

–

Hannah had never before set foot inside the chapel her father attended. One of the prime tenets of the religious sect to which he belonged was that the role of the husband was to guide his wife and any other female members of the household in religious observance and hence all Hannah's knowledge of the Bible had come entirely from him. The premises used by the brethren were strictly a male-only province.

The illicit reading of library books had given her clear awareness that in the wider world things were done very differently and, piqued by curiosity, she had occasionally slipped inside a church – mostly a Catholic one near her home – to see for herself what they were like. She had only dared to go in when there was no service, sitting at the back, enjoying the quiet, the scent of incense still in the air from an earlier Mass mingling with the perfume from the flowers on the altar. She would stare, in fascination, at the painted statues, the stations of the cross, the rows of wooden benches and the ornately carved altar with its shining tabernacle. There was something beautiful and mysterious about the place and on the odd occasion when she had a spare coin she always lit a candle.

Today, as her father walked briskly with her to his place of worship, she therefore expected it to look something like that church – a place designed to reflect and celebrate the glory of God. Her expectation was confounded when she entered the small wooden building that resembled the kind of hut Boy Scouts and Girl Guides might use. Inside, it was empty, apart from a half-circle of wooden chairs, and a lectern placed at the top.

As she entered the room with Dawson, the heads of the men seated in the semi-circle all turned to look at her. Her father took one of the few empty chairs. Hannah hesitated, unsure whether to sit on one of the others, both of which were a distance from the one Dawson had taken. For a moment she thought of turning on her heels and running but knew she had no chance of escape with all these men ready to chase after her. And another look from her father chilled her to the bone.

Her dilemma was resolved when the pastor appeared from behind a curtain at the rear of the room and indicated that she kneel on the floor in front of him. Conscious of the many pairs of eyes trained on her, and still wanting to get up and run out the room, she felt like St Joan bound to the stake – but without the consolation of belief in her imminent eternal salvation. Why hadn't she realised her father would do this – use the element of surprise to force the issue? If only she'd run away, hidden in a corner of a warehouse until Will's ship returned. What a fool she had been.

Pastor Henderson's voice veered between a low monotonous drone and near hysterical hectoring. She wasn't entirely sure what he was speaking about, but she knew it was in some way designed to demonstrate to her that her presence and her personal feelings were of little or no consequence to the men gathered around.

Oh, where was Will? When would he find out what had happened to her? Would he even find out at all? But she knew that he would. And she knew it would be too late. He would go to her house if she failed to appear on the shore or on the dockside and her mother would tell him she had been married off to somebody else. She suppressed a sob. If only he could appear now – before it was too late – burst through the door, sweep her up and take her to safety, away from the hostility of these grim-faced men and her husband-to-be.

And what of him? Of Samuel Henderson? She lifted her eyes from the rough wooden floor and tried to spot him, but without lifting her head, which she feared would be interpreted as disrespect, all she could see was a curving row of feet, all uniform in their polished black lace-ups. Which were his?

After what seemed an eternity that was a slow torture and yet which she wanted to prolong as long as possible – buying time for the impossible dream of Will somehow coming to rescue her – she was told to stand up. Her head spun as she righted herself and at last, she was able to look around. Sam Henderson was now standing beside her, his face as unreadable as a marble statue, his expression frozen in a fixed stare into the middle distance.

Henderson senior's voice broke through her thoughts. "'A virtuous woman is a crown to her husband:'" he intoned "'but she that maketh him ashamed is as rotten-ness in his bones.'' Proverbs Chapter 12, Verse 4'. She thought of the words Sam had spoken when they were in the back room at her home – about their fathers being like sepulchres painted white on the outside but filled with rotting bones within. The rottenness he had referred to, arose from their hypocrisy not from the shameful behaviour of any woman. And what might constitute shameful behaviour anyway? But she knew the answer to that one already. To these men, shame came from women who spoke their minds, who dared to read books, who showed even the slightest hint of disobedience – in fact who did anything that was not a direct fulfilment of the wishes of a man.

The pastor had now moved on to a subject that made her feel even more uncomfortable – and looking sideways at Sam she saw he was squirming too. This time, he quoted Proverbs 5 "'May your fountain be blessed, and may you rejoice in the wife of your youth. A loving deer – may her breasts satisfy you always, may you ever be intoxicated with her love.'" The pastor looked around at the assembled men and Hannah could feel all their eyes upon her. It was worse than the catcalls and wolf-whistles of the dockers. She knew they were all imagining her naked breasts. All except Sam Henderson. He was studying the floor and she could see his face was angry.

Henderson went on to pronounce the couple man and wife. The actual marriage part of the ceremony was so brief as to be almost an afterthought. At this point, the pastor signalled Hannah and Samuel to follow him and he led them over to a table at the side of the room where they were to sign the marriage registry. Dawson signed too and two other men acted as witnesses. The deed was done. She was now Mrs Samuel Henderson.

No ring. No flowers. No bridesmaids. No wedding breakfast. No gown. Not even the presence of her mother and sister. Was she really married? All there was to show for it was her signature in a book.

The men gathered around Sam to shake his hand and wish him well. Her future happiness was evidently inconsequential. She stood to one side waiting, her eyes still stinging, the pain in her arm smarting and her spirits lower than they had ever been in her life.

Chapter Nineteen

Hannah experienced no immediate difference in her status as a married woman compared to her single state. When the wedding ceremony, such as it was, had concluded, she was ignored by all present.

Sam approached her, his face gloomy.

'What happens now?' she asked him.

'I'm to take you back to our house. I think my father's rather hoping you'll give it a good clean.' He had the grace to look apologetic.

She turned to Sam. 'What about you?'

He looked at her blankly. 'What about me? I'm going back to work.'

'I don't even know what you do.' She looked across the room nervously to where her father was now deep in conversation with the pastor and three other men.

'I'm an accounts clerk,' Sam said. 'I work for the council and I need to get back there now.' He stretched his lips into a semblance of a smile. 'I'll drop you off, then see you at home tonight.'

They took the bus. She had no idea where Walton was or how to get there. Nor was there any question of her going back to Bootle. Not with Sam guarding her and not so much as a ha'penny in her pocket. Her offer to go alone was met with a refusal — Sam was clearly under orders. He was silent on the trip, evidently irritated at the need to escort her and delay his arrival at work further. Hannah looked out of the window of the bus, trying to gain her bearings, hoping to recognise a landmark and find out where exactly she was and how far away from her mother and sister in Bootle and the docks. But what was the point of knowing that. She was stuck now. None of them could help her. She was now Mrs Samuel Henderson and might as well start getting used to that, no matter how much her heart screamed against it.

Descending from the bus at Walton Vale, they trudged up the road to their destination in Moss Lane. Hannah's spirits were at rock bottom. What lay ahead? Tied in marriage to a man who clearly wished he wasn't married to her – or possibly married at all, and living under the roof of the stern and cold pastor, doubtless subject to frequent tirades from him. Her father had barely spoken a word to her after the ceremony. No affectionate embrace – not even a handshake or a word of congratulations. There was no doubt in her mind that he viewed her nuptials as akin to a business transaction.

For a moment, Hannah wished that she'd never set eyes on Will Kidd as, if she hadn't, her present situation might not seem quite so terrible. But she *had* met him, fallen for him and couldn't stop thinking about him in every waking moment. Why was God so cruel to put this man in her path, let her fall in love with him and then send her away from him? It was a nasty vicious joke. Just the kind of trick that the vengeful petty God her father so respected would play. A God who'd order a man to murder his own son and then send an angel in the nick of time to admit he'd been testing him. God didn't even have the courage to tell Abraham himself, leaving it to an angel to do his dirty work.

Hannah supposed it was at least some consolation to know that she had loved and been loved in return. But unable to show that love, all she had now of Will was the memory of a few tender kisses, and a proposal of marriage she couldn't act upon.

Sam halted outside a big house. The Laurels was at least as substantial as the former Morton family home, Trevelyan House. An imposing, detached, Victorian villa, it was partly concealed from the road by an untrimmed privet hedge. The garden had once been laid to lawn but was now reduced to a scruffy tangle of weeds and litter blown in from the street. Unlike the surrounding houses, all smartly painted and with neat gardens, this one had an air of neglect.

'I'm going now. I'm late. See you this evening. She'll let you in.' Then he was gone.

Hannah stood on the front path. Who was 'she'? The pastor was a widower, but perhaps he kept a servant.

Ringing the doorbell produced no jangle, so taking a deep breath, she knocked on the tarnished brass knocker. Sensing movement inside, she waited in the porch, anxiety eating away at her. The door opened and a blonde woman leaned against the frame, looking Hannah up and down. 'And who might you be?'

'I've just married Samuel. I'm the new Mrs Henderson,' she said, thinking as she said them that the words sounded ridiculous.

To her astonishment the woman burst out laughing. 'Are you indeed? Nobody tells me nothing.'

'I'm sorry. Who are you? Nobody tells me anything either.' Hannah smiled at her.

Ignoring the question, the woman said, 'You'd better come in.' She stepped back into the gloomy interior, holding the door for Hannah to enter. Inside there was a stale smell of boiled cabbage.

'No bags?'

It was the first time Hannah realised she hadn't even brought a change of clothes. It had all happened so quickly. 'No, I will need to collect my things from home.' Again she felt foolish saying it.

'And where might home be? Well – until now.' The woman chuckled.

'Bootle. Quite near the Huskisson Dock.'

'Not that it means anything to me. I'm a Londoner.' She offered no explanation as to why she was here or what her role in the house was. 'I s'pose you could do with a cup of the old Rosy Lee.' By now they were in the kitchen. A wooden clothes rack hung overhead, and Hannah had to step aside to avoid the drips from the assorted stockings, socks and underwear hanging there. The woman told her to sit and went into the scullery beyond to make the tea.

Hannah sat down, then jumped with fright as she felt something brush against her ankle. A ginger cat. It slid past her other leg and then wandered into the scullery too. She heard the woman open the back door. 'Git out of 'ere, you little bugger!'

She returned with two cups of tea, minus the saucers. 'Saves washing up,' she said. Once seated she offered her hand to Hannah. 'I'm Nancy Cunningham. But you can call me Nance. Everybody does.'

Accepting the handshake, she answered, 'I'm Hannah.'

While she sipped her tea, Hannah studied the woman. She was whip thin, sharp-boned, her narrow mouth heavily coated in bright red lipstick that had strayed beyond the natural line of her lips onto the surrounding skin, possibly by design. Her hair looked as though it had more than a passing acquaintance with the peroxide bottle. Dark roots showed in a wide band where the hair parted. There was a roller behind her right ear that she had evidently forgotten to remove when she'd brushed her hair out that morning. Hannah guessed her age at between thirty-five and forty.

'You've left a curler in your hair,' she pointed out.

Nance lifted a hand and removed the offending article. 'Always doing that. No bleeding mirrors in this house. Thanks.' She looked at Hannah in undisguised appraisal. 'So you've got yourself hitched to young Sam then. Hadn't got him down as the marrying kind. If you get what I mean.' She gave a little snigger. 'He kept quiet about you then. When did it happen? Short engagement, I presume?'

Hannah was embarrassed. 'We were married this morning. It was all quite sudden. Our fathers are friends.'

'Don't worry, love. I imagine neither of you had a lot of say in the matter.' Another little guffaw. 'Not exactly romantic is it? Did they send you home on your own in a taxi then?'

Hannah felt herself blushing again. 'We got the bus. He came with me as far as the front gate.'

The woman burst out laughing then stopped herself and gave Hannah what appeared to be a kind smile. ''Ow old are you, love?'

'Twenty-two. Almost.'

'Going on fifteen. Where did you get that dress? Looks like something my late mother would wear.'

Indignant, Hannah said nothing.

'Maybe I'll see if I can find summat to fit you. Us girls 'ave to stick together.'

'Excuse me, Nance, are you Mr Henderson's daughter? Sam's sister?'

The woman roared laughing again. 'Blimey! You got to be joking! I'm his floozie. His bit on the side. His fancy woman.'

'Sam's?' Hannah struggled to hide her shock.

'Gawd, no! The old man's. The main man.'

'Mr Henderson! But he's a pastor, a man of God. Surely that can't be right. Isn't it adultery if you're not married?'

'More than plain adultery, girl. He's a walking advertisement for all the sins he condemns from his platform. Kinky ain't the word. Then he toddles out of here and goes to that chapel of his and tells the buggers they'll all burn in hell for doing half of what he gets up to.'

Hannah's face burned in embarrassment. 'I'm sorry. I didn't mean to pry.'

'Look, love, I don't believe in beating about the bush. I came to Liverpool to get away from a rotten husband. Used to beat the blazes out of me, so I upped and left him. Came to Liverpool because it was as far away as I could afford to pay for a train ticket.' She twirled the lid of the teapot around idly. 'To cut a long story short I ended up on the game. His Lordship was one of my best customers.'

'His Lordship?'

'Mr High-and-Mighty Henderson. Old Fire and Brimstone himself.'

Hannah gasped. 'The pastor went with prostitutes?'

237

The woman laughed. 'You really are an innocent abroad aren't you? He was legendary. But he has some unusual tastes, shall we say? Not all the girls were happy. I'm up for anything if the money's right and there's no bruising. So he always asked for me. After a while he decided to cut out the middle man and moved me in here. For his exclusive use.'

Hannah was lost for words. She stared at Nance across the table.

'Never met a prozzie before?'

She shook her head.

'Not that I am any more. A kept woman is more accurate. But as far as you're concerned I'm 'is late wife's sister.'

'His sister-in-law?'

'He'd like me to say I'm the 'ousekeeper, but I told him I'm not 'aving that as it might give people the idea that I'm going to be doing the cooking and cleaning. One thing you need to get straight right from the start, Mrs Hannah Henderson, is I ain't doing no 'ousework. That's strictly your department.'

'I see.'

'Now, mind you don't let on I told you all this. His Lordship wouldn't like you to know about his inclinations. He likes to keep up the appearance of a man of God. Although he makes so much bloody noise I imagine the whole bleeding street knows what he gets up to.'

'So, he isn't a man of God then?'

'He is when it suits him. It can be a lucrative busi-ness, religion. At least he's found a way to make a tidy profit from it. Not that I'm supposed to know about such

238

matters.' She got up from the table. 'Right. If you've finished your tea, I'll show you around.'

Ignoring the rest of the ground floor, Nance led her upstairs. 'He keeps the ground floor rooms for 'is own use. The front one is for when men from his church come to visit. He sometimes 'as meetings with them. And then there's the drawing room and study. Keep out of the study. Well, if you're smart you'll keep out of all of them. Stick to the parlour with me, girl, if you want to keep out of trouble.'

The upstairs landing was dark, with heavy, begrimed net curtains on the only window which was anyway shaded by a tree outside. All the doors were closed.

'Bathroom in 'ere,' she said. 'Only use it when he's not at home. There's a privy in the back yard for when he is.' Hannah looked inside. The bath was heavily stained, the linoleum floor covering cracked, and a couple of greying towels were slung over a rail. 'You'll need to do some washing if you want a clean towel. Like I say, I'm not the bleedin' 'ousekeeper. You can have a bath once a week, but remember, only when he's out. He'll not be pleased if he wants to take a shit and you're soaking in the bath.'

Ignoring the unpleasant image that conjured up, Hannah asked, 'Is he out a lot?'

'Both of them are. Gawd knows where – Sam goes to evening classes, I think. I'm certainly not complaining when they're out. It's nice to 'ave some peace and quiet. Sometimes I go to the flicks and there's a gang of us girls who have a game of bingo every now and then.'

She opened another door off the landing. 'This is me in 'ere. I insisted on 'having me own room. I do what I 'ave to do for him but I'm darned if I'm going to spend all night in his bed, kept awake by his snoring.' She rolled her eyes. 'I 'ad enough of that when I had a ruddy husband. No thank you!' Before Hannah could look inside, Nance had pulled the door shut again. She indicated the adjacent room. 'In 'ere's His Lordship's room. Biggest in the house. Out of bounds to you, of course. There's stuff in there you're better off not seeing.'

Hannah shuddered. The idea of crossing the threshold into the pastor's bedroom was not something she was tempted by.

'This here's a box room. It's full of junk as far as I can tell.' She held the door open wide and Hannah saw a dismantled bed frame, a collection of battered looking suitcases and trunks, and several tea chests. 'It would make a nice nursery.' She gave her a nudge in the ribs.

Nance flung open the door to the last room. 'And I suppose you'll be in here. With him. Sam.' Inside, was a neat, sparsely furnished space, containing only a brass bed, a rug on one side, a washstand in the corner and a night table with a lamp and a copy of the Bible.

Hannah tried not to think about lying in that bed beside Sam Henderson. The whole day had been surreal so far and she didn't want to imagine having to climb under the bedclothes to spend the night with a virtual stranger. Her knowledge of sex was limited to what she had read in books and the noises she had heard from her parents' room – which in recent years had mostly ceased or been replaced by screams and blows. In the books she read, the details were usually skated over, but she got the impression that the participants were overwhelmed by a consuming passion. That was something she found impossible to imagine would occur between herself and

Sam, but she'd recently begun to anticipate it with a frisson when thinking about Will.

Remembering she had no luggage, she turned to Nance. 'I have to go home and collect a bag. I don't even have my toothbrush or nightgown.'

Nance laughed. 'A woman doesn't usually need a nightgown on her wedding night, love.' She paused. 'But then again since it's Sammy Boy, maybe you will. Somehow, I can't see him as the sort to tear a girl's clothes off. Much the pity, as he's a good-looking lad. I'd rather have a bit of the old slap 'n tickle with him than with his old man. But somehow I don't reckon slap 'n tickle's his thing.'

She gave Hannah a quizzical look. 'How well do you know him?'

Hannah walked over to the window and looked out. The view was over the street and the overgrown front garden. She turned back to face Nance. 'I don't know him at all. Before today I'd met him once and that was brief.'

Nance gave a long tuneful whistle. 'Blimey, love. How do you feel about that then?'

'If you really want to know. I don't feel happy at all. In fact, right now, I wish I were dead.'

Nance moved across the room and gave her a quick hug. 'It's not as bad as all that, love. Could be a whole lot worse. He's a decent enough fellow, is Sam. Always civil. Minds his own business. He's clean. Polite. Dresses smartly. Has a job. Quite a good one, I believe. As long as you keep out of the old man's way. Yes, you could have done a lot worse. And unlike my ex, I can't see him lifting a hand to clobber you. Not Sam.'

'But he's a stranger to me.'

Nance sat down on the bed and patted the candlewick bedspread to signal Hannah should sit beside her. 'Listen love, don't expect me to feel a lot of sympathy for you on that count. When you're on the game, every man's a stranger until you build up your regulars. And a lot of them are old, smelly, foul-breathed, ugly, and expect you to do all kinds of things for them. When you're desperate and need the cash, you just have to get on with it.'

Hannah was indignant. 'How can you possibly compare being a prostitute to being married?'

'Because I've been both. You, on the other hand have been neither.' She patted Hannah on the knee. 'When it comes down to it, they're all just men. Most of them only want one thing. And my guess is Sam Henderson will neither be beating you up like my husband used to do to me whenever he'd had a skinful – which was most nights – or expecting you to do the kind of kinky stuff his father expects me to do.' She got up. 'Put it this way, love. I think you'll be lucky if he gets it up at all for you.'

'What do you mean?'

'I mean if he manages to "do the dirty" with you at all, you'll be doing well. I'll bet if he can get you up the duff he'll leave you in peace after that. Once he can show his father he's produced a child. So you'd better hope that happens sooner rather than later. Now, I'm going to see if I can find you a nice nightie to wear tonight.' She looked back and winked as she left the room.

Chapter Twenty

As soon as the *Arklow* docked, Will couldn't disembark fast enough. His head was filled with thoughts of Hannah and eagerness to see her again and tell her that everything was arranged for her in Dublin. He wondered if she had tried to get down to see him before he sailed and imagined her arriving after the ship had departed. More often than not they were late setting off, delays caused by all manner of things, but this time the ship's master had decided to cast off more than an hour earlier than planned, with the intention of avoiding the worst of the weather, forecast for later that day. As it happened, they'd hit the squalls anyway and Will had felt angry, frustrated and out of sorts until the kindness and practicality of the O'Connors had lifted his spirits again.

Now he was going to put all that behind him. He wasn't going to be put off by all the talk of how monstrous Hannah's father was. In fact, it made him more determined to get her away from him. Once he'd found out that Dawson had raped Elizabeth he wanted to tear the man limb from limb. Lovely Elizabeth, the woman who had lit up his life during those last years in Australia. If he could rape her and break her sister's arm, what might he do to Hannah? No. It was right that he act fast and get her out of the country in the next few days.

After they were married he might even give up the sea. They could move to America, or he could take her home to Australia. He realised it was the first time since he'd left it eleven years ago that he had been able to think of Australia as home. Anywhere where Hannah was would be home to him from now on.

He tried to recreate Wilton's Creek in his mind's eye. The long low wooden house with its veranda, the eucalyptus trees, the scrub, the creek where he fished, the well-worn track leading to town. But the picture was marred forever by the memory of his brother grabbing at Elizabeth as she was hanging out washing, by the anger that had risen inside Will as he lunged towards Nat to pull him away from her, by the pain of a cold steel blade sinking into his body, by the blackness that followed. No. Even now, Wilton's Creek was contaminated forever to Will as the scene of his father's last moments of liberty before being led away to jail and his eventual fate.

Instead, Will thought of the canyon. The beauty of the blue haze that rose above the sea of gum trees that covered the craggy mountains and gave them their name. The sound of the waterfalls, tumbling down through rocks and ferns. The splash of colour from the rainbow lorikeets, a sudden flash of white or green from a parrot. The clean crisp unpolluted air. The sight of a possum disappearing up a tree, or a kangaroo, disturbed as it grazed, hopping away into the distance.

Now, here on the Liverpool docks, the air was heavy with the smell of diesel. All around were coal blackened buildings, the clank of the overhead railway as it thundered past, car horns, the rattle of trams, whistles and curses from the dockers as they went about their work, the long low lament of a foghorn and the feeling of damp and drizzle under his collar. He longed to be away from Liverpool and determined that he would convince Hannah to leave with him at once. Regardless of what she had told him, he was going to the house in Bootle now and he wasn't going to leave without her.

–

Will sat at the table with his head in his hands. In the background he was aware of the rattle of cups and the hiss of a boiling kettle but all he could think about was Hannah. Lost to him forever.

Sarah returned with a tray of tea and poured it. 'Here, drink this, Will. It will make you feel better. There's lots of sugar in. Good for shock.' She handed him the cup, then put the freshly-laundered handkerchief he'd lent her last time on the table in front of him.

'How's it possible? Why so fast? Why didn't she tell me it would happen so soon?'

Sarah shook her head. 'None of us knew it would happen so quickly. I'd no idea he'd arranged everything. When the man and his father came here to meet her, we thought we'd still have some time. I told Hannah to get herself down to the dock to find you but she was too late. You'd already sailed. Then two days later while we were sitting here eating our breakfast he told us she was to be married that day.'

'Couldn't you have stopped it?' He thumped the table in frustration. 'Couldn't you have stood up in church and yelled out an objection when they asked if anyone has just cause? You know how it works – I saw a film where that happened.'

Sarah dropped her eyes. 'I wasn't even there. At my own daughter's wedding. I doubt they'd have asked that anyway. It was all done at the place where my husband worships.' She stretched her lips into a narrow line. 'They were married by her new husband's father. He's the minister.'

'Is that even legal?'

She shrugged. 'Apparently so. Not that it would stop Charles if it wasn't.'

'No, but it would be grounds for annulling the marriage. Wouldn't it? Surely?' He looked at her in desperation. 'I've spent my whole adult life expecting to be alone and now that I've met the one woman I love she's stolen from me.' He slammed his fist into the table. 'Where is she? I have to find her? I don't care whether she's married legally or not. I'm going to find her and get her away.'

Sarah shut her eyes. 'I don't know. All I know is the name of her husband, Samuel Henderson. She's living with him and his father but I haven't a clue where that might be. My husband refuses to tell me anything.'

Will squeezed his hands into tight fists, frustration mounting. 'For Pete's sake, Sarah. How is this even possible? You're her mother! You of all people should be allowed to know where she is.'

'He says I can see her eventually when she's settled into her new life. He said it would be "disruptive" for us to meet sooner. Says she needs time to adjust.' Sarah began to cry. 'Oh God! How could this be happening. My daughter.' Her sobbing intensified, and Will pushed the clean handkerchief back across the table. While she wiped her eyes, he drank some tea, desperately trying to think of a plan.

'When do you sail again?' Sarah asked.

'Tonight. But I'm not going. How can I?'

'You must. There's nothing you can do here. While you're gone I'll try to work on him. Try to find out where she is. I can surely find out the address. There must be directories. There can't be that many Samuel Hendersons in Liverpool. But it will be his father's name, won't it? I don't know what that is. Charles always refers to him as the pastor.' She rubbed at her cheeks with the damp handkerchief. 'I can find out. I'll do it. You go to Ireland and I promise you, I'll have tracked her down by the time you come back.'

'I had a plan. I was going to bring her over to Dublin. I'd got it all worked out. Too bloody late – sorry Sarah. I didn't mean to swear in front of you.'

'Swear away. You don't shock me.' She smiled for the first time. 'I've let that pig of a husband walk all over me and my daughters for too long. I'm getting my life back. And somehow I'm going to help you get Hannah back.'

–

Hannah assisted Nance in preparing the supper – with the older woman making it clear that in future this would be entirely Hannah's responsibility. 'Shopping too. You won't need any cash as there's accounts at the greengrocer, the butcher and the general store, but mind you watch the pennies. His Nibs settles up at the end of the month.'

Nance evidently preferred not to use whatever was Mr Henderson's Christian name. Hannah wondered what it was but decided not to enquire.

The two women stood side-by-side in the scullery, Hannah peeling potatoes while Nance slow-boiled a piece of ham and washed a cabbage.

'I presume you know how to cook?'

'I did it at home. But nothing fancy.'

'Well, that's great. Means I get my life back.' She didn't elucidate what that might entail. 'And don't worry – His Nibs don't like fancy. Meat and two veg usually. Fish once a week but never on Friday as that's Papist he reckons. He can't abide Roman Catholics. I've never told him I was born one.'

'Are you religious, Nance?'

'Me? You're cracking jokes! I reckon God gave up on me when I had to go on the game. And I gave up on him when he let the bastard I was wed to beat the living daylights out of me night after night. What about you?'

'My father is one of the brethren who follow Mr Henderson's ministry. I've been familiar with the Bible since I was a toddler. The only book allowed in the house.'

Nance didn't show any surprise. 'You believe all that stuff?'

'I believe in God. Well most of the time… sometimes I find my belief gets tested rather too much.'

'Like now?'

Hannah nodded.

'So which one's your father? What's 'is name?'

'Charles Dawson.'

Nance gave one of her signature long whistles. 'I'd never have guessed that.'

'You know him?'

'Oh, yes, I certainly know him.' Nance looked as though she were about to say something but changed her mind. Eventually she said, 'He's been here to the house. Henderson sometimes has meetings here. They're friends.' She put the lid on the pan of ham, turned the gas down low and told Hannah to keep an eye on the supper. 'I'll see you later. I'm going for a nap. He likes it on the table at seven o'clock sharp. Except Fridays when it's six-thirty. Cutlery's in the drawer over there.' Then she was gone.

Chapter Twenty-One

Henderson senior arrived home punctually before dinner that evening. He took his place at the head of the table, with Nance seated to his left. There was an empty space to his right where the absent Sam was to sit. Hannah took the chair beyond that.

When she put his plate in front of the pastor, he said, 'You've met my sister-in-law then?'

'Yes.' She thought it a stupid question.

'Do as she tells you. She's in charge. Don't go getting ideas or trying to throw you weight around.'

He began to eat, masticating loudly. Hannah was nauseated. He was a big man, jowly and clean-shaven with beetling eyebrows, cavernous nostrils, steel grey hair that was cut long so it went over his collar, and cold grey eyes. Sam must have inherited his mother's looks. Hannah wondered how Nance could bear to share a bed with him and shuddered to imagine what were the acts she was expected to perform with him. It wouldn't surprise her if one day Nance enlightened her – but she hoped that day was a long way off.

After a few minutes, Henderson looked up from his meal and spoke directly to Hannah. 'Where is my son?'

'I don't know, sir. He's not returned from work yet.'

'Make it your business to know. Now that he's a married man I expect you to ensure he's home at the appointed hour. It's your responsibility as a wife.'

She swallowed, bewildered by her new situation and baffled as to how she could be held responsible for the late arrival of the husband she didn't know at all.

The three of them ate the remainder of the meal in silence, the ugly brass carriage clock on the mantelpiece ticking loudly, as though to underline the absence of conversation.

Hannah was washing up the supper plates in the scullery when Nance came in. She jerked her head up at the ceiling. 'Time for me to go to work.' Winking at Hannah, she added. 'If Sam's not in by ten o'clock, you can go to bed, but you'd better start praying he is or there'll be hell to pay and I'm not taking bets as to who'll get the blame for that. I'll give you a wee clue: I'm looking at her right now.'

Hannah sat in the parlour drinking a cup of tea. Above her head she was unable to avoid hearing a range of noises, from furniture being moved, to suppressed cries and groans, deep moaning, then after a while the sound of loud animal grunting and eventually the rhythmic creaking of bedsprings and a sound that she realised must be the headboard banging loudly and rapidly against the wall. The whole noisy episode lasted over an hour. When it finished, there was a long silence then the sound of a flushing toilet and a series of doors opening and closing.

Her situation was bizarre and intolerable. If her father knew what kind of immoral things went on under this roof, he would surely never have expected her to marry into the Henderson family. She had to escape. What was to stop her walking out of the house? Now. Before Sam returned and while her new father-in-law and Nance were sleeping. No matter that she'd no idea how to get home. If she walked for long enough and kept heading in a downhill direction she had to reach the Mersey eventually and she could find her way home to Bootle from there. Once she'd told her father what was going on here at The Laurels, he'd have to agree that she couldn't stay with the Hendersons, and since the marriage was unconsummated, he could arrange for it to be annulled. Filled with a sense of purpose and hope, she got up from the table, washed her teacup and saucer and tiptoed from the room.

Creeping along the dark hallway she fumbled in the vestibule for her coat and slipped it on. She reached for the large doorknob and turned it but the front door didn't budge. It must be locked with a deadbolt and there was no sign of a key. She went back along the hall, treading softly, shoes in her hand, and through into the scullery where she tried the back door. The same. Locked and no key. All the downstairs windows were painted closed and she couldn't shift the sashes. She pulled open the kitchen drawers and cupboards, hunting for the keys. She looked underneath the tea towel hanging on the back of the scullery door thinking they might be on the hook there, but nothing. A search of the hall and vestibule produced nothing either.

Returning to the kitchen table, she sat under the canopy of Nance's now dry stockings still dangling from the wooden drying rack, and wept her heart out.

Sam Henderson let himself in through the front door at a quarter to midnight. Without coming through to the back of the house where Hannah was sitting, he went straight upstairs and she heard the creak of the bedroom door. What should she do? Follow him up there? Stay down here all night?

She waited for half an hour in the darkened parlour surrounded by a deathly silence, then, exhausted, crept up the stairs. Sam must surely be asleep by now. After quickly undressing in the dark, she pulled the flimsy night dress Nance had lent her, over her head and slipped into the bed beside Sam, trying not to disturb him.

His whispered voice sounded eerie in the darkness and made her jump. 'You were still downstairs then? I thought you must have gone.'

She told him she'd been waiting up for him in the back parlour.

'I'm sorry. I didn't want to come home tonight. I've nothing against you, Hannah. You seem a nice girl. I just don't want to be married to you. Well, to anybody.'

Hannah thought they must look like a pair of Egyptian mummies lying side-by-side on their backs, motionless, both staring up towards the now invisible ceiling in the pitch-dark bedroom.

'I don't want to be married either,' she said.

'Well, we understand each other at least.'

She hesitated then said, 'I did try to leave tonight. After your father had gone to bed. But the doors were all locked.'

He twisted onto his side in the bed beside her. She could feel his eyes on her but the room was too dark for them to see each other. 'He'll have guessed you'd try to do that so he locked them. It's usually just on the Yale. Lucky I had my full set. What would you have done if you'd got out anyway? Where would you go?'

'Back home. To my family.'

She heard him snort. 'You can't do that, Hannah. You need to get used to the idea. We're stuck with each other.'

'Where did you go tonight? Your father was angry that I didn't know. He told me it was my job to know.'

'I'm sorry.' He rolled onto his back again. His voice was a disembodied whisper. 'Look, I have a proposal to make to you. I promise to leave you alone if you'll cover for me.'

'What do you mean?'

'When I go out at night.'

Hannah was completely bewildered.

'Look, I can't be a proper husband to you, Hannah. Do you understand what I'm saying? You do know what we are supposed to do as husband and wife?'

Hannah said nothing, too confused to answer.

'I'm talking about how babies are made.' He sounded as embarrassed as she felt.

'Yes,' she whispered into the dark. 'I do know.'

'If you cover for me and say I'm at evening school when I go out in the evenings, I promise to leave you alone. I think that's what most women prefer don't they, given the choice?'

'I don't know. Do they?' She wanted to cry but swallowed and bit her lip to hold back the tears.

She wanted to be home in her bedroom with Judith beside her instead of this peculiar man. Even more, she wanted to be lying beside Will Kidd. Somehow, she knew that being 'left alone' by Will was not something she would want – even if her lack of knowledge of the finer details of what they would do was sketchy. She just knew she wanted him. To be close to him. Wrapped around him. To have him holding her and loving her. But she was never going to lie beside Will. Never feel his arms around her. Never discover what it would be like to make love to him. Now, it seemed she wasn't even going to discover what it was like to be with a man at all. Hannah didn't know whether to be grateful or sad. Marriage to a man who didn't even want to father a child with her. Who didn't want to touch her, caress her, kiss her.

At last she said, 'Don't you want to have children? Why did you marry me then?'

He gave a long, exaggerated sigh. 'I did it because of my father. Look, Hannah, I can't think about this now. It's all a mess and I'm dog tired. Go to sleep and we'll talk tomorrow.'

The following day was a Saturday and over breakfast Sam announced that he and Hannah were going out for a walk. Nance gave Hannah a cheeky smile and the pastor grunted what she assumed to be approval.

They walked side-by-side through the streets of red brick houses. The homes, although mostly smaller than the villa that was the Henderson dwelling, were bigger than the terraced house she had lived in and looked more cared for than those in Bluebell Street. Some had tiny patches of garden behind low red brick walls between house and pavement.

Once they were five minutes away from The Laurels, he turned into a road that passed along one side of a public garden surrounded by privet hedges and consisting of gravel paths and rose beds. He led her inside and they sat down on a bench.

Sam cleared his throat then said, 'Here's what I propose. I'll come home after work and eat with you and my father and his tart, then, after he's gone out or upstairs,

I'll be going out myself, but I don't want them to know. Most evenings he attends his so-called chapel anyway. I need you to pretend that I'm at home all night even when I'm not.' He took a pack of filter-tipped cigarettes from his jacket pocket and lit one. 'If I'm not around and he asks where I am, you'll need to tell him I'm at my evening class. I'm meant to be doing more accountancy examinations. And if he asks, tell him I was home and in bed by ten o'clock. But he won't ask. As you'll probably have gathered, on the nights when he's at home he's far too occupied behind a locked bedroom door with his mistress to be aware that I'm not home.'

'Where will you be?'

'Out and about. Seeing friends. You don't need to worry about that.'

She turned sideways and looked at him. His face was handsome, a long aquiline nose, clear blue eyes, a chiselled jaw. His blond hair looked the sort of hair it would be nice to touch. Soft. Silky. 'Do you already have a wife, Sam? A secret one?'

He gave a little guffaw, smiled at her, his eyes sad and then to her surprise he leaned forward and kissed her lightly on the brow. 'No, I have no other wife but you, Hannah. No girlfriend. No secret woman. Only you.'

'Then I don't understand.'

He smiled at her again and shook his head. 'Such innocence.' He took her hand. 'I may as well tell you the whole truth, if you promise not to be shocked and never to let my father know I've told you this.'

She nodded, fearing what was to follow.

'I don't have feelings for women. Not the kind of feelings men are meant to feel for women. I prefer men.'

Hannah gave a gasp of surprise.

'As you can imagine, this is not something my father is willing to accept. I've had the Book of Leviticus and passages about the eternal damnation that awaits me, drummed into me until I could recite them backwards. I have tried, believe me, I have tried to be otherwise, but it's not in my nature.'

'Have you explained that to your father? That you've tried to change but you can't?'

'Time and again. He won't accept it. To him it's the worst possible abomination. He believes it's pure wilfulness on my part. He says if I go with a woman I will start to feel differently. But to be honest, I don't think I could face it.' He leaned forward, head in his hands. 'It wouldn't be natural.' He coughed and ground out his cigarette stub under his heel. 'For years I kept it hidden. My father either didn't know or chose not to believe it. But then there was a threat of scandal. He had to pay to hush it up and that's when he decided that if I were to be married it would solve the problem. Or at least cover it up. So, you, poor Hannah, are my cover. Since I am a respectable married man, I can't possibly be one of those terrible perverts.'

Hannah could hardly breathe. She was completely unprepared for dealing with something like this. It was outside her sphere of knowledge – certainly not something ever discussed in her home. She had known no one who was like this. Her own reading of the Bible and other books had never revealed any example of a man preferring other men. She started to wonder if it was naivety on her part. 'But how is it possible?' she said. 'Is there something wrong with you?'

'My father would have you believe so. Your father too. The Book of Leviticus says, "If a man lies with a male as with a woman, both of them have committed an abomination; they shall surely be put to death; their blood is upon them."'

Hannah gasped, horrified. 'If the Bible says that—'

'The Bible says lots of things that I choose to ignore. And it says things that are contradictory. Remember David and Jonathan: "Thy love to me was wonderful, passing the love of women".'

Hannah squeezed her hands together, twisting and turning her fingers. 'It's too much to take in. I don't know what to say. I know nothing of the real world. Only what I managed to read in books.' She was trying to think, but her brain didn't know how to compute what he had told her. 'Are you saying we will only ever be married in name?'

'I suppose I am. I'm sorry, Hannah, if that's not what you wanted.'

'And you will never have a child with me?'

'I haven't said that.' He groaned and kicked at the gravel with his foot. 'Maybe eventually. I know there will be a lot of pressure from my father for me to produce an heir. But it's not something I really want to think about now. I'm sorry, Hannah, this is evidently a big shock to you.'

'Did my father know?'

Sam didn't answer, continuing to scrape his shoe through the gravel.

'Please, did he know?'

'Yes.'

She tried to absorb this but couldn't believe that her father would have agreed for her to be married to such a man.

'Look, you might as well know everything. The whole dreadful mess. Your father is the one who found out what I was doing. He happened to see me leaving a place… somewhere where men like me go to meet each other. Your father saw me leave with another man and he followed us. He caught us… we were… we were… well, never mind what we were doing… it was in an alleyway. Late at night. Down by the docks. He made me pay him money to keep it from my father and my employers. I'd have been dismissed. I had no choice. I had to pay him.'

It was like a punch in the stomach to Hannah. 'He blackmailed you?'

'Yes, I suppose that's what you'd call it. It went on with him demanding higher sums, until I refused to pay any more so he went to my father. Told him everything and threatened to tell my employers too. Said it was his Christian duty. His moral obligation.'

Hannah felt the tears stinging her eyes, but she was determined not to shed any caused by her father. 'My father is a bad man. I didn't realise how bad until recently. I'm ashamed that I'm his daughter.'

Sam gave his head a little shake and scuffed the gravel again.

'Isn't the pastor supposed to be his friend? How could Father do that? If he believed what you were doing was wrong and against the teachings of the Bible why would he seek to profit from it by extorting money from you and your father?' Hannah felt sick to her stomach. 'So what happened then?'

'My father doesn't appreciate being blackmailed, but he didn't want word to get out that his son is a pervert. Rather than give in to the blackmail, he decided to settle the matter once and for all by buying Charles Dawson's silence with a lump sum and agreeing that you and I should be married. That way he guarantees that Dawson won't expose his daughter's husband without bringing shame on himself and his family. So, you see, this marriage is not about bringing together the offspring of two men who share a common religion. It's all about venality and greed and hypocrisy.'

The sun was shining and the little park was bathed in light that lit up the colour of the early roses. It contrasted sharply with the world of darkness that Sam had revealed to her, which Hannah had never imagined existing.

Sam reached for her hand and held it between both his. 'I'm sorry to have shattered your illusions, Hannah. I'm sorry to have had to tell you all this. You seem such a nice girl. A good woman. I hope we can be friends.'

She pulled her hand back. 'We should go to the police. We should tell them about the blackmail. We could get the marriage annulled.'

'No!' His voice was a screech and he grabbed at her hand again, jerking her round to face him. 'We can't do that. I'd be ruined. They could throw me in prison. I'd lose my job. Don't you understand, it's not just the Bible that condemns men like me – it's against the law of the land too.'

Hannah felt trapped. How could she go against Sam's wishes when it could cost him everything? Yes, she owed him nothing, but she'd already decided she liked him. Trusted him. He was as much a victim of a cruel father as she was – and in his case her own father had conspired to put him in this situation.

Sam leaned forward and reached for her hand again. 'Will you help me? Can you cover for me?' His blue eyes fixed onto her and she looked away. 'Please, Hannah.'

Realising she could use this as a bargaining chip, she turned back to face him. 'I'll need you to do something for me too.'

'Ah, the *quid pro quo*. I thought there might be one. What is it?' He smiled at her.

'Actually, it's two things. Firstly, I want to see my mother. Can you take me there? Or at least tell me how to get there. Maybe you could give me some money for bus fare.'

'Right,' he said slowly. 'I'll have to think about that. My father said he doesn't want you seeing your family until you've had plenty of time to settle in.'

Impatience hit her. 'That's ridiculous. My own mother? My sister? Anyway, I don't even have a change of clothes. Just what I'm standing up in. Nance had to lend me a nightdress.'

He looked thoughtful for a moment. 'Very well. But for goodness sake don't tell Nance, or my father will find out and then there'll be hell to pay for both of us. Here's what we'll do.' He reached into his breast pocket and pulled out a wallet. 'Here's ten shillings to be going on with. If you walk down to Walton Vale, you'll find a bus there going to Bootle. Now what's the other thing?'

Hesitating a moment, she wondered whether she should confide in him. But he had confided so much more to her. 'I want to get a letter to someone' she said.

'You've got money now for a stamp. I'll bring you paper and envelopes on Monday.'

'It's not as easy as that. It's to a ship. I have no idea how you write to a ship.'

Sam laughed and she thought how much nicer he seemed when he relaxed. 'And why would you want to write a letter to a ship?'

'I wasn't exactly honest with you when you asked if I had a boyfriend.' Tears came in a sudden rush, after being pent up so long.

'Bad as that, eh?' He passed her a handkerchief.

'I love him.'

'And he's a sailor?'

She nodded. 'We were going to be married.'

Sam squeezed his eyes tightly shut for a moment. 'I'm really sorry, Hannah. That must make everything so much worse for you.'

Blowing her nose, she said, 'I'll never see him again.'

'God, that's awful. Did your father know about this?'

'I don't know. I don't think so. If he'd known he'd have been angry. He'd have hit me again.'

'He used to hit you?' Sam's expression was appalled.

'Only once, but then he knocked Mother down and she broke her arm. He's pretending it was an accident. I'm sure if he knew about Will he'd have taken it out on me and Mother.'

Sam drew out his packet of cigarettes and lit another, puffing on it slowly. 'That's so wrong. Hitting women. How low.' He shook his head. 'What are you going to tell your sailor, Hannah, in the letter you write him.'

She started to sob again. 'I have to tell him to forget about me. To get on with his life.'

'And will he?'

Covering her face with the palms of her hands she gave a long deep sigh. 'He must. But he won't want to. That's why I have to write the letter. I have to tell him that I don't want him to try to find me.' She looked at Sam, who was listening intently. 'It will break my heart, but I have no choice. I have to make the best of the situation. Perhaps it's God's will.'

'You don't believe all that stuff!' He twisted round to face her, then turned his head to blow smoke over his shoulder away from her.

'Of course I believe in God. Just not all of the Old Testament stories. I do believe God watches over me, and if it is his plan for me to be married to you I just have to get on with it. It must mean that no matter how much I love Will, we aren't meant to be together.' She began to cry again. 'It's like my aunt, my mother's older sister. She was supposed to marry someone and he was killed in the war. I look like her. That's how I met Will. He thought I was her.'

'Can't she help you? If she knows what it's like to lose someone.'

'She's in Australia. Our family lost touch with her.' Her body was shaking as she was convulsed in tears. She tried to pull herself together. What if someone should see them. But the park was empty.

'This is all my fault. If I wasn't a queer, none of this would have happened.' He thumped his fist on the back of the bench.

'It's not your fault. If Father hadn't forced me to marry you, he'd have had me marry someone else of his choosing. He made that clear. And it could have been someone much worse than you – sorry, I didn't mean to

263

sound rude.' She gave him a watery smile. 'I thought at first he wanted me to marry your father.'

'Good grief – that would have been a fate worse than death.' He pulled a face. 'But surely you could have run away with your sailor.' He looked puzzled. 'Why didn't you?'

'I'd no idea it would all happen so quickly. I thought there'd be time. After I met you and knew it was all arranged I went to find him, but his ship had sailed. He goes back and forth to Dublin and he's usually gone for three or four days, sometimes longer. Then I thought there'd still be time. You know – while all the arrangements for our wedding were being made. I'd no idea there wouldn't even be any. Just a bunch of old men and a signature in a book.'

'Not exactly every girl's dream, eh? And I don't imagine most girls would be too thrilled about marrying a queer.'

'Is that what they call people like you?'

'We get called all manner of things. That's the mildest.' He took her chin in his hand and tilted her head back slightly. 'Such a pretty girl. It's a damn shame your beauty and charms are wasted on me.' He dropped his hand and said, 'Very well, Hannah, I will help you get a letter to your sailor. Even though it will probably break the poor chap's heart.'

A thought appeared to give him pause. 'How do I know you won't write and tell him where you are, so he can come and take you away. Your father could start the blackmail all over again.'

She hesitated, bit her lip then said, 'I'll let you read the letter.'

264

'I can't read your declarations of love. It wouldn't be right.'

'It won't be a declaration of love. That would make him more determined to come and find me. I have to make it clear that there's no hope for him. It's the only way I can protect my mother and the only way I can get on with my life. Living in hope is more than I can stand. Do you get that?'

He nodded solemnly. 'You are a very special woman, Hannah. I don't deserve you. And you deserve so much more than I can ever give you.'

'Thank you.'

He jumped up and pulled her to her feet. 'Enough of all this sadness. We need to get back. I have to pretend I'm studying and you have to cook the lunch.' He crooked an arm out to offer her. 'Shall we?'

Hannah slipped her arm through the proffered elbow and they made their way out of the park.

'I must say, you have very good taste. I have a bit of a weakness for sailors myself.'

'Really?' Her eyes widened. 'Even sailors can be…'

'Perverts? Yes, they can. Not all queers are gentle little flowers with a penchant for dressing up, you know. Some of them are very masculine. What we call in the trade, a bit of rough. I've had some regular trysts with a nice Australian sailor.'

Hannah stopped in her tracks. 'Australian?'

'Yes, we queers come in all shapes and sizes and even nationalities.'

'Will is Australian too.'

'I don't think this can be the same chap. I certainly hope not anyway. For your sake.'

'Of course he isn't.' Remembering the fervour of his kisses, she knew there was no possibility of Will harbouring any feelings for men. 'There must be lots of sailors from Australia. Liverpool has sailors from all over the world. What's his name?'

Sam frowned.

'I've told you Will's name.'

'You have an extraordinary way of winkling out all my dark secrets. His name is Jacob – but he calls himself Jake.' Sam's eyes drifted away from her to gaze into the middle distance as if recreating a memory. He's a regular at the club I go to. Short and stocky, with a dark beard and a very strong Australian accent. I can't see him as being remotely like the man of your dreams, Hannah.'

'But he's yours?'

'Yes, but I fear I'm not his.'

'What makes you say that?'

'I think he's ashamed of who he is, how he feels, what he does. Lots of queers are like that. They can't bear to face up to it. Some of them even go with women in the hope that it might cure them. It doesn't – it just makes them more unhappy. I could never do that myself.' He glanced at her sideways. 'Sorry.'

'And you said it's against the law?'

'Yes. That in itself makes some men ashamed. I suppose even me. I'd die if anyone in the office found out about me.'

'And your Jake? Does he try to keep it secret?'

'The navy is probably the most tolerant of any profession about queers. But it's one thing at sea and another on land. And Jake's out of work. He was a bosun but he

266

can't get another ship as he was blamed for a man going overboard.'

'How awful. It wasn't his fault?'

'Of course not. But he got a bad report and no one else will take him on so he's working on the docks now.'

'But if he didn't do it, why can't he argue about the bad report.'

Sam shrugged. 'They don't actually mention it in the report. They just give a rating with no explanation. He got Satisfactory which is evidently code for unsatisfactory. You have to get a Good to be hired.'

'Well, I hope he'll stop feeling ashamed of you, Sam Henderson, and start to realise how lucky he is to have someone like you.'

Sam gave a wry smile and shook his head. 'I wish. But I'm afraid his feelings for me are only in the moment. Afterwards, it's as if he wants to kill me. The other night we met on the shore. It was a beautiful moonlit night and I wanted to stay longer, talking, holding hands. Doing all the things you probably did with your sailor, but as soon as he got what he wanted he ran off and left me there.'

'I'm sorry, Sam.' She was about to tell him she hoped he'd find someone who would love him back, but it felt wrong talking like that about two men. Listening to Sam it seemed completely natural but there was something inside Hannah that made her feel that being like him must be wrong.

–

As soon as Hannah had written her letter to Will, and Sam had taken it from her and promised to find a way to deliver it, Hannah was overwhelmed with sorrow. It was as though she had slammed a heavy door on Will and it meant she would never see him again.

Knowing it had been the right thing to do to find a way to free Will from the burden of pointlessly trying to find her, didn't prevent her from imagining the pain her words would cause him. The letter was the result of several drafts and the only one that she felt certain was incapable of misinterpretation. She had made it crystal clear that she didn't want to see him again. But how fickle it must make her appear to Will, how shallow, how cruel.

Torturing herself, she tried to picture him reading it. How would he react? With anger? Sorrow? Bewilderment? She pictured his brow furrowing, his hands pushing his hair back from his forehead, then his head slumping forward, defeated. Once he read it he would hate her, despise her – and already that was how she felt about herself. Yet what choice did she have? If she didn't get in touch with him, he would surely try to find her – even though by now he must have discovered it was too late. Even if she'd tried to explain that she didn't want to be married to Sam Henderson, told him she was in a big old house in another part of the city, effectively working as an unpaid housekeeper for a corrupt preacher, his ex-prostitute mistress and his homosexual son, it would still have been too late for them.

Chapter Twenty-Two

Will was on the quayside watching the dockers unloading the *Arklow*. The short frequent runs across the Irish sea had done little to feed his sense of adventure. Crossing a murky sea, often under cover of darkness, from one English-speaking port to another with a ship full of cattle was not the stuff of dreams. The cloudless blue skies of Africa, the scent of spices and the unfamiliar smells of a vast continent were far away. Now his days were dark, drizzling, dull.

But he knew his melancholic mood was little do with these superficial complaints. Were Hannah Dawson in his life, there would be nothing dull about it. Her presence would light up the darkest, dreariest day for him. And were he to be under that hot African sun he knew that he would feel as gloomy as he did now. After only a brief spell in his life, Hannah had left a void he believed could never be filled. Meeting her had wiped out the eleven barren years he had wasted since leaving Australia. It was as though he had been reborn, but now she was gone he was beginning to die again.

It was a cruel hard world. How had he ever entertained the illusion it might not be? Hadn't all those empty years taught him that there was no meaning in life, that the world owed him nothing? It was all about serving time, living in the moment, then moving on.

There were two types of sailors: those men who went to sea as a means to living a life free of responsibilities and attachments, and those who travelled the world thinking only of home. Will had spent his time firmly in the first camp, and believed he would always feel that way. Then, when he met Hannah, he had been catapulted into the second. He had begun to imagine a life settled in one place, a life shared with another person, willingly fastened to the anchor that was Hannah.

But that brief dream was shattered. Happiness and love had been dangled in front of him like the carrot held over the donkey's head, only to be snatched away just as it opened its mouth to bite.

Will had always enjoyed women, sought their company, taken pleasure from their bodies, but none had ever come anywhere near to making him believe that love was possible. None since Elizabeth – and he now knew his feelings for her had been boyish dreams and genuine affection. Not the all-consuming love he felt for Hannah. A love that combined physical desire with a tenderness he had never felt for anyone before.

He struggled to remember any of the pretty faces, firm bodies, wide smiles he had known until now. They all melded into each other – an everywoman who was nobody. Apart from Rāfqa – she'd been different. She'd had an instinctive understanding for him and for exactly what he needed. Probably because, like him, she had been trying to obliterate sadness and loss. Rafqa had been a balm to him – he'd been fond of her – but he could never ever love her. It was only now that it was snatched away from him that he was absolutely certain that real love was what he felt for Hannah.

Over the past few days at sea Will had been thinking about her and how he had to find her and help her escape from this insane marriage that was clearly performed against her will and her best interests. But how could he help her if he didn't know where she was?

Tomorrow he would call on her mother again. Perhaps by now she'd found out the address. If necessary, he'd break down the door of Henderson's home and take her away.

He leaned against a huge iron capstan and puffed at the remains of his roll-up. The *Christina* would be ready to sail again in a matter of weeks. But how could he think of leaving Hannah behind in Liverpool?

He tried to picture the bum boats of Port Suez, the gully-gully men in their long white robes and red fezzes selling leather goods and performing magic tricks, the deep green of the water, the enormous straw baskets full of fruits and spices, their scents mixing with the smell of bunker oil. But he could only see Hannah's face, upturned to look into his, those soulful eyes and that mouth that he hungered to kiss again.

He tossed his cigarette butt into the water and turned to look back down the waterfront towards the Pier Head. It was a few seconds before he realised that the figure walking in his direction was familiar. The gait, the slight swagger in the movements, the tumble of dark hair under a jaunty cap. Paolo Tornabene. It must be six or seven weeks since they'd parted. Will moved towards his friend and broke into a run. They flung their arms about each other in a warm embrace, then broke apart, grinning, slightly embarrassed.

'*Ciao amico!*'

'Am I pleased to see you! What the hell are you doing back here, cobber? I thought you'd gone back to Italy?'

Paolo twisted his head to look away, but Will had already seen the sadness in his eyes. 'I had to get way from *Italia*. I will never return.'

'What? We have to talk. Hold on a second, will you.'

He went to speak with one of his crew-mates and then returned to his friend. 'I've got an hour. Let's go and have a mug of tea and you can tell me what's happened.'

Five minutes later they were sitting opposite each other across a table in a quayside hut that served as a café for thirsty dockers.

'What happened?' asked Will.

Paolo took a sip of his tea, pulling a face as he did so. 'My Loretta *è morta*. Dead.'

'Strewth! Hell, Paolo, mate, I'm sorry.'

'She was made to marry a bad man. One of the Camorristi.'

'But she said she'd wait for you.'

Paolo lifted his eyes and looked at Will. 'I know. But she didn't. She couldn't. She was shut away in a big house in the hills outside the city, guarded by *i fascisti* – the Blackshirts. The man they made her marry is a leader in the Fascist party.'

'So, who made her marry this goon?'

'Her brothers. All they care about is power and money. They made her marry an old man. In his sixties. She would never choose to marry a man like him.' He thumped his mug down on the table, slopping some of the contents onto the oilcloth that covered it. 'A very bad man. Her family are mixed up with the fascists.'

'What happened? How did she die?'

'It was *colpa mia*. My fault. I tried to see her. I went to the house and they wouldn't let me in. Maybe they punished her. I don't know. Or maybe seeing me made her do it.'

Will waited, dreading what his friend was about to say.

'She did what your sister did. Killed herself. She threw herself off a cliff.'

Will bent his forehead into one palm. 'I'm gutted for you, mate. That's terrible.'

'Now you know. We won't speak of this again.' Paolo wiped the back of his hand across his eyes, took a swig of tea then pulled a face. 'Disgusting! *Madonna!*' He gave a forced smile. 'What about you, Will? *Come va?* You still doing the ship to Ireland?'

Will gave him a rueful look. 'Yes. I'm still sailing with the *Arklow*. Back and forth like a yo-yo. Deck full of bloody cattle on the way back. Stinks to high heaven.' He began to roll a cigarette. 'But never mind the ship. You're not going to believe this, but I'm in the same boat as you. Well, almost – she's not dead though.' As soon as the words were out he cursed his own tactlessness. Why was he always so thoughtless towards Paolo? Perhaps it was because he felt as close as family.

'What you mean?'

'I fell head over heels for a girl and her old man forced her to marry someone else.'

Paolo spluttered his tea, sending spray flying. He crashed his mug down again. 'Who? How? When?'

273

So Will told him about meeting Hannah and how from the first sight he had been drawn to her and then fallen for her in a way he had never experienced before. 'I got it bad, Paolo. Real bad.'

'*Non ci credo!*'

'You better believe it.'

'But you! What was always your motto? Love them and leave them?'

Will grinned at him. 'Well, I fell and I fell bad, mate. But it's no good as she's married now and I don't even know where she's living.'

'You really love this *ragazza?*'

Will nodded, feeling sheepish.

'Then you must fight for her.'

'But—'

'Don't say but. Believe me, Will, my friend, I wish I had run away with Loretta when I could. Now she is lost to me forever.'

'I've no bloody idea where Hannah is. And I told you, she's married.'

'But if you find this Anna and get her to go to Ireland with you then you can marry her there? It is another country.'

'Don't be daft, mate. You can only marry once. Even in a different country. And her name is Hannah not Anna.'

Paolo rolled his eyes, then said, 'But even in England it is against the law to force a woman to marry. No?'

'In theory, yes.'

'*Va bene.* You can go to the police.'

Will pulled a face. 'First I have to find her, then convince a lawyer to take on the case. And her father will move heaven and earth to argue that it was a free marriage and I doubt Hannah and her mother would be in a position to prove him wrong.'

'How so?'

'Because he is supposed to be a pillar of the church. Well, some church. That makes him very plausible. But more importantly he's violent. He's beaten Hannah before and would do it again. He broke her mother's arm. They'd be taking a huge risk going against him.'

'*Che bastardo!*'

'You're right. He's a complete bastard. And a Bible-basher. He uses his religion as a cover for his violent behaviour.'

'Bible-basher. What's that?'

'He goes on about God all the time. Believes he has some kind of divine right to choose who his daughters marry. Says God talks to him.' Will shook his head and raised his hands in despair. 'He's a bloody religious maniac.'

'Like the brothers of Loretta – only their religion is money not God.' Paolo leaned forward. '*Caro* Will, if you don't try to stop this now you will regret it for the rest of your life. Believe me.'

Will closed his eyes, trying not to imagine Hannah, like Loretta and Hattie, throwing herself into the Mersey and drowning. 'Maybe you're right. Her mother is a decent woman. I got on well with her. She wants Hannah to be with me. She told me she wants to help us. Said she was ready to stand up to her husband. Maybe I can talk to her and find out more about this sham marriage.'

'*Bravo!*'

'What are you doing later?'

'Drinking a beer with you, I hope.'

'I'll meet you in the Baltic. Right now I'm going to talk to Sarah – Mrs Dawson.'

'*In bocca al lupo*'

'Stop talking Italian as if I'm supposed to understand it.' Will knew he sounded irritated and it was wrong to take it out on his friend.

Paolo's dismay showed in his face. 'I mean to say you good luck.'

Will put a hand on his shoulder. 'Sorry, mate. I'm a bit snappy at the moment.'

'*Non fa niente* – I mean, don't worry, it's fine.' The Italian corrected himself quickly.

As Will walked through the streets, he desperately hoped that Sarah Dawson would be able to give him information about her daughter's whereabouts. Otherwise, trying to find Hannah in a city the size of Liverpool was likely to be a fool's mission – particularly as he was at sea or in Dublin most of the time.

He hoped that Charles Dawson would be safely out of the way at work and cursed himself for not passing by the Morton's office first to make sure. Deciding to exercise caution he went to the alleyway that ran behind the row of houses and was relieved to see the numbers were on the gates and that the gate for the Dawson home was on the latch. Opening it cautiously, he slipped into the small backyard. He crouched behind the coal bunker, then edged slowly and quietly towards the scullery window. Sarah was standing at the sink, in front of the window. Waves of relief washed over him and he gave a light tap on the window, seeing her jump and move towards the door.

'What are you doing here, Will? I told you I'd find you if there was anything to report. You need to go. Right away.' He saw her left eye was purple and puffed up. The blow must have been direct.

'Did he do that?' Anger rose up inside him, like water through an open lock.

'Go. Now. Please. You'll make it worse.' Her eyes pleaded with him. 'I don't know where she is. If I find out I'll come to the docks and tell you.'

'But I might be at sea.' Then he remembered Eddie. 'Ask for a docker called Eddie O'Connor down at the Gladstone. He's usually rostered there – knows the foreman so always gets picked. He's a friend. I trust him. You can leave word with him if I'm not in port.'

She was already pushing the door closed on him, mouthing that her husband was in the house.

As he turned to go he could hear her through the door saying. 'There was a stray cat in the yard, but I got rid of it.'

For a moment Will thought of pushing the kitchen door open, going in and confronting Dawson. If the bully wanted a fight he could have one with a man instead of always picking on women. But something made him hold back. Flattening the man with a few punches might give Will satisfaction but Sarah and Hannah's sister would have to live with the consequences. Better to find a solution that would get them away from Dawson or – preferably – put him safely behind bars. And Dawson was the only way to find where Hannah was. It made no sense to cut off that possibility.

It was almost a week before Will returned to port. Paolo was waiting for him on the dockside when the *Arklow* edged into its berth.

The trip to Dublin had been a miserable one, as he had been beset by thoughts of what might have been. Everywhere he went he couldn't help himself imagining Hannah walking beside him. When he called on the O'Connors to let them know that their new lodger wouldn't be arriving as she'd married someone else, he was met by open mouths. The lads wanted to sweep him off to the pub to drown his sorrows, but Will wasn't interested. He wasn't interested in anything.

When he left the tenement building, Bridget ran after him. The last thing he wanted was her pity – or her prayers – since they had done nothing for him so far. But she had no homily to offer him, no repetition of her previous offer to remember him in her prayers. Instead, she took both his hands in hers and squeezed them. 'You are a good man, William Kidd. May God watch over you.' Then she turned on her heels and ran back to the family home.

Seeing Paolo waiting patiently on the quayside, he realised the Italian was now the only person he wanted to spend any time with. Paolo too had lost the woman he loved. Their situations bore remarkable parallels.

'Maybe we are cursed, you and I,' the Italian said later as they sat in the pub, neither finding much to say to the other, but both knowing that words were no longer necessary between them. 'Perhaps an evil spirit came on board and brought these troubles upon us.'

'Don't be daft.'

'In Africa they believe in such things. In Italy too. Even though we are told by the priest that such thoughts are the work of the devil.'

Will looked up from his beer. 'The only devils I believe in are Hannah's father and your Loretta's brothers.'

'*Hai ragione.* You are right.'

They lapsed into silence again.

Neither noticed Jake Cassidy approaching. The first they knew of it was when Will felt a hand on his shoulder. The former bosun pulled up a chair and turning it around, sat facing the back of the seat, arms folded and legs splayed. 'G'day, me hearties,' he said sarcastically. 'Fancy seeing you two here. Thought you'd gone back to Eyetie land, Turneybainy. How about you give me a few minutes with my cobber here? We Aussies have a bit of catching up to do.'

Paolo started to get up but Will put a hand on his arm. 'Stay put, mate.' He looked at Cassidy. 'You're not my cobber. And how come you're not in jail?'

'No thanks to you, Kidd, but the magistrates thought a fine upstanding man like me, with no previous record, didn't deserve to go down. And funnily enough none of the witnesses showed up in court.' He winked. 'The beaks had to let me off with a caution.'

'So, what do you want with me?'

'More like what can I do for *you*. I have something for you. I've a letter here from a young lady. Asked that you got it as soon as possible. Most anxious she was, according to my friend.' He took an envelope out of his jacket pocket and held it towards Will, drawing it away as Will went to take it. Married to a friend of mine she is. Name of Hannah. I hear she's a nice-looking girl. Sounds far too good for the likes of you. Not the kind of sheila who'd have any time for a man whose father was hanged for murder. And who was the brother of a drugged-up bird who topped herself and with a brother so rotten his own dad shot him in the back. No. Not the kind of family a nice young lady would want to be associated with.' He shook his head in pantomime solemnity. 'That's why she married my friend.' He waved the letter in the air.

Will resisted the urge to try to snatch the envelope from his hands. He knew all too well that was exactly what Cassidy wanted – and equally well that, if he did, the former bosun would move it out of reach again. He decided to bide his time, even though every fibre of his being longed to get his hands on Hannah's letter – and punching Jake Cassidy would be a welcome bonus. He leaned back and crossed his arms, waiting.

Frustrated, Cassidy turned to Paolo. 'Did you know he was sniffing round a woman here? Wanted to marry her but she had other ideas. She's married a good-looking fella, lives in a big house. Plenty of quid. I reckon she was just toying with your friend Kidd, here.'

Paolo said nothing, taking his cue from Will's silence.

Realising this was going nowhere, Cassidy got to his feet, knocking his chair over. He spat on the sawdust covered floor. 'My friend is said to be a real stallion. Your lady friend's getting lots of this. He tells me she can't get enough of it.' Cassidy executed a crude pantomime of the sex act, thrusting his hips back and forth rapidly. Will jumped to his feet, anger exploding from him.

But Paolo got between the two men before Will could strike a blow. '*Basta!* Enough!' He pushed Will back into his chair, then squared up to Cassidy. '*Vai a fare in culo, stronzo*'. Neither Cassidy, Will, nor anyone around them need a translation. The intent was clear.

Perhaps mindful of his night in the cells and narrow escape in court, Cassidy stepped back. He flung the letter onto the table. 'Read it and weep, you miserable ocker!' Then he was gone.

It was only then that Will realised the whole pub was silent – all watching the drama take place. He looked at Paolo.

The Italian downed the remains of his pint and said, 'Drink up. Let's go.'

Paolo was staying at the Seaman's Home so the two friends headed there. The sitting room was almost empty, most men doubtless in the local hostelries or over at Atlantic House. The only other occupant was an old tar in the corner snoring.

Will ripped open the envelope, impatient to read what Hannah had written, hoping it would tell him where she was so he could go and find her. Right now the fact that she was married was immaterial. He had to get her away from this husband, take her safely to Dublin and then they could investigate how to get the marriage declared invalid. His heart pounding, he began to read.

> Dear Will,
>
> I expect by now you will have heard that I have married. When we last met I said I didn't want to follow the wishes of my father and marry the man who has now become my husband. That was before I met Sam. Once I did, I felt differently. He is a good man, handsome, prosperous and as soon as we

met there was an immediate understanding between us. A strong feeling.

You and I barely had time to get to know each other and now that I have had a chance to reflect, I have come to the conclusion that our relationship was not suitable. As a sailor you would not have been able to provide me with the home and stability I need. Also your family connections have caused me some concerns.

You are a good man and I am sure that, as my aunt once told you, you will one day find someone with whom you can settle down. I regret that I am not that person. I was caught up in the excitement of discovering you knew Aunt Elizabeth and this clouded my judgement.

Please don't try to find me and seek to change my mind. I am very happy with my new life and my husband.

Yours sincerely,

Hannah.

No address. No clue where she was. Will stared at the page, at the neat handwriting, the flowing signature. This couldn't be Hannah. How was it possible? How could she have changed her mind so utterly and completely? Had someone forced her to write it? He read it again. As he absorbed the words it occurred to him that perhaps it was indeed true. He had nothing to offer her other than his love. That love was unconditional, whereas here was the proof that hers had not been. Could he blame her for not wishing to marry a man who spent most of his time at sea? He remembered what Mrs O'Connor had said when Will had first met her – *'The sea's a hard mistress. There's not many women willing to share a man with her.'* And his thoughts about taking Hannah to Australia with him, or to America... why had he entertained the notion she would she want to do that? To expect her to cross the world and build a new life so far from her mother and sister and everything she'd ever known was absurd. Then he realised, he hadn't even raised this as a possibility with her – they'd had so little time together. So many of their conversations had been rehearsals in his head. There had been so little time to talk about the future, other than to agree they wanted to spend it together.

And yet – how was it possible that she could have changed so much in so short a time? When her eyes had gazed into his, Will had been certain he saw her love there. His own feelings for her were unmistakeable. Absolute. Unchangeable.

But he had made that mistake before. He'd convinced himself all those years ago that Hannah's aunt might have romantic feelings for him and he'd been proved wrong then – so why not again now? Maybe he was unworthy of a woman's love. Perhaps there was something about him that had made Hannah suddenly cautious and had driven her away. Something that had caused her to shy away just as he thought she had given him her heart.

Was there something in him that made him unworthy, and both Elizabeth and Hannah had seen it? It was wrong of him to make the comparison between Hannah and her aunt: Elizabeth had never shown the slightest indication of anything other than a maternal love for him, the warmth of friendship and affection – but never romantic love. That had been in his head only. Puppy love. Infatuation. Hannah, was different. She had responded to his kisses with passion. She had declared her love for him too. And wouldn't her father stop at nothing to prevent her going against his wishes? Was this letter written under compulsion?

Looking up he saw Paolo was watching him intently. He passed the letter to him. 'Read it.'

Paolo looked astonished. '*Ma non posso*. It is private, no?'

'Read it,' he repeated. 'There's nothing to cause you blushes there. It's my discharge papers. Unsatisfactory husband material.' He leaned back in his seat, exhaled, and stared unseeing at the ceiling.

Paolo looked puzzled and read the letter slowly. 'I don't understand it all, some words… but it seems bad.'

'I don't understand it *at all*. And yes, it *is* bad. Very bad. As bad as it could be.'

He took the letter back and read it again. Surely if it had been written under duress she would have given him some clue. Something to make it clear only to him that the words were not her own. A re-reading offered no such hope. No secret message encoded within the stark words. She had dumped him of her own volition. He had believed he had known her, yet she was making a choice now based on material factors. On survival. On a chance of a better future than he could offer. He slumped back in his chair, a terrible emptiness hollowing him out inside, sucking his hopes and happiness away and leaving a hollow void.

Paolo looked at him, his dark eyes telegraphing his sadness for his friend. Immediately, Will clenched his fists and put on his emotional armour. What had possessed him to take it off in the first place? He gave a dry laugh. 'Oh well, you win some, you lose some.'

The Italian frowned at him, evidently seeing through this display of bravado. 'I am sorry, *amico mio*. I don't know what to say.'

Will jumped up. 'You don't need to say anything, mate. Let's just go and get drunk.'

The two men headed to a nearby pub, but conscious of the cost and their desire to drown their sorrows, decided the cheap beer at Atlantic House would be a better bet.

Will was determined to brush off what had happened – the last thing he wanted was pity. Yet he knew he wasn't kidding Paolo. His forced nonchalance had evidently not convinced the Italian.

He realised he actually envied his friend. While both of them had loved and lost, at least Paolo had not suffered the terrible pain of his beloved choosing someone else. Loretta had been forced into marriage yet, were Will to believe the words of the letter, Hannah had embraced it with open arms. Paolo had the clear knowledge that Loretta had loved him deeply, enough to take her own life. But given the choice of Hannah alive but apart from him, or Hannah dead, he wanted her to be living. He hoped, for her sake, she was as happy as the letter indicated, no matter how much that felt like a knife cutting into his own heart.

There was no dance tonight at Atlantic House – just men playing snooker and crowding inside the bar to enjoy the cheap beer and the company of the local girls. Father

O'Driscoll was, as always, very much in evidence. He nodded a greeting to Will, who ordered three pints and sent one across the bar to the priest.

Will and Paolo found a table in the corner, away from the throng. As Will drank his beer, he became increasingly melancholy and fatalistic. He was a fool to have believed in Hannah's love for him.

Paolo leaned over the table and raised his voice above the hubbub. '*Ho deciso*, Will. I have decided. I sign to sail with the *Christina* again,' said the Italian. 'It will leave the dry dock next week. *Tutto pronto*. Sailing back to east Africa via the Cape.'

Will didn't respond.

'*Il Capitano* Palmer, he ask me if you come too. Please, Will. *Vieni, vieni con me!* Let's go together to Africa. Leave all this sadness behind. All this shit. We will both forget the past and the women we have lost. We leave them behind and start a great new adventure. What you think, Will, my friend?'

Will thought for a moment, then drained the remains of his pint. 'You're on, mate. I'm in. I can't face another bloody hop over to Ireland. Let's go where the sun shines every day.'

Paolo leaned over the table, took Will's head between his hands and planted a friendly kiss on his friend's brow.

'Steady on, fella. You're not in Italy now.' He shoved his empty beer glass towards Paolo. 'Now let's have another beer.'

Chapter Twenty-Three

Hannah was asleep when Sam came home. The sound of the bedroom door opening woke her. He was standing at the foot of the bed and even though it was pitch dark and she could only see his outline, she knew at once something was wrong.

'What's the matter, Sam?'

She reached over to the small lamp on the night stand and flicked it on. Gasping, she crawled to the end of the bed where he was standing head lowered.

'What's happened? Your jacket's torn.'

He lifted his head and she gasped again. His face was red and swollen and his lip was cut. Tomorrow he'd have a massive bruise. On her knees at the end of the bed she lifted a hand to touch his face. He winced and drew away.

'Who did this to you, Sam?'

He moved round the foot of the bed and sat down on the side. She swung her legs over to sit beside him.

'Jake.' He made a little sobbing sound.

'Wait here,' she said. 'There's some witch hazel and iodine in the bathroom cabinet.'

She returned with the bottles, and taking his handkerchief from his top pocket, she soaked it in witch hazel and began to dab at his face.

'Why?' She asked eventually. 'Why did he hurt you?'

Sam closed his eyes. 'I gave him your letter and he said he knew your friend and would make sure he got it. We arranged to meet later in our usual place – a disused warehouse on the docks. When he turned up, he was drunk and angry.' He leant forward and put his head in his hands. 'I was trying to make him feel better. I didn't know why he was upset. I wanted him to know that no matter what, I was there for him.' He made a choking sound as he tried to suppress the sobs. 'I told him I loved him.'

Hannah reached for Sam's hand and gave it a squeeze.

'He didn't say anything at first. For one magical moment I thought he was going to say he felt the same, but he didn't. He didn't say anything at all. He just swung his arm back and punched me in the face. I was so shocked I couldn't move. I landed on the floor, up against some grain sacks. Then he kicked me. As if he were taking a penalty in football and wanted to hammer it in the back of the net. Here.' He pointed to his left thigh. 'Twice.' Then there was the sound of a ship's foghorn so he ran away. Left me lying there on the ground. It was so painful I don't know how I managed to get as far as the taxi rank to get home.'

She told him to take off his trousers. The skin on his thigh was already blooming into an enormous bruise like a chrysanthemum. Despite his trousers, the skin was broken and there was copious dried blood all down the leg. Hannah dabbed at the cuts with the iodine. 'Now get into bed and try to sleep. Would you like me to make you some cocoa?'

Sam shook his head. 'Thank you, Hannah. I am so lucky to have you. Your kindness is the only good thing in my life right now.' He slid under the covers. She got into the other side of the bed. 'Can I hold you?' He asked. 'Just until I fall asleep?'

'Of course you can,' she whispered, switching the light out. He slipped an arm around her waist and was soon breathing with the heavy breath of sleep. Hannah remained awake, staring into the dark of the bedroom, wishing that it were Will's arm around her, knowing that if it were, neither would be sleeping.

—

As time passed and in an attempt to stop dwelling on her impossible situation, her lost love and her bleak future, Hannah threw herself wholeheartedly into the task of getting The Laurels into better shape. Nance Cunningham had not exaggerated when she said she didn't like doing housework. The windows probably hadn't been cleaned since the pastor's late wife had been alive. The bath was ingrained with a tidemark of grime and the toilet stained and smelly. Dust had gathered on every surface and there were cobwebs in the corners of the ceilings. There was evidence of the presence of mice and they were probably only kept in check by the frequent intrusion of the cat she had encountered that first day, and which she now knew to belong to the elderly man who lived next door.

Nance, evidently eager for company and conversation, liked to follow Hannah from room to room, perching on a chair or leaning against the window ledge, watching her work while smoking cigarettes. Not once did she offer to lend a hand, but she did provide a steady flow of cups of tea and occasionally went so far as to open a tin of sardines or make cheese-on-toast, for their lunch.

Her idleness didn't concern Hannah, who was glad of the consolation of physical activity and the distraction of Nance's monologues. The woman rarely showed any curiosity about Hannah or her background, but had no hesitation in revealing her own life story in detail. She told Hannah that she had married her childhood sweetheart as soon as he was demobbed after the Armistice, but the young boy who had gone to war was not the man who returned. Her husband had escaped physical injury but his happy-go-lucky nature had been transformed into dark moods, a tendency to heavy drinking and consequent aggression, which he took out on his wife.

One morning, Nance surprised her by asking her how she was getting on with her new husband.

'Well enough,' Hannah replied, looking up in surprise.

'Have you done it yet?'

'Done what?'

'Had sex.'

Hannah gaped at her, astonished.

'I suppose you think it's none of my business and you're right, it isn't, but I can't help being curious. It's in me nature.'

'Then you must stay curious. What happens between a husband and wife should be private.'

Nance snorted. 'I'll take that as a no then.'

Hannah turned her back on her and carried on polishing the wooden dining table.

'You do know he's a queer don't you? You must have worked that out by now. A nancy boy – though why they should call them after me I can't imagine.' Her laugh was like a little trill. 'Although I've got nothing against them personally. Each to their own. I'm not one to judge.

And I've always felt sorry for Sam, having a father who's convinced him he's going to burn in hell for ever. It must wear a man down in the end. Lower his spirits. I expect that's why he agreed to marry you. No offence, mind.'

Hannah wasn't going to rise to the bait. She moved over to dust and polish the sideboard.

Nance carried on regardless of her failure to produce a response. 'I don't believe in hell, but I'll say this. If there is one, it won't be the likes of Sam who'll end up burning there – he's never done anyone else any harm. Oh no.' She shook her head in an exaggerated fashion. 'The real perverts are the men like his father and yours. They're very good at covering up their sins to the world. But if their God does exist, they can't hide from him. He's meant to see everything. Gawd knows why they choose to forget that in their own cases.' She gave another laugh, a lower one this time.

'What do you mean?' Hannah's curiosity had now won through.

'When Amos Henderson asked me to go private and move in here, he suggested I take on your father too. Not a threesome, mind – His Nibs don't like sharing. I think he was trying to do your dad a favour. But kinky stuff is one thing, pain and violence is another. I don't mind a good spanking – so long as it's on me bottom – although His Nibs prefers to be the one spanked rather than doling it out himself. He takes pleasure from being disciplined.' She chuckled to herself. 'I have to play the part of his mother and pretend he's been a naughty boy. He likes me to hit him with a cane or a ruler until he gets excited enough to get his little dick up. But he's not violent towards me. Not like your old man.'

'I don't understand? What about my father?'

'Look, love, I know he's your father but he's a bleeding sadist, isn't he? Makes me husband seem like a lamb in comparison.'

Hannah put down her duster. 'How did you know he hit me and my mother? Who told you?'

Nance whistled. 'I didn't know, doll. I'm sorry to hear that. And glad you've got away from him. You're safe here. Sam'll never raise a hand to you. Nor the old man.'

'So, what did you mean about him being a sadist? And about Mr Henderson asking you to take on my father too?'

Nance pursed her lips, sighed, then said, 'All right. I may as well tell you. Your father used to be one of my customers – before I went exclusive for old man Henderson. At first it was all right. He were no worse than any other customer, although he liked to shout out passages from the Bible when he was coming. But that didn't bother me. Whatever turns you on.' She narrowed her eyes. 'Then one night, he was sucking on my tits like a hungry baby, when he bit right into me. Nearly took my nipple off. Drew blood, he did. Couldn't stop the bleeding for ages. I wasn't going to put up with that. Not blooming likely.'

Hannah gasped, nausea rising up in her. She slumped into one of the chairs.

'That was it. I wasn't having any more of that. And I weren't the only one. Every girl he went with complained. In the end he were banned from the place as no one would do him. Dunno where he goes now to get his end away.'

It was all too much for Hannah. In just a short space of time she'd learnt more about sexual perversion than she wanted or could imagine. The idea of her own father going to prostitutes was abhorrent. How long had it been going on? Did her mother know? Sarah had told her about him attacking their former maid but nothing about prostitutes and compulsive violence. No wonder her mother had been worried about the way he sometimes looked at Hannah. The man was evidently capable of anything. Was Judith safe under the same roof as him? She jumped to her feet, ran into the scullery and vomited into the sink.

—

That night Hannah cried herself to sleep, grateful that Sam was out late and not there to witness her grief.

After the men of the house had left the following morning, she told Nance she was going out to do the grocery shopping.

'No, you won't love. I've blooming well got to do it. His Nibs says you're not to leave the house.'

Hannah gasped. 'But there's things I need to get.'

'Tell me and I'll add 'em to the list.'

'You're telling me I'm to be kept prisoner in my own home?'

'I suppose I am. Strict orders. Just until you've had time to settle in.' She looked thoughtful. 'I reckon he's scared you'll go running home to your family.'

Hannah felt herself blushing. Was it that obvious? Of course it was.

'Mind you, you'd be a blinking idiot to try that on. You know your dad's in cahoots with Henderson. And knowing what we all know about Mr Charles Dawson's temper – I'm sure you don't want to be on the business end of his fist.'

Hannah winced.

'They'll be watching your every move. My advice to you, duckie, is to learn patience until the buggers trust you, before you try anything on. That's just supposing you still want to try anything on, which if you've half a brain, you won't. You and Pretty Boy seem to be getting on well enough, and at least no one's going to give you a good clobbering here. And don't forget Ol' Man Henderson has plenty of money that'll come to Sammy boy one day. Gotta learn to play the long game, girl.'

'Is that what you do?'

'Maybe it is. But that's for me to know.' Then she relaxed a little, her face breaking into a conspiratorial smile. 'Actually, I've made sure there's provision for me.'

'Provision?'

'In his will.' She lit a cigarette. 'A nice little nest egg and a small allowance to get me started. Enough for me to buy a little place by the sea in Southend.' It was a moment before Hannah realised where she meant as Nance pronounced it 'Sarfend'.

'Is that where you're from?'

'No, but I went there one day with me 'usband before the war, when we was courting. Beautiful it is. There's a pier they say's the longest in the whole country – goes on for miles right over the sea. Me and our Alf had cockles from a stall. Maybe that's what I'll do – open a cockle stall. I could go round the pubs at night selling them. Nice little earner.' She blew a series of smoke rings, then grinned. 'And no more blooming sex!'

Hannah offered to make another pot of tea.

'Oh go on then, doll, twist me arm!'

When they were drinking the fresh tea, Hannah leaned forward and said, 'Can I ask you a special favour, Nance?'

'Depends what it is? Answer's no if it involves letting you out of the house, girl.'

'It doesn't. Is there a library nearby?'

'How the hell would I know that? Do I look like someone who wastes their time reading books?'

'Maybe not, but you must have gone past one near here. Please think.'

Nance closed her eyes, stubbed out her cigarette and reached to pick up the pack and take another one. 'Mmm actually, now I think about it, maybe I do know where there's one. It's got them fancy pillars outside. Walk past it when I go to bingo. Why?'

'I was wondering if you could get some books out for me.'

'Books? He don't like books, His Nibs. Won't have them in the house. He found Sam had a stash hidden down the back of the airing cupboard and he threw a real fit. You'd think the airing cupboard was Sodom and Gomorrah. Threw the lot of them in the fire.'

So, burning books was a passion Henderson shared with her father – and Adolf Hitler. She shivered.

'I was hoping you'd hide them in your bedroom for me. You said he doesn't go in there.'

Nance sucked on her cigarette, thinking. 'What's in it for me, then?'

Hannah looked blank. Everything had a quid pro quo in Nance's world – although she'd likely describe it as 'you scratch my back and I'll scratch yours'. She said, 'I don't know. What do you need? What do you want me to do?'

295

'I'll 'ave to 'ave a think about that. Just remember you owe me one. Now how do I get a book out the library? Just go in and take it?'

'You'll need to be a member. You have to fill in a form and they'll give you a ticket. I can write a list of the books I want and you give it to the person behind the desk and she'll tell you where to find them.'

'I must be nuts taking that kind of risk.' She thought for a moment. 'One book at a time. I'm not tramping back up the hill with a bagful of heavy books.'

'I read fast. You'll be going back and forth all the time.'

'No, I won't. You'll make do with what you're given and you'll have to read it again if you finish too quick. I'm not your lady's maid. And if he finds it I've had nowt to do with it. Understand?'

'Of course. But he won't find anything. I'll be careful.'

Later that afternoon Nance returned with a copy of *The Weather in the Streets*, which Hannah fell upon like a starving crow on a small animal. After waiting so long, at last she'd be able to finish it. Life would be marginally more bearable.

–

At breakfast the following morning, the pastor addressed Hannah directly.

'You have had time to settle in, now you must do the work of God.'

She put down her piece of toast and waited, curious as to what he was about to propose. Her housework couldn't possibly be of an insufficient standard. The house now gleamed, polished brass, well-buffed wood, windows you could actually see through, thoroughly beaten carpets, and not a cobweb in sight. The bed linen and towels had been boil-washed and bleached. Surely the pastor couldn't be dissatisfied with the quality of her work – although not even the shining white bath had elicited any comment from her father-in-law.

'Women, of course, are unworthy vessels, designed for the pleasure and service of men, and are not capable of fully understanding and explaining God's teaching. They all carry the sin of Eve.' He was addressing her but, as usual, made no eye contact, projecting his words into the middle distance. 'God's teaching is the work of men. Only *we* are capable of the level of knowledge and the depth of understanding to communicate the scriptures and spread the word.' He leaned back in his chair, savouring his own words as though they were fine wine. 'The role of the woman is to serve God by serving man.'

He coughed, his face reddening, and they waited for him to recover and finish speaking. 'I have decided you will take those leaflets and go door-to-door in whichever neighbourhood I select, each day.' He indicated a bundle on the sideboard behind him. 'Starting tomorrow, you will knock at the door, ask for the lady of the house, recite the verse I have selected, and instruct the woman to deliver the pamphlet into the hands of her husband and master.'

'What do the pamphlets say?' She asked the question expecting him to rebuke her for failing to mind her own business. To her surprise, he nodded and waved a finger in the air.

'Good question. They are invitations, requiring the men of the neighbourhood to attend a service at my meeting hall so they may find out how to save their immortal souls from eternal damnation.' He handed her a leaflet. 'You may read one. Although not now. First you must ready yourself by learning the verse I have chosen for you.'

At last, here was her opportunity to get away from this house and call on her mother. She could easily dump the flyers in a rubbish bin and she still had the ten shillings Sam had given her for bus fare.

'I will be testing you, Hannah Henderson, as well as the various neighbourhoods and the verses I give you each day.'

'Testing me?'

'By results. The power of mathematics. Each day we will see how many men come along to hear the truth of God and bear witness. I will know which roads and districts prove the most fruitful and which Bible verses the most effective. I will also know whether you have been fulfilling your mission as directed.'

'How?'

'What do you mean, woman?' The word woman was spoken as if it were a curse.

'How will you be able to tell the difference between the different districts, the verses and my own role? If every day I call on a different neighbourhood, reciting a different verse how can you tell which factor was most influential? And how will you know if other things might dissuade people from coming on a particular night – such as whether there's a sporting fixture or a programme on the wireless that no one wants to miss?'

'I will know because I am God's instrument. God will guide me,' he thundered. 'And how dare you presume to compare the chance to bear witness to God and hear my preaching of his word with a football match or a wireless broadcast. Has your father taught you nothing? The wireless, the cinema and the library are all creations of the devil. God will punish you for saying such things, for bringing your sinful thoughts under this roof and casting shame upon my son!' He thumped the top of the table with his fist, scraped back his chair and left the room. A moment later the three of them heard the front door crash.

'Blimey, love, you ought to know better by now.' Nance shook her head and went into the scullery to stick the kettle on again.

Sam gave Hannah a meaningful look and got up from the table. 'Don't provoke him. It will only come back to make things worse for you. You'll never win by trying to be clever.' He went into the hall, to put on his coat and hat and collect his briefcase, then stuck his head back round the door. His voice low, he said, 'Don't do anything silly, Hannah. Bide your time.' Then he was gone.

She went over to the sideboard and saw there was a piece of paper with the chosen verse, from the Book of Malachi, written down.

> *Behold, I am going to send you Elijah the prophet*
> *before the coming of the great and terrible day of*
> *the Lord. He will restore the hearts of the fathers*
> *to their children and the hearts of the children to*
> *their fathers, so that I will not come and smite the*
> *land with a curse.*

The next morning, Henderson demanded that she recite the rote-learned verse. In spite of feeling self-conscious and foolish she correctly recited the verse.

'Use more enthusiasm,' he said. 'You make it sound as though you don't believe it. If you are to persuade the women of the urgency of their husbands answering the call of God, you must speak with conviction.'

'But they'll think I'm crazy if they open their doors and I just start incanting the words. Can I say something else first?'

'Do as I tell you. Say the verse then hand them the pamphlet and instruct them to give it to their husbands so that they might be saved by the Lord.' His face telegraphed his impatience. 'Are you stupid, woman?'

'No. Of course I'm not. But—'

'Then do my bidding for it is God's bidding.' He looked at his watch. 'Time to go. Bring the pamphlets.'

Hannah followed him out of the room and out of the house, the bundle of leaflets in her arms.

They began a few streets away in a road of terraced houses, each with a front 'garden' that was little more than a strip of concrete or soil less than a couple of feet wide. Low walls provided somewhat extravagant boundaries, separating these meagre plots of land from the pavement in a symbolic aspirational gesture.

Henderson indicated the first house she was to call on.

'You mean I'm to do it alone?'

'I will be watching.'

She was about to answer back, then decided her best option was compliance if she were to earn the trust of this man and so be allowed to do the missionary work alone. Detaching a leaflet from the bundle, she approached and knocked at the door.

Almost immediately, it opened. A woman wearing an apron appeared. Her hair was in rollers under a head scarf, stockings rolled down to her ankles. 'Yes?'

Hannah launched into her Bible recitation. Before the first sentence was finished the door was slammed in her face. She turned back to the pavement. Henderson swept his hand forward, indicating she was to knock again. Mortified, she complied.

The door opened again. 'Piss off. We're Catholics. And if you knock on this door again you'll get a bucket of water in your face.'

The reception was similar in the next house, and the one after that. Humiliated, embarrassed and wanting to run a mile, Hannah turned to her father-in-law. 'Please, Mr Henderson, this is pointless. No one is interested. It's clearly a Catholic district.'

His eyes narrowed. '"*Many are called but few are chosen.*" This is God's work. Hold up your head and do His bidding.'

They trudged the streets for several hours. As door after door was closed in her face, Henderson told her to push the pamphlets through the letterbox. She asked him if it might be better to do that in the first place and cut out the door knocking, which was raising hostility.

'Women don't want to be interrupted while they're doing housework. If I just posted the leaflets through the doors, it would be less likely to antagonise them. They'd probably read them out of curiosity, whereas if they're annoyed they might throw them in the bin.'

He glowered at her but must have acknowledged the truth of what she said as while he didn't voice his agreement, he didn't object when she started to put this plan into action. Eventually, all the flyers posted, they returned to The Laurels.

The following morning there was no mention of distributing more leaflets. The pile remained on the sideboard. Perhaps Henderson didn't want to spend another morning tramping the streets with her and wasn't ready to allow her to go alone without his supervision.

After the men of the house had left, she told Nance she was going to carry on with the missionary work today.

'He didn't tell me that.' Nance was clearly suspicious. 'Never said owt.'

'Really?' Hannah injected a breezy confidence into her voice. Remembering a road sign she had seen on their door-knocking yesterday, she said, 'He wants me to do Walton Hill today. I'm to distribute another hundred leaflets.'

Nance folded her arms. 'I'm not so sure. He'd have said summat just now.'

'He told me yesterday. He was most specific.' She added some fabricated details, pleased at her capacity to lie convincingly. 'As far as Chestnut Avenue, then back down Northport Road. And I can change my library book at the same time. Save you having to do it.'

'Well, if you say so.' The woman frowned. 'Odd that he said nowt to me. Oh well. I'll have to come with you. I'm not knocking on any doors mind. I'll just be there to keep an eye on you.'

'There's no need for that. I'll be back by noon.'

Nance harrumphed. 'He should have bloody well told me. I'm the last to know everything round here.' She inspected the back of her hands. 'I'm going to go upstairs and do me nails then. You'll have to sort something for us to eat when you get back. I won't want to risk scuffing them once they're painted.'

Remembering to take a pile of leaflets with her, Hannah checked in her pocket for what was left of Sam's money after she'd paid Nance for the trip to the library, and left The Laurels. She set off for Walton Vale to find a bus going to Bootle. As she walked briskly down Moss Lane she felt a huge surge of relief to be free of the oppressive atmosphere in the house.

It wasn't safe to dump the flyers in a bin anywhere in the local neighbourhood in case they found their way back to Henderson. Better to hold onto them for now. Then she remembered she wanted to return her library book. She could leave the bagful of leaflets in there. A library would be the last place Henderson would find them.

Her mission accomplished, she caught a bus for Bootle. Picking up a discarded newspaper she glanced idly at the front page, which bore pictures of men digging trenches in Hyde Park in London, barrage balloons – described popularly as 'silver sausages' – being inflated and set in place to offer protection from the possibility of airborne attack by Germany, and the news that gas masks would now be supplied to the whole population, starting with the major cities including her own. She had lost touch with what was happening in the wider world. The threat of Hitler and war had left her largely unmoved when the smaller domestic war she had become caught up in seemed so much more sinister.

Here, gazing out at the rows of soot-stained buildings from the top of the bus, she indulged herself for a moment to wonder about Will. Where was he now? Might he be thinking of her too? The harshness of the words she had written convinced her he would not. She brushed away a tear and thought instead that soon she would be seeing her mother again.

As she walked up the street towards her former home it seemed as though it were a lifetime ago that she had been living here. In that time, she had lost her innocence, her belief in the possibility of happiness and every last vestige of respect for the man who was her father. In contrast, she had gained a new hardness inside her, a resilience. Nothing could shock her any more. She had undergone a baptism of fire but felt a nostalgia for her naivety and innocence of just a few weeks ago.

Only a few steps short of the house, she froze as the door opened and her father stepped outside. For what seemed like an eternity they stood facing each other down. Hannah's heart was hammering so loudly it felt as though it might burst through her chest. She thought of turning and running. But there was nowhere to run to – and no point.

Dawson strode towards her, grabbed her by the wrist with one hand, swung the other back and struck her across the face. It was like a whiplash. Her cheek flamed under the searing sting of the slap.

Across the road, two women, chatting across their doorsteps, stopped their conversation to watch the display. Neither made any attempt to intervene. Probably frequent recipients of their husbands' blows, it was an entertaining sideshow to see someone else getting a bit of a lashing. Hannah's father saw the women too, and evidently conscious of his dignity and desire always to project the image of a man worthy of respect and standing, a cut above the other residents of the street, he dragged Hannah away by the wrist.

He didn't take her into the house as she expected. Instead he led her back to the main road, where he pushed her in front of him to the rear of a queue boarding a waiting bus. They were going back to Orrell Park.

When they arrived at The Laurels, instead of knocking on the front door he dragged her round to the back door and pushed it open. He had said nothing for the entire journey.

As soon as they were inside the scullery he landed a blow. Hannah fell against the enamel sink, smashing her elbow on the edge and releasing a cry in agony. Trying to protect her head with her arms she stumbled into the back parlour where an astonished Nance was finishing her manicure.

Heedless of her newly-applied nail varnish, Nance grabbed the poker from the fire and brandished it above her head, advancing towards Dawson. 'Get the hell out of here before I smash this through your skull, you filthy bastard.'

Ignoring the warning, Dawson moved towards her. Instantly the poker slammed into the side of his head, sending him reeling. He staggered backwards, eyes wide in shock. Nance, now with the upper hand, swung her arm back and swiped again. This time it cracked into his upper arm with a force that was audible. 'That one's for Madge's black eye.' Swinging again she caught him on the hip. 'And that's for the time you broke Tina's nose.'

By now, Dawson was cowering, arms over his head. 'Don't hurt me! Please!' He backed, still half crouching, towards the door. He looked at Hannah in appeal.

'Don't look to her for help. Not after what you done to her, you bloody great bully. She knows all about you. Everything. I've told her all your dirty little secrets. There's a few more details she'll hear too before I'm done. About how you've been bleeding money out of your family business into paying for prostitutes. And paying off girls to stop them going to the police and exposing your perverted games.'

Hannah was open-mouthed. Her father was whimpering now.

'If you know what's good for you, you'll get the hell out of here right now and you won't darken the door again. She don't wanna see you and I sure as hell don't. And Old Man Henderson ain't going to be too pleased to know you've just walked right into his house, assaulted his daughter-in-law and tried to assault his lady friend.' She waved the poker to underline her point. 'Now hop it!'

Dawson didn't hesitate. He grabbed his hat from where it had been knocked onto the floor and went out of the back door.

Nance sat down at the table and picked up the bottle of acetone. 'Now I'm going to have to do me bleeding nails again. Stick the kettle on, doll.' She looked up at Hannah. 'You all right? Did he hurt you?'

'I'll be all right. Thank you for doing that.'

'My pleasure, ducky. I'd have liked to break his skull. Only I don't fancy going down for it.' She wiped an acetone-soaked rag over a nail to remove the polish. 'But let's got one fing straight. If you lie to me again I'll go straight to His Nibs. And from now on, you're confined to barracks.'

'Do you think my father will tell the pastor?'

'Nah! And have him know what 'appened? Not bleeding likely. He'll stay away from here from now on if he's got half a brain. Now you going to tell me what you were up to?'

'I wanted to see my mother. It's not right that we should be kept apart like this. I miss her.'

'Poor cow your mother must be, married to a bastard like him. Let me have a think. We'll see if I can come up with a plan.'

Chapter Twenty-Four

Two days later, Hannah was chopping vegetables for a soup while Nance sat flipping idly through a women's magazine.

'Does Mr Henderson know you read magazines – or have them in the house?'

'Not blooming likely. It'd be turned into kindling for the fire if he saw this. But what the eye don't see... Besides, he knows only too well that I'll pack my bags and go back on the game if he crosses me. He knows which side his bread's buttered on. Not many girls can give a good spanking like I can and put up with all his nasty habits. Have I told you—'

'I'd rather not know if you don't mind.' Hannah tipped the peelings into the bin. 'I'd like to hang onto what little innocence I have left.'

'You are a card, ducky!' Nance burst out laughing. 'Innocence, eh? Something I can't even remember.' She tossed the magazine aside. 'What a waste of time that was. All knitting patterns and recipes and tips for keeping your house clean. "*Ten ways to please the man in your life*" – apparently it's about having his dinner on the table, his slippers warmed in front of the fire, and a smile on your face when he comes home from work.' She snorted derisively. 'I tell you there are better ways to keep a man happy than that – and that don't involve having to be a slave to housework. I could tell you a thing or two, doll – but it would all be wasted on young Master Samuel.' She giggled. 'He'd have kittens if you tried some of my little tricks on him. Hey, maybe you should – perhaps you could convert him from being a nancy boy. I bet if you—'

'No, thank you, I've no intention of learning any of your tricks. And I'm perfectly happy with things the way they are.'

Before Nance could respond they were disturbed by a tapping noise. They both looked up and there was Hannah's mother, Sarah, looking at them through the scullery window.

Hannah jumped up and rushed to open the door. Launching herself into her mother's arms she cried, 'I'm so happy to see you! How did you find me? Nance, did you arrange this?'

Nance put her hands up. 'Nowt to do with me, love.'

'I saw you and your father when you came to the house. I was at the window when he took you. I followed you and nipped onto the bus just in time and went upstairs. Thankfully the conductor didn't get to me 'til you were getting off anyway – I'd no money for the fare and told her I'd left my purse at home. I kept you in sight 'til you came in here then I walked home. I didn't want him to catch me. Today's the first chance I've had to come. He's been watching me like a hawk.'

Hannah hugged her mother, squeezing her tightly, unable to believe that at last they were reunited.

'How's Judith?'

'She's fine. Working hard. He takes every penny from her on pay day.'

Nance shepherded them into the back parlour. 'I'll make a brew then leave you to catch up.' Addressing Sarah, she said, 'Make sure you're gone by five o'clock when His Nibs comes home.'

Tea provided, Nance left them alone and mother and daughter sat on opposite sides of the narrow kitchen table. Hannah told her mother what had happened when her father had dragged her to the house. Sarah let her tea go cold, so caught up was she in concern at the violence Charles Dawson had meted out to her daughter.

When Hannah got to the part about Nance attacking him with the poker, she decided to omit any references to Nance's prior connections to her father and his consorting with prostitutes. It was bad enough anyway.

After a while, Sarah asked, 'Are they treating you well here?'

Nodding her head, Hannah told her that she had plenty to eat, the house was big, Sam was courteous and Nance was kind to her, even fetching her library books.

'Sam hasn't hurt you, has he? I mean he isn't rough with you? Inconsiderate?'

'No. He's a kind man. He'd never lay a finger on me. In fact...' Should she tell her mother everything? 'He doesn't touch me at all.'

'You mean in bed?'

Hannah nodded, feeling the blood coursing to her cheeks. 'He doesn't like women. He prefers men.'

'You're serious? So you're still a virgin?'

'Yes.'

Sarah's face broke into a smile.

'He goes out at night. To meet men.' Hannah's face was burning

'That will make getting an annulment easier.' Sarah clasped her hands together. 'But to do that, we first need to get you away from here. Then we can go to the police.'

'No, we can't.'

'But we must. We'll find Will. He'll be able to marry you after all.'

Hannah started to cry.

'What's the matter, love? Don't you want to be with Will? I thought you loved each other.'

She sniffed and fumbled for a handkerchief. 'I wrote him a letter. I told him to forget me. I said some cruel things.'

Her mother put her head in her hands, slumping forward. 'So that's why he's left Liverpool.'

'He has?' Hannah didn't know whether to feel relieved that her letter had achieved the desired effect or devastated that it had.

'I went to find him this morning to tell him that I'd found out where you were living. I thought he'd want to come and get you out of here. I went to the dock and since the *Arklow*, his ship, was out of port, I asked for the Irishman Will told me would know when it was due back.' She stretched her lips. 'The fellow told me Will had signed up with a ship going to Africa. Left a few weeks ago. Says he'll be gone for at least eighteen months – possibly two years. Completely out of the blue apparently. I couldn't understand why he didn't come to see me first and tell me what he was doing and why.'

'Well, now you know.'

'But why did you do it, Han? It doesn't make sense. He was going to try and find you. He and I talked about it. He loves you.'

'I didn't want to wreck his life. I wanted him to forget me.'

'That's silly, love. It's a sham marriage. You had no say in it. You were forced. We could have gone to the police. We still can. We'll get the marriage annulled. I've a piece of good news. It's why I came to see you as soon as I could.'

Hannah looked up at her bleakly, incapable of believing that anything could be described as good news any more.

'I've found out that the place your father took you to be married isn't a proper religious institution. There's no licence to perform marriages. Pastor Henderson is not even a recognised religious official. You're not legally married to Samuel Henderson.' Her mother was grinning and reached across the table to take her daughter's hands. 'I went to the registry office and they said no such place or clergyman was listed. I asked them for a copy of your marriage certificate and they said there wasn't one. They told me to go to the police.'

This was like a body blow to Hannah and she slumped onto the table, now sobbing loudly. 'It's no good. It's too late. Will's gone and it will ruin Sam.'

'What are you talking about?'

'If you go to the police about this, it will mean Sam's life is wrecked. He'll lose his job.'

'That's Sam's problem not yours.'

'I can't do that to him. He could be arrested too. It's against the law to be a homosexual.'

A voice came from behind them and Nance entered the room. 'Actually, it isn't. It's just against the law to be caught performing a homosexual act.'

Hannah flinched and looked at her mother. Neither wanted to imagine what that might entail.

'If you ask me it's only a matter of time before that happens.' Nance raised one eyebrow. 'She covers for him when he goes out at night.' She jerked her head towards Hannah while addressing Sarah.

Hannah gave a little gasp.

'I wasn't born yesterday. The Old Man might sleep like a log but I hear Sam creeping up the stairs at all hours. Unless he's very careful he'll get caught one night.' She pulled herself up to perch half-sitting on the edge of the table. 'Most of the time the police turn a blind eye, but every now and then they have a bit of a purge. Just to keep the politicians happy – and the papers. They're always going on about cleaning up the docks.'

'You seem to know a lot about it.' Sarah looked at Nance curiously, then glanced at her daughter, who looked away.

'I bloody well should do.' Nance laughed. 'When I started out I used to walk the streets round the docks.'

'You were a policewoman?'

Nance collapsed into peals of laughter. 'Cor blimey! That's rich. No. Love. I was a prozzie. On the game. When I first came to Liverpool I used to work the streets but then I got a place in an establishment. Much classier. Pastor Henderson was one of my clients and he paid me to go private about a year ago.' She turned her hands out theatrically. 'So here I am.'

Sarah's mouth dropped open. She turned to her daughter. 'Did you know this?'

Hannah nodded, mutely, praying that Nance wouldn't mention her father's role in all this. It was too much to spring on Sarah at once. She felt protective towards her mother.

Nance evidently recognised this and instead said, 'If Sam's got any sense, he'll steer clear of the docks.'

'He has a special friend. A sailor.' Hannah was blushing. 'They had a quarrel so I don't think he goes near the docks any more.'

Nance rolled her eyes. 'A sailor, eh? Likes a bit of rough, does he, young Sam? If it's not the docks then it's likely it's up a dark alley or in a queers club. Either way, he'll get caught eventually.' She looked towards Sarah for support. 'I keep telling your Hannah she ought to try and coax him out of it. I could give her some tips. It's worth sticking by young Sam as he's going to inherit all of this one day.' She swept her arm through the air. Dropping her voice to a conspiratorial tone she added, 'And between you and me, the Old Man has a tendency to over exert himself. I won't be at all surprised if he pegs out on top of me one night.'

Sarah gave her a look that would have frozen a boiling kettle. 'My daughter has no interest in financial gain. She needs to be free of this sham marriage. And I'm going to do my utmost to make that happen. Now I want to talk to my daughter in private.'

'I've more right to be here than you have, love.' Nance folded her arms. She was still sitting on the edge of the table. 'Besides, you may find I have some useful information.'

Ignoring this, Sarah turned her attention back to Hannah. 'I need to gather the evidence.' Looking at Nance again, she asked, 'Were you present at the so-called marriage?'

'No.'

Hannah said, 'There were only men there. About twelve of them.'

'It's not just the wedding. I want to find out everything I possibly can to incriminate your father. I want him to be taken somewhere he'll not be able to harm you and Judith.'

'If you need a witness to him assaulting Hannah, then I'm your woman. He's a piece of work, Charles Dawson. The most violent man I ever came across.'

Hannah sighed inwardly. It was all coming out.

'You know him?' Sarah frowned.

'Oh yes. I was on the receiving end of his nasty violent tendencies. None of the girls would go with him by the end. He got banned. And believe me that takes some doing.'

If Sarah was shocked, she hid it well. Curling her lip at Nance, she turned to Hannah, and said, 'Didn't you say you had suspicions about what was going on at Morton's?'

'There was more money going out than there should have been. I couldn't get to the bottom of it. I tried to check one of the invoices. It was to a firm that doesn't exist and was for over £40. Merseyside Maritime Services.'

Nance laughed. 'Well, I can help you with that, ladies.' She looked pleased with herself. 'Lots of the gentlemen attending the establishment I used to be part of liked to hide their expenditure there from their wives – and use it to offset their taxes as well probably. They wanted invoices. We had them made out from Merseyside Maritime Services as that was a believable name for a creditor for most of our clientele. Clever, eh?'

'You're saying that my husband spent money on prostitutes and paid for it through our family business?'

'I certainly am.' Nance winked at her.

'Are you willing to testify to this?'

'No. That I'm not. I'd do it gladly to help bang up your rotten husband, but there are a lot of decent enough men who'd risk getting dragged in too. Men who've done nothing wrong except try to keep things private. Most of my clients were family men who just weren't getting it from their wives. Nothing wrong with that. We were providing a public service.' Nance glanced up at the clock on the wall. 'Now, Mrs Dawson, I hate to break up your reunion with your daughter, but it's time you scarpered. The old man will be home soon and he's not going to be pleased to find you here.'

Hannah threw a look of appeal at Nance. 'Please give us five minutes alone.'

'As long as you don't think about doing a runner. If you disappear I'm the one will get it in the neck. You may not realise which side your bread's buttered on, but I certainly know mine. You can have five minutes then I'll open the door.' She locked the back door.

When she'd left the room, Hannah hugged her mother. 'I'm so sorry you had to hear all that, Mother.'

'It's not you who should be sorry, my darling. It's me. I'm the one who let you get caught up in all this. Now, are you absolutely sure you're all right living here, with that creature?'

'Nance is all right. She's been kind to me.'

'I'm not resting until I've got you safely home again and your father where he should be. Behind bars. It's just going to take me a bit longer than I'd hoped. Especially if she won't help.'

'Don't worry about me. I'm fine here. Father won't come back. Nance nearly brained him with that poker.'

Sarah smiled. 'I imagine that was a sight to behold.'

'He was snivelling. Like a frightened child.' She squeezed her mother. 'That was when I realised he's just a pathetic coward.'

'Most bullies are.'

'You will come again, Mother?'

'I'll try. But I don't want to raise his suspicions. I only managed to come today as he's in Manchester. It's a meeting with one of our last remaining customers. I wouldn't be surprised if that one's going the way of the others.'

'As bad as that?'

'I had a chat with Mr Busby. He says sales have dwindled to a trickle. He showed me a letter from a long-standing customer cancelling their account. Uncompetitive pricing and poor service according to the letter.'

'Mr Busby told you that? Whenever I tried to ask him anything he said it was none of my business and told me to ask Father.'

Sarah stroked her hair. 'I've known Mr Busby since my papa was running the business. Since I was a child. Now I must go before that harridan flings me out of the door. We must be patient, my lovely girl.'

Chapter Twenty-Five

Most of the crew aboard the *Christina* were different from those who had sailed into the port of Liverpool back in March. The majority had signed articles for other ships during the *Christina*'s long layover. Fred, the second mate, along with the chief engineer, had signed up again, and Will was also pleased to see Abuchi, and one or two others. Although he would miss Eddie and the O'Connors he had no regrets about walking away from the Irish crossings.

He had stowed his kit bag in his cabin and was heading up the companion way when he bumped into Mr Palmer.

The master gave him a clap on the back. 'Good to see you, Kidd. How did you like Dublin? Quite a change doing those short hops.'

'It was a bit of a deck chair job, sir – apart from the cattle.'

The master gave a wry smile. 'Ah yes. I forgot about that. We don't go to sea to become farmers, do we son?'

Will grinned. 'Cattle's no fun in a rough sea.'

'All good experience, man. You studying hard?'

Will thought of lying but decided to tell the truth. 'To be honest, sir, I got a bit distracted while I was in Liverpool. But I'll be working hard now I'm back on the *Christina*. I'm determined to get my mate's ticket.'

Palmer chuckled. 'A woman, I'll bet. Serious?'

'It didn't work out.'

'Sorry to hear that. It's good for a man to have a woman to come home to. But then I suppose I've always thought of you as a "blue water man", so perhaps I shouldn't be surprised. There are some men who are never happy unless they're at sea and as far away from home as possible.'

Will nodded agreement, while thinking that whilst once that might have been true of him, he'd give up the sea in a heartbeat if it meant he could be with Hannah again.

The master narrowed his eyes. 'I've been talking with the first and second mate, and as you know, we need a new bosun. I'd like you to take the job, Kidd. You ready for that?'

Just a couple of months ago, Will would have been delighted but now he had to force a smile. More money – but for what?

–

After calling at Casablanca and Tenerife, the *Christina* had an uninterrupted run down to Dakar in Senegal and from there a series of trips back and forth bouncing between various west African ports such as Lagos and Accra. This part of Africa wasn't popular with the crew. The countries they visited were poor, the towns shabby, the atmosphere hot and humid, so most of the crew were happy to see Table Mountain at last. After several days in port in Cape Town – always a crew's favourite – they would be collecting and discharging cargo up and down the east coast of Africa, going wherever the loads were.

It was as they docked in Cape Town that news of Prime Minister Chamberlain's momentous meeting with Hitler in Munich reached them. Cheers went up among the crew with relief that the once imminent outbreak of war had been forestalled. 'Peace for our times' was a far better alternative than getting sucked into a war just twenty years after the end of the last one. The men aboard the *Christina* were all too aware that should war have been declared their lives would have changed radically.

In particular, Paolo Tornabene was relieved to hear the news. If war had broken out it wasn't too hard to imagine which side Italy would be on. Chamberlain and Mussolini had recently signed another treaty in which Britain conceded Italy's right to Ethiopia on condition that Italian troops left Spain – but what was that in the face of Mussolini's continuing courtship of the German Chancellor?

Will spent most of his time studying for his mate's ticket. After so many years at sea, much of the syllabus was already familiar to him, but he found his concentration frequently wandering and always in the same direction. He couldn't get Hannah out of his mind. Whenever the distraction proved too much, he would take the now well-thumbed envelope out of his locker and re-read her words in an attempt to drum into his head that she didn't care for him. Constantly thinking about her was fruitless.

Hannah couldn't have loved him. It had all been a lie. Otherwise she couldn't have reconciled herself so quickly to marrying someone else. Even if Sam Henderson was a remarkable man, it was such a rapid turnaround in her affections that it was hard for Will to accept. It just didn't make sense. Every time he tried to push the image and memory of her away, her face was there in front of him: her eyes gazing deep into his, the remembered feel of her mouth on his, the love shining from every pore of her. He saw her face in the cloud formations above, in the shimmering water of the ocean, in the patterns on his retina when he closed his eyes.

Could she really be such an accomplished actress? So fickle in her affections? If she'd cared nothing, why had she led him along? Had he done something to make her suddenly change her feelings for him?

All this self-torture was leading nowhere. He had to forget her and get on with studying tide tables and navigational charts.

Paolo too was finding the voyage hard. He never spoke again of his grief over Loretta, but Will often saw him staring blankly into space, gazing out across the empty sea, lost in thought. Neither of them needed nor wanted to tell the other any of this, but there was an unspoken bond between them. When the other crew members went off to explore the local attractions in each port, the two friends tended to stay on board, Will studying, and Paolo reading or writing to his family. Occasionally, they ventured ashore for a few beers or some local food but avoided the fleshpots of the ports they visited.

Christmas 1938 was spent on board, at sea between Durban and Lourenço Marques in Mozambique. The cuisine on this voyage was significantly poorer than on their previous African roundtrip. They had taken on a new cook in Liverpool who had a tendency to drink and a heavy hand with the salt. The meals on board were known by the crew in the common merchant naval parlance as 'chew and spew'. In Durban, the offending cook had failed to return on board, presumably having fallen down drunk in a bar somewhere. The master had no hesitation in setting sail without him – leaving him to find his own way home to England as a DBS, a distressed British seaman. To replace him, one of the assistant cooks, a Lascar, was promoted to head cook to the delight of the crew, thus ensuring that their Christmas festivities, such as they were, would not be impaired. Food was the last thing on Will's mind. The hilarity of the crew as they enjoyed extra rations of rum and beer was like a mockery to him. As they sang Christmas carols in a tropical rain storm, he imagined the rainy streets of Liverpool, the cold winter temperatures, fir trees lit up with fairy lights and families gathered around coal fires.

–

They had been away from Liverpool for seven months when they sailed into Zanzibar in early January. It was their first call there on this voyage.

'Let's go to Rafqa's,' Will said to Paolo.

The Italian looked at him with astonishment. 'You want to see Rafqa?'

'Why not?' said Will. 'Enough studying. Enough misery. It's 1939 and we've avoided a war. Rafqa's food is the best in east Africa and I feel like getting drunk.'

'Is that *all* you feel like?'

'Well, I can't live like a monk for ever, can I?'

Paolo shrugged. 'Maybe you're right, Mr Bosun, perhaps that's what you need.'

'What about you?'

Paolo shook his head.

'Come on! At least come for a meal and a few drinks. There's always a good band playing at Rafqa's. We both need cheering up.' Will hoped his forced jollity rang truer to Paolo than it sounded to himself.

The friends, along with Fred and Abuchi, headed through Stone Town to Rafqa's. As usual, the bar-café was packed with people, the air smoky, and the music lively. They found a table at the rear and ordered drinks. There was no sign of Rafqa.

After several beers and a spicy Lebanese fish stew, the second mate suggested a change of venue. 'Some of the lads were heading to a bar that's just opened near the quayside. How about we give it a go? We can always come back here later if it's not up to much.'

There was general agreement, but Will said he was staying here for a while. 'I might wander over there later, lads.'

Paolo voiced his doubt at Will. '*Non penso.*' He gave Will a departing wink.

Will called the waiter to bring him some rum. There was no rush to get back to the ship as they were not leaving port for another day or so. With still no sign of Rafqa, he leaned back in his chair and listened to the band. They were performing with a female singer, an African woman, who was singing in French. The nature of the music had changed, with the upbeat swing jazz replaced by a haunting ballad. Will couldn't understand the words of the song, but the sentiment was unmistakable.

> *J'attendrai*
> *Le jour et la nuit, j'attendrai toujours*
> *Ton retour.'*

He let the sad and soulful music wash over him and tried not to think about Hannah.

After nearly half an hour had passed, Will was about to give up the wait for Rafqa, when the curtain at the back of the room parted and the German he recognised from a year ago, emerged. As Will knew all too well, the only place that curtain led to was the stairway to Rafqa's private apartment. The sudden twinge of jealousy caught him by surprise. The man walked past without giving Will a glance and went straight out of the building through the main door at the front.

Some minutes later, the beaded curtain parted, and Rafqa came in. She passed between the tables en route to the bar without seeing him. Will took advantage of this opportunity to watch her closely. Behind the smiles and greetings she offered to customers, she looked anxious, with a tired look playing about her eyes and a slight downturn of her mouth. She was still beautiful – an exotic beauty, with dark eyes and rich black hair and Will felt a little surge of desire.

He drained his glass and was about to move to the bar, when she lifted her head and saw him. She threw him the merest hint of a smile, communicating through her eyes while her mouth remained set. She held an open palm towards him, behind her back, the five fingers splayed, while continuing her conversation with Bebe, the barman. Then without looking again at Will, she disappeared back through the curtain.

Will waited the five minutes as instructed, then leaving the cash for his drink on the table, he took advantage of a burst of applause for the band, to slip through the curtain and climb the stairs after her.

She was waiting in her room, but this time she wasn't naked. Wearing a green silk evening gown, elegant in its simplicity, she was standing by the window, a glass of wine in her hand, staring out over the moonlit rooftops of the city. Beneath them the faint sound of a plaintive saxophone solo drifted upwards.

How long ago it seemed since the last time they had stood here in this room together. A year that felt more like an eternity. Rafqa turned to face him, her expression unsmiling. 'It's been a while, William. I had a feeling I wouldn't see you again.'

Will said nothing, but moved towards her.

She crossed over to a side table where there was an open bottle of wine. 'I can go down to fetch you something stronger if you prefer,' she said, holding up the bottle.

He noticed it was already half empty. Glancing behind him, he saw there was another glass on the drainboard beside the tiny sink. He couldn't help looking towards the bed, but it looked neat and unruffled. Perhaps she had remade it.

'Wine's fine,' he said, taking the glass from her and moving over to sit in the window seat. 'Why didn't you think I'd be back?'

'I don't know. Just a feeling. Female intuition.'

He wanted to ask her about the man, but he suppressed the urge. Better not to know. And anyway, he had no right to ask. Rafqa owed him nothing.

But she seemed to guess what he was thinking. 'You saw my friend leaving?'

'Yes. The German I saw you with last time. The one you pretended not to know.'

'Why do you say that?' She frowned.

'Because you denied talking to him when I asked you that night.'

'Yes, I lied to you. I was being careful.' She looked at him with a steady gaze.

'So, you and he—'

'Had business to discuss. He came up here tonight so we could speak in private.'

Will shrugged. 'You don't have to explain to me, Rafqa. I'm just someone who sails into town once in a blue moon. You owe me nothing. Just because we've slept together a few times—'

'Don't! Don't say things like that, William. I thought we had more respect for each other. You know I don't have casual relationships.'

'I didn't say it was casual.'

'I don't have *any* relationships. I made an exception for you. Perhaps I shouldn't have done.'

Will smiled at her, feeling suddenly very sad. 'I should go.'

She touched his arm. 'Don't go. I don't want you to go. There's nothing between me and that man. Just business.'

He pulled her towards him, kissed the top of her head, ran his hands over her hair then drew her against his chest. 'Oh, Rafqa, Rafqa.' It was like a sigh.

Rafqa looked up at him, her eyes fixed on his. 'You're different, William. Something's changed in you.' She cradled his cheek in one palm, still watching him intently. 'I think you have fallen in love. I can see it in your eyes. Sadly, not with me.' She gave a little bitter laugh, then smiled. 'But you are sad. You have been hurt.' She stood on her toes and kissed him softly in the middle of his forehead. 'My poor, dear William.'

He forced a laugh. 'You have a vivid imagination, Rafqa. There's no one.'

She smiled, reached behind her and unzipped her gown, letting it fall to the floor. 'Come then. We will make love and then you can tell me all about what has happened to you since we last met – if you want to tell me.' He looked at her naked body and let her lead him over to the bed, where she undressed him as he kissed her. He'd been right: the best way to forget a woman and heal a broken heart was in the arms of another woman.

She kissed him again. Looking into her eyes he told himself that this was what he wanted, what he needed, but all he could see was that her eyes, beautiful as they were, weren't Hannah's eyes. He rolled over onto his back. 'I'm sorry, Rafqa. I can't do this. I just can't. It doesn't feel right any more.'

In the moonlight from the open window he could see her bite her lip and fight back incipient tears. She reached for her glass of wine and pulled herself up to lean back against the pillows. 'A pity,' she said. 'Now, are you going to tell me why?'

'You're right,' he admitted. 'I met someone. She's everything I ever wanted and didn't believe it was possible to find in a woman. I can't even say why. Yes, she's beautiful, yes, she's kind and good and clever and interesting. But it's more than that. It's as if I have always known her, but never been able to see her, as though I were searching for her without knowing what I was looking for – or even that I was looking for anything at all.'

Rafqa took another sip of wine, then slid down the bed to lie on her side, facing him, propped up by one elbow.

He reached for her hand. 'I feel bad telling you this, but you and I have always had a special understanding. I feel closer to you and more able to trust you than any other woman – apart from her. I wish I could be a better man for you. I wish I could feel for you in a different way. You deserve so much more than I could ever give you. You are a true friend. You have always been a wonderful lover, but no matter how much I'd like to, I can't love you, Rafqa. Can you understand that?' He lifted her hand and kissed her fingers softly.

She nodded, then sighed. 'You and I have a beautiful time together and I would like to have you in my life more often, but perhaps I'd be kidding myself if I said I truly love you, my darling. I too have been lucky enough to have known true love, but in my case it was snatched from me when my husband died.'

Will frowned. She'd never spoken of him before. He'd always assumed her late husband had been an older man and that it was an arranged marriage.

'Perhaps that's why I recognised it in you tonight. Will you marry this woman?'

'She's married to someone else.'

'Ah! Like that, is it? You should know better, William.'

'She wasn't married when we met. She agreed to marry me, then she went and married someone her father chose for her.'

Rafqa pulled a face. 'You couldn't stop this happening?'

'I didn't find out until it was too late. Even then I was going to try to find her, take her away with me. Look for a way to get her out of the marriage. But it seems I got it all wrong. I read her wrong too.' He told her about Hannah's violent and tyrannical father and how the marriage was

328

arranged and effected in a matter of days while Will was out of the country.

'Then you must help her. This is terrible.' Jerking herself upright she plumped up the pillows behind her and sat up, with her knees drawn up in front, arms around them.

Will reached out of the bed and pulled his cotton jacket off the floor, fishing in the pocket for Hannah's letter. 'Read it. It shows I was living in a fantasy world.' He saw her hesitate. 'Go on. There's nothing private or personal in there. It's like a business letter, dismissing me. I can't believe it's written by the woman I was in love with.' He shook his head. 'Who am I kidding? – *Am* in love with.'

Rafqa took the letter, but before reading it, she asked, 'How do you know it's written by her? Maybe her husband or her father wrote it or coerced her into writing it.'

Will shook his head again. 'No. It's her. I can tell. Give me some credit.'

She unfolded the paper and read it quickly, then again more slowly. 'If you hadn't got the letter what would you have done?'

'Hunted for her of course. Even if it took me forever, I'd have knocked on every door in Liverpool if I'd had to. But I'd have found her.'

'And she would know that?'

Without a moment's hesitation he said, 'Of course.'

'Then she's written it to protect someone. Maybe you yourself? Perhaps someone in her family? Possibly herself. But I don't believe these words and her claim that she'd never loved you.'

'Why do you say that?'

'Because I know you, William. You don't give your love easily. If anyone knows that I do. To give it so completely you must have had something back. You're not the kind of man who is so vain not to be aware of how a woman thinks and feels. If you believed she was in love with you then she *was* in love with you.' She handed the letter back. 'In here she is playing a part. She has written this with the clear intention of making you angry with her. Of encouraging you to go away from her. To stop looking for her. Which is exactly what you have done. And exactly the opposite of what you were going to do.' She reached for her wine glass and drained it. 'Writing this must have caused her great pain.'

'How do you know that? You don't know Hannah. What makes you so certain?'

'I don't know Hannah but I do know you and I know that she must be a very special woman to have caused you to feel so much pain and so much love.' She swung her legs out of the bed and pattered across the room to fetch the bottle of wine. She poured what was left into their glasses. 'You must go back to Liverpool, William. You must go to find her. I am certain she needs your help.'

'What?'

'I mean what I say. You love her. You believe you are meant to be with her, yes?'

He nodded.

'Then you mustn't give in so easily. If she's worth fighting for, you must put on your armour and go to war.' She lifted her glass and chinked it against his. 'Now, much as I would like to spend some time trying to persuade you to make love to me, I'm not stupid enough not to know when I'm beaten. Put your clothes on, my love, and let's sit

330

and watch the stars together. I have a feeling that tonight is the last time you and I will meet, and I want to spend some more time with you. Do you think your Hannah would begrudge me that?'

Will dressed and Rafqa slipped on a silk dressing gown and they went to sit together on the large rug by the window. He reached for her hand, remembering the last time they had sat here, smoking hash together between making love.

As though conscious of that memory too, Rafqa changed the subject. 'So, your Mr Chamberlain pulled you all back from the brink of war.'

'Apparently.'

'I hope he won't one day live to regret appeasing Hitler, but I fear that he will. We all will.' She gave a little smile. 'Or are you still determined to keep your head in the sand about politics?'

'It's been impossible to do that in England. It was all anyone talked about: Hitler and the Sudetenland. They were building up civil defences, digging trenches and giving everyone gas masks. Waste of time that proved to be then.'

'I don't think so. Not at all. I hope they have been building ships and planes and armaments too. I think they'll need them.'

He leaned back. Her face was partly in shadow, the rest illuminated by the moonlight. 'Is that what you were talking to him about?'

'Who?' she said, clearly deliberately pretending not to know.

'Your guest this evening. That's what you do, isn't it, Rafqa? Collect information for him. But which side is he on?'

'You mean which side am I on?'

He grinned. 'You're clever enough to play both sides.' Then he frowned. 'Are you so sure we're not going to have "peace for our time" after all?'

She hugged her knees and pushed a strand of hair behind her ear. 'I wish I knew. I hope it is a lasting peace. But I fear it won't be.'

'You will be careful, won't you? Only, I don't like the look of that German. Are you sure you can really trust him? He looks shifty.'

'I'm a big girl, William. Don't worry about me. And anyway, I'm far too unimportant to be any danger to anyone.' She smiled.

They sat in silence for a few moments as the music played. An upbeat jazz number ended and the tempo changed. It was the same song the woman had sung earlier.

'This song's a beaut,' he said. 'I really like it. Even though I can't understand a bloody word of it.'

'That's because it's speaking to your heart.'

'What's it mean?'

'It means "*I will wait for you. Day and night. I'll always wait for your return*" – she's calling to her lover who has left her to travel far away to distant shores.'

'You're kidding me?'

'I swear. French is my second language. And you know I never lie. *J'attendrai toujours ton retour.*'

He repeated the words and she corrected his awkward French pronunciation, until he had mastered the short line. 'I won't forget that,' he said. Getting up, he pulled

332

her up to her feet. 'I must go now. Thank you, Rafqa. From the bottom of my heart.'

'What will you do? When does your ship return to England?'

'Not for a year. I need to find another way home. Even if it means going DBS.'

'Talk to your captain. He'll understand. You don't want to jeopardise your future career.' She stroked his hair. 'As it happens, I know there's a British coal tanker due in later this week. They're heading back to England via the Cape.'

'And just when I'd been promoted to bosun. It'll be back to being a deck hand for me.'

'Does that matter?'

'Not any more.' He leaned forward and kissed her softly on the lips. 'Thank you, Rafqa. You are and always will be a dear friend to me.'

'Goodbye, William. And God bless.'

A few minutes later as he was walking away, he looked back up the street to the café bar and saw her watching from the window.

Chapter Twenty-Six

It took Will three weeks to reach Liverpool. He had left the *Christina* with Palmer's blessing and the promise that there'd be a berth for him if things didn't work out with his quest to rescue Hannah. The well-connected Palmer fixed for him to work his passage on the coal tanker Rafqa had mentioned.

After depositing his bags at the Sailors' Home, he went straight to Bluebell Street. On the voyage back to England he'd had plenty of time to rehearse what he was going to say to Hannah, but first he had to find out where she was.

Mindful not to endanger any of the Dawson women by attracting the ire of Charles Dawson, a man he had yet to meet, Will approached the house via the back alley. It was early evening and already dark. The sky was moonless and there was no lighting in the back lane so he felt his way along with his hand on the brick wall, almost sending an empty dustbin clattering down the cobbles, but righting it just in time. When he estimated he must be close to the house, he lit a match and held it up to the gate. The number painted roughly on the wooden panels showed he must be outside the house next door. When he tried to open the right gate, this time it was bolted shut. The corporation dustcart must have been emptying the bins that day as several were lying about in the alley.

He upturned one of them and used it to help him climb up and over the wall, grateful that, unlike most of their neighbours, the Dawsons hadn't embedded broken glass into the top of the wall to deter burglars.

Feeling like a housebreaker, he landed in the yard and crept towards the light from the scullery window. Peering in, he thought at first the room was empty. He was about to try the back door, then realised that, as it was evening, Dawson could well be home. Cursing his stupidity, he was about to head round to the street to knock on the front door and, if Dawson answered, pretend he'd come to the wrong house. It was then that he noticed the shoe. A black leather ladies' shoe with a bar strap and a small heel. It was sticking out from behind the kitchen table in the room beyond. As his brain processed this information, his heart leapt inside his chest as the adrenaline sent a shock wave through his body. It wasn't just a shoe. There was a foot attached to it and beyond that the curve of an ankle.

Without hesitating, Will grabbed the door handle and tried to turn it. Locked. Throwing his whole weight against it, he shouldered the door. Nothing. It must be dead bolted. He shoved his hand inside his jacket pocket for protection and smashed the glass window panel in the door. The sound echoed as the glass shattered. In just two steps he was inside the back parlour.

Sarah Dawson was lying in the space between the table and the closed door to the hallway. It took no more than a second to establish that she was dead. Blood was pooled underneath her and her eyes were glassy like a china doll's. Will could see that she had been hit over the head with some form of blunt instrument. On one side her singed hair was matted with blood and her skull had clearly taken a heavy blow. An ironing board was collapsed on the floor beyond her. The still warm iron, evidently the instrument of her death, lay against the skirting board.

Knowing that Hannah's sister might be in danger, he stepped over Sarah's body and pushed open the door into the tiny hall space. The door to the front parlour was wide open and the room empty. He turned to go up the stairs and came face to face with Charles Dawson for the first time. Dawson froze momentarily, then his eyes moved wildly and his head jerked as if twitched by an electric shock.

'Accident.' Dawson tried to push past him. 'The police. Someone broke in and attacked my wife.'

Will stepped in front to stop Dawson from coming down the last stair and into the hall.

'You're going nowhere, you bastard.'

'You don't understand. My daughter's upstairs. I was just checking she's unharmed. I must find a telephone box to call the police and an ambulance.'

'I told you, you're going nowhere. And your wife won't be needing an ambulance. She's dead. You've killed her. But you know that as well as I do, don't you?'

'Stand aside!' Dawson began to scream. 'Whoever you are, you're going to pay. God will smite you as he smote the evil in the cities of Sodom and Gomorrah. I am God's instrument!' He hammered on the wall. 'Help! Murder! Help! Call the police.' His fist pounded into the dividing wall. In a moment there was banging on the front door and someone shouted through the letterbox, 'What's going on?'

Will shouted. 'Get the police. NOW!'

He heard the man say, 'Madge, run and get the bobbies. Oy Frank, gissa hand. There's something up in the Bible-basher's house!'

Dawson took advantage of the commotion outside the door to try again to push past Will. This time he lunged at him, throwing his body weight against Will and knocking the breath out of him.

Will saw red. Sarah was dead and Hannah's sister was upstairs, possibly harmed herself. He righted himself and grabbed Dawson's arm just as he was in the act of opening the front door. He twisted the arm behind him into a half Nelson, pushing Dawson's face hard against the wall.

By now there was a small crowd on the pavement and the first man stepped through the open door into the cramped space. 'What's going on? Who the hell are you?' He was addressing Will.

Another man pushed past them and went into the back room. 'Oh my God. The wife's dead. Head bashed in.'

As he said it, there was a muffled scream from the top of the stairs. 'No! Mother!'

The two men converged on Will in the narrow space of the hall, each grabbing an arm and freeing Dawson. Before Will could do anything, they'd pushed his head against the wall. Dawson was through the open front door running and down the street.

Judith stumbled down the stairs. Her voice was distorted as though she had strained it. 'Let him go!' she rasped. 'It was my father. He's killed Mother. Smashed her head with the iron.' She collapsed into a heap at the bottom of the stairs.

Will turned to his assailants. 'Is there someone who can look after her? She's in shock.' He reached for Judith's hand and squatted in front of her. 'I'm Will. Hannah's friend. I need to know where she is.'

'I know who you are. You have to get to her before he hurts her. I think he's gone mad.' She began to sob, the intensity of her crying mounting.

'Tell me where she is, Judith. What's the address?'

She said nothing, her tears now turned into big gulping sobs.

A voice boomed into the hall. 'Police. Everybody out unless you live here. We'll get to you later if we need you.' The constable's physical size and the authority of his uniform filled the hall. 'Now what do we have here?'

'There's a dead woman through there. Her husband killed her and this is her daughter. You need your men to get after him. He's just run away.'

Judith looked up at last and Will saw for the first time that her neck was red where her father must have been trying to strangle her. With mounting horror, he realised that he must have got here just in time. He could take little satisfaction from that, knowing that had he come straight here without dropping his kit bag off, Sarah might be alive too.

'And who might you be?' The policeman had his little notebook out, pencil poised.

'Never mind who I am. We have to stop him. His other daughter is in danger. I have to get to her.' He turned back to Judith. 'Tell me the address, Judith.'

Her voice was a weak croak. 'I don't know. It's a house with a name to do with trees and it's in Orrell Park.'

The policeman called over his shoulder to another constable waiting outside the door. 'Get onto Orrell Park nick and tell them to go to any house called by the name of

338

a tree. The Oaks, The Chestnuts, The Limes, whatever. Tell them it's a murder and the killer could be heading there.' He turned to Will. 'Now where's the body?'

But all Will could think was that Hannah was in mortal danger. He pushed past the copper and ran down the street. He could pick up a taxicab on Stanley Road if he was lucky. He ran as fast as his legs could carry him and was relieved to see that if any of the coppers had tried to follow him they had abandoned the chase before he got to the main road.

He was lucky. There was a cab dropping a group of men off outside a social club. Inside, he told the driver to head for Orrell Park.

'Whereabouts, lad?'

'I don't know. It's a house named after a tree. That's all I know.'

The driver gave an exaggerated sigh.

'Look, fella, a murder's just been committed and unless you get me there in time there might be another one.'

Alarmed, the driver slammed on the brakes.

'Not me, mate. I'm trying to stop it.' He held up his hands. 'It's my girlfriend. Her father's just killed her mother and is probably heading there to kill her too.' As he spoke the words the urgency of situation hit him and he yelled. 'Now, step on it!'

The driver took off with a scream of tyres. Leaning over his shoulder he said, 'Most of the houses round there have numbers. If it's got a name it'll might be in Orrell Lane or Moss Lane. There's some big houses there with gardens and trees.'

Will leaned forward in the seat, anxious. He had to get to Hannah before her father did. The driver, now enjoying the fact that he was caught up in a drama, kept his foot down, screeching round corners like a rally driver. When they approached a fork in the road by the Orrell Park Ball Room, he showed down. Which one shall we try first? Moss left or Orrell right?'

'Left.'

The car turned into Moss Lane.

'I'll get out and do it on foot. We can't see the house names from the car.' He handed the driver half a crown.

'You want me to come with you?'

'No. I'm sure I'm ahead of him. I'll find it.'

'If it isn't along here, when you hit the parade of shops, turn right and it'll take you to Orrell Lane.'

'Cheers, mate.'

'Good luck!'

Will's heart lifted when he saw the first big house was called Cherry Tree Lodge. He raced up to the door and knocked loudly. An elderly woman opened it.

'I'm looking for the Hendersons.'

She looked him up and down. 'Wrong house.' The door closed on him before he had a chance to ask if she knew where they lived. The next house was a doctor's surgery, and the following pair were conjoined and called Galway Villas. Ahead, he could see the row of shops the taxi driver had mentioned. After Runnymede and Kelvinside, he approached the last but one property with a growing sense of urgency. The Laurels. The house appeared to be in darkness, but when he hammered on the knocker he heard footsteps, a hall light spilled through the glass panel above and the door swung open.

A peroxide blonde stood on the threshold, appraising Will as though he were a colt at a bloodstock sale. She wore a silk dressing gown patterned with a display of red rambling roses. A cigarette dangled nonchalantly from the corner of her mouth, like the bad girl in a gangster movie. 'And what can I do for you, sailor?' she said. 'You are a sailor I presume? I can always tell.'

Will thought it must be the wrong house, but desperate not to make a mistake, he said, 'I'm looking for Hannah.'

No sooner were the words past his lips than there was movement behind the blonde, who took a step aside. Hannah was standing, frozen, in the middle of the hallway. For a fraction of a second that seemed to stretch forever, she stared at him and then he held his arms open and she cannoned into them.

Will held her against him, feeling her heart thumping against his own, her breath coming in little jerks. It was really her. He'd found her. In time. Unharmed. His overwhelming feeling was of gratitude. She *did* love him. Rafqa had been right. There was no mistaking it. How could he have ever doubted her?

'I thought I'd never see you again. I'm so sorry for sending that terrible letter. I can explain why. Oh Will, I can't believe it's you.'

Before he could reply, Nance's London accent cut across their reunion. 'Well, *I* can't believe it's so bleeding cold this evening. Get your arses inside and I can shut the bloody door.'

They did as instructed, still clinging onto each other as though if either let go both would drown.

'Now, is someone going to tell me what the hell's going on?' Nance removed her cigarette and leaned back against the wall.

A door at the rear of the hall opened. 'What's the commotion? Who are you? What are you doing in my house. Take your hands off my daughter-in-law.' Amos Henderson stood in the middle of the hallway, hands on hips. He reminded Will of a hippopotamus: his face jowled, with a disproportionately large jaw, enormous nostrils, short legs and a fat stomach. He bellowed up the stairs, 'Get down here, Samuel. At once.'

Hannah swung round to face Henderson. 'I'm not your daughter-in-law. Sam and I are not legally married. My mother has the proof. She's going to the police. Your church is a sham. My wedding was a sham. It has no legal standing.'

Henderson's lip curled. He went on the attack. 'You've been living as man and wife with my son and in the eyes of God you are married.'

'That's not true.' Sam's voice broke through the tension. 'We have never been man and wife.' He came down the stairs and stretched a hand out to shake Will's. 'You must be Will. You're a lucky man. Hannah is a wonderful woman. I only wish I could have been a husband to her, but I could not.' He smiled. 'But I imagine you, sir, are happy about that?'

Will drew Hannah closer. She looked up at him. 'It's true. He never laid a finger on me.'

Amos Henderson's face was scarlet and he looked as if he were about to have a heart attack. 'You're a useless excuse for a son. A pansy! I'm ashamed of you. Your late mother will be turning in her grave to hear you.'

'No, Father. The truth is Mummy always accepted me for who I am. I didn't have to play a part for her. She loved me just the same.'

'Then it's as well she's dead.'

In the face of this talk of the late Mrs Henderson Will was acutely aware that Hannah didn't yet know about the death of her own mother. He felt his throat constrict. How was he going to break the news to her? How could he shatter the joy of their reunion?

Before he could do or say anything, there was a hammering on the door.

Before Will could warn her, Nance, nearest to the door, reached behind her and opened it. Charles Dawson stood on the threshold, a carving knife in his hands.

The pastor stepped forward. 'Charles! What's going on? Do you know this man?' He waved a hand in Will's direction.

Dawson reached for the nearest person, who happened to be Nance. Moving fast, from behind, he threw his arm round her neck, gripping her in a lock hold. She tried to scream but the pressure from his elbow against her throat prevented it.

With his other hand he moved the knife up so that the point was above his arm and against her throat. Her eyes widened with fear and she stopped struggling. Still holding her, Dawson drew her against him and lifting one leg kicked the door shut behind him. Everyone waited. The long case clock at the rear of the hall rang the hour. Seven o'clock. Dawson looked crazed, eyes wild, traces of spittle at the corners of his mouth. He seemed to have developed a nervous twitch. Will was the only person who knew he was now a murderer. Where were the police? If he'd found The Laurels why hadn't they? He tried to think what to do. He could feel Hannah's body shaking as he held her against him. Her safety was paramount.

'My wife is dead and that man has killed her.' Dawson's voice rose in pitch. 'Now he wants to kill my daughter.'

As he spoke, everything happened at once. Sam hooted in derision. The pastor turned towards Will and was about to grab hold of him. Will felt Hannah's body jerk, then she slipped forward, slumping towards the floor as a moan came from her that was chilling in its intensity. A cry of grief, loss, fear and anger. He supported her then helped her onto a chair that Sam pulled towards them. Will dropped to his knees beside her, cradling her in his arms. She looked at him her face white, her lips pale. 'Is it true? Is Mother dead?'

Will nodded and held her against him. Her breathing was jerky, laboured, and he felt her tears against his face. In that moment he wanted nothing more than to plunge that knife straight through Charles Dawson. He turned to look at him and saw that there was a thin line of red blood under Nance's chin and the woman was whimpering.

'Let her go.' The pastor's voice was like thunder. 'Now! Or I'll kill you myself, Dawson.'

'I'll let her go as soon as you hand this man to the police. They'll be here any minute. He must pay for what he's done. Spawn of the devil!' He jabbed a finger at Will, while the other hand continued to hold the carving knife against Nance's throat. 'He seduced my daughter and filled my wife's head with lies and calumnies against me. The Lord will smite him dead as he smote the armies of Israel. Like Judah's son, this man *was wicked in the sight of the Lord and the Lord will slay him.*'

Before anyone could respond, Nance brought her right leg up and jerked her heel backwards into Dawson's groin. Dawson bent double, screaming in pain, still clutching the

344

knife. Freed from his grip, Nance crumpled to the floor in a heap. A stain spread across her dressing gown joining up the roses into a continuous sea of red.

The sight of Nance in peril stirred Hannah and she broke away from Will and knelt on the floor beside her friend. Dawson was lying against the skirting board, nursing his injury with one hand, still moaning. Will stepped forward and pressed a foot down hand on the arm that held the knife. Dawson yelped again. Sam swung his leg back and landed a kick in the small of Dawson's back.

Nance was still breathing and Hannah felt herself pushed out of the way. The pastor was now on the floor beside her, trying to pull Nance upright. Tears were coursing down his jowly cheeks and the front of his white shirt was coloured with her blood. His face was crimson.

Before Hannah could do anything to help Nance, there was a hammering on the door and Will opened it to reveal four policemen on the doorstep. At the end of the drive was a waiting ambulance and a Black Maria.

'Right. What's going on here?' The first policeman, with stripes on his epaulette, stepped over the threshold and saw the blood which was all over the neck and chest of the now unconscious Nance. He called over his shoulder. 'Ambulance. There's an injured woman. Move!'

The ambulance men rushed into the hall and within moments had Nance on a stretcher and out of the house. A sobbing Henderson was held back by one of the policemen.

'Can I go with her?' asked Hannah.

'Right now, no one's leaving. When we're done with you, you can go and see her. They'll be taking her to

Walton Hozzie, just down the road. You'll only get in the way now and I have some questions for you all.'

He turned his attention to Charles Dawson who was cowering and whimpering, the knife hand still pinned under the weight of Will's foot. A pool of urine spread out underneath him to mingle with the blood on the Minton tiled hall floor.

The police sergeant turned to the two constables. 'Cuff him and take him in. And tell the Desk to call Bootle to let them know we've got him. He's pissed his pants so hold your noses, lads.' As the policemen pulled Dawson to his feet, he dropped the knife and allowed himself to be led away, still muttering Biblical curses and calling on God to avenge him.

'What's in here?' The sergeant gestured at the first door.

'The drawing room.' Sam held open the door to show him.

'Right. We'll use that. The Detective Inspector will be here soon. You first.' He jerked his thumb at Will to indicate he should go inside and then told the remaining policeman to take the Hendersons and Hannah into another room. 'Keep an eye on them. I'll see them one at a time, when I'm done with the other fellow. Starting with him.' He pointed at the pastor, who looked as though he were in shock.

–

Hannah was numb. In the space of less than half an hour her entire life had changed. Joy at the return of Will and at the knowledge that he still loved her was tempered by the terrible news she was struggling to absorb, that her mother

346

was dead. And now Nance was in hospital fighting for her life. All at her father's hand. The hatred and the madness she had seen in his eyes were in themselves shocking. His past unpredictable outbursts and violence had not prepared her for the sheer evil of what she had witnessed in him tonight. Evil mixed with cowardice and weakness. Just as she had seen that day when Nance went for him with the poker. Charles Dawson was a liar, a hypocrite, a bully, and now a cold-blooded murderer. She sat at the kitchen table between Sam and his father, with the policeman standing guard beside them. Laying her head on her folded arms she allowed herself to weep quietly for her mother. A hand was placed on her back and she lifted her head as Sam passed her a cup of tea.

Then it hit her. What about Judith? Where was she? How was she?

'My sister!' she cried, jumping up from the table. 'I have to find her and see if she's all right.' She tried to leave the room but the policeman blocked her. 'Please! I have to go to her.'

'Sit down,' the constable growled, but his eyes showed some compassion. 'Now, don't move so much as a muscle or you'll be in trouble. I'll go and find out about your sister.' He disappeared for a few minutes.

When he returned he smiled at Hannah. 'Apparently your sister's fine, love. At least according to your friend, Mr Kidd, next door.' He indicated the drawing room. 'He was the one who discovered your mother's body and he saw your sister before he came over here. She was distressed, but unhurt. The Detective Inspector's arrived now and he's going to ask Bootle nick to send your sister over here in a car.'

Hannah heaved a sigh of relief that Judith was safe. Losing her as well as their mother would have been more than she was able to bear. Sam gave her arm a little squeeze. As she turned to look at him there was a thump. Amos Henderson's head hit the table.

Hannah and Sam jumped to their feet but the constable got there first. Henderson was slumped forward, head turned to one side, open eyes staring sightlessly into a void. The constable felt for a pulse.

Nothing.

With Sam's assistance the policeman pulled the pastor upright, but his head lolled unsupported by his neck. It was clear he was dead.

Nance was in hospital for two weeks. She had lost a lot of blood but fortunately the knife had not severed her jugular vein. Hannah and Sam sat at her bedside and broke the news to her that the pastor was dead.

'Poor old bugger. I was actually quite fond of the old pervert, despite all the fire and brimstone. Felt sorry for him in a way. God rest his soul.'

'I doubt that.' Sam frowned. 'No man has the right to pour judgement on another when he's full of sin himself.'

'Sin? Cor blimey, Sammy. What bleeding right do you have to talk about sin?'

'As much right as anyone. Including my father. Wasn't it a sin to force me into marriage? A sin to make Hannah marry me against her will? And a sin to consort with prostitutes while my mother lay dying? To preach about sinful women while exploiting them to satisfy his own lust?' His voice was angry. 'And a sin to create a church solely as a means of generating money?'

Nance closed her eyes. 'I'm not going to argue with you. There's a bloody hornet's nest of bad things, but I put most of the blame on Dawson. Old Henderson was a blithering idiot with a liking for a bit of corporal punishment but he never did anything really bad. Least not to me.'

Hannah thought for a moment then said, 'He colluded with my father to force me into a marriage. A marriage that he wasn't legally allowed to perform. And he must have known about my father's violence – how could he not? Yet he went along with all that. He paid money to him to keep him quiet about Sam.'

Nance said nothing. Her eyes closed again and Hannah looked at Sam. 'Time to go,' she said.

Chapter Twenty-Seven

Will proposed to Hannah on the sands at Crosby. This time it was a warm spring day and cotton wool clouds skittered across a pale turquoise sky.

'When your mother died, I was more terrified than I have ever been in my entire life,' he told her. 'The thought of your father getting to you before I could... I don't know what I'd have done. I couldn't have gone on living myself if anything had happened to you.' He looked down at her face. 'As soon as we can, I want to marry you. I can't bear the thought of another day without you.'

'I want it too. More than anything. But, please, let's wait until the trial's over. I can't think about the future while that's hanging over us. I want it all behind us when we marry. I want it to be a day of complete uninterrupted happiness.'

'The trial's a foregone conclusion, Hannah. No jury could fail to convict your father.'

'He'll hang for it, won't he?'

Will kept his gaze steady. 'Yes.'

'So we'll both have fathers who were executed for murder. I doubt there's many couples who can say that.'

He said nothing but reached for her hand, wrapping his own around it.

'My father deserves to die. Yours didn't,' she said.

He pulled her against him and cradled the back of her head with the palm of one hand. 'I love you so much and I wish I could protect you from all this. From the trial. From the probable verdict. From everything.'

'I don't need to be protected from any of it. The only thing I want to be protected from is losing you.'

'I'll make sure that won't happen.' He held her face in his hands, locking his eyes onto hers. 'When we're married, I'm going to give up the sea.'

She was startled. 'But that's your life.'

'It was. But now you're my life and the thought of sailing across the world and leaving you behind in Liverpool for months is not going to work. It's not what I want. Not what I want for you. For either of us. Those months when I was at sea after I got your letter were unbearable. The knowledge that I might never see you again. It was too painful to think about.'

'Then don't think about it. I'm still ashamed about that letter. Even though I wrote it because I loved you so much that I wanted you to be free.'

'But it was only my believing that you didn't love me that made it possible for me to go on that voyage. How can I do that now, knowing I'll be leaving you behind for months, knowing how much we love each other? No, Hannah I can't do that.'

'You could do the Irish ships again.'

He shook his head. 'That's no life. Not much better than working the ferries.'

'So what will you do?'

'I want to take you back to Australia with me.' Feeling her body stiffen, he added, 'Judith too of course. I know how much you mean to each other. There'll be nothing

351

for her here if you're gone. We can all make a new life for ourselves there, away from all this. Away from all the terrible things that have happened. But we need to do it as soon as we can. Everyone's saying there'll be a war after all. That peace treaty wasn't worth the paper it was written on. If war does happen then they'll expect me to go back to sea. This could be our last chance to get away.'

He led her over to the dunes and they sat down on the soft sand, her head resting on his shoulder.

'Australia,' she said, savouring the word. She frowned, her mouth stretched tight, thinking, then she smiled. 'It sounds like the perfect adventure. Tell me about it. Is it very beautiful there?'

'It's a bonzer country. Vast empty spaces with nothing but canyons and miles of gum forests. Rolling plains for sheep and cattle. Small friendly towns, like MacDonald Falls, where I come from. Big cities like Melbourne and Sydney. Clean cities with trees and skies and shimmering water.' He swept an arm in the direction of Liverpool. 'None of these blackened buildings and squalor and crowded houses. If we were there now, we'd be looking out at Sydney Harbour instead of that grey dirty Mersey. It's the most beautiful place on earth, if you ask me – and I've seen plenty. Water the colour of your dress, brilliant sunshine, none of the smog we have here, warm water you can swim in, lots of little coves and inlets and islands. It's a beaut, is Sydney.' He thought for a moment. 'Here, it's all black and white and grey, even when the sun's out, like today. There, the colours are so bright it makes your eyes blink.'

'It sounds beautiful. Is that where we'd live? Sydney?'

'Maybe. We'll certainly visit it. But I was thinking I'd like to buy a plot of land and farm it.'

Hannah smiled. 'Really? So I'd be a farmer's wife?'

'How would you like that?' He grinned at her.

'As long as you're the farmer I'd like it a lot.' She lifted her face to kiss him.

When they eventually drew apart, he said, 'I've written to the school teacher in MacDonald Falls. Her name's Verity Radley and she was your aunt's best friend. I've asked her to pass on a letter to say that I've found you and we're going to be married. If anyone knows where Lizbeth is it'll be Miss Radley.'

'You didn't mention Mother, did you?'

He brushed a finger over her lips. 'No, I thought that was something you need to tell her yourself. When you finally meet her again.'

'That would make going to Australia even better. To know that Judith and I might one day see Aunt Elizabeth again. Oh, Will, that would make me so happy.'

'That's all I want to do now. Make you happy, my dearest love.'

–

While they waited for Charles Dawson's trial to begin, Will returned to the Irish runs on a temporary basis. He needed money if he were to bring both Hannah and her sister to Australia. While he could work his passage, he would need to pay for theirs. He also wanted to save as much as possible for a down payment on some land when they got to Australia.

Four months after Sarah's death, Dawson was arraigned for the murder of his wife and the attempted murders of his daughter, Judith, and Nance Cunningham. To her intense relief, Hannah was not required to testify.

She visited her father on one occasion only, while he was still on remand awaiting trial, but the visit was distressing. He showed no remorse at all over the murder of her mother. He continued to rant and spit forth verses from the Bible to justify what he had done as part of his divine mission. By the end of the brief visit, Hannah had come to the conclusion that he was insane. Perhaps he had always been. Maybe her fear had prevented her from recognising that he was a psychopath.

Criminal insanity was offered up in court in mitigation by the defence, but carried little weight with the judge. The prosecution summoned a wide range of witnesses. The neighbours admitted they had frequently heard Dawson's violent outbursts through the walls but had not realised they were so serious or life-threatening. Sam Henderson attested to the attack on Nance Cunningham. A string of women, including Nance Cunningham herself, testified to Dawson's violent attacks with much salacious detail to the great entertainment of the public gallery and the lasting gratitude of the Liverpool Post and the Echo, which had record sales for the duration of the trial. Will told of the discovery of Sarah's body, the marks on Judith's neck and the subsequent attack on Nance.

The most incriminating evidence came from Judith. Hannah's fears that her sister would crumble under questioning were unfounded. The eighteen-year-old stood tall in the witness box and gave her answers clearly and succinctly. She was asked about the circumstances immediately prior to the death of her mother.

'Mother was in the scullery washing up. I was in the back parlour, pressing a dress I was making. When my father came home, if it wasn't for the fact that he's a teetotaller I would have thought he'd been drinking. He immediately started shouting at Mother. He called her names.'

'What kind of names?' The prosecuting counsel asked.

'He called her a shameless harlot. A sinful daughter of Eve.'

'And how did your mother respond?'

'She didn't. Well, not at first. She carried on doing the dishes.'

'Then what happened, Miss Dawson?'

'He got angry. He went into the scullery and grabbed her by the hair and pulled her into the back parlour. He was hurting her. She begged him to stop. I begged him too. Then he pushed her hard against the wall and she fell over. When she got up she made a terrible mistake.'

'A terrible mistake?' The Counsel echoed.

'She told him she'd got proof that the marriage between my sister and her husband was invalid.'

A murmur ran around the court.

'They were forced by my father to marry and the wedding was carried out in a place that was not a proper church by a man who was not authorised to perform marriages. And Mother had found out he'd been black-mailing someone. He'd also been spending money from the company that he shouldn't have. She'd found false bills.'

The defending barrister got to his feet and said, 'Your Honour, this has no bearing on the case. My client is not being tried for fraud or blackmail.'

'I imagine there was no room left on the charge sheet,' muttered the judge sarcastically to much laughter. Dawson's counsel sat down again, scowling.

The judge turned to Judith. 'Continue, please, Miss Dawson.'

Judith looked across the court to where her father was sitting in the dock. For the first time she seemed to waver, to look nervous. Her eyes wandered round the room until she located Hannah, who gave her a smile of encouragement.

'Then Mother got back on her feet. She said that my father had no right to call her names when she had found out he had been visiting prostitutes and had been paying them out of the company money. She called him a dirty hypocrite.'

Another buzz ran around the courtroom and the judge banged his gavel.

Judith's lip trembled and she began to cry. Fumbling for her handkerchief she dried her eyes and after another quick glance at Hannah, stood tall again. 'That's when he grabbed the iron. He picked it up by the handle from the ironing board and smashed it over her head.' Tears streamed down her cheeks. 'My mother didn't make a sound. She just crumpled into a heap. I ran out of the room. I was going to go for help but he'd locked the front door, so I ran upstairs and locked myself in my bedroom. Almost immediately he came upstairs and kicked the door in.'

'What happened then?'

'I thought I was going to die. He tried to strangle me. He had both hands round my neck and was squeezing. Then there was a sound of breaking glass from downstairs.

He let go. For a moment I thought it was Mother. That she was all right. That she was trying to raise the alarm.' She dried her eyes again. 'But it was Mr Kidd breaking the glass in the back door. That's when my father went downstairs. That was the last time I saw him until today. After that, I heard all the people in the house, neighbours and police, so I thought it was safe to come downstairs. By then my father had gone. The police interviewed me, then the doctor looked at me. He tried to persuade me to go to hospital, but I felt alright and I just wanted to be with my sister.' Her voice quavered. 'So, finally they took me to her in a police car.'

The only question from Dawson's lawyer was whether Judith could be certain it was her father's blow that proved fatal to Sarah Dawson. If he was about to launch into a theory that someone else – no doubt William Kidd – was the actual killer he had no chance to pursue it as the judge cut him off immediately. 'Don't waste the court's time, Mr Davies, we have already heard medical evidence from the pathologist that the victim was killed by a single blow to the skull. Miss Dawson is not a medical expert. Any more diversionary tactics like that and I'll hold you in contempt.'

The case for the defence was feeble. The decision to call members of Henderson's church as character witnesses backfired when, under cross examination by the prosecution, it was revealed that both Dawson and Henderson had extorted substantial and increasing sums of money from them in so-called religious tithes.

When the jury took just an hour to find Charles Dawson guilty, the court was bursting at the seams and a cheer went up from the public gallery as the death sentence was intoned by the judge.

Since the night of her mother's death, Judith remained with Hannah in the Henderson house along with Sam and Nance. The sisters now shared what had been Sam and Hannah's bedroom, while Sam cleared out the whips and canes and moved into his father's old bedroom. The whole house felt different now. The joy of knowing there was no risk of an angry or violent outburst, the pleasure at bringing books home, entertaining guests, listening to the wireless and sharing meals around the dining room table was a new experience for them both. Will was a frequent visitor at dinner whenever he was in port.

On the day of the verdict, Judith and Hannah stayed behind at The Laurels, not wanting to be in court to witness their father being sentenced. They waited for the other three to return.

'You don't have to tell us,' said Hannah. 'We all knew what to expect.'

Will nodded and took Hannah in his arms. 'It's all over now, my love. We can get on with the rest of our lives.'

Hannah shed no tears. She'd cried herself out over the loss of her mother and she wasn't going to waste any tears on her father. As Will held her, she reached out a hand and grasped Judith's. Easing herself away from Will, she turned to face Nance and Sam. 'We are a family now. All of us.' She looked at Will, who nodded. 'We want you three to be the first to know. Will and I are going to be married. As soon as we can get the licence.' She gave a little smile to Sam. 'A proper licence. And we will be married in a proper church. I was wondering if you'd give me away, Sam?'

'I'd be honoured.' A wide grin broke across his face.

'And we'll make sure you get a proper wedding this time, ducky. A real party.' Nance rubbed her hands together.

Judith was jumping up and down with glee. 'At last. Something happy! I can't wait to start making your dress.'

'You a dressmaker, love?' Nance raised her eyebrows. 'You and I are going to be the best of friends, I can tell.' She put her arm round Judith's shoulder.

–

British law required that a minimum of three Sundays must elapse between an individual's sentencing to death and the execution, to allow for the emergence of any new evidence. None was forthcoming, and early in the morning of Monday 28th August 1939 Charles Henry Dawson was hanged at Walton Jail, less than a fifteen-minute walk from The Laurels. No one sitting around the breakfast table in the house that morning spoke of it, but the four of them were all acutely aware of Dawson going, unrepentant, to meet his maker.

Hannah's wedding to Will was set for the following Saturday. When they'd booked the date and made their plans, neither of them had expected that Hitler would invade Poland the day before. But by then, Will already knew that their planned voyage to Australia would probably need to be postponed. Some passenger liners had already been 'taken up from trade', fitted with guns and readied to act under Royal Naval command to protect merchant convoys. Britain would be dependent on the merchant ships to keep the island in food, raw materials and armaments. Now, with war an inevitability, Will had a big decision to make. The night before their marriage, with news of the invasion of Poland very much on their minds, the couple were alone in the drawing room at The Laurels. After all the years of music being banned under his father's roof Sam had bought a gramophone player, and music at last filled the house regularly.

Will produced a record from behind his back. 'I've been looking for this everywhere, but today I found it in a shop in Bold Street. I heard it in a bar in Africa and as soon as I did, I couldn't help thinking about you. It's in French.' He took it out of its paper cover and slotted it onto the player. Before he eased the arm back and placed the needle on the disc, he spoke the words he had remembered so carefully. They sounded awkward with his Aussie twang. '*J'attendrai toujours ton retour.*'

Hannah put her head to one side, puzzled, then as the music filled the room, she smiled. 'What a beautiful song. How sad. Do you know what the words mean?'

'I will always wait for you to come back.'

Hannah placed her hand on his arm. Moving in front of him she put her other hand on him and looked deep into his eyes. 'I knew you were worried. You don't have to tell me why.'

He looked startled. 'What do you mean?'

'We can't go to Australia. Not yet anyway.'

Will's jaw dropped. 'How did you know?'

'Because I know you so well. You're a man of honour, the bravest man I've ever known. You won't be able to become a farmer, knowing that there's a war going on here.'

'Oh, Hannah, I don't know what to do. I'm in a turmoil. I can't bear the thought of leaving your side ever again, but I can't just run away from Hitler. I went to a meeting this morning. Everyone reckons war will be declared any day now. Probably some time this weekend. Chamberlain is giving Hitler a chance to pull back – but we all know he won't. The Prime Minister has no choice now. No more appeasement, he has to take the country to war, and that means the whole empire including Australia will be sucked in. I can't stand by and do nothing.'

'Will, you don't need to explain. I understand completely. I wouldn't love you the way I love you if you were a man who put himself first.'

'I put *you* first. That's what my problem is.' He drew her close against his body, her head resting on his chest. 'Look, I want you and Judith to go to Australia without me. My old ship, the *Christina* is already heading back to Liverpool. I'm going to rejoin it if they'll have me. I'm ready to do whatever we have to for the war effort. But I want you to go to Australia where you'll be safe. Hitler's Blitzkrieg won't stretch that far.'

'I'm not going. Not without you, Will Kidd. I want my first view of that beautiful harbour you talked about to be with you standing beside me, your hand in mine. Until then, I'm staying in Liverpool. Wherever they send you, it's likely you'll come back into port here. I'm not budging.'

'Liverpool's the most important port in the country – especially for shipping between Britain and America. Once the war starts, Hitler's going to blast the hell out of it.' He paused, brushing his hair back from his eyes, nervous. 'If you won't go to Australia, then will you and Judith go to Dublin? You're going to meet Eddie O'Connor's sister, Bridget, when she comes to the wedding tomorrow, and her family are all good people who'll look after you and Judith. I think you and Bridget will get on well.'

She shook her head, her mouth set firm. 'I'm sure we would. But my family is *here*. I don't just mean Judith, but Sam and Nance too. We'll all take care of each other. I want to stay so I can be standing on the Pier Head whenever your ship comes into port. Don't send me away, Will. Please.'

He pulled her into his arms and kissed her, both of them longing for tomorrow, when at last they would be married, but both fearing what the coming war might bring.

'Whatever happens, we'll face it together. I love you, Will.'

Acknowledgements

I drew on the support of both Liverpool and Everton supporters in researching this book. My extended Merseyside originating family is divided along football lines – although probably united in their condemnation of me for being a Chelsea supporter! Cousin David McFarlin (Everton) for his insights into life in the merchant navy and his kind gift of a book which was a very helpful glossary to all the complicated terms used by sailors and for the various parts of ships. Cousin Tony Lundy (Liverpool) very kindly went to Crosby Library and photographed local street plans of the waterfront between Seaforth and Blundellsands from before the war. This was an invaluable aid.

My thanks as always for the fresh eyes and consistent encouragement of my critique group here in Eastbourne – Margaret Kaine, Merryn Allingham, Jill Rutherford, Jay Dixon and Paula Lofting.

Thanks also to all the team at Canelo, in particular my editor Laura McCallen, and Louise Cullen, who approached me and brought me on board.